THE DISAPPEARANCE

By T. V. LoCicero

TLC *Media*

Also By T. V. LoCicero

FICTION
The Obsession (The Truth Beauty Trilogy, Book 1)
The Car Bomb (The *detroit im dyin* Trilogy, Book 1)
Admission of Guilt (The *detroit im dyin* Trilogy, Book 2)
Babytrick (The *detroit im dyin* Trilogy, Book 3)
When A Pretty Woman Smiles
Sicilian Quilt

NON-FICTION
Murder in the Synagogue
Squelched: The Suppression of Murder in the Synagogue

COLLECTION
Coming Up Short

Praise for *The Disappearance*

"T. V. LoCicero just gets better and better in this cosmopolitan thriller of betrayal and corruption in the shady world of Swiss banking. Unpredictable, twisty and clever, the intrigue draws you in and won't let go." — Victoria Best

"...a gripping novel of high stakes banking, fraud and money laundering. The chase is on to uncover the perpetrators. Paramount to Lina and Marc, however, is the safe return of Clara Marche. LoCicero has created a dichotomy between kind, caring characters in direct contrast to many reprehensible ones. The twists and turns lead to an unexpected ending." — Fran Hoffman

"Another fabulous thriller with the lovely Lina Lentini...all the main characters are thrown into a maelstrom of fraud, fear, danger, betrayal and death...This book is another great treat that I can whole-heartedly recommend." — Rosemary Standeven

"...an intriguing and cleverly plotted thriller... a complex net of lies, cover-ups and diversions... far from obvious or predictable." — Christoph Fischer

"...a mash-up of genres, principally romance and crime fiction. The conventions of neither genre ascend, which speaks of the author's ability to balance them. That said, Mr. LoCicero's true gift, on full display in this book, remains exposition. As this story progresses, the reader learns a great deal about its characters, which of course aids greatly in divining their motivations...the movie rights, in the hands of the appropriate screenwriter and director, would turn this, I think, into a compelling film." — Mark Feltskog

"A great storyteller, T.V. LoCicero delivers again in The Disappearance. Suspenseful with twists and turns that leave me begging for more. The characters are extremely believable and the writing is top notch. Fast paced with intricate details. I love how the plot unfolds and the endings are never predictable." — Cathy Morgan

"Holy molly!!!! What the heck did I just read!?! The plot of this story is so thick you won't see your way through. I found myself lost from reality just because I needed to read the next page. I had to find out what was going to happen! Don't start this book if you are running a busy schedule, clear some things first, because if you don't, this book will make you!" — Peggy Salkill

"This is an action packed, cleverly plotted thriller with lots of intrigue. It's hard for Clara to know who she can trust. Check it out for a great read! I see too that it's a trilogy; I can't wait for Book 3!" — Valencia Redd

"The twists and turns don't let you down, loads of things revealed and answers I'd never even considered. The plot moves along so intriguingly I couldn't have read it faster." — Angel Love

"It has tons of twists and turns and a great plot as the mystery continues. I'm waiting for number 3 with baited breath." — Debbie Carnes

"Another excellent book by T.V. LoCicero. This time we follow Lina in a search for the truth in the disappearance of a friend. Lina and a new friend cross country boarders and oceans to discover the complicated and emotional facts in this latest installment of her life." — Sue Wardle

T. V. LoCicero

T.V. LoCicero has been writing both fiction and non-fiction across five decades. He is the author of the true crime books *Murder in the Synagogue* (Prentice-Hall), on the assassination of Rabbi Morris Adler, and *Squelched: The Suppression of Murder in the Synagogue*. His novels include *The Obsession* and *The Disappearance* (the first two books in The Truth Beauty Trilogy), *The Car Bomb, Admission of Guilt* and *Babytrick* (The *detroit im dyin* Trilogy), *Sicilian Quilt* and *When A Pretty Woman Smiles*. His collection of shorter works, **Coming Up Short**, includes the stories and essays he has published in various periodicals, including Commentary, Ms. and The University Review, and in the hard-cover collections *Best Magazine Articles, The Norton Reader* and *The Third Coast*.

THE DISAPPEARANCE

By T. V. LoCicero

The Truth Beauty Trilogy
Book 2

TLC *Media*

The Disappearance
by T. V. LoCicero
Copyright 2012 by T. V. LoCicero

For more information on this and other works by T.V. LoCicero please visit:

www.tvlocicero.com

For A. J.

Chapter 1

Clara knows this is not exactly a whim. Over the past several weeks she has thought about doing this more times than she cares to remember. But tonight? Certainly she has not thought about doing it tonight.

Until now. Even though over lunch on Monday she listened to her new dear friend Lina reading aloud from Clara's old e-mails to and from Marc—all those words flying back and forth across the Atlantic that neither of them could understand without the idiot translation machine—and she suddenly knew without question that if she and her lover were genuinely hopeful about their future, one or both would have made the requisite effort to learn the other's language. It was time to end it.

Until now. Even though Marc's e-mail this morning on her office computer strained as usual for upbeat, disguising despair about somehow finding a free-lance job that would send him to Europe so he could be with her for at least a few precious days. She could have done it this morning, a quick, cold note meant to set them both free. But she was busy and bothered, and it was worse in the afternoon, and then she had to leave early to pick up those matching little sailor suits the twins ended up loving and their mother hated. She would wait until tomorrow to write back.

Until now. Even though at the twins' fifth birthday party this evening, her two adorable grandsons began chanting, for no discernable reason, "*Le folie de Grandmaman! Le folie de Grandmaman!*" Grandma's folly. Honore, their mother, who has no doubt uttered the phrase about Marc so often that the boys picked it up, tried with a cross look to shush them, while Vera, who seems as flighty lately as her older sister is predictable, simply laughed. Clara's two daughters have been impossible lately. Only Louis came to her rescue, telling his sons with a smile and a wink, "Yes, you two scamps are definitely Grandma's folly."

But on the way back into Geneva from their home in Carouge her eye glimpsed the little Italian place where she and Marc had their last dinner together way back in March, eight months ago now, and that started a train of thought to which she has finally surrendered.

She parks her four-year-old red Opel Astra near the front of the Banque Privee Morneau on the rue de Hollande, the heart of the financial district quiet at this hour on a Thursday evening. A wave and a smile through the glass of the front entrance, and Marcel, the former policeman at the night desk in the lobby, buzzes her in. Walking across the sparkling, high-ceilinged space, she digs in her large purse and pulls out her badge. Just one of the many changes she has seen over the past three decades in this proudly unchanging institution. In the old days, coming at this hour, she would have needed to sign in and out and notate the times.

Now as she says brightly, "*Bonsoir,* Marcel," he simply scans the bar code on her badge and punches a key on his computer. She glances at the large gold clock above his head: 9:32.

"Forget something?" he asks in his clipped French. As usual he looks morose.

"No, I just need to answer an e-mail I neglected this afternoon. I won't be long."

"Monsieur Lyon is up there."

This stops her, and she nearly turns to leave. With Julian in the office does she really want to sit there writing an e-mail ending it with Marc? Her boss has been obnoxious about her lover lately. "Your American Casanova," he calls him. But if Julian is actually working at this late hour, maybe he'll be so engrossed he won't bother her. Or maybe he'll finish soon and leave. In any case, she's determined to do this tonight. Get it over with, this one of too many things in her life she cannot control. At least she'll be out from under this one.

"So," she says finally, "our man burns the midnight oil." She heads for the lift. "*Merci,* Marcel."

On the second floor when she opens the door to the suite and walks in, Julian's office door stands wide open, the lights inside glowing. Not to startle him, she calls softly, "Julian? *Bonsoir.*" There is only dead silence. She puts her purse on her desk and moves a few steps to rap twice on the jam and look in. His chair is pushed back away from the desk, and his computer screens are bright. But no Julian. She walks in, a slow step at a time, feeling somehow drawn. And then she stops, telling herself not to do this, not to be in here

2

without him. His firm rule (only one of the things she finds annoying about him) was established from the beginning: Do not enter this office unless your presence is requested. He could walk in any time, in the next second or two, from wherever he went—the men's room maybe, or chatting with Giles, if the chairman has also stayed late? And yet, feeling strangely compelled, she moves slowly to the desk and around its edge.

Now she has a good look at the two large flat panel screens angled together to one side of the glass top desk. At first glance the pages they display seem familiar. Certainly the one on the left has digits in a configuration she has seen many times before on the client account printouts she has delivered to Cecile every quarter for much of the past five years. Except—and now she is moving closer to the screen on the left—there are differences here, rows of numbers that vary markedly from what she has seen before. But then, of course, this must be someone else's account. Except—and now she moves even closer—Cecile Eaton's name is exactly where it always is in the upper left corner. And in the upper right the quarter listed is not from some decade or two past but is in fact the most recent, completed 30, September, 2009.

With her stomach beginning to twist, she moves her gaze to the screen on the right, and scans slowly, steadily, back and forth across its lines and totals. Then she looks again at that familiar screen on the left, and with one more long look at the screen on the right, she knows with a certainty that lands like a terrible blow to the chest that her life has just changed forever.

She feels dazed, stunned for several seconds, until the perfect silence in this office is cut with the distant rush of a flush from the men's room down the hall. And suddenly she feels her heart slamming. If the fastidious Julian stops to wash his hands, she will have maybe 30 seconds to flee unseen.

Moving quickly now, she pauses for a second at her desk, wondering if she should just sit there and start her computer. No, she grabs her purse and, feeling her mouth quiver, heads for the hall. Pulling the door open, she looks up the corridor to the men's room entrance, then slips off her heels and shoves them in her bag. Go, go! Silently she closes the door behind her and, with a soundless dash that feels like forever, she reaches the near end of the hallway and turns the corner just as she hears the soft creak of the men's room door opening. Pressing herself against the wall next to the lift, she stares at the door to the stairwell. As she listens to his footsteps coming closer, she wonders if he caught a glimpse of her rounding the corner. If so, would he have called, or simply continued to follow her down here? But the footsteps stop, and the sound of the door opening to their suite brings her some relief. Finally when it clicks shut, she breathes.

On the landing heading down the stairs, she slips on her shoes, and when she reaches the lobby door, she stops, shakes her hair into place, takes one deep breath and practices the smile she will give Marcel as he again scans her badge and she wishes him *"Bonsoir."*

Chapter 2

It is Friday morning, October 16, 2009, two weeks before Clara's evening visit to the Banque Privee Morneau. Lina Lentini, professor of comparative literature on leave again from the University of Bologna, is sitting on an old stone bench next to her friend Cecile Eaton in the ample, smartly tended garden behind Cecile's villa where Lina has been staying since early September, six weeks now.

"Ah, well," says Lina, "the good pope and the bad pope."

"Yes, dear, but for both a mistake is out of the question." Cecile offers an ironic smile, then gazes off at the lake and the Alps in France beyond.

"But, of course, infallibility extends only to matters of doctrine," says Lina. "Neither John Paul nor Benedict presumably had a word from God on the acceptability of popular music or whether to allow Dylan to perform for all those impressionable young people."

Both women are in light sweaters. Lina feels the warmth of the sun on her face but also the chill in the breeze that hints at what's soon to come. She feels her own red curls ruffle and notes a few fly-away strands from Cecile's snow white bun. Lina has been telling this 88-year-old American woman, who has lived here outside Geneva for nearly a quarter century, about the day a dozen years ago when she attended an extraordinary event in Bologna, along with 300,000 enthusiastic young Italian Catholics. The World Eucharistic Congress in the fall of 1997 included a concert much opposed by then Cardinal Ratzinger (now Pope Benedict), who generally considered pop music the devil's work and thought the featured performer, Bob Dylan, a dangerous false prophet. But the famously hip John Paul had no problem with the concert and delivered a homily on Dylan's "Blowin' in the Wind," saying the answer was certainly in the wind, not the one that blows things away, but "the wind of the spirit" that would lead these young people to Christ. Then he listened to Dylan sing "A Hard Rain's A-Gonna Fall," "Knockin' on Heaven's Door," and "Forever Young."

"The moment was extraordinary," said Lina. "When he finished singing, this little Jewish man with the hook nose, who had become a born-again Christian two decades earlier, took off his cowboy hat and walked over to John Paul in his white robe, and they shook hands."

"That's right, I'd forgotten Bob was born again."

"Then it is one of the very few things you have forgotten."

Now stirring on the bench, Cecile takes Lina's hand gently. "So remind me, dear, why God won't let the pope make a doctrinal error but feels it inappropriate to offer guidance on a concert that might corrupt young people."

Lina knows this is one of her friend's favorite ploys, making a point by asking a question she does not need answered. "Because God will not intrude on our exercise of moral freedom."

"Except when the very foundation of faith is at stake."

"Yes, except then. Some things are just too important to let freedom get in the way."

After they are silent for a few moments, Cecile asks, "Did I ever tell you about the night a very young Mr. Dylan almost picked me up?"

They have never talked about this, but Lina recalls it from the second of Cecile's four books, all memoirs. What was the title? The first was *Getting Started*, the second, *Getting Over*. Because it is always a pleasure to hear the woman spin stories, Lina says, "No, please do."

"Well, it was the early '60s," says Cecile, "and I was 39 but still looked pretty good."

"No, you were stunning. I've seen photos."

"Oh, dear...."

"I'm just setting the facts straight."

"Anyway, he was at one of those clubs in the Village where he was always singing in those days, Gerde's, I think, and my friends persuaded me to come down and listen to this scrawny little fellow who rattled out all these words and held the room spellbound. Afterward my friends introduced us, and almost the first thing he said was, 'Would you like to take me home with you, Miss Eaton?' Very mock politely, like I was his homeroom teacher. I thought fast and said, 'Bad luck, I have houseguests.' He said, 'No problem, I can

6

sleep on the floor.'"

"And you replied?"

"I said I was sure he'd find himself a better offer. I learned later that within a week or two, he met Joan Baez."

When she met Cecile in the spring of 1999, Lina was attending a conference in Geneva and with a colleague went to a dinner party at a large villa just up the lake. The colleague, a Swiss linguist, had long been friends with their hosts, and on the way to the party he filled her in. Cecile Eaton had met Claude DeRocheford in New York in 1983. She was then 62 and he five years older, and there was a fairy-tale-for-seniors quality to their transatlantic romance.

Widowed at 22 and divorced at 33, she had been single for nearly three decades. In New York art and literary circles, she was a woman with a wide and often racy reputation, a respected editor who had worked at two major publishing houses with some of their most prominent writers, and over the years she had been linked romantically with authors, actors, playwrights and painters. He was a tall, distinguished-looking businessman who had made a fortune in pharmaceuticals, a widower, who had lost his wife and daughter 20 years earlier in a car accident and whose son, an adventurous young man, had gone off on some humanitarian mission in what is now Congo and was never seen again. Still in his 40s, Claude had thrown himself into his work and never married again, until Cecile. When she left for Geneva to wed and live with Claude, she told friends in New York, not entirely tongue-in-cheek, "A major attraction is that he thinks I would be great at giving away his money." They all predicted she would be back in Gotham inside two years. She never returned.

Instead Cecile was re-inventing herself and soon began writing the first of her series of memoirs. In her late 70s at the time of the dinner party, she had just published her third volume, *Getting Rich*, dealing with how dramatically her life had changed in the move from Manhattan to Switzerland. After dinner Cecile signed a copy of the new book and gave it to Lina. The two women, despite the half-century difference in their ages, seemed powerfully drawn to each other and ended up in a corner talking non-stop for most of the evening.

If asked back then to explain the attraction, Lina would have mentioned how wise Cecile seemed, especially about men and relationships, and how hopelessly in love with art, literature and life itself she continued to be. If asked that question today, Lina thinks her answer would be the same, but over the past decade they have swapped and exchanged so many books, ideas, experiences and intimate pieces of themselves, that her friendship with this extraordinarily literate old woman seems simply beyond words.

That first evening Cecile and Claude, an animated, gracious man then 83, prevailed on Lina to move from her hotel in Geneva to spend her final two nights of the conference as their guest at the villa. It was the first of several stays Lina enjoyed with them over the years, and she quickly developed admiration and affection for Claude as well. Trained as a bio-chemist, he was a rare combination of scientific savvy, business brilliance and unwavering ethic, and he never completely retired, still going into his office in Geneva a few times a week. But with no close family and consumed with work while accumulating his wealth, Claude had never given much thought as to what to do with it. Then Cecile entered his life. He trusted her to choose wisely, and so she picked a few clear-cut causes — food and education for the poorest of the poor, environmental and clean-energy research — and found trustworthy conduits.

Six years ago Claude died suddenly from a heart attack. Cecile was alone now in the villa and "missed terribly that princely husband of mine." But Zazu, who cooked and cleaned for her, still came everyday, someone in her circle of devoted friends often stopped by for lunch or invited her for dinner, and she always kept busy with writing and tending her garden. In short, her life continued comfortably but without extravagance, and most of the money, from the trusts and investments Claude had set up through a privately owned bank in Geneva, still went to those same good causes, as always anonymously. That was the way Claude had arranged it with the old acquaintance whose family owned the Banque Privee Morneau.

Actually, it was three years ago that Lina last saw her friend. Back then Cecile had announced in an email that she was quite tired of "moping" and wanted to "get out and about," and so Lina suggested she make her first visit to Bologna. Staying for five days with Lina in the large apartment on Via San Vitale, the older woman was filled with energy and devoured the city. And then, surprisingly they lost touch.

The following fall Lina spent almost a full term lecturing in the States at St. Thomas University in mid-Michigan. There she fell in love with John Martens, a married professor, and became an obsession for his young graduate assistant, Stanford Lyle, the affair bringing both a thrilling connection and a litany of troubles. Her life quickly filled with the kind of duplicity she had always abhorred. Forced to return to Bologna, she was followed, first by Stan and then by John. Schemes, threats and murder ensued as Stan stalked Lina and John through the streets of the ancient university city and finally to the legendary beauty of the Sicilian mountain town of Taormina. There, with the cancer in John's prostate having returned and moved to his brain, his loving support was taken from her, and she was left alone to confront and ultimately put an end to Stan's murderous intent.

During her vigil at the hospital in Taormina, Lina finished her third book, exploring aspects of the novel in times of terror, as she waited for her lover's inevitable end. It was three months before John finally expired in her arms. Seven weeks later she joined his parents in Cleveland for a memorial service, attended by several people from Michigan, including Fr. Robert Redding, who had invited Lina to lecture at St. Thomas, a few of John's colleagues and his wife Marissa.

But once back in Bologna, Lina could not shake the memories that seemed to enervate her. She was teaching again, seeing her friends and making notes for a new book, but the spark seemed to have gone out of all these efforts. She gave into her old lover Paolo's entreaties and traveled with him as he researched a case in Paris. But her heart was a locked box and nothing worked, nothing allowed her to feel normal and truly engaged again after John. And after Stan. At one point she actually considered going to the Carabinieri and confessing to murder.

Then after more than a year of *dibatte* (her Italian for floundering), one morning on her patio, she was making her usual rounds on the Dell and checked the book page of the New York Times. There she found a review of Cecile's new memoir, *Getting On*, which Lina had not even known was in the works. The review was glowing, and there was also an author profile:

The essays in this, her fourth book, hopscotch

from horticulture to atheism to anti-aging schemes. "It's my best seller," says Eaton, "maybe because I've never before dealt with such forbidding taboos. Oh, I've written about extra-marital sex, abortion, even an orgy, but nothing like aging and death. I've seen smart, hip people simply walk away when the subject comes up. But now that I'm heading for my 90s and can still walk, chew gum and even have a good time, I suspect people take heart and say, Hey, maybe it's not so awful."

For Lina the profile wove together facts known, unknown or forgotten. Born Cecile Watkins in 1921 into a wealthy Baltimore family, she graduated from Wellesley College in the middle of WWII. Despite the war, she expected a smooth transition to marriage and children, and at 22 she married her first love, a Harvard grad named Nels Eaton. She had no doubt she would always be faithful. "And then," she said, "he went off to the Pacific and got himself killed just before the end of the war. My heart was completely broken, and the condition lasted for another decade before I finally fell again." The second marriage was to a prominent photographer named Philip Newsome, "who also went off and got himself killed, but this time not before he betrayed me, divorced me and met his fate when his new girlfriend's old lover stabbed them both in the heart."

After that came a series of affairs in which Cecile was often the other woman, and usually quite content to be so. "Possessiveness is a poison," she says. "Love someone, don't possess them. Of course hurting others is not an option, so either have an open marriage — which most cannot seem to manage — or keep your affairs extremely discrete." Sex was "both a tangy pleasure and an unmatched way to explore a man when he can't really hide." Viewed this way, and after the pain of her first two marriages, it was also insurance against emotional involvement for the next three decades. Along the way there were a couple of abortions (illegal then) and in her 40s, after she had finally decided she wanted a child, a miscarriage. The piece concluded:

As for regrets, she will admit to a few: being without the glow of love and the complexity of

10

commitment for close to 30 years, being childless, and not sitting down seriously to write until her 60s. "I was lazy for much too long," she says.

Lina's email was full of congratulations and apologies for having been silent for so long. In return Cecile sent her a copy of the new book and an invitation to come to Geneva: "Dear, you sound like you could use a respite, and I am often lonely these days as I am losing so many of my old pals. One by one they're dropping like flies."

Lina wrote back to say that her life has felt for some time now like an "unending respite, but your offer is too good to pass up." She opened the new book and read in the prologue:

> This little volume germinated when it occurred to me that all I had left to write about was being old. An absurd idea, I told myself, a dreadful bore. But a few days later I found myself thinking, well, maybe, if it were a very short book.
>
> Now it's a common observation that older authors write shorter books. Yes, there are exceptions, some of them famous, like old Henry James. But leaving aside the diminution of powers issue, it is a simple actuarial fact that time is no friend to the elderly. Better to embark on something short, and hopefully less demanding, so that once completed your brave little opus can at least have a shot at being praised for its artful simplicity and pared-down wisdom.

Lina finished the book in one sitting but then went back and re-read graphs that have continued to stick with her:

> Does a man have at 50, as Orwell put it, the face he deserves? And if so, does Orwell's rule apply equally to a woman, who on average will spend considerably more time, effort and expense over the years on maintaining her face? If it's true at 50, is it even more true at 80, or does time at a

certain point begin to move things in the opposite direction, muddling the message of your visage?

As always there was her delightful irreverence:

> Some say the death of people you love is a kind of psychic blow, and that the accumulation of such blows is what ultimately kills you. But it seems just as possible that the death of a significant other can prompt positive feelings of a sort. When my beautiful Claude passed, I was of course deeply saddened but almost equally grateful for that wholly unexpected gift of his presence in my life for two decades. There is also at times that distinct elation at having been spared once again by the Reaper, the self-regarding notion that you, unlike the dead ones, have been favored by Mistress Fate. How else to explain, as we get on, our search of the obit page? Surely we are not looking there for another blow to our aging and vulnerable psyche, but rather for the grim satisfaction of continued survival even as those around us fall away."

And her good-hearted unbelief was unrelenting:

> Of course, as an atheist my position on these things is much different than those of my God-fearing, or God-loving friends. By the way, while the love angle seems much more in vogue these days, I have always thought fear is much more appropriate when it comes to an Entity so often capricious. Believers claim that God knows what's in store for you. But my question is does God really give a hoot? As I see it, omniscience is greatly over-rated. So what if God knows everything? The real question is, does God also care? What exactly is the evidence that God has emotions, that HeShe gives a rat's patootie what

happens to anyone?

So in this fall of 2009, living with Cecile in her beautiful home with this lovely garden overlooking the lake, Lina has begun to feel more like herself. There has been much to tell her friend about the past two years, and Cecile, as always, has been the perfect listener, those blue eyes—the bluest Lina has ever seen other than John's—lit with an intelligence both penetrating and inviting. Despite the loss, pain and disappointment of a lifetime, Cecile has not a single sharp, severe or rigid line in her face, nothing hard or dissatisfied. Everything is soft and rounded, nothing slack or uncaring. After nearly nine decades, there are wrinkles, naturally, but they all live in pleasant networks that seem to say with quiet confidence, "We are here, exactly where we should be." Overall, her look is comely and makes Lina want to be close, even to hold her. And yet she seems perfectly self-sufficient, her aura speaking softly of needing no one. Still, when those steady blue eyes turn Lina's way, she feels wanted, included, chosen in a way that seems privileged and extraordinary.

"Oh, did I tell you?" asks Cecile now up and moving to water her mums, "Clara is coming for dinner this evening."

"Good," says Lina watching her move with a slow grace, "we will have fun then." Clara Marche works at Cecile's bank, and soon after Lina arrived for her stay in Geneva, she met the woman and liked her immediately. As Cecile explained, after Claude's death there was a need to occasionally check on the performance of the organizations receiving those millions in annual donations. Her contact with the bank settled into regular visits from a manager named Julian Lyon, an impeccably courteous man in his 30s and very good-looking. Probably too beautiful to be anything but gay, she decided. His reports, though, seemed essentially the same each time, and Cecile thought them boring. "The details made my eyes glaze over," she told Lina. And soon Julian was sending his secretary, Clara, in his stead, which was just fine with Cecile, who found her a bright, attractive woman with a luminous smile. "Ah, yes," Cecile told Lina fondly, "I have known men who would have paid handsomely just for that smile."

Clara was into her 50s but appeared ten years younger, and as her connection with Cecile became more personal, her bank-business visits turned into monthly lunch dates. That's when Cecile began hearing about Clara's unusual love affair with Marc White, an

American video producer, a black man from Detroit who spoke only English, while Clara managed only French and Italian.

"This is a love affair that could not have happened even a decade ago," Cecile told Lina. "But it's possible now because of the Internet and those free translation services."

Having met three years ago when he covered Geneva's annual motor show, Marc and Clara have been able to spend only a handful of times together, a week here and there, once all of ten days. But nearly everyday they've exchanged emails with detailed personal and family histories, private thoughts and fantasies that have deepened and enriched their relationship.

"I've seen those computer generated translations," said Lina. "They can be awkward, funny and at times misleading, but usually you can get the gist."

"Yes," said Cecile, "And the irony is, the communication they've afforded, even if limited, is often much more effective than anything possible between the two of them in person—beyond, of course, the love making, which it sounds like he's very good at."

Having met him on a few occasions, when she served the couple as a personal translator, Cecile is clearly fond of Marc. Two days ago she showed Lina a copy of the correspondence that Marc and Clara had agreed to give her, a collection of all the email exchanges printed out, complete with their computerized translations.

"See what you think," said Cecile, handing Lina the fat stack of printed emails. "I'm toying with the idea of turning them into an epistolary novel."

Now in the garden Lina tells her friend, "You know, I am engrossed in Clara and Marc's emails. They are fascinating. And I think you are right: they could make an interesting novel."

Cecile looks up from her ancient watering can. "Oh, good, good. Now I want you to consider finishing it if I don't manage to before I'm gone."

"Oh, Cecile!"

"No, I'm serious, dear. Promise me you'll consider it."

Lina gazes at the serene blue of Lake Geneva and the gauzy haze over the mountains beyond. "Of course, I promise."

Chapter 3

Late in the afternoon of that same mid-October day, at the Banque Privee Morneau Clara is deeply annoyed at how she has just been summoned. She tries to calm herself by delaying her response and counting the ways this man is being inappropriate.

First, instead of using the intercom and thus being able to speak in a quiet, gentleman's tone suitable to the halls of this very civilized institution, he called in a high-pitched bleat that shot straight through the thick, solid oak door between their offices, "Clara, I need you in here!"

Second, not in French but in English no less, continuing his recently initiated effort "to help you become more proficient in the language of that American boyfriend of yours," a campaign so inapt and unpleasant that she has actually thought about asking Martine, her attorney friend, if it might be considered actionable workplace abuse.

And third, a summons delivered with such uncalled-for volume that it could surely be heard through the east wall of his office by Mercedes in the suite beyond, of course to the delight of that pretty young thing so obviously infatuated with Client Investment Manager Julian Lyon that she has been casting envious glances over the past few weeks at Clara, whose job she so clearly covets.

Clara slides her keyboard in, rises from the steal-and-mesh ergo chair in which she spends most of her day and moves to his door. She twists the polished brass handle and slowly, silently pushes into the man's office. He is turned away from his desk, his back to her and facing the large window looking out over the rue de Hollande. He says in a normal tone of voice, "Ah, finally, there you are."

This, she knows, is one of his favorite little stunts. He still seems amused by it, acting as if he were preternaturally aware, as with eyes in the back of his head, but of course using the late afternoon glint on the window for a half-mirrored glimpse of her standing in the room behind.

"Julian?" she says quietly.

"Clara Doloro Marche," he replies swiveling to face her. His use of her maiden name along with her long-ago ex-husband's family name (which she has so often regretted keeping) fuels more annoyance. And once again she observes that this man—with that glistening black hair curling along the forehead and neck, the amused dark eyes and all-seasons tan, the fine features and cheekbones—is more beautiful than she is. "I have sent to your computer a report I just finished on investment strategies for the next two weeks…"

She interrupts. "*En français, s'il te plaît.*"

He looks at her for a second and shrugs. In French he says, "You will be sorry when your American Casanova drops you."

She says firmly, "*Pas ton affaire.*" Not your concern.

Again he shrugs, and in French continues, "The report needs to be proofed, reformatted and blasted to our clients, I'm afraid before you leave this evening."

"This evening." She knows that what he has sent will be a mess that she will need to re-write and fact-check as well."

"Yes, and be sure if you have any questions to ask them quickly. I'll be leaving very soon for the day."

Not trusting her face or her voice, she turns quickly and moves out the door. She stops closing it behind her when she sees Giles Morneau, the bank's chairman, walking into the suite from the hall. As usual, he greets her with a warm smile. She has known this man since he was ten, meeting him on his very first visit to the bank with his father, Albert Morneau, and it was clear, even back then, more than thirty years ago, that this slight, fair boy would someday run this august and trusted institution. Now that boy is a man, and every molecule a banker, the short brown hair always well-brushed, every strand in place, the physique a bit pudgy, especially in the belly (he likes to eat and it shows), large brown eyes that seem both trusting and sincere, and a calm, un-dramatic manner, very low key. He tells her she looks very attractive today, as usual, and asks if that is a new suit.

Yes, she says, and thanks him.

Very chic, he says. And then he spots on the corner of her desk the newly published French translation of Cecile's book, *Getting On*. It has just been released in Geneva, and Clara immediately bought and read it and will bring it with her to dinner this evening to get another personalized inscription from the author, to match those in her copies of the first three books.

He says, "Ah, so I see you are reading the new one from our favorite client. And how is it, may I ask?"

"Wonderful, like all of them. I've been invited for dinner at Madame Eaton's this evening." She glances quickly back into Julian's office. He is obviously listening to all this.

"Well, marvelous," says Giles. "Please give Madame Eaton our best."

"I will," she says sitting at her computer, anxious to learn just how bad this new, last-second job is going to be.

The door between the offices has been closed less than ten seconds when she hears laughter from Julian and a low (embarrassed, she thinks) chuckle from Giles. Are they laughing at her? No doubt it was something Julian said. But then why does she care? She has been stewing for weeks about how full of himself this man has become, how often he has been unpleasant, demanding, even foul of mood with her lately. Why does this upset her so? They are not friends. He's her boss. Why does she need a pleasant relationship with him?

Later, after six, well beyond the time she is usually off to fitness or heading back to her apartment, she is still working intensely on Julian's report. It is not as bad as some, worse than others. She still has at least a half-hour of work left, and she is grateful the suite is empty; there are no interruptions, and silence envelops the place. Then Emmanuelle, Giles Morneau's secretary and her best friend at the bank, comes through her door. For many years the two women have shared all their secrets at work and most of those that are private as well.

Emmanuelle raises her eyebrows and says, "Again?"

Clara smiles and nods.

Her friend says, "I'm so sorry, darling. Can I help?"

"No, dear, thank you. I'll see you in the morning."

"Of course."

The break is brief, but Emmanuelle's understanding and support are bracing, and Clara races through the rest of her assignment without a pause. She makes sure everything she needs from her desk is in her purse, grabs the book and is out the door. With luck she will only be a few minutes late at Cecile's.

Downstairs, walking across the marble of the bank's large echoing lobby, she spots a man she has not seen in quite some time. In a short black leather coat, he is standing next to Marcel at the night desk. As she passes they both turn to look at her. Running behind schedule, she does not particularly want to stop and talk. But the man she has not seen in at least 3 months smiles and says in his German accented French, "Ah, Clara. *Bonsoir.*"

As much as she does not wish to, she pauses. "*Bonsoir*, Willem, Marcel." After all, Willem Tanner is a man she was with for more than a year, until he ended it, what, four years ago now? He looks good, she thinks. A thick, stocky 5'10" but he never seems to gain an ounce. The blond buzz cut may now be showing a little more white, but at 55 that ruddy face is still smooth. Of course there is still the earnest, brutal look of an ex-cop and—as she learned only after they started dating—also an ex-con. That last surprising fact had come from Emmanuelle, who would not tell her how she had learned it. "Please, Clara, you never heard it from me. Better yet, you never heard it at all."

Now Willem, still smiling, remarks that she has been working late today.

She smiles also and replies that he knows the saying, no rest for the wicked.

Yes, he says, but in this case it does not apply.

She should thank him for that but only shakes her head. Instead she says she has not seen him here at the bank for some time. He nods and says he's been traveling, on assignment.

She senses he would like to keep this going, but she gives him one more smile, wishes both men a good evening and moves on. He calls to her, asking if she might let him buy her a drink sometime. They could catch up. Without breaking stride, she looks back, cocks her head and says, maybe. Then she pushes through the glass door of the main entrance into the gathering dusk on the rue de Hollande.

As she walks briskly to her Opel in the garage, she surprises herself by thinking about Willem Tanner the whole way. What would she say if he actually called? And why, after all this time, would he even want to catch up? Could she ever touch that man again? After he crushed her? With no explanation at all? Afterward she had been forced to see his face so often around the bank where he functioned as a kind of one-man security detail. Usually he would report directly to Giles, as chairman, but there were also times when he met with Julian, and then she rued those moments of awkward silence as they waited for the intercom call.

Things really improved only after the relationship with Marc took root, and for a long time now she has rarely even thought of Willem, until this evening. But then lately, as the connection with Marc has felt increasingly difficult, she has actually found herself thinking of breaking it off. Hope for a real future together seems to be slowly slipping through her fingers, and the irony now is that she and Marc have agreed to let Cecile write a book about their unlikely romance. A novel, yes, but probably only a thinly disguised version of the real story, one that her friends and family would surely recognize, if it ever reached the public. Maybe she agreed to all this because of her doubts and dwindling hope. A way, perhaps, of "immortalizing" their strange affair?

As she drives across the Mont Blanc Bridge where the southwest end of Lake Geneva flows into the Rhone, really the city's center, she has put these thoughts of both Willem and Marc behind, and now on her mobile she pushes the speed dial number for Honore. Louis answers, and she can hear little Henri and Michel yelping in the background until he gently quiets them. She loves her son-in-law. Sometimes, it seems, even more than her own daughters. Unlike them, Louis is so solid, sweet, centered and loving. Honore is a good mother, but she might be less so without Louis. And despite all her education, she was floundering until Louis made her the office manager for his landscape design firm. When he quickly puts Honore on the phone, Clara wishes she could have spoken with him longer. As it is, in the middle of making dinner, her older daughter sounds harried. Clara says she won't keep her, is just wondering if she has talked to her sister.

Why? What's wrong now?

Nothing really, but Vera, divorced at 27, is talking again about quitting at the clinic, without finding another job first. The last time this happened she ended up sleeping on Clara's couch for weeks. "Please," says Clara now, "when you speak with her, just make sure you tell her to line up another job before she gives her notice."

"Of course, Mother. What else would I say?"

"Maybe Louis could talk to her?"

"Why don't you talk to her, Mom?"

"I try, but I have trouble these days even getting her on the phone."

"Mom, I have got to go. She's a big girl. She'll be alright."

"How are my beautiful twins?

"They're hungry, Mom."

"Okay, go. I'll talk to you soon."

* * *

Sitting with these two extraordinary women in this large, high-ceilinged room — a space with at least twice as many square meters as her entire apartment — Clara wonders again at how comfortable she feels. They are after all so highly educated, literate and accomplished, and she is not even a secondary school graduate. Driving up to the imposing gray stone mansion with the brown tile roof, she thought of her first visit here five years ago now, and how warm and welcoming the old mistress of the manor had been. That was how she had thought of Cecile before she met her. But from the beginning the woman had never made her feel inferior, diminished or any kind of lower rank. Her opinions, thoughts and observations on life, and even on art, literature and politics were always sought and seemingly valued.

And with the addition of Lina, nothing really has changed. Quite simply, she is taken seriously. When she talks about why Paul Auster, the American novelist who translates his own books into French, is her favorite writer, or about the love affair she's had with Dali's work ever since she visited his museum in Paris 20 years ago, or when she mentions how pleased she has been with Obama, both women listen closely and ask questions with genuine interest in her answers. There is nothing patronizing, or condescending about these women, and she loves and trusts them both.

She holds up her copy of *Getting On* and says, "So now that I have read this beautiful book, which I have loved just as much as the first three, I have a question."

Cecile's smile glows. "Well, thank you, dear. I will try to answer."

"So, yes, actually, you raise this question in the book yourself. You ask, what is the best way to go at the end. Quick and easy, even if you have no chance to say goodbye to anyone you value? Or slow, and probably painful, so you can take a proper leave? And then you add the question of whether you would rather be aware of what is happening at the moment of death, or not. Would you prefer to be

20

conscious or in a coma? But in the book, you do not really answer."

"Yes, dear, they are not easy questions. So I left them for the reader to answer whatever seems best for her."

"I understand, but I am curious what your personal preference might be."

"I am not really certain. As I wrote in the book, I have lost people close to me in each fashion and in ways that mixed the two. But no one has come back to tell me what the experience was like. My Claude, for instance, sat with me that evening in this very room. We were both reading, and as far as I could tell, he was feeling good. I went into the kitchen to get us some tea — Zazu was off that night — and when I came back I found him slumped in this chair, his book on the floor, as he clutched his left arm with a grimace on his face. He looked at me across the room and whispered just loud enough for me to hear, 'I love you, darling.' And by the time I put the tray down and rushed to him, he was gone.

"Now he was 89 and had some terrible sadness in his life and some great good fortune. That day he had spent time at his office. So he had a long, productive life, a good life, and I think it's safe to assume that while he had some pain at the end it was very brief, that he knew what was happening to him and that his 'I love you' was his goodbye. Overall a good death, I'd say, much better than many, maybe even most. But what about you, dear? What kind of death would you choose?"

Clara nods. "I think your husband's death would be, as you say, preferable to many. I am just not certain I want to be aware of what is happening. That seems terribly frightening. So maybe I would prefer a coma." She stops, then shakes her head and starts again. "But who knows what your mind is doing in a coma or what you are really aware of?"

"True," says Lina. "But I think I would want to know, to be fully aware of what is happening to me. Of course, the one thing no one wants is to linger in pain, or to be so drugged you do not even know who is in the room and then to realize in any lucid moments you might have that you are a terrible burden to anyone who cares about you."

"Yes," says Cecile. "That would be the worst."

A silence holds the room for several seconds. "So speaking of the book," says Lina, finally, "I've been meaning to ask if there are aspects of aging you avoided writing about, things so grim or unpleasant that you chose not to include them because you thought they might frighten or depress your readers."

"Yes," says Cecile raising her eyebrows pleasantly at Clara and tilting her head. "Well, incontinence, certainly, which, thank my lucky stars, I have not suffered, and indigestion, which I have. Generally speaking, decaying physically is no fun, but living in Paris for a while and then here in Geneva, also, of course, very French, I've picked up anti-aging and beauty secrets from women I consider world-class experts. If you keep at it and have some luck, it can help."

Clara asks, "And what about sex? Since you were never reticent before, I was surprised you did not write about it in this book."

"Well, dear, I just thought there's been so much written lately about senile sex and most of it obscene and absurd. Anyway, I gave it up years ago along with wine. I missed both for a while, but when your stomach can no longer stand alcohol and you keep running out of partners and lubricant, I mean, what's the point. You just move on."

"Yes," says Lina, "I think the right partner is key. I have been without for some time now, and it is like everything else. You adjust."

Cecile says, "For you, darling, this is strictly temporary."

Lina looks grateful and then shifts those bright green eyes. "But what about you, Clara, may I ask? You have Marc in your life, but he is rarely with you. This must be difficult."

"It is difficult," says Clara. "But what can I do? I am faithful to Marc, and I think he is to me. But we never ask each other or even talk about it. The hardest thing is to look ahead and not see how it could become better, and when we might be together more often."

She stops, wondering if she should elaborate on her doubts, her thought of breaking it off with Marc. But Zazu, small, dark, in her 60s and wrapped in a white apron, appears to announce in Italian that dinner will be something called *Uove in Purgatorio*. Eggs in Purgatory. A Ragu Napoletana, she says, with four different cuts of pork over chestnut polenta, with an egg fried on top for each serving.

They move into another large room with a long, lustrous walnut table set at the far end for the three of them. Cecile sits at the head and says, "So, Purgatory, a temporal Hell. Sooner or later you will have suffered long enough to purge all remnants of your earthly wrong-doings and be worthy of Heaven."

"I never liked the idea," says Clara. "The sisters said we must pray for the dead, that God would add up the prayers and decide if there were enough to let you go. But what if there was no one to pray for you?"

"Indeed," says Lina, "a quaint metaphor, perhaps, for waiting through pain for love."

Over Zazu's perfect Crème Brule, they finally turn to Cecile's desire to make the emails into an epistolary novel. Clara is fine with the idea that Lina too might work on this project, if for any reason Cecile cannot. Clara first met Lina back in September at her monthly lunch meeting with Cecile. The presence of this younger woman, so attractive and brilliant, was a surprise. Lina had only arrived the day before and was just beginning to recount events from two years earlier. The professor wanted to suspend her story, but both Cecile and Clara urged her to continue. And so out poured the joys and miseries of Lina's stay in the States, and the frightening tale of what happened in Italy thereafter. Clara quickly felt a bond with this woman who offered a narrative so intimate that it seemed as if they were already friends. Together again two weeks ago for Clara's October visit, the talk continued nonstop, both of them offering family histories and childhood tales.

Now having read much of the correspondence with Marc, Lina is full of observations. "I was surprised," she says, "at how quickly and easily Marc describes his affection for you. And once your exchanges deepen, and you begin to tell each other about yourselves and your lives, you obviously knew he had left with your heart. You were so open and honest about your feelings early on, but he responds so beautifully. You must have been thrilled."

"Yes," Cecile chimes, "So the first time you two were together must have been stunning, full of sweetness and lightning. But then he goes home, and you really get to know each other."

Clara nods but says nothing.

Lina says, "I had no idea his maternal grandfather was Italian. A poor young man from Calabria who ends up in Tunisia where he meets and marries a black woman. An extraordinary story. And then after the Great War, they somehow find a way to get themselves to the States and by sheer accident end up in Detroit, where Ford Motor finally gives him a job. When Marc writes in those early exchanges about his family, he has real insight into what that experience must have been like for them a hundred years ago. And everybody, except that one Italian grandfather, is black."

Cecile takes Clara's hand. "Well, dear, you know what I think of your Marc. So smart, kind, sensitive and loving to you."

Clara smiles but feels suddenly exhausted. Both women gaze at her with warmth and concern. And with every word about Marc, she feels more certain that she can't go on much longer with this strange purgatory of the heart.

Chapter 4

Lina's bedroom is a comfortable space on the villa's second floor, a large, square, high-ceilinged room with a handsomely wrought brass bed and a vanity to one side and to the other a good-sized desk and an armoire with carved and mirrored doors. Dominating the room at mid-morning is a marvelous light streaming in three large lattice windows facing the lake and looking down on Cecile's garden.

It is Monday, a week and a half since Clara's visit for dinner, and Lina is at the desk with her Dell, again reading through the email exchanges between Clara and Marc that she now has electronically stored. Over the two-and-a-half years of their correspondence, with no computer at home in her apartment, Clara printed out each day's exchange at the bank, including the translations, to take home with her to read again that evening, or whenever she wished to warm herself with Marc's words. At the same time in Detroit, Marc was going paperless, saving everything electronically. That evening, after Zazu's *Uove in Purgatorio* and Crème Brule, Lina asked if Clara thought Marc would send his digitized version of all two-and-a-half years of their messages. Of course, said Clara, and by mid-week the whole electronic slew arrived attached to several emails.

So she is taking seriously her promise to Cecile to finish this project if Cecile cannot. There is something compelling about this glimpse into the lives of these two interesting people, and she finds herself revisiting the early exchanges, marking passages to cut and paste in a "Selects" file of prime examples of the computerized "auto" translations.

In English Clara's perfectly good French often became awkward: "Your message very pleases to me and I thank you for it. I am in form and I hope that you too. The life is beautiful!" Sometimes it was a bit puzzling: " Today it done beautiful and cold east." Once she quoted Matthew's famed New Testament line: "Many are called but few are chosen." And it ended up butchered almost beyond recognition: "It of called there much and few elected officials."

Clara said she and Marc had tried several free translation websites and finally settled on one, but they all had strengths and weaknesses. At one point Clara wrote these lines: "*Ne pas oublier: Nous avons tous droit au bonheur! J'ai été très bien dans tes bras et les sentir à nouveau serait un grand bonheur et un miracle. Je t'ai vidé mon coeur!*" And the computer offered an English version that was by turns opaque, humorous and stilted, though still decipherable: "Not to forget: We have straight to happiness! I was very well in your arms and to smell them again would be a great happiness and a miracle. I emptied you my heart!"

The gender of pronouns usually overmatched the computer program, so it was not uncommon to find constructions from Clara such as: "I liked my grandfather. It died when I was 9-years-old." And once in a while the language was so confounded that meanings were actually reversed: "I am bored also of you," the computer rendered at one point. Had he somehow conveyed with his last email that he had grown tired of her? Certainly not. Rather she had used an expression, *Je m'ennuie aussi de toi*, by which she simply meant "I miss you too." Later he wrote that after some confusion he had decided the expression meant literally something like "Without you I am bored." Of course, as Clara made clear at one point, it was the same going the other way: "The translations in French are very funny, but I arrive to understand the meaning of your words."

The Dell's clock says it is past time to get ready for her lunch with Clara in town. At the windows she finds Cecile walking steadily below on the garden's outer path. This morning she wears a tam pulled down at a rakish angle, a black jacket and long skirt and a purple scarf. It must be chilly, but nothing short of a raging downpour seems to keep Cecile from her walk.

"That's my motto," she told Lina last night, "always keep moving."

They were about to retire to their bedrooms, and Lina used the line to let her old friend know that it was time for her return to Bologna. Her stay with Cecile has been nothing short of idyllic, a perfect chance to make peace with herself and find her core again, but she now felt a powerful need to walk those ancient streets, be among those bustling crowds of students buzzing with excitement, intelligence and purpose, and to finally pick up her life again. She would always be indebted beyond words for Cecile's deep kindness and understanding, her enormous generosity in opening her home and her heart to her, but after two months it was time now, and this coming weekend she will pack up the VW and drive back through the Alps to Italy.

The old woman said nothing for a few seconds, her blue eyes watery. Finally she moved forward, took Lina's hand and said, "Of course, darling, I understand. It's just that you have been such a gift to me. Just your presence has been a lovely gift these past two months, and I will miss you so much." Holding Cecile in her arms, Lina sensed a frailty that seemed new.

* * *

At Brasserie Lipp, a large French bistro on the edge of Geneva's charming Old Town and around the corner from the financial district—Clara said it took little more than five minutes to walk from the bank—Lina has the duck galantine and Clara the pot-au-feu, a beef stew specialty of the house. The place is filled with suits and secretaries, most of them speaking French. Lina is in a dark green sweater and slacks with Clara dressed for work in a well-cut navy suit over a beige shell. Her unlined face has only a light make-up, the brown eyes wide and warm, the fine blond hair pertly coiffed. Professional and attractive.

"So this is where Marc and I had our first date. Not really a date. We all met here—Marc, Derrick, Adele and me—exactly one year after we happened upon each other at L'Entrecôte."

"Ah, yes," says Lina. "But again, you and Marc have been so generous."

Clara smiles. "It's my pleasure. You have opened your heart to me also as a friend."

"So, since I am leaving soon, I wanted to ask about how this unusual love affair got started. Cecile mentioned some things, but I brought along a few passages I thought could be a starting point, and maybe you can fill in what I do not know."

Clara says, "Okay, of course."

Lina pulls a couple of typescript pages from her bag. "So about a month into your emails you wrote this to Marc: 'I need to speak to you about my life. I was married for 17 years, and I've been divorced for 14 years. I did not remarry, even though I had proposals. I did not find the right man, so I waited. I am not complicated, and I have only one requirement: to feel good when I am with a man. If not, then I prefer being single to being unhappily attached. I am not a grasping woman. I have had well-to-do men in my life, but if I had married one of them, I would certainly have divorced again. I am not interested in money for its own sake.'"

She stops and says, "I love how honest and direct you are in these messages."

Clara just shakes her head.

Lina says, "And then this," and reads again: "'You often talk of our first night together. I never talk about it. Not out of modesty, but because of my fear of revealing too much of my feelings. So today I will write honestly about what I felt. In 2006 our meeting was brief. In general, I have no preconceived ideas about the people I meet. They seem friendly to me or not. You and Derrick I thought were very nice. I noticed you more because you were facing me, but there was nothing more than that.'

"So tell me," says Lina, "how that first meeting happened."

Clara says Marc told her later that he and his cameraman Derrick were in the mood for beef that night. First they tried Boeuf Rouge near the city center, but there was no table available. So, hungry after a long day of shooting cars at the Pal Expo, they walked down the rue Des Paquis to L'Entrecôte Couronée, a local favorite specializing in the popular French-cut steak. There the maitre d' seated them at the last open table, near the entrance and only a few centimeters from the table where Clara was waiting for her friend Adele, who as usual was late.

Obviously, if the men had been in the mood for fish, none of this would have happened. But only after Adele arrived finally and sat next to Marc and across from Derrick was there any interaction. An attractive, trim-figured woman with a glamorous look, Adele could speak decent English, and when the men started talking about a video job waiting for them back in Detroit, she broke the ice by saying she had worked on Swiss TV, a show about cultural affairs. So for the rest of the meal the four of them chatted away, with Adele providing translation. She said Clara worked at "one of our very important banks," and Marc and Derrick explained that they came to Geneva every year at this time to cover the motor show. They had credentials as journalists, but they actually worked for General Motors and did a kind of "polite industrial espionage," shooting all the World Premieres, not just here but in Detroit, Paris, Frankfurt and Tokyo, and later producing a video on each show for the company's executives, designers and engineers. "So," said Adele, "you are spies!"

When the men finished their meal, they all ended up exchanging business cards and saying how much they had enjoyed this chance meeting. Maybe, they agreed, the four of them could meet again when Marc and Derrick returned to Geneva next spring for the 2007 show.

"Thank goodness Adele finally showed up," says Lina.

Clara nods, and Lina asks how she and Adele know each other. They were best friends in secondary school, lost touch in the years after Clara left to find work and help support her family and Adele went off to college. And then they met again about eight years ago when Adele visited the bank to consider opening an account. Adele's then-lover, an aging actor who co-hosted the TV show with her (and at home offered both verbal and physical abuse), told Adele to place her money in another bank. But she and Clara renewed their friendship, began meeting for dinner and found they had much to talk about. Clara's shoulder was good for a cry when Adele's lover kicked her out of his life and installed a younger woman as his new co-host.

A sad story, says Lina. Yes, but many women have sad stories, Clara replies coolly. She says within a few weeks, Marc wrote from the States a pleasant note to both Adele and herself. Clara put off a reply until returning from her family home in Italy that summer, but Marc sounded pleased to hear from her, and eventually they set up dinner right here at Brasserie Lipp on Marc and Derrick's last night in Geneva.

"So," says Lina, "here's what you wrote in that same email, where you promised to tell Marc about your honest feelings: 'Our second meeting, at Lipp, was a chance to renew acquaintances and share a meal. During the meal, sometimes you touched my leg or my arm. I liked that. When Adele left us, she simply said: "He wants to spend time with you." I was surprised, because I had not thought about that.'

Lina glances up and says, "And then you write: 'Now I have to tell you something very important: I had never followed a man I did not know to his hotel room. That was a first. The most important thing for me is that it was the first time I felt so good, truly, as a woman, unashamed in both my body and my mind. And I loved it.'"

Finding Clara on the edge of tears Lina reaches to touch the woman's hand resting on the white tablecloth and says, "I am so sorry, dear. This upsets you."

Clara smiles. "No, please ask me. It may help us both."

"Well, then how did you end up in that hotel room?"

Clara gestures across the room. "We were at that table in the corner, and he was sitting next to me, close, on the bench. And we were all having a good time talking. Now Marc is a very warm and naturally friendly man. So when I wrote that he touched my arm and leg, I meant nothing presumptuous or aggressive. As I said, I liked it. Just an occasional soft touch as he made a point to Adele, who would then translate to me. So later as we were walking to our cars, I was surprised when she said he would like to spend more time with me. Instead of a taxi taking them back to their hotel, near the airport, I had already insisted that I drive them back. And when we got there, Marc told Derrick he wanted to talk with me some more. That was quite humorous since we hardly seemed able to say two understandable words to each other. So Derrick went inside, and I drove around to the side of the building. And when I turned the car off, Marc kissed me. Very softly and gently. And then he did it again, and again. And after a few minutes, with gestures, a few simple words in English and a few in Italian, he asked me to come to his room. I thought, and I said nothing, and I thought. And he asked me again. And finally I nodded yes. Even now I am not sure why. Except by then I felt he was warm and gentle and kind. It was a moment I did not want to lose."

Lina nods and smiles and says, "So Marc knows a little Italian?"

"Yes, very little. He studied a year in college, he says because of his grandfather. But only a year and that was three decades ago."

"And so you went inside. Please, if I ask too much, just do not answer."

"No, it is not too much. I know you need to understand, if you write this story. So inside, you know, we did not really need words. His bed was a single, very narrow, so we had to be careful not to fall off." She flutters her hands and laughs.

Lina laughs with her. "Yes, but it was good."

"It was very good And so beautiful. And so easy. I don't know how to say it. It was beautiful and easy. And it was like nothing I ever experienced before with a man. And there I was, a woman of 50."

"Wonderful," says Lina.

"Truly. And after the first time, I managed to say — again a little English, a little French, a little Italian — 'So you do this with women all over the world.' Because I thought this man must have so much experience in how to please a woman. And he said, 'No, only with you.' And of course even now I do not really know, and I do not ask. But then I tried again to find words to say, teasing a little, 'And so you are a gynecologist.' And he looked at me and turned his head a little, and he said, 'It's good, or bad? *E' buono, o male?*' I said, 'Good! No, *tres bien!*'"

Lina asks, "So you still see Adele?"

Clara's face turns unexpectedly sour. "About two years ago, when Marc wrote one of his emails expressing his love and then saying please give his best to Adele, I sent it on to her and told her about our love affair that had started of course in part because of her. So Adele called me and was very friendly and said she was very happy for me. And then she said it was a good thing she was seeing someone at that time when we all met for dinner at Lipp. Because otherwise she would have 'plucked Marc in a heartbeat for myself.' So I was stunned. I did not know what to say, and we have not seen each other or spoken since."

Lina shakes her head. "Such a sad boast must mean she is unhappy."

Clara nods but says nothing. And then comes a man's mellow, pleasant voice: "Clara, so nice to see you here, and with such a lovely friend." Lina suddenly notices two men standing at their table. Looking up, she thinks one of them is surely among the most beautiful males she has ever seen. His gaze seems to be consuming her.

"Ah, Julian, " says Clara, "And Giles. Lina, this is Giles Morneau, Chairman of Banque Privee Morneau, and Julian Lyon is my boss. Gentlemen, this is my friend Professor Lina Lentini from the University of Bologna. She is staying with our client, Cecile Eaton."

Both men make a fuss over Lina. A pleasant, staid-looking fellow somewhere in his 40s, Morneau asks about her field at the university, and Lyon, the gorgeous one, says she is clearly a rare mix of brains and beauty. And then he winks. "Of course, your friend Clara here, is no slouch in either department. As you see, she is fond of teasing, calling me her boss, when we all know she is the one who runs the entire bank and kindly allows us to pretend we do!"

Their pleasant chat goes on for another minute before the men take their leave and head for a nearby table where the host is waiting.

Lina says, "Well, you and Cecile are correct. Julian is stunning and, I must say, quite charming."

Clara without expression: "He is two-faced. In the office lately he has been impossible, and I think it really affects my mood."

"Ah, that's unfortunate. So there is tension at the bank?"

"Yes." After a pause, she starts again. "And lately I've even thought about ending it with Marc. Really, I am losing hope that it will ever be anything but an email exchange."

"Clara, I am so sorry."

"Thank you, but I hesitate to do that because you and Cecile seem so excited about this love affair of mine. And you have both been so kind to me."

"Look, Clara, this is your life and your decision, and you must forget about Cecile and me. If it is not good for you, if it makes you feel bad, then maybe end it. But do it for yourself. I know what it feels like to lose a man you love beyond words, but if you look ahead and feel no hope, then…"

Clara shakes her head.

Lina says, "I know you need to work here to make a living, and you're devoted to your family here. But what about Marc? His work is completely tied to Detroit?"

"Yes, I think so, and now General Motors is bankrupt, and his projects there have disappeared. As for money, I think he is better off than I am, but not much."

"And like you, he has two daughters?"

"Yes, like mine. The older one is successful, an attorney, although she has health problems, diabetes. She is divorced and has a young son. But the younger daughter is a lost girl, often on the streets, addicted to heroin, and prostitutes to feed her habit. So many times she has broken Marc's heart. And he tries so hard to help her, even kidnapped her once and brought her to a therapy program in Minnesota. She ran away. The mother, his former wife, has completely disowned her, and so it is all on Marc. I don't think he could ever leave this girl alone for long."

Picking at a fruit plate, they continue talking about whether Marc and Clara might still somehow find a future together. When they finish and leave, they pass the table where the two bankers seem deep in discussion. To Lina's surprise, when Lyon's dark eyes lift to hers, he quickly gets to his feet and takes her hand.

"Professor…"

"Monsieur Lyon. Lina, please."

"Lina, of course. And I am Julian. I would love to see you again and have a chance to talk further. Perhaps I could show you some of my favorite places in Geneva."

This is all so unexpected that Lina finds herself saying, "Well, how nice of you, but…"

"Good, then. I will get your number from Clara. It will be my great pleasure."

Just saying "Thank you" and moving on seems the easiest thing to do.

Waiting a short distance away, Clara asks, "What does he want?"

"A date."

"Incredible."

Chapter 5

Usually, when Clara has trouble sleeping, it comes as a surprise. She falls off quickly but then wakes after an hour or so feeling a strange kind of energy, as if riled by a dream she can't recall. And then, sometimes for hours, nothing works. It matters not which side of the bed she faces, or which side of the pillow she tries, whether one pillow or two, counting up to a hundred, or down from a thousand, thinking a pleasant thought, or striving for a mind completely blank. Followed by the dreaded check of the clock to learn how long all these efforts have failed.

Tonight, though, after her evening visit to the bank and her shocking look at Julian's twin monitors, there is no surprise. As she lays on her back in the dark, her mind is troubled with a kind of fever, and as the digital clock keeps a silent vigil, she only occasionally thinks about trying to clear her head. There is too much to consider.

Long before her sudden stop at the bank, the day was emotionally ragged. This chronic nervous feeling has been building for weeks and intensified a few days ago when she and Lina lunched at Lipp. Do what you think is best for you, her friend urged, and then the thought of ending it with Marc, the man she loves as she has no other, would not leave her alone. If she banished it at times, she would find herself even more edgy, unhappy and cross. When she arrived this morning she knew Marc would be waiting on her office computer, the message sent, as she has long ago come to expect, well after midnight in Detroit. She knows he's an early riser, often trying to get by on four or five hours. She has told him many times it's not healthy to skimp on sleep, but lately she has given up writing such things. Her day jammed with tedious tasks and last-minute demands, she did not write back, not even a few words to say she was too busy to respond and so would catch up tomorrow. This has happened more than once over the past few months,

His words, as always lately, tried hard to be hopeful. Maybe there will be some way, somehow, over the next several months that he could come to Europe on a job. But she knows even the motor show in Geneva in March seems out of the question now. In crisis, GM is slashing everywhere.

Returning from the bank to her dark apartment, she had a strong urge to tell someone about what she just saw. She came close to calling Emmanuelle. The phone was in her hand when she finally decided that she already knew what she must do and that telling Emmanuelle anything — even hinting at something amiss — might end up putting her friend in Clara's own dreadful position.

There is Marc, of course, but she would have to go back to the bank, use her computer and then wait for his written response. Not an option. And if she tries using the phone, they'll need a translator. Cecile or Lina maybe? Not at this hour. Yes, in the morning she could use her Gmail account at the Internet Shoppe, but this feels absurd. Just hours ago she was about to send him a note that would end their relationship, and now she's thinking about telling him something enormous and asking for his loving advice? No, dealing with Marc is on hold now. Maybe later she'll break it off. Or maybe down the road she will really need his help.

But what of Cecile? It is her fortune being robbed, her hugely generous charity thwarted. Shouldn't she call Cecile or arrange a meeting with her, at least give her some kind of warning? For the next hour she wrestles with that one and tosses in the bed trying to decide on the words to convey such a massive betrayal. Finally she decides she does not know enough with certainty yet about the extent of the fraud or the looting or whatever it is. Only Giles has the power to fully determine the nature and extent of what Julian is doing, and her first move really must be to go to Giles and tell him as accurately as possible what she saw last night on Julian's computer screens. And then? Then let Giles take it from there. It is his bank, certainly his responsibility.

But there are two worrisome things about meeting with Giles in the morning. One is the likelihood of encountering Julian. She dreads this so much that her stomach feels like it's tied in knots. The other is what she will say to Giles about why she entered Julian's office last night, not just stepping through the door and finding her boss not there, but moving all the way inside, far enough to see what was on those monitors. She finds it troubling that she will have to lie somehow about that.

Finally, about the time the alarm on her mobile normally wakes her, she works out the details of the story she will tell. Last night, she will say, she stopped by the office to pick up some pills she needed and had forgotten in her desk drawer. In the drawer also was an unopened bar of Toblerone, and on a whim, because she thought he might appreciate it working so late, she brought it in to place on his desk, and that's when she glanced at the screens and could not look away. She was so stunned that she simply dropped the bar in her purse and left.

When she calls Emmanuelle at 7:50 am — the woman is always the first to her desk, usually by 7:30 — Clara tries the line she has been rehearsing for the past 20 minutes. Could she please give Julian an excuse for why Clara's arrival will be delayed this morning (say there is a family emergency — one of the twins is ill, and she is needed at the hospital) and then could Emmanuelle please schedule a meeting for her with Giles as soon as possible?

As she expects, Emmanuelle immediately says, "Dear, what's wrong?"

Clara begs, "Please, Elle, don't ask. I will tell you when I can, but I can say nothing for now. It is just very important that I see Giles this morning."

"Can I at least ask if you're all right?"

"Yes, I'm fine."

"And the twins?"

"They're fine too. Please, dear."

After a pause, her friend says, "Well, the first part is easy. Julian just called in to say that he worked late last night, and to tell Giles he won't be coming in until the afternoon. Actually he said he might take the day off entirely."

"Good."

"And I will make certain that you get in to see Giles, no later than 11."

Sitting with Emmanuelle in the outer office waiting for him to call her in, Clara feels tense and uncomfortable as she listens through the closed door to the soft murmur coming from Giles on the phone. Though her old friend has honored her request and asked no further questions, the silence between them feels awkward and somehow wrong. To distract herself she turns in her chair to get a better look at a frame propped on the end table next to her. It holds a photo of the bank's Wikipedia page, and she reads the first few lines:

"Banque Privee Morneau was founded in 1919, soon after the Treaty of Versaille and the end of World War I, by Edmond V. Morneau. Established as a strategically small bank, a kind of boutique institution with strict limits on its growth, it was designed to insure superbly personalized service."

Soon after he arrived, almost six years ago, Julian had adapted the bank's musty old history for this Wikipedia article. Emmanuelle had come up with the idea of putting the page in a handsome frame and placing it in the office waiting area. Giles was not at all sure it was appropriate, but Julian thought the office display brilliant and carried the day. Clara had no opinion on the subject. Of course she knows many interesting things about the bank and its history not to be found in the Wikipedia entry.

For instance, rumor was that for some reason old Edmond, Giles' grandfather, had a special affinity for the number 37, and he had decided never to serve more than 37 clients at any time. And there were limits as well on the kind of clients that would be acceptable. New accounts could not be opened for less than 2 million francs. Among Morneau's clients after Edmond's son Albert took over operations was a distant cousin, the recently widowed Claude DeRocheford, who opened an account at the bank in 1961, and who decades later married the remarkable Cecile Eaton.

The story goes that Edmond Morneau was something of an eccentric and that his son Albert was even more so. Edmond had two daughters before Albert arrived, and to ensure that Albert would be certain to work hard and devote himself to the bank, Edmond had it written into the bank's bylaws (and into his own will) that the family enterprise could never be sold and that if Albert did not want to run it, it would need to be dissolved. Also to ensure his son's devotion and hard work, Edmond arranged various trusts for his son that would keep him hungry and striving for several years, and until he had proven himself by running the bank efficiently and strictly according to those bylaws.

Albert had adored and idolized his father and felt himself properly challenged by this arrangement and pleased with this chance to prove himself worthy. Geneva society was shocked when the 57-year-old Albert, seemingly a committed bachelor, married a girl in her 20s and then produced a son named Giles. Ironically, given the circumstances of most of their depositors, both father and grandfather secretly despised the idea of inherited wealth and what they saw as the danger it carried of sapping ambition and purpose. And so in his turn, Giles was confronted by the same challenge so successfully met by his father.

Emmanuelle had been Albert Morneau's secretary for many years before Giles finally became chairman, and Clara knows from some of her friend's remarks that during Giles' first years at the bank, after taking his advanced degree from the University of Zurich, there were rough patches between father and son. Voices raised behind closed doors would precede the younger Morneau stalking from his father's office, the steam almost visible as it escaped from his very red ears. And then when he turned 30, something had changed. Giles had apparently rededicated himself to his work at the bank, found himself an appropriate young woman to marry, and within three years had given his father two beautiful grandchildren. It had been a complete turnaround for Giles, and six years ago, shortly before Albert had passed away from a heart attack, the dour old man had expressed a firm confidence that his only son could now handle the demands of this trusted and prestigious family institution.

Personally, while Clara had always found Albert to be a cold and difficult man and had never cared for him at all, her connection with Giles has always been good. From his first days at the bank after college, she has found him to be invariably kind and friendly, not only to her but to everyone at the bank down to the lowliest janitor. She is proud of how he apparently grabbed hold of his life when it seemed perhaps to be running off the rails, how he found a way to make peace with his impermeable stone of a father.

And so how has Giles performed as chairman? Again from Emmanuelle's comments, it seems he has been diligent and reasonably successful. Until perhaps lately, when the waters the bank has sailed have been particularly troubled and its health a bit more problematic. Recent investment losses appear to have been heavy, some clients have left and now bottom line projections may be less than favorable. Because of Julian's obsessive secrecy, Clara has not been able to confirm or counter any of this. But then what bank, practically anywhere in the world, has not felt threatened, frightened, or close to crisis over the past year or two?

If this bank really does have problems, maybe what she is about to tell Giles will help him pinpoint at least one cause or source.

Chapter 6

In Giles' office she smiles at two framed photographs on a low shelf behind the chairman at his desk; one is of the old man Albert, stern as always, the other a typical family portrait—Giles with pretty, petite Hilde sitting with proud smiles behind Eric, 9, and Isabelle, 7, both bright-eyed and cute. She has met the family several times on their visits to the bank, has watched the children grow, and always feels happy for Giles. He and Hilde, she knows, are very active in Geneva's social and cultural life, pictured often at opera and symphony events and most recently at the dedication of a new hospital wing.

Normally she would ask first about his wife and children, but there is nothing normal about this moment. She thanks him for meeting on such short notice.

"Of course," he says with his kind smile, "Not a problem."

There is nothing to do but plunge right in, and so nervously, feeling a small patch of skin under her left eye twitch in a strange way, she tells her pills/Toblerone story. A quiet version of his smile lingers right up to the point at which she says that what she saw on Julian's screens was so disturbing she immediately left the bank. And then the smile disappears.

"And so please, Clara, what exactly did you see?" His face now seems very serious, but gives nothing else away.

"What I saw on one of the screens was something I've seen many times before...."

He nods, and she continues. "A page from the quarterly report I have delivered many times to our client Cecile Eaton."

He stops nodding. She says, "Her name was on it, and in fact it was the report for the most recent quarter, with the date—30, September, 2009—right there in the upper right corner. Except that all the totals of those anonymous donations to each of her charities were only about ten percent of what they are in the report I gave her earlier this month."

Giles looks grim. "And on the other screen?"

"The other screen is more problematic but still important. It was a listing from an investment account, but the page was scrolled down, so I could not see the names of either the account holder or the investment firm. I should have scrolled it up to look, but I was too stunned and frightened to touch his keyboard."

"Understandable," he says. "But still important, you say?"

"Yes, because they matched up in a way. I mean, in each case, the ninety percent in effect taken from each of the charities equaled the amounts listed as recently invested in several different securities. I mean, it was clear he was moving funds from Cecile's — Ms. Eaton's — account to another account entirely."

There is what feels like a long, thoughtful silence. Finally, Giles nods as if there is something about this terrible story that has finally clicked into place and made sense. Then he asks if she has told anyone else about any of this. And she says no, she did not think it was proper to say anything until she had "at least spoken to you." With some fervor for a man who always seems calm and under control, he replies that she has done exactly the right thing, and that many people are in her debt, he first among them, for her "honesty, integrity and devotion to the bank and its clients." It is exactly what she wanted to hear from Giles Morneau.

"Now the first thing I want to do," he says, "is to lift the terrible burden that has so suddenly and unfairly descended onto your shoulders. But forgive me, Clara, I need to ask more questions to make certain I am absolutely clear on what you saw in Julian's office. I know you understand this is an extremely grave and serious matter, and we must be very careful here."

"Of course, please ask, and I will try to answer as completely as possible. I just want to say again that I was extremely shocked by what I saw. At first I could not believe my eyes, and so I looked again and again. Of course I do not have a photographic memory, but I am certain that what I have told you is what I saw."

"I have no doubt," he says and proceeds for the next 10 minutes to ask questions about every detail of her story, at one point focusing on those securities she mentioned. Unfortunately she recognized none of them, recalled none of the names, but thought they sounded mostly like bonds and maybe private investment pools. Finally, he thanks her again profusely and demonstrates, she feels, a full understanding of her feelings, her fear and concern for Cecile and her deep discomfort at being placed by a capricious fate in the middle of all this.

To make certain he can lift this burden from her and deal with this situation in the most effective way, he asks only that she continue her silence on this subject, not mention a word about this to anyone, either inside or outside the bank. Actually, he wants her to take the rest of the day off, go home as soon as they are done here, and relax as much as possible. He will call, probably within a few days, when it is time for her to return to work.

As they get to their feet, Giles says he knows she has developed something of a personal relationship with Cecile and that she might feel obligated to share this information with their esteemed and long-time client. But that really needs to wait until he has gotten to the bottom of this and has done what is necessary to fully restore Cecile's position. Really from this moment forward, it will be his most important duty and responsibility to keep Ms. Eaton fully informed and, of course, fully protected.

Escorting her out of the office, he moves her past Emmanuelle (who glances at her with eyebrows slightly raised) and then down the hall to the lift. There he surprises Clara with a hug, the first she has ever had from him, brief but firm. His soft brown eyes look sadly into hers, and he says, "Clara, thank you for helping to save our bank."

Unable to speak, she nods with emotion as the bell chimes, and she boards the lift.

Back in the apartment she sits in her favorite reading chair and wonders what she will do now. It feels strange to be here at mid-day on a Friday. Maybe she will spend the afternoon reading, something she has done very little of lately. Auster's new one, *Man in the Dark*, is waiting right there for her on the coffee table. And then just the thought of reading sends a wave of exhaustion over her, and she remembers again that she hardly slept at all last night.

In the bedroom she slips off her clothes, removes the plain gold necklace and hoop earrings and, not even bothering with the t-shirt she usually sleeps in, gets under the covers. She is just falling off when her mobile sounds next to her. The ID says it is Emmanuelle. Not surprising. Her good friend is no doubt concerned and hoping for answers. But, with the admonition from Giles, this is not a good time to talk. She lets the call go to voice mail, then waits for the beep and, curious about whether Emmanuelle will report some telling comment or behavior from Giles, picks up the message. Her friend's voice sounds worried, but she does not push Clara. "Just want to know you are okay. Call me, dear, when you can." Clara turns the phone off and falls asleep.

* * *

The room is dim when she wakes, and her clock says it's nearly 5 pm. She has slept away the whole afternoon. She wonders first how Giles has spent his day. Has there already been a confrontation with Julian? Turning on her mobile, she is surprised there are no calls, no messages left. Perhaps going to Giles with her story still seems so momentous, that she expects some kind of seismic response or reaction almost immediately.

With the apartment warm, the way she likes it, she throws on a thin wrap and takes the mobile with her into the kitchen. She suddenly feels famished. As a cup of coffee brews, she pulls out a half-loaf of crusty day-old bread, a sharp cheese and some mortadella and begins munching. In the living room she uses the TV remote to turn on TSR's news at 5. More concern about security in Iraq after those two suicide bombings in Baghdad killed 155 and wounded 500 more. And in the U.S. the latest on that H1N1 flu outbreak that Obama declared a national emergency. Nothing yet about scandalous criminal charges against a brilliant and handsome young investment manager at the Banque Privee Morneau.

Clara thinks of Cecile. She promised Giles she would tell no one, but shouldn't she at least let her friend know that she is thinking about her, maybe simply say that she'd like to move their next lunch up a few days, given that Cecile will be alone now with Lina leaving tomorrow? She picks up her phone, calls and, when she gets the answering machine, leaves her message. As soon as she rings off she wonders if she sounded too urgent. If Cecile had answered, could she really have not said a word about Julian's computer?

And now out of seemingly nowhere comes a thought that she immediately brands as nonsense but is soon followed by a constriction in her chest and slightly labored breathing. This she knows is fear. The thought is that she might actually lose her position at the bank over what has just happened. She tells herself this is

43

absurd, that in word and demeanor Giles could not have been more grateful and reassuring, that the idea of her consistently faithful employer of more than 30 years severing its connection with her is totally irrational.

And yet she cannot stop wondering if she will somehow end up being the one to blame. After all she contravened Julian's law about entering his office when he is not there. She lied to Giles about why she found herself in front of those monitors, and perhaps she somehow completely misconstrued what was in fact on those two screens.

Again she tells herself this is entirely ridiculous, that it makes no sense at all. And yet she still feels dread about her future. What if she were in fact to lose her job at the bank? Then what? At her age and with no recommendation from her former employer? With her woefully limited savings, she is certainly not ready to face a forced retirement.

Finally, sternly and aloud she tells herself to stop thinking like a fool. And almost in an effort to put this silly fear behind her, she calls Vera. Her daughter is really the only one who might be impacted if Clara were unemployed. She has helped support Vera as an adult at times, and so what would happen if Clara lost her ability to even support herself? As she listens to the rings, she is sure voice mail is coming, but then for the first time in close to two months Vera answers. And so, of course, without saying why, she nags her daughter again about not quitting her job without lining up another. And Vera is no more receptive to this advice than she has been in the past. The conversation quickly turns unpleasant, and before she catches herself, Clara says, "Look, there may be trouble at the bank."

"What? What kind of trouble?"

"Nothing. I didn't mean that."

"Mother," says Vera, "If there is one thing I've learned from you lately, it's that before I ever reach menopause I should certainly kill myself."

And then her daughter claims someone is knocking on her door — which Clara does not believe for a second — and hangs up.

Almost immediately there is, weirdly, a knock on Clara's own door. With no buzz from the intercom, it's probably a neighbor with mail placed in the wrong box. But when she looks through the peephole in her door, Willem Tanner is there, staring at the floor. No doubt sent by the thoughtful Giles out of concern for her. Willem must be here to make sure she is okay, to ask if there is anything she needs or wants. Or maybe to underscore the importance that Clara say nothing to anyone. When she opens the door these thoughts prompt her to give the man a full, warm and grateful smile. Willem stands there, looking what? Somber? Even when they were together, she was never very good at reading his face, and now she is doing no better.

Chapter 7

In her easy, fluent French Lina says, "So you have the big three: brains, beauty, wealth. You're irresistible. How is it you're still single?"

Smiling irresistibly across the two glasses of Cab they've just clinked, he says she'd be surprised. And then launches into an unlikely story of unrequited love—betrayal and rejection by a beautiful woman he adored with two small children he loved. The woman claimed to be divorced when in fact she was only separated, and finally her husband returned to reclaim her. He had disappeared somewhere—Africa, he said, Sierra Leone, setting up an export business—but realized finally he had made a huge mistake. All he wanted was his family back. The woman claimed she was crushed but had to take the husband back for the children's sake.

Julian says he is still certain he and this woman were a perfect match, and yet it all fell apart. The breakup happened earlier in the summer, and he's been fighting depression ever since. Actually he decided to change his life because of it, and that's why he pursued the job in Hong Kong. The fact is Lina is the first woman he's encountered since to catch his eye and intrigue him, and now they are both leaving Geneva.

A sad story told with those gleaming dark eyes looking anything but sad. All intended to make him appear a very hetero victim? Would he make up such an elaborate tale? And now he goes back over his story, spicing it with all kinds of details: names and descriptions of the kids, endearing little moments with the woman, where and how they met, how the woman at first was sure he was gay. Something he's lived with most of his adult life. "Too beautiful to be straight!" At one point in his 20s he held a razor to his cheek, thinking if he disfigured himself, women might more readily accept that he could want them.

"I know, absurdly stupid, but it did cross my mind. Actually I was trying to decide which cheek when the phone rang. My mother. By the time we rang off, I knew I couldn't do that to her."

Lina shakes her head. Finally she ventures, "A woman, I think, can usually tell if a man is really there for her. If a man really wants her."

"How about you? Do you think I really want you?"

She is tempted to evade. Instead she looks at him steadily and says, "Well, do you?"

He smiles and says simply, "I think I've already made that clear."

His call came just after noon, a big surprise. He was starting his weekend early, skipping school, he said, and wondered if she might be free this afternoon for a little romantic getaway, a visit to Annecy, just a short drive to the south. She will love the place.

She does love the place, she told him. She had been there a couple of times, though not for several years.

Wonderful then. He'll pick her up, about 3? They can spend a while walking along the lake and through the town, then pick a place for dinner. He'll have her home by 9 at the latest.

When he arrived punctually at the villa, he was perfectly charming with Cecile, asking her to join them, no doubt certain she would not. The old woman was in high spirits and seemed amused by the interest in Lina affected by this absurdly handsome fellow she had long ago decided was gay. In a rakish brown leather flyer's jacket over a black sweater and slacks, he winked at Lina and said the three of them could have "some real fun."

Cecile replied that her last ménage a trois was more than 40 years ago and hadn't turned out all that great. No, she would stick with her book—for the third time *For Whom the Bell Tolls*—and give Zazu the day off.

In his sleek black 5 series BMW she asked what possessed him to call her.

Well, he said, he had given her fair warning. He had told her he would call when they met at Lipp. She is brilliant, gorgeous, and fascinating. Exactly why would he not call? Besides, Clara had told him she was returning to Bologna this weekend. So this was a last chance to spend some time and get to know her.

As he drove, fast and skillfully, down through the pleasant countryside, they exchanged bio details. He had grown up in Lucerne with a loving, protective mother and no father. The man had left them when Julian was only months old, so, while he had seen photos, he had no recollection at all. University was in Zurich, heavy in math and sciences, then the graduate banking program. Stepping-stone jobs in Zurich, New York and the Far East, and then five years ago Giles had tapped him to be his investment manager at Banque Privee Morneau.

He spoke easily about himself, clearly a favorite topic. But to keep him talking and, she hoped, revealing himself, she bemoaned her "abysmal ignorance" about the world of high finance and even economic basics, wondering if he could help her understand what has happened over the past year or so to land us in this crisis. And so he gave her his views in fairly simple, easy-to-follow terms, and it was nothing really she hadn't heard or read before. All about sub-prime mortgages, greed, lust for new and easier ways to accumulate obscene amounts of wealth, credit default swaps and collateral debt obligations, the trading of risk and various kinds of monetary insurance that blew up when the real estate bubble burst in the States and the U.K. In Julian's telling, the Swiss giant UBS is one of the villains and the determinedly small and conservative Banque Prevee Morneau is one of the good ones, playing by the rules and doing the right thing for its clients, even though the bank has been hurt by the crisis more than others.

Curious because Clara has been so sour on this man, she asked what it was like to work so closely with her. "She seems like such a pleasant, competent woman."

"No, not competent, she is superb, and I don't know what I'll do without her."

"How do you mean?"

"Well, I've told no one, except Giles, of course, but I've taken a significant job at a major firm in Hong Kong. I'll be at the bank only another week or so."

She offered surprised congratulations, and he said it was another step up for him, but he could only hope he would find someone half as good as Clara to work with there.

In Annecy he parked near the lake front, and they walked in the late afternoon sun along the lovely blue lake surrounded by the spectacular Alps, then back into the charming old town with its Venice-like canals, a postcard around every corner. He flirted, trying hard, she thought, not to seem like a gay man straining to appear straight. Would he actually come on to her? And if so, would it really prove his sexual interest? At one short flight of steps he took her hand and then held it for a while as they walked. Then he kissed her, rather chastely, she thought. When they were moving again, he asked if she believed in true love.

"True love?" she said. "Of course, and you?"

"Yes," he said simply. And a few minutes later he asked if she knew that the famous French film "Claire's Knee" had been shot here in Annecy.

"Yes, it's one of my favorites."

"Really. I could never understand why it was so important. I mean we studied it in the class I took in Zurich in Modern French Film Classics. But nothing really happens. Just a lot of talk and then Jerome, the central character, a diplomat, I guess, rubs the girl's knee for a long time and that's it. Frankly, I wondered if he really might be gay."

"An interesting thought, but there is nothing in the film to suggest he is."

"Nonetheless, I wondered."

And then they found themselves standing in front of a small canal-side restaurant called the Chez le Pere Jules. He said, "It's good. Unpretentious and this time of year there aren't many tourists."

"Sounds perfect," she said and inside found he was correct on all three points. There was an Alpine feel to the old wood-paneled walls, red-and-white checked tablecloths and cured meats hanging from the ceiling. They both have the Tartiflette, a mix of potatoes, wine, cream, pork and melted Roblechon cheese. Certainly there is nothing fay or delicate about what this man says was his favorite childhood dish.

Chapter 8

As Julian urges the BMW swiftly through the darkness up the two-lane road back to Geneva, she thinks of the book she's been reading, the one she found on a shelf in her bedroom at Cecile's, and feels anxious to get back to it this evening. She asks, "So what if I tell you a story?"

He glances at her. "Ah, good. I love stories."

"Yes? This will be a pleasant game then. It's about a very famous man, and we'll see how long it takes for you to guess who it is."

"So may I ask questions as we go?"

"No, for now no questions. Maybe later. Agreed?"

"Agreed."

"So the man was born to a Protestant family in Geneva, and, though he would spend his life in many other places, he always referred to himself as a citizen of Geneva."

Julian nods with his eyes on the road.

"His father was educated and a lover of music and made his living as a watchmaker. His mother was the daughter of a Calvinist preacher and died of a fever within days of the boy's birth. He and his older brother were brought up by the father and an aunt."

"This sounds like a long time ago."

"Yes, let's just say hundreds of years ago, but no questions!"

"Okay."

"So when the boy was five, his father wished to foster a love of reading, and every night after supper they would read together in a collection of adventure stories. They would be so consumed by these stories that sometimes they would read all night, and the father would berate himself for being more of a child than was his son. After a time the boy became enamored of Plutarch's *Lives of the Noble Greeks and Romans*, and he would read the book to his father while the man made his watches.

"When the boy was 10, his father got into a legal scrape with a

50

wealthy landowner and fled Geneva. The boy would rarely see his father again and was left in the care of relatives who soon packed him off to a minister outside the city. There he boarded for two years and learned the rudiments of mathematics and drawing. At 13 he was apprenticed, first to a notary and later to an engraver. But the engraver often beat him, and so at 15 the boy ran away. Somehow he turned up in Annecy."

"Ah, so he may have taken this very road."

"Perhaps he did. In any case, a Catholic priest sent him for refuge to the home of a noblewoman in Annecy. She was 29, attractive, separated from her husband, and supported in part by the King of Piedmont, receiving a stipend for helping to bring Protestants to Catholicism. The woman was quite taken with the boy, and he was quickly enthralled with her, calling her mother. But concerned that it would appear unseemly to harbor a 15-year-old boy under the same roof, she arranged to send him to Torino to learn the basics of Catholicism and complete his conversion. Then for a while the boy was on his own, wandering through Italy and France and as far as Paris, working at times as a servant, secretary and tutor, finally finding his way back to the woman he called "Maman," who was now living in a house in Chambery.

"No longer concerned about appearances, she gave him a room along with guidance and support. He had access to her large library and her circle of educated friends and was given formal music lessons. In short, an entre to the world of arts, letters and ideas. And when he turned 20 this woman he idolized taught him a few other things. Concerned, she said, that he had become a target for the wiles of the women of Chambery, she took him as her lover, even though she already had a lover, the steward of her house. Somehow all three lived together without a problem. But while the young man continued to adore this woman for her beauty, intellect and kindness, and would always refer to her as the love of his life, the sex between them, as he would describe it later, was constrained, dutiful and a bit confusing, perhaps because he never stopped thinking of her as his mother."

Julian moves his eyes to her. "That would do it, I'd say."

"Yes, maybe so. Anyway, in his 20s, despite bouts of hypochondria, he became a serious student of not only music but also philosophy and mathematics. Finally at age 27 he left his

'Maman' for a job in Lyon as a tutor. By 30 he was in Paris and presenting his own newly invented system of musical notation, certain that it would change the world of music and make his fortune. It did neither, and for years he was close to penniless. But in Paris he took up with a pretty seamstress named Therese, and they lived together with her mother and other family members. Eventually over the years he and Therese had five babies, each of whom they gave away to a foundling home. Strange behavior, it would seem, for a man who would later be celebrated as a major theorist on education and child-rearing.

"So until his late 30s, the man led a life of poverty and obscurity. But in Paris during those years he became friendly with the famed philosopher Diderot, and by age 37 he was contributing articles to his friend's renowned *Encyclopedie*. Then a year later he entered an essay contest, writing on whether the development of the arts and sciences had been morally beneficial to mankind. No, he argued, before their development people lived in ways that were simple and virtuous, but now with the flourishing of science and the arts, life had become complex, corrupt and unhappy, with governments assuming powers too great and suppressing individual liberties. Princes, he wrote, encouraged involvement with the arts because it helped to "wind garlands of flowers around the chains that bind" their subjects. His essay won the contest and, when it was published, brought him considerable notoriety.

"This was in fact a man of great heart, intellect, and also contradiction. Soon after writing sternly against the higher value of the arts, he composed an opera that was performed for King Louis XV, who loved it so much that he offered our man life-long financial support."

"Nice," pronounced Julian, his profile cast in the high-tech glow from the dashboard.

"Yes, but he rejected the King's prestigious gift and continued to snub other advantageous offers, to the consternation of his friends. At 42 he returned to Geneva briefly and converted from Catholicism back to Calvinism. But in the surge of books and essays he would produce over the next several years, it became clear that he valued all religions alike, as long as they brought man to a higher moral plane. Back in Paris he found himself increasingly at odds with both critics and friends, and with support from wealthy benefactors he lived outside the city. As he approached age 50 he published a long and very popular romantic novel based in part on his relationship with his "Maman." That was followed the next year by a didactic novel that also had substantial impact. But his most important work was a political treatise he published between the two novels. It began with these words:

"'Man is born free; and everywhere he is in chains. One thinks himself the master of others, and still remains a greater slave than they.'"

"Ah," says Julian lifting both hands off the steering wheel for a second, "'Liberty, equality and fraternity.' It's Rousseau!"

"Yes, *Of the Social Contract*. Bravo!"

Julian with a quick glance of triumph at her: "I was pretty much in the dark until those words. But they've always stuck with me, ever since my university days at Zurich, second year, Political Philosophy. They seemed so important to me then. The still do, actually."

"Yes, well, in their way they helped change the world."

"They certainly changed my world."

She wants to ask how but lets it pass. After a pause he says, "But I don't recall learning anything about his personal life, as in the story you told. Except, didn't he go out of his mind toward the end?"

"Not really. He had always been emotionally volatile, perhaps a bit unstable at times, but as his writing and his ideas became more famous, his life became more complicated, difficult and overwrought. His deeply critical views of monarchy and government branded him a dangerous foe of those in power. His attitude of religious tolerance angered both Catholics and Protestants. And his notions on the spiritual origins of man made enemies of the secularists, atheists and materialists who were formerly his friends. There was a bitter public feud with the great Voltaire. And even his old friend Diderot ended up describing him as 'false, vain as Satan, ungrateful, cruel, hypocritical, and wicked.'

"Of course, this was a time of enormous intellectual ferment and excitement. Big ideas were wildly important, argued and fought over with vigor and sometimes violence. His books and essays were banned and burned in Geneva and Paris. He was condemned by the Parliament of Paris, a warrant was issued for his arrest, and he was banned from France. He took refuge in Switzerland, but his house was stoned. Finally, he fled to England and stayed for a while as a guest of David Hume, but then they had a falling out."

"So," says Julian, "it's not paranoia if they're really out to get you."

"More or less. Back in France under an assumed name, he spent his last years in seclusion and died of a brain hemorrhage on a solitary walk. Voltaire had disparaged him unmercifully, but much later, their remains were placed across from each other in the Pantheon in Paris, along with those of the other heroes of the French Revolution."

They drive in silence for a time. Then he asks, "So, Lina, tell me, do you just walk around with this kind of data in your head?"

She looks at him. "You mean about Rousseau?"

"Yes, I find it incredible."

"No, no, I have been reading a book I found at Cecile's. His *Confessions*, written toward the end of his life, a long memoir and self-justification."

He is silent the rest of the way back to the villa. When he pulls up to the front entrance he shifts into park and turns to her. She can see him better now in the bright glow of the torch lights on either side of the massive door. Cecile must have turned them on for her.

He says softly, "I'm so pleased this worked out."

"I am too." She wonders if she should invite him in and then realizes she is finished with this man. Telling Rousseau's story, she knows now, was only to learn a few last things about him, and there is no longer any interest. She can't wait to see Cecile and spend the rest of the evening with her.

When he leans in to kiss her, she gives him a cheek and then quickly the other. Reaching down for her bag, she says, "I'm sure Hong Kong will be another triumph, and I wish you a wonderful life, Julian."

"And I hope the same for you."

Does she seem too anxious to leave? Not when he appears even more ready to part. He waits until she turns the key and opens the heavy front door, then with one last exchange of waves he's off.

Inside the large house is silent. The entrance hall is dimly lit, but she can see that the great room, to which it gives access, is brighter. Cecile is probably in there reading in her favorite chair, the one that used to belong to her husband.

Not wanting to startle her, she calls in English, "Cecile, darling, I am back." No response, but in the living room the lamp is lit next to her chair, and the Hemingway is open, pages down, on the arm.

Lina remembers that Zazu is off and calls again, louder this time, thinking she will most likely find Cecile in the kitchen. Still only silence. On the ornately carved mantle, the antique clock says it is just before 9.

She moves through the dining room thinking the older woman may have retired early, though that would be unlike her. With a push through the door to the kitchen, she says "Cecile?" one more time.

And then she finds her friend sprawled, unmoving, on the red tile floor. Her right arm is extended, the fingers of her hand spread, as if she had been reaching for the phone on the counter when she fell. The usual warm pink color of her face is gone, her right cheek is pressed against the tile, and drool glistens next to her open mouth. The one eye Lina can see, the left, is closed. Does it flutter just once, for an instant? Rushing to her, she cannot be sure.

Chapter 9

He hasn't been in this bar since before he went away, close to a decade now. Off the rue de Berne in Geneva's tame, tiny (a few square blocks) red light district, close by the Gare Cornivan, the central train station, with porn shops, a few shows, a couple of cheap hotels and some obvious whores. A young one, actually rather cute, at the far end of the bar has been eying him since he walked in, probably thinking she's made him for the cop he used to be, as if that made any difference. If they keep themselves clean, no one cares what these girls do.

A glance at his black Movado tells him it's nearly 10, his call long past due. "That's our little Will," his mother used to say, her voice grating with sarcasm. "Never today what you can shove off for tomorrow."

"Leave the boy be," his father would say. Or not. Sometimes with enough booze he'd use those huge construction worker paws to beat the shit out of him. "The Ice Princess," was his father's favorite term for her. Hardly appropriate, except for the "Ice" part. The woman was a cold, grim presence in their ugly little apartment, her thick waist, common features and lank blond hair never reminding anyone of royalty. Firmly attached in mutual loathing were his parents, so viciously fixed on each other that the boy was mostly left to shape himself and to impose some kind of order on a life that seemed only ragged, pointless and unhappy. He used to wonder if that's why he became a cop. He had grown up with a cold, brutal streak of his own and at 20 thought his peculiar, self-styled, black-white notion of good and evil might best be employed by the Geneva Municipal Police.

Early on he learned he enjoyed hurting people who flouted the law, especially in ways he found particularly odious. Yes, it was well-known and granted that this town's biggest criminals wore suits and that those men occupied a different plane altogether; they made the world go round and were generally not to be touched. Drugs

56

were of some concern only if the product offered not bliss, surcease or oblivion, but rather bodily harm, or if the trade's collateral damage became excessive and bystanders were hurt. But robbers and petty thieves, disturbers of the peace, assaulters and murderers, those who preyed on weakness and took what belonged to others, whether their watch or their life? Those were his special concern and got his special attention.

He soon acquired a reputation in the department as an especially effective interrogator, particularly adept at using fear, intimidation and sudden, shocking violence to elicit the desired response. Because of his intense dedication and swift, clean efficiency, he was eventually assigned to the chief's security detail. There his loyalty was highly valued as was his willingness to carry out assignments that others found distasteful. He was particularly adept at dealing with certain criminal types—those who showed no respect for societal order or the authority of the force, thus refusing to pay the tribute due the chief—making them more acutely aware of their responsibilities, or on occasion simply arranging their permanent disappearance. Finally, he became the chief's most trusted enforcer and bagman and held that post for several lucrative years, and then everything got fucked.

At the center, not surprisingly, was a woman, beautiful, alluring and absurdly careless, a cartel operative fingered by Interpol, then nabbed by the Swiss national police. He had seen it coming and strongly suggested that he make her disappear, forcing the group to use someone more responsible for their monthly exchange. But the answer was no, she was a favorite of the man in charge, and thus untouchable. When she saved herself by giving them Willem, he knew exactly how things would work. In exchange for his stony silence he would get three years reduced to 17 months and upon re-entry a good-sized pot of gold. Except the pot failed to materialize. Instead, while he was away, the cartel, with a suggestion from the chief, made a laundering arrangement with Giles and his bank, and so Willem was set up in a new job, a kind of special security agent for Banque Privee Morneau. The position has paid quite well and involved very little work. There's been some international travel involving a few less-than-challenging assignments, and only one bit of unpleasantness that he should have foreseen.

Soon after he joined the bank, he discovered an opportunity that seemed too good to refuse. Easy access to a goodly sum of the bank's cash and a chance move it unnoticed to his own account. He was, of course, caught red-handed and told that he would be given one more chance, but that he must do whatever was needed by the bank, carry out any and all orders, or the evidence of his fraud would be turned over to the national police, and Willem would be returned to prison for a very long stay. Still, none of his work assignments has been odious in any way. Until he was called to Giles' office today just after noon.

Actually, the visit with the old woman was not much of a problem. It took him less than two hours to get the compound he needed from the hospital orderly who owed him, and after a call from the bank about some paperwork needing a signature, she answered the door herself and cordially invited him in. It was on the way to the dining room table to sign the papers that he stuck the syringe in her upper arm. The old woman was feistier than he expected, crying out, flailing her arm and striking him in the nose with the back of her hand. Had the needle come out perhaps before all of the compound had entered her body? He was almost certain it did not, and by the time she reached door to the kitchen, she was already staggering. Uncertain whether the housekeeper might still be there, he left immediately.

The little blond whore at the bar has finally decided to make her move, carrying her drink and walking straight up to him with an odd twist of a smile.

"I think I know you," she says.

"No, I think not."

"Well, then I think I would like to know you."

Some things change. Some never do. Back in his first years on the force, when he used to frequent this place along with his partner Savoneau and their pal Tremelyn, they liked it because it was not popular with other cops. They pretty much had it to themselves along with the whores who would offer a quickie or a blowjob, thinking they and their trade were safer that way. There were no preliminaries. Just a look or a nod or at most a "want to?" Sometimes he'd partake, sometimes not. Now he's tempted by this girl's proffered distraction. But her small attempt at a smile somehow reminds him of the fateful one he received earlier this evening.

Waiting in front of that apartment door, he found himself filled with dread, hoping almost desperately that when the woman saw him, she would not smile. "A smile that would warm the dead," Savoneau had said after they ran into him on the street one day. But it was the smile, as much as anything, he thought, that broke them up after several months together, more than four years ago. Yes, when he was caught at the bank, trapped like a dumb animal doomed by it's own instinct, he was told also to break it off with Clara, and he knew that was for the best. As a cop he had many women but never let any of them get close. Clara was his first after prison and for a while, it was different, and he wondered if maybe he had changed. But he was a hard man, with hard things to do, and this woman made him soft. That smile, as the saying went, turned him to butter. And so he broke it off, never giving her a reason, other than that he was just a man who had always played the field, and it was time again to play. Despite the brave face she put on, he knew she'd been hurt, and with any luck she would remember that pain now as she unlocked the door and opened it to him.

No such luck. When she looked into his eyes, the smile he dreaded came quickly, and she invited him in. He did not move for a second or two, stopped by a sinking in his chest. When he finally crossed the threshold, he felt almost hopeless.

She offered him a glass of wine, and he accepted, thinking maybe it would help. But as she moved to the kitchen, and he sat alone in her modest little apartment, he thought of the many nights he had spent here, and it only got worse. She returned quickly with a glass for each of them, and he fumbled with an explanation for his unexpected appearance at her door. He was passing by and just got a sudden urge. He hoped he wasn't intruding.

No, of course not, she said, and, no doubt sensing his discomfort, began filling the silence, rattling on about her daughters and grandchildren.

This did not help at all, and so he stopped her and said, "Look, I must tell you why I'm really here."

She looked at him, again with that damn smile, and said simply, "Yes?"

He tried to speak brusquely, with as few words as possible. "Yes. Well, I've been assigned to make you disappear."

She stared at him, the smile slowly dying, as if she were trying to process words she had never heard before. "Assigned to make me disappear."

"Yes." He needed to be more blunt. "There are men who want you dead."

"What?"

"Clara, there are men who want you dead."

"What men?"

"You know what men."

She shook her head. "Why dead?"

"You know why."

"Because I saw something?"

"Yes, I don't know what you saw, but because of that."

She got to her feet. "So I will go to the police."

He also got up. "No, even if I allowed that, it would do no good."

"You would not allow that?"

"Look, you have no idea how incredibly well connected these men are."

"These men! These men?" She is suddenly more angry than he has ever seen before. "Stop playing this game! It is Giles?"

He nodded silently.

"And Julian?"

"Yes. And it would simply be your word against theirs. You have no evidence of what you saw."

"I have my eyes."

"That is nothing, and in any case, by now they will have wiped it all away."

She sat down, and he did too.

"Clara, I know you are frightened and angry. But please think clearly. You must flee tonight, leave here and contact no one, especially the police. Do not make me hurt you."

And with a soft cry the tears began. To keep her focused he continued talking, trying to make sense. He said that anyone she contacted—friends, family, anyone who knows she's alive, even if they don't know where she is or what she knows—would be in grave danger. He will tell these men she is dead, and for them she must be. Maybe not forever, maybe only for a while, until certain things happen here in Geneva. But for now, she must be dead.

"Dead," she said wiping her cheek.

"Yes, dead. There must be no calls, no emails, no texts, no communication of any kind. They'll probably believe me, but still, they'll be watching everything. Along with their friends at the police. So if you use your mobile, a credit card, anything, you will leave a trail they might easily access. Do you have any cash here?"

His question made him realize he had not thought any of this through. The odds against her staying "dead" for long seemed suddenly astronomical.

She looked toward the kitchen. "A little." She was no longer crying. "I always keep a few hundred…"

"Okay…"

"But I can go to the bank machine now and get five hundred more."

"No, Clara, think! You're already supposed to be dead and so you do the one thing that's easiest for them to check?"

She shook her head and said what he was already thinking: "This is hopeless."

"No, it's not. You just have to be careful and resourceful. Extremely careful and resourceful. Look, I'll give you this, as a loan." From his days on the force he had always carried a substantial wad of cash. And from his pocket now he unfolded and counted out eleven hundred.

She hesitated, then took it and said, "Thank you, Willem."

"So where could you go?" He was feeling a sudden, uncharacteristic attack of nerves.

"The States?" she said after a brief hesitation. "I could maybe go to the States or…."

"That's okay, I don't even want to know. Just think quickly and go."

"When? Tonight?"

" Of course, tonight! Now! You have already died."

He waited impatiently while she took too long to pack a small carry-on suitcase on rollers, then waited again while she donned her dark blue car coat and wrapped a gray woolen scarf around her neck. As they walked out, she grabbed a sweater hanging by the door and shoved it in her large purse. Finally, he carried the suitcase for her down the two flights of stairs.

"Will they be watching us?" she asked as they hurried along the cold, dark, nearly empty street to her car in the garage two blocks away.

"No, they trust me," he said but wondered the same.

With the case in the car, she gazed up at him, not smiling. She looked as if she wanted to kiss him, but all he saw was her neck wrapped in that scarf. Under the wool it was so slender, he knew. He could snap it in an instant. Instead he kissed that pretty mouth, firmly and finally, then without another word, put her in the car and watched her drive away.

The blond whore's neck is short and rather thick, but having done it with more than one other neck, he knows it would not take much. Just walk her to a nearby alley, shove himself into her a few quick times, then break it quickly in his hands. It's surely what he should have done with Clara in the garage. He has not the slightest doubt that he should have made the woman, her smile and her red Opel all disappear forever. And this thought makes him very angry.

The whore, he notes now, has one gray eye and one green, a fact he finds disorderly and off-putting. He says, "Sorry, not in the mood. You should leave now."

She looks at him for a second or two, then places her half-filled glass on a table and walks out of the bar. He gazes after her, then pulls out his mobile. Fuck making the call Giles is waiting for. All he'll get tonight is one word. He slowly taps out the text.

"Done."

Chapter 10

Waking, she finds herself staring into the hazel eyes of a young girl, maybe 8-years-old. The eyes are only a few inches away from hers and possibly magnified a bit by the glass between them. The girl's stare is somehow familiar and seems to hold some kind of accusation. Does she know this girl? She has the strange notion that this may, in fact, be her own 8-year-old self gazing at her. Perhaps in a dream from which she is just now waking? Moving her head slightly she finds it resting against the driver's side window of a car.

The girl screams, backs away and starts running. As Clara lifts her head, the folded sweater she was using as a pillow falls away, and she recalls now where she is and how she got here. Squinting in the bright morning light that must have wakened her, she sees the girl running toward a woman maybe 30 meters away, her mother probably, who is pulling something from her purse. A mobile. Clara grabs for her bag but then spots her keys dangling from the ignition and, with a pounding in her chest, starts the Astra.

Yes, last night she parked in the darkest end of this small lot, positioned for a quick get-away, and grateful now for her own forethought, she jams in the gearshift and squeals away. In her rearview mirror, as the car bounces out of the lot and onto the street, she sees the woman holding the phone to her ear and then dropping it to her side. Probably wondering what she would actually say to the police. On their morning walk, her daughter, now clinging to her, has just wakened and frightened a woman who was sleeping in her car. "Yes, madam, and so you would have us do what?"

It's all coming back now as she swings past the apartment buildings of the residential neighborhood she found shortly before midnight almost immediately adjacent to exit 15 on the A9. It is the off-ramp she always uses when she visits Montreux, to stroll the lovely lakeside promenade, meet a friend for dinner at one of their favorite restaurants or attend one of the music festival events she loves so much. Now with the need to appear dead, will she ever do any of those things in Montreux again? There's no time for such mournful, impossible speculation. Just find her way to the A9 entrance, get back on the toll road, speed past the city and head south. What, she wonders again, will the Alps and Italy bring?

That question helped her decide finally to stop last night at Montreux. Fight or flight. Fight was her visceral response in the apartment as she jumped to her feet. But Willem's cold, awful logic sat her back down. There was no proof of what she had seen, the evidence had already been erased, no one would believe her word against theirs, and beyond all that, they had the police in their pocket. Yes, their wanting her dead filled her with rage, but the urge to act against them was trumped by fear and the instinct to survive.

The idea was to drive straight through the night, across the Alps all the way to Stresa, some 4 or 5 hours without stopping. She was running on adrenalin, but after only a half-hour or so, by the time she approached Lausanne, she was feeling a new kind of anger. She realized now that she had been an instrument of Giles and Julian as they deceived and bilked Cecile. With Clara's help they had robbed her old friend blind for who knows how long. She suddenly felt a kind of personal guilt for what they had done to Cecile, and to the good and important causes for which all that money had been intended. This she knew was more than a little irrational — she had not knowingly done anything wrong — but she felt anger nonetheless for being a tool of the bankers' cruel and selfish ends. She had a strong urge to stop and call Cecile, even at that late hour, to warn her about the crimes perpetrated against her. But how could she do that without any tangible proof and without endangering herself and probably Cecile as well. She fumed with frustration.

After another half-hour, as she reached Montreux on the opposite end of Lake Geneva, she was feeling exhausted. Maybe if she stopped and found a place to sleep for a while, she could think more clearly. Besides, the prospect of making that drive through the Alps in darkness was daunting. Occasionally, as early as this month, heavy snow could close some parts of the route. She had made the drive many times over the years but never at night, except once as a girl when she slept in the car with her father driving. And so she had pulled into that quiet place off the highway, folded up that bulky sweater she had grabbed at the last minute as she was leaving the apartment with Willem, leaned her head on it and promptly fell asleep.

Now driving south on the A9 toward Martigny, she keeps it at a cautious, steady 80 km/hour and again feels tossed with confusion and fear. Maybe she should have called Cecile last night and told her everything. But now she is even worried about the call she made yesterday after her meeting with Giles and before Willem came to kill her. Had she sounded suspiciously strained or urgent in the message she left? If Cecile had answered, would she have told her about Julian's computer? As it was, all she really said was that she'd like to move next month's lunch up to the next day or two, if that would work with Cecile's schedule. Now there is probably a message from her friend on the answering machine in the apartment. She could pick it up, but Willem warned that her calls and phone records might be monitored, and so with the risk involved it seems pointless.

Actually, one of the last things Willem told her was that her mobile was not her friend. "Do not use it," he said flatly. "And make sure to remove your battery and keep it separate. They can use the phone, even if it is turned off, to trace your location. If you absolutely must make a call for some reason I can't imagine, use someone else's or a pay phone."

She feels hounded, surrounded by risk. Occasionally she beats back hunger pangs, vowing no stops until she reaches Italy. Well, at some point she'll need petrol and a toilet, and then she can buy a bottle of water and maybe a breakfast bar of some kind. But until then, no stops. That's what her father used to say, in that gruff, mostly put-on voice, "No stops. No food, no toilet until Martigny." Of course once she or Claudio made their need sound urgent in their small child voices, he would soon relent. Her mother was actually tougher about it, telling them they would not die from hunger or from holding it a while longer.

With her parents and her brother long-since gone, Honore and Vera are her only close relatives. Along with Louis. What is this, Saturday? Would they already be missing her? She always calls both daughters on the weekend, so surely by Monday they will worry that she hasn't called. Or will they both just be grateful their annoying, pestering mother has left them alone for once. Yes, she remembers now. To give Honore a little respite this afternoon, Louis is scheduled to take the twins on an outing, a movie and a pizza, and so she and Honore had made vague plans to go shopping together. But again maybe Honore will be just as happy when she does not hear from her mother and won't have to spend all those hours with her.

How different Louis is from her own former husband, Honore's and Vera's father, who never lifted a finger with child rearing or domestic chores. It took her many years to find the gumption to stand up to Nicholas, ever the superior, successful businessman and ruler of the roost, not to cringe, submit, acquiesce or sulk in silence, but rather to embrace herself and the right to her own opinions, desires and preferences. Once she got there, she could see no way back, and their fights became raw and ruthless. Until one day when she got tired of fighting and decided she and her teenaged girls would somehow get along without him.

Now as the A9 turns past Martigny and heads sharply east through foothills, valleys and tunnels into the Alps, she decides to stop at the petrol station she usually frequents on this trip. And then she changes her mind. The people at that place know her well, even greet her by name. She is, she knows, a gregarious person, perhaps friendly to a fault, ready to talk with anyone about anything. She makes acquaintances quickly and friends easily, including the old couple who operate that station and its shop.

Obviously now she must change her ways, stop only at unfamiliar places where people don't know her, and then keep her overly friendly mouth firmly shut. Outgoing, warm, cordial, almost everyone thinks of her that way. Even her family. And beyond Cecile and Lina, Emmanuelle and the girls at the bank, she has so many dear friends — married, single, divorced, old, young, straight, gay, shop-keepers, tradesmen, business people, professionals. She actually begins ticking them off...Martine a lawyer, Hector a doctor and his wife Lucien, Serene a nurse, Luc a schoolteacher...but soon stops. Not all will miss her quickly, but it won't be long before many will wonder about her silence and try to get in touch. She stops at a place new to her and buys petrol, water, grape juice, cheese and a baguette. Back in the car, she is suddenly ravenous and rips off a crust of bread,.

Less than an hour later she urges the Astra into the most spectacular part of this trip, the Simplon Pass, that famed stretch heading down to the Italian border, first developed in the early 1800s at the command of Napoleon, who wanted a way to move his artillery pieces between the Rhone and Italy. She knows how it will go as she starts on this remarkable passage through these always amazing Alps. She will find herself lost in the beauty of their stunning vistas and astonished again that men actually found a way to build this road, a highway now on which autos can move faster than drivers can safely manage with the visual distractions.

With vigilant eyes only briefly darting away, she has no time or inclination to wonder what might be happening back in Geneva. Streams and rivers often run next to the highway, sometimes hundreds of meters below, or slide down sheer rock from above in silver rivulets and cascades. Snow-capped summits hover over massive evergreen stands and hillsides covered with the gold and russet of a thousand trees turning. Rough white torrents race under ancient rock bridges while mammoth stone gorges and sweeping green valleys are somehow traversed by giant cement spans whose construction must have once seemed well beyond possible or even the wildest imagining. Ragged peaks are shrouded in puffy clouds. One-way highways are stacked on double decks, bending their way around the high rock cliffs. An astounding drive and as usual she is almost numb with pleasure and relief as she reaches the old nondescript border buildings, unmanned in this new Europe.

On the Italian side she drives without a glance past a restaurant and a deli she knows well and heads south. In Stresa on the shores of Maggiore, she will stop somewhere and stock up on provisions for a stay in her house in the hills above the lake. A stay for how long? Another question she cannot answer.

Chapter 11

When the knock on the front door comes, she has been in the house for less than an hour. It took two trips from the car to the kitchen door at the back to get her suitcase and the groceries in. She opened only one set of shutters, over the kitchen window, and then turned up the furnace and the hot water heater. The old, rough-hewn house is a decent size, three bedrooms and a bath upstairs and the kitchen, small bath, dining and front rooms down, and it is still chilly, just beginning to warm up when the knock startles and frightens her. The police already? Or maybe Willem has changed his mind about letting her disappear.

A furtive glance through the small round window in the door, and she sees it is Anna, her favorite neighbor from down the hill in this tiny town called Speranza, which means hope, about the last thing she has right now. She knows immediately she will need to answer the knock—Anna is nothing if not persistent. She no doubt saw the Opel parked in the back—at a time of the year when it's almost never here—and she will continue to come by until Clara answers. Putting this moment off will only heighten the woman's curiosity and speculation.

And so she opens the door to expressions of surprise and delight, an exchange of hugs and kisses, and word that Anna was out for her walk and to her great pleasure spotted Clara's car. Despite this sudden intrusion, Clara surprises herself by quickly going on about work at the bank lately being especially demanding, and how she simply felt the need to get away for a few days. Just a quiet little respite, and everything will be fine.

Anna says, well, her timing is perfect. She and Giorgio are having company tonight for dinner, the Strozzis—Clara doesn't know them but she will like them, and they will love her—and Giorgio is making his Vodka sauce.

Unfortunately, says Clara, in the car she began to feel like she is coming down with something, a cold or maybe the flu, and she is probably very contagious. Of course, the invitation is deeply appreciated, but she will take a warm bath and cuddle up in bed with a book. Anna commiserates; she will come by tomorrow with the left-over pasta and maybe some soup.

With the door closed again, Clara still feels the fear drumming in her body. The dread is probably making her look pale and drained, ill with something. But coming to this house was clearly her worst possible move. If the bankers or Willem are looking for her, wouldn't this be the first place they'd check? Then again it's been less than a day, and she has given them no reason to think she is anything but dead. She has used no check or credit card, has been seen by no one who knows her, other than Anna, and whom would she tell? Still, what about calling Marc? Yes, and exactly how would she explain this desperate, complicated story on the phone? In a way he could understand? Even just the basics, how much and why she needs his help immediately? In what language?

Now she is afraid to leave the house and afraid as well to stay. Her mind and heart are roiled with debates, and there are times when she is strongly tempted to at least let her family know she is alive. However they might feel about her, whether there is love or annoyance or both, all families have petty differences. Certainly they will be worried sick about her, if not by now, then very soon.

Late Sunday afternoon Anna returns to check on her and deliver the left-over penne with Vodka sauce and some of her special chicken soup, as always heavy on the garlic, with big chunks of white meat and some chopped vegetable mixed in. Clara tells her she is still feeling bad, but the worst should be over in the next day or so.

As soon as her friend leaves, the questions swirl again. When will her family file a missing person report with the police? As early as tonight? And tomorrow what will happen at the bank? What will Giles and Julian be saying about her, other than that she went home on Friday after meeting with Giles? But why? Maybe Giles will say she complained of not feeling well and needed some time off. What will Emmanuelle think, knowing that Clara requesting time off would be highly unusual? How about Cecile and Lina? Lina is probably already back in Bologna and no longer thinking about life in Geneva.

Clara sleeps only fitfully Sunday night, and Monday feels like a replay of the past two days, a jumble of anxiety, notions that feel half-baked, resolves that last all of two minutes, and flat-out despair. She wonders again whether to believe what Willem told her, especially about the advisability of going to the police. Could the bankers really be so powerfully connected that her accusation would be totally dismissed, or might only backfire, bringing harm to herself and her family? And then there's the possibility that Willem could change his mind, track her down and kill her. On the road out of Geneva, she was actually tempted to go to the police in Lausanne or Montreux and tried to think through what would happen if she did. Wouldn't their first step be to contact the Geneva Municipal Police, who, Willem said, have close ties with Giles and the bank? But what she came back to every time was that it would be only her word against theirs, a lowly secretary versus respected bank officials. Then what if she told the police about Willem and what he said the bankers had ordered him to do? Again, he would deny everything, and it would only be her word against his.

And now she wonders if it's possible that for his own twisted reasons, Willem has made this whole story up. Is it really possible she has in fact been betrayed by Julian and Giles? Especially Giles, whom she has known and respected for 30 years. But then what possible reason, twisted or otherwise, would Willem have to make up such a story? And has she already forgotten what she saw with her own eyes on the screens in Julian's office?

By the middle of Monday afternoon, she is also wondering how much longer she can possibly keep this up. How much longer can she live with all the fear, loneliness and unanswerable questions? How much longer can she run away, pretending to be dead?

The idea of going to the Carabinieri comes to her when she's having some of Anna's soup. And try as she might, she cannot shake the thought. Why not go to them and tell the whole story, beginning to end, including everything she heard from Willem? Why wouldn't the Carabinieri believe her or at least give her a fair hearing? After all, Cecile will surely vouch for her. So will Emmanuelle. Certainly anyone who knows her well — other than Giles, Julian and Willem — will say she is a person of honesty and integrity. And think about it, why would she possibly tell such an outlandish story, if it were entirely made up and untrue? She finally must trust someone. She cannot simply remain "dead" to everyone she knows for the foreseeable future, whatever that amounts to. By the time she is putting the rest of the soup back in the refrigerator, she has decided on her course. This just feels right, and her resolve has a real firmness. She knows this time she will not waver.

In the Opel heading back toward Stresa, it feels good to be moving, to actually be doing something with conviction and purpose. She doesn't have to think about exactly what she's going to say. She will just take her time and let it all come out. Does this mean bad things will happen to Willem? She hopes not, but she can no longer be concerned about anyone else now. She must save herself.

It helps that her one experience with the Carabinieri a few years back was a good one. Returning from Geneva to open the house for the spring, she found there had been a break-in. No real damage, other than a broken window, but lots of drawers pulled out and left on the floor, and a few small appliances — a TV, radio and microwave — taken. She was surprised to be dealing with a female officer, who thanked her for taking the time to report the crime. Over the past few weeks, there had been a series of break-ins reported in the area around this northwest corner of Lago Maggiore, and a "gang of young idiots" was suspected. Nothing had ever come of her report, but at least now she knows exactly where she is going, about 15 kilometers up the road from little Stresa, in the much larger city of Verbania.

At the front desk in a busy waiting room, she says she needs to report a crime. What kind of crime? asks a bored-looking fellow at a computer. Fraud, she says. When he asks for her name, for some reason she says, "Doloro," giving him her Italian maiden name. He nods, offers a weary gesture and tells her to please take a seat. Someone will be with her shortly.

It's nearly 5 pm, and at least six people seem to be ahead of her. A worried-looking businessman, an old man with one eye, a mother with a teenaged daughter who definitely doesn't want to be there, two couples — one young, one old — and an attractive young woman who is constantly texting. Clara studies them and tries to imagine the trouble each of them has to report. After 10 minutes the old man and the young couple have been escorted through a door to a hallway that she knows from her last visit leads to a series of offices.

After another several minutes, when the door opens again, a young officer, tall and thin, heads for the mother and daughter, but as Clara watches, he is called back to the door by an older supervisor type with a heavy mustache and a clipboard. Only a meter away from where she sits, the two men stand in the open doorway and speak in low voices. And then she hears her own name. Clara Marche.

She turns to them with a smile but they aren't looking at her. Instead, handing the younger man a slip of paper from the clipboard, the supervisor is saying that a request has come from the Municipal Police in Geneva concerning this woman, who is apparently responsible for some kind of bank fraud. They're asking if the office can send someone to check out her family home in Speranza, just outside Stresa.

Geneva, says the younger one with a quizzical look.

A favor for an old friend, says the supervisor.

Nodding and folding the slip of paper, the young officer says he can go out there in about a half-hour.

Clara feels stunned. She's afraid her hands will not work, but somehow she manages to reach into her purse and pull out two pieces of tissue. As she carefully blots her face, the tall, young officer, the mother and her troubled teen exit the waiting room.

Chapter 12

Shortly after her return to the villa early Monday evening, the phone rings in the great room, and unlike several other recent calls, she decides to answer it. The woman's voice is unfamiliar and asks in French for Cecile. For perhaps the tenth time in the past three days, Lina gives the short version of what has happened. There is silence, and finally the woman says she is very sorry to hear about Ms. Eaton. Her mother has always spoken so highly of her.

"Your mother."

"Yes, my mother is Clara Marche. She works at Ms. Eaton's bank."

"Ah, of course, this is Lina Lentini. I know Clara. How is she?"

The woman hesitates, then says her name is Honore. Her mother has also spoken fondly of Lina. Actually, she is calling about her mother. Everyone in the family is very concerned because they have not heard from her at all since last Friday, and that is very unlike her mother. Her sister Vera was the last to speak to her, sometime Friday afternoon when their mother called and sounded, Vera thought, a bit strange, saying something about some kind of trouble at the bank and then quickly saying she misspoke. Honore was supposed to go shopping with her on Saturday but could not reach her and never heard back. Vera, who has a key to their mother's apartment, went over there last night, and there was no sign of her. A suitcase was gone, and when Vera checked their mother's garage, so was her car. Vera also checked Clara's phone messages, but other than those left by Vera and herself, there were none.

Lina asks if she has called the bank today, and Honore says, yes, this morning. Julian Lyon, her mother's boss, said she had gone home Friday around noon complaining of not feeling well, and the bank has not heard from her since. They too were concerned, because not showing up at work, and without a word, is so completely out of character.

Lina says she can offer nothing other than that Clara left a message on Cecile's phone on Friday, wanting to move up their monthly meeting for November. Nothing unusual about the call: Clara sounded like her always pleasant self.

They speak for a while about Cecile's condition, until Honore wonders if there might be some connection between that and her mother's disappearance. "But what it might be I can't imagine," she says finally.

"Nor can I," says Lina.

After they ring off, she thinks Honore's last speculation was odd. But obviously the woman is very upset about her mother, and after three days of her own grief and regret, Lina certainly understands. Last Friday evening after that awful discovery on her return with Julian from Annecy, she found a note card taped next to the phone in the kitchen. On it was the emergency number for the Clinique de Gervais, which turned out to be a nearby private hospital. Over the next day or so, it became clear that Cecile had planned carefully for just such an emergency. Zazu told her that Madame had patiently explained exactly what should be done and fixed that card to the wall.

The ambulance was there within 10 minutes, and one of the efficient young techs said "Most probably a stroke," echoing Lina's own guess about her dear friend on the kitchen floor, breathing but unresponsive.

Lina followed the ambulance to the hospital and answered a nurse's calm, yet urgent questions. The most salient fact, she already knew, was how long she had been away from the villa and from Cecile. Had Madame DeRocheford complained of feeling off in any way before she was left alone? No. Any slurring of speech? No. Any mention of a headache or numbness? No. Any vagueness in her thoughts or expression? No, she was sharp as ever, and that was very sharp indeed.

The wait for some word from the medical team was excruciating, close to three hours. A man with salt-and-pepper hair and a kind but weary air came in finally to speak with her and said his name was Dr. Monrovian. "The news is not good," he said, looking steadily at her. "Madame DeRocheford has suffered a massive stroke, an ischemic stroke, meaning one caused by a blood clot in the brain. The prognosis is frankly not encouraging."

Lina nodded but could not speak.

"As you may know, with a stroke, the time elapsed between the onset of the event and the initiation of treatment is always crucial. The sooner we can treat a situation like this, the better."

Lina shook her head with self-accusation.

"From what you told us when she came in, there was a period of about six hours between the time you left her and when you returned. So those were the parameters we were looking at to begin with. When we did the scan and could see the blockage, where it was and the substantial area of the brain affected, it was our estimate, a guess really, that the clot had lodged in its position somewhere between 3 and 4 hours before she was admitted. At that point, it was a borderline call whether to apply the clot-busting medication we like to use within 3 hours of onset. But recent guidelines have extended that limit a bit, so we felt it was worth a try. The drug works very quickly and that clot has been dissolved, but the damage already done has most likely been extensive. We continue..."

Lina interrupted. "Doctor, from what you say, I take it that crucial areas of the brain have been destroyed and that when you refer to damage, you mean that all or most of the brain cells in those areas are dead."

The doctor's tired eyes held hers. "That is correct. Unfortunately. When those cells are deprived of blood, oxygen, etc., they die."

Lina pushed for more of a prognosis. She wanted the doctor's best guess on what kind of future Cecile now faced. Again, he said, at this point things did not look good for her recovery, but really it was much too early for a definitive call. Yes, a recovery, one that would give her some desired quality of life, did not look likely, but it was not absolutely out of the question. They were going to have to watch and wait and hope. In the meantime, she was on a ventilator and an IV for both nutrition and medication to guard against another clot. Of course, they would keep her as comfortable as possible.

Lina asked if she could see Cecile. The doctor said, yes, but madame would not know anyone was there. It was now after midnight, he said, glancing at a clock in the ICU waiting room, and maybe the better course was to go home, get some sleep and come back in the morning.

Saturday dawned bright and clear. Heartless, thought Lina, gazing through the lattice windows in her room at the sparkling lake and snow-covered Alps in France. She tried visualizing Cecile in her black tam and long coat walking in the garden. It did not seem likely that her old friend would ever do that again.

At the hospital Dr. Belleveau, a young woman with bright blue eyes in a stern face, said there had been no real change. In her Intensive Care Unit room Cecile appeared dominated by contraptions, particularly the ventilator, and seemed to show her displeasure with a perpetual frown. Lina asked Dr. Belleveau if Clinique de Gervais was the best place for Cecile.

The young doctor replied calmly, "We are very good here. We have a dedicated stroke unit and even train our ambulance techs to recognize stroke and to call ahead when they do. Which is what happened in this case, so we were ready to move as quickly as possible once they arrived. Of course, the Clinique Generale-Paquis in Geneva has one of the best neuro-vascular departments in Europe, but in the case of Madame DeRocheford, unfortunately the damage appears so extensive there is little anyone can do, at least for now. Perhaps that will change, and, in any case, we certainly encourage consideration of all options."

A half-hour later Lina was having breakfast in the hospital's cafeteria when Julian called her mobile. Sounding upbeat and pleasant, he just wanted to thank her for making Friday such a memorable pleasure.

When she told him about Cecile, he expressed profound shock. "I cannot believe it. She seemed so bright, engaged, even feisty yesterday when we left her. I am so very sorry for her, and for you, Lina. I know how close you two were."

Past tense, she noted. He offered to come to the hospital and be with her. It was Saturday after all, and he had no plans. She thanked him and declined. About the last thing she wanted was to have him around now. He said just let him know if there was anything he or the bank could do to help.

Later in the day Giles Morneau called her mobile as well. Upon hearing the news from Julian, the bank chairman had also been "shocked and devastated." He had been calling around to people he knew, doctors, experts and the like, who were all of a mind that it would be wise to move Madame DeRocheford to the Clinique Generale-Paquis, the hospital mentioned by Dr. Belleveau. "Our family has close connections there. In fact, the family name Morneau is on the pediatric wing. If Madame DeRocheford were moved there I could make absolutely certain that she would get the extraordinary care she deserves and that all of us want for her."

Lina told him what the doctor had said about Cecile's condition and care. Morneau paused and then replied, "Well, please think about it, and let's talk again tomorrow."

She thanked him for his thoughtful concern, and Morneau responded by also offering to provide someone in the bank's employ, actually a security specialist, a very responsible fellow, who could stay in the room with Cecile or as nearby as possible in the hospital to give Lina a break in what must be a very trying and difficult time for her. This man could make sure the care being provided Madame DeRocheford was vigilant and everything it should be. Of course, if there were any change, for the better or worse, the fellow would call Lina immediately.

As she had explained to Julian, Lina said she had been sitting in the room reading aloud from Rousseau's Confessions, and whether or not Cecile could hear or understand a word, Lina herself found the activity reassuring. She had no problem at all staying with Cecile, and she had already come to trust this hospital's doctors and the staff. They had all been wonderful.

Morneau sounded reluctant to let the matter go and again asked that she please think about his offers. Actually, while impressed with the generous concern shown by both bankers, with Cecile seemingly locked in a vegetative state, what Lina thought about were conversations in the past in which her old friend had been very clear about not wanting any heroic measures taken to keep her alive, especially if her mind were gone.

Late in the afternoon, Lina met again with Dr. Monrovian, who said he had been in touch with a Dr. Fugazy, Madame DeRocheford's primary care physician. Fugazy had mentioned that his office had a letter on file concerning Madame DeRocheford's wishes regarding treatment under various medical circumstances. A copy of the letter had been sent to the hospital. "I have not seen it yet," said the doctor, "but from what I understand, in a situation similar to the one she is facing now, she wanted all special efforts to be discontinued no later than two weeks after arriving at such a condition. Palliative care, keeping her as comfortable as possible for those two weeks, and then she directed that she be removed from all life-extending devices, methods or medications. Fugazy said she specifically mentioned

77

wanting her letter to be the final word on the subject and forbidding any further consultation with friends or family. She wanted no one who knows her to be put in a position where they felt forced to be part of the decision."

'Sounds like Cecile," said Lina.

"Yes," said the doctor. "She appears to have carefully thought about everything."

On Sunday Lina was again at the hospital much of the day, mostly in Cecile's room reading Rousseau aloud but prompting hardly the flicker of an eyelid from her dear old friend. At mid-day she spoke again on the phone with Morneau and explained there had been no change. After a pause, he agreed to put off the question of moving Madame DeRocheford until tomorrow, when perhaps it would be good for Dr. Odile, the chief of neuro-vascular medicine at the Clinique Generale-Paquis, to speak directly with Dr. Monrovian. When Lina thanked him again for his thoughtful concern, he said, "I'd like to think we take this kind of care and concern for each and all of our clients. After all, that's what our small, private bank is all about. But I must admit that Cecile—Madame DeRocheford—is particularly special to us."

Privately Lina felt Cecile was exactly where she wanted to be under these circumstances, in the Clinique de Gervais. It was where she had wanted to go in an emergency, and it was where Lina could be sure Cecile's wishes would be followed. When she met with young Dr. Belleveau, she asked if anything had surfaced about what might have brought on the stroke.

The doctor said, "We have of course done all the blood tests, and there are several sets of numbers that are well off what they should be, what we would want them to be, and well off what they were four months ago when Ms. Eaton had her last check up with her regular physician Dr. Fugazy. We've spoken with him, and he was surprised at how much things had changed, but then she is 88-years-old, and at that age problems can develop very quickly. The bottom line is, with what we see in her blood work now, she was a stroke waiting to happen."

Late Sunday afternoon, for the first time, Lina took the advice of the nurses, went home to the villa and had dinner with Zazu. She finally listened to messages on the phone at the villa. There was one on Friday from Clara and several over the weekend from concerned friends. There was also a message from old Charles Mercier, Cecile's attorney. Lina had met the courtly old fellow more than once at the villa, the last time about a month ago. He had heard the terrible news about his old friend and client, and while all his prayers were of course for the best possible outcome, he thought it might be helpful for Lina, and especially Zazu, to know that Cecile does have a will on file. Its provisions were really quite simple. In the event of Cecile's passing away, Zazu's income is to be continued for as long as she lives. And all of Cecile's belongings, including the villa and everything in it and all of her investments and holdings are to be sold or cashed in, and all proceeds are to go to the same charities to which she currently gives.

Now on Monday evening, a half-hour after speaking on the phone with Honore, Lina is still thinking about Clara's strange disappearance. The woman seems the very essence of reliability. Then another call comes, this time on her mobile. It's Julian. She does not want to answer but then thinks maybe she can learn something more about Clara. In his usual polite fashion he asks about the latest on Cecile, and she recounts her conversation at the hospital with Dr. Belleveau. He says he's sorry that all this has come down on Lina. It seems such an unfair burden. He knows how anxious she is to return to her work in Bologna.

There really is no burden, she replies. She can work here, and feeling closer to Cecile than just about anyone else in her life, she would not dream of being anywhere other than by her side in this crisis. By the way, when is he scheduled to leave for Hong Kong?

Oh, he says, that's been put off a bit. Some things have come up that Giles needs his help with at the bank.

Lina asks if one of those things might be Clara's disappearance. There is silence, and then Julian says, in fact, yes, and goes on to describe the shocking discovery he made earlier in the day. Clara has been involved in a fraud on the bank that has been going on secretly for years. Small amounts steadily accrued to a considerable sum. Actually, she had found a way to access Julian's own accounts and devised a method of taking small sums every month and cleverly hiding the fact that they were missing. The total, from what he has been able to determine so far, comes to about 40,000 Swiss.

Lina is dumbfounded but finally manages to ask if he has spoken about this yet with anyone in Clara's family.

He has just hung up, he says, with her older daughter. He had spoken with her this morning when she was very concerned about not having heard from her mother, and he had given her his mobile number to call if she heard anything from or about Clara. Actually, his talk with her this morning got him checking on things, and of course he was stunned by what he found, shocked and deeply saddened, as is everyone at the bank, from Giles on down.

How did her daughter take the news?

"Not well," he says. "Of course, like everyone else she was in an initial state of shock, but then she became very angry and accusatory. I guess no one likes to hear that her mother is an embezzler, but that appears to be exactly what's happened here. Giles is trying very hard to keep it out of the media, but she is now a wanted person, with notices for her arrest going out to police agencies all over Europe."

Chapter 13

"What I would like to know," says Julian, hearing the nerves and the annoyance in his own voice, "is why you allow him to stonewall you on something so basic." He is not pleased with the way he sounds and wants his cool, unflappable self back. He stares hard at Giles behind the chairman's big desk and, as if Tanner is not sitting right there less than two meters away, adds, "I mean, the man works for you. He knows full well what will happen if he disappoints us."

Giles' face is a mask, but his eyes shift. "Willem?" he says.

The security factotum gives a light shrug of his large shoulders. "What I said," he says slowly, "was, you don't want to know."

"And what I am saying is I certainly do want to know." Julian has still not even glanced at the repellent lout sitting next to him.

"No, in my professional opinion, with my experience in such matters, you should not know. You are both better off not knowing. What do the politicians call it? Deniability?"

"Oh, Jesus Christ!" Now he has turned in his chair, looking straight at Tanner, just to his left. "You let us decide that. I want to know where she is. At the bottom of the lake? Somewhere underground? In a trash compactor? And how did you handle the termination?"

Tanner raised his large hands, thick fingers splayed. "I used these. And she's in a place where she'll never be found."

Giles stirred, leaning forward a bit and gazing only briefly at Julian. "I think that's all we need to know. But let's get back to the purpose of this meeting. At the moment it seems, without our raising a fuss and perhaps appearing suspicious, that Madame DeRocheford will be staying for now at the Clinique de Gervais. The doctors have spoken and exchanged opinions, and while Odile feels the patient might be somewhat better off at the Clinique Generale-Paquis, Professor Lentini seems intent on keeping her where she is. So Willem, you've scouted the place, what are the chances of getting in there and finishing your work?"

The fellow shakes his head, and Julian already knows he will not like the answer. "Well, the fact is, she is not in the best place for going in and doing what you want. I mean, the ICU rooms are wide-open, glassed-walled and with at least one nurse almost always monitoring. Even presuming I'm not discovered, how do we get a result that looks normal and not suspicious? You say yourselves they think her prognosis is poor with little chance of recovery. My advice for now would be to let nature have its way."

"Nature is a dice game," snaps Julian. "We are not leaving this to chance. We've all heard stories of brain-damaged people suddenly coming back, and if that happens, we're all fucked. You're the one who's supposed to be good with these things, and frankly, it seems to me you failed on this the first time, and now you don't want to risk your skin to make it right."

"It would not be my skin only. I'm discovered, and you're likely to be implicated. No matter what I say. I work for the bank."

In the silence that follows, everyone hears a mobile buzz, and Tanner extracts his from a shirt pocket, looks at and shakes his head. "It's blocked," he says, getting to his feet, "I should take this."

"Take it outside," says Giles. "We're finished for now. We'll let you know."

Tanner nods, pushes a button and holds the phone to his ear. "Yes." And after a pause, "No, wait a minute." He is already on his way out of the office.

As usual lately, Julian has a different take on what should have just happened here. He does not like the way the man glanced furtively at each of them but avoided their eyes as he heard the voice on the phone. Giles should have kept him in the room. But then once again, things have changed between them. Giles is the more decisive, somehow stronger one now.

Of course, everything started with that horrid bout of explosive diarrhea. He did not think he was going to make it to the men's room, actually running the last several steps. What he had eaten or where the bug had come from he still doesn't know. "Nervous stomach," Giles said. "You've been nervous about everything lately." No, not really, not until after they learned the rotten-luck consequence of that mad dash to the john. Yes, now he was nervous about everything. Especially Willem Tanner.

82

So way back when, how did Alain Dubonne, chief of the Geneva Municipal Police, prevail on them to hire the guy after his release from prison? According to Giles, Alain said, yes, the bank would certainly be doing him a favor—and Giles had already been most generous to his old friend—but put this Tanner in a special security position, and it could be a very good thing for Giles and the bank. Alain then assumed his most earnest police chief face and pronounced:

"This is a man with significant resources. He knows how to do unusual things, has access to unusual people and services that can come in quite handy. He is not a squeamish man, if you know what I mean, not afraid to get his hands soiled doing certain unpleasant tasks, and of course I will personally vouch for him as a completely trustworthy agent. As I mentioned, he has been in prison for the past year and a half—not a pleasant sojourn, I can assure you. He's been there for one reason only: when necessity demands it, he knows how to keep his mouth clamped shut. Bottom line, he can do a wide variety of things for you, things you may not dream you'll ever need, until the day arrives when you clearly see you do."

Giles told Julian that he knew the chief had his own agenda on this, one totally unrelated to the bank's welfare. Giles said whatever this man might be able to do for the bank, there could well come a day when suddenly the downside would appear. Giles argued against the hire, until Julian (who had not yet met the fellow) finally talked him into it, saying with their long-term plans to create an idyllic new life, a man such as the chief described, could be very handy indeed.

It was an argument whose success Julian came to regret once he got to know Tanner, and it was beyond a matter of personal dislike. Yes, there was something ugly and brutal about this ex-cop/ex-con, something in him that surely had no use for a man like Julian. Until now they had never clashed; there was never an unpleasant word between them. But he also hated the way the guy talked and walked and smelled and looked at you when he thought no one was watching. So perhaps nothing rational, but, despite the chief's strong affirmation, Julian definitely knew that Willem Tanner was not a man to be trusted. That was why he came up with the devious plan to catch him in the act of doing something for which he could be thrown back in prison. Just a little insurance, he told Giles, who, despite his earlier misgivings, had come to like the fellow and only reluctantly agreed to Julian's plan.

Roles reversed. Usually Julian was the calm, confident one, always able to read Giles more acutely than Giles could read him, Julian dreaming and scheming and then pushing Giles to take the big steps that have brought them to the brink of everything they desire. Now everything seems upside-down.

It's been five days now since Cecile's stroke, and every day she continues to hang on makes Julian more nervous. He has always playfully accused Giles of being a jittery old biddy. Now it's Julian who better fits the description.

The looting of the DeRocheford account actually began as pillow talk. About a year into Julian's position at the bank, he and Giles were at a conference in London, and together on the king-sized bed in their lush suite at the Dorchester, he found Giles sad and unresponsive — the hooded eyes and limp dick tell-tale signs he knew well. When pressed about what was wrong, Giles reluctantly admitted that he was deeply concerned about the bank's future, that he had been left a losing hand by his fucking old man, that with an aging client base and the lingering effects of the absurd strictures his father had insisted on keeping in place, they would have to work like crazy over the next several years just to keep the hamstrung institution from failing. He felt terrible that he had not been more honest and up front with Julian before offering him the job, and he was afraid now that the bank's dead weight would soon drag them both down.

"I fear," he said, "we might simply go under. Not immediately, of course, but quite possibly within the next four or five years. And I am so sorry for doing this to you, darling. You deserve so much better, and I will certainly understand if you decide to leave."

Julian had stared into those dull brown eyes and said he had accepted the job "fully aware" from what Giles had told him that the bank's health was not sterling. Then while playing lightly with his lover's sad little prick, he said, "Let me fantasize for you an alternate future. First I'll tell you what it can look like, say five years hence, and then I'll suggest how we can make it happen."

Giles had given him a dismal look and said, "Okay, fantasize for me."

And so Julian talked quietly but with increasingly detailed

enthusiasm about a breath-taking, state-of-the-art villa, designed by Giles and decorated to their brilliant collaborative taste, built on a low bluff overlooking a gorgeous and deserted white sand beach lapped by an impossibly blue-green sea somewhere in the tropics. The two of them would be living there and doing anything their conjoined hearts desired. And when the urge came over them, they would leave this phenomenal dream for a while to pursue other, perhaps more lurid fantasies, jetting off to any of the world's pleasure capitals to indulge whatever whim they might imagine before returning again to the quiet refuge of their lovely island paradise in the sun.

"So how does that sound?" Julian smiled and felt Giles getting hard.

"Not bad." Giles opened his eyes. "And how does this happen?"

"Well, each of us has a role to play. You must do whatever is necessary to keep the bank afloat for at least the next four years, six at the outside, and I continue to do what I have been doing for the past three months—taking 90 percent of Madame DeRocheford's wasteful charitable contributions and placing those funds in a secret account controlled by us."

Giles eyes were closed, his penis melting again. "Jules, darling, tell me you are joking."

But Julian said he was not joking, had never been more serious in his life, and by the time he had explained exactly how this absurdly simple, boldly ambitious scheme was fool-proof, Giles had a rigid hard-on that Julian proceeded to service with a fervent glee.

Now he stares past Giles at the two photos on the shelf behind. Julian sometimes uses them to gauge his own feelings about things. Of course, he knows the way he should see the stolid old man and the smiling woman and children. He knows very well that if they had not played their fate-assigned parts in Giles' story, he, Julian, would not be sitting here today on the verge of bliss with the love of his life. But there are also times when his anger beats up against the small-minded cruelty of old man Morneau toward his only son, and when that charming family portrait fills Julian with a secret, nagging fear.

He shakes himself out of this useless line of thinking and asks Giles if he has heard from Dubonne.

"You mean since yesterday?"

"Yes."

"No, the chief only calls when he has something new."

Julian knows the strange tale of how the bank chairman and the police chief came to be friends. It began a long time ago when Giles and Alain Dubonne went through primary and secondary school together. At first, when they were 9 or 10, Alain was fond of bullying little Giles. One day at school he pulled down Giles' pants to slap his bottom, but a teacher caught him in the act, and later he was beaten by his father. Giles always suspected that Alain's father had been overly impressed with Albert Morneau and his bank, but, for whatever reason, thereafter things changed quite radically. Alain became Giles' protector, and in high school he took Giles under his wing on the fencing team. In recent years, serving together on the hospital board and meeting often at civic and cultural events, they renewed their friendship.

Then a while back, shortly before Julian joined the bank, Alain had introduced Giles to a "friend" named Galeano. The little Chilean man was looking for a new bank because his old one in Zurich had begun acting like a nervous old crone, asking too many silly questions and generally making his banking experience "a pain in the buttocks." Senor Galeano said he owned a nice little company called Moyano Exports based in Chile and dealing in everything from jewelry to leather goods. Giles suspected from the start that the chief himself might well be the beneficiary on the account, and when he upped the bank's usual percentage and fees, there was no objection.

Two years later (during Willem's 17 months in prison), the Chilean introduced Giles to one of his "friends," a fellow named Calvino, whom he described as a wealthy Brazilian and also a friend of Alain Dubonne. This man represented a larger firm, a heavy machinery broker, which would be making much more substantial deposits. Giles strongly suspected that Fernandez Industries was another company that existed strictly on paper, but when he mentioned the new applicant to the chief, Dubonne vouched for him as well: "Ah, yes, Calvino, another good man, highly reputable."

Back in those early years when he was at terrible odds with his father, Giles' favorite line was from Bertolt Brecht, something about how it was crime to rob a bank but a bigger crime to found one. He was particularly fond of reciting the sordid details of Swiss banking's rich history of innovative laundering, everything from Hitler's gold to the torrent of narco bucks to the filthy lucre of the world's most vicious dictators, corrupt politicians and brilliantly successful tax dodgers. In the annals of banking discretion, there was little that could measure up to the Swiss role in facilitating the Iran-Contra debacle, or insuring crucial monetary support for the globe's most ambitious terrorists. It was a remarkable history, a clear demonstration of how a firm commitment to secrecy at the right time and place can make life so much better for certain select beneficiaries.

And now faced with another unexpected opportunity to carry on this long Swiss tradition, at a moment when the troubled Banque Privee Morneau could certainly use some help, Giles, in close consultation with Julian, had decided to fully embrace the moment and say yes to Senor Calvino. Of course, they would have to deal with the Due Diligence Agreement that Swiss banking had come up with many years ago, and the more recent Money Laundering Law as well, but a key element of these strictures was self-regulation, and with Julian's wizard-like ability to create convenient electronic trails and corroborating paperwork, the size of the gain to be achieved was deemed certainly worth the risk.

Both of these accounts, belonging to or, perhaps more accurately, fronted by the Chilean and the Brazilian, had become very important to the bank, especially over the past two years when the global financial tsunami hit full force. And next to the billions cleansed and hidden over the decades for some of the world's bloodiest butchers— Nicaragua's Samoza, Haiti's Duvalier, the Congo's Mobutu—and next to the Mexican drug river flowing through respected giants like Citibank and UBS, the totals little Banque Privee Morneau was handling would look like a piker's sum.

Back in his own office Julian tells the new girl Mercedes he is not to be disturbed. No calls accepted from anyone except Chairman Morneau. This is the week they were scheduled to put their long-gestating, carefully calculated plan into action. This is the week he would bid everyone adieu to return to the Far East. And then leave Geneva in the opposite direction. Now who knows when they might initiate that so-often-dreamed-of scheme?

Lounging at his desk trying to find some way to make himself feel better, he thinks of Lina Lentini, and how he made a fool of this brilliant and beautiful woman. His favorite part was how she had stupidly swallowed the often re-polished story of his desperately sad love affair with the unhappily married woman and her two kids, told perhaps at the very moment Willem Tanner was doing his dirty work at the DeRocheford villa—albeit with something less than complete success. The story has been worked and re-worked so many times over the years, he could tell it in his sleep. Actually, perhaps he has, with both women and men whose only common denominator has been wanting to get too close.

Maybe it was time to call Lina again and invite her to dinner. And quietly yet firmly persuade her that the best possible chance of Madame DeRocheford coming back to us with her remarkable faculties regained is to allow the move to the world-renown stroke care at Clinique Generale-Paquis.

Yes, Willem Tanner is not to be trusted, but even if pretty, nosy Clara is in fact still breathing somewhere, they definitely have her in an airtight box. She has no way to prove her absurd accusations, and no way to defend herself against the bank's evidence of her own serious fraud. The return of a cogent Cecile DeRocheford, on the other hand, would pose a problem they certainly do not wish to confront.

Chapter 14

"A magical place."

She can hear Marc voice those words with quiet amazement as if it were yesterday and not a year and a half ago when the two of them, her arm in his, strolled Lerici's promenade, golden sand beach and sparkling blue sea on one side, and on the other a cascade of centuries-old pastel buildings built down to the harbor. She wonders again why she has come here, whether to pleasure or to torture herself with this beauty and these memories.

In Milano she told herself that lovely Lerici would help her feel less desperate. Just south of the tourist-clogged Cinque Terre, the town is so beautiful that Italians have long kept it a secret for themselves. And yet she has been walking back and forth on this marvelous two-kilometer stretch of waterfront, trying in vain to clear Willem's barking voice on the phone from her cluttered, worried head.

"Yes."

"Willem, it's Clara. Can you talk?"

"No. Wait a minute." And then after a long pause, his voice low but intense: "I told you never to call me."

"No, Willem, I am sorry, but you said yourself there is no one else I can call. Please, tell me what has happened at the bank? I am charged with a crime? How can this be?"

"I told you I cannot talk. It's not safe."

"But fraud, Willem. I am charged with fraud?"

"It means," he growled like a dog, "only that you must disappear even more completely."

"But you said I would be able to return after a time. How long..."

And then he disconnected the line.

By the time she blocked her number and dialed again, he must have turned off his phone. It went straight to voice mail. She started to leave a message, "Willem, please..." But tears caught in her throat, and she rang off.

In a blur she climbed down from her tiny rented room to walk this promenade, trying to regain her composure. Twice now, once down and once back, she has passed an older gentleman who each time nodded to her and touched the brim of his black bowler hat. Someone sent by the bank? Have they already found her? Maybe it's her new mobile. Maybe they have already traced it? No, she is thinking like a crazy woman again. Many men have tipped their hats to her, even in recent years as her beauty faded. No, how could anyone possibly know she is here in Lerici?

Once again she retraces her route here. With the officer at the desk engrossed in his computer screen, she had slipped out of the waiting room of the Carabinieri office in Verbania, raced back to the house and packed up her things. Her mind still reeling, she shuttered the kitchen window and tried to make sure it looked like no one had been there recently. She thanked her lucky stars that Anna and Giorgio had gone off to Milano to spend a couple of days with their daughter, who was in school there. So she did not have to worry about the tall, thin officer, the one who would soon come here to the house, talking to the only people who knew she had been in Speranza over the weekend.

Driving fast, she made it to Milano in about an hour, before dusk. She found an inexpensive room in a small motel tucked in a less-than-attractive neighborhood on the other side of this very large city from the university district where she imagined Anna and Giorgio would be staying while visiting their daughter. Still, she worried about even the minute chance she might run into her friends there, and though she had been sure she would feel better in the anonymity of a large city she doesn't know, she did not sleep well and in the morning was so nervous that she decided to leave and drive to Lerici.

Over the past decade she had spent a few August days in Lerici nearly every year with a couple of her best girlfriends, Emmanuelle from the bank and Monica, who owns a clothing shop in Geneva. It had always been a kind of a girls-only long weekend, the other two being married but never bringing their husbands. And then 15 months ago, on her most recent visit, she had come with Marc, not the girls. They had more than understood, happy as could be for Clara's romantic interlude.

On her two-and-half-hour drive from Milano southwest to the

Ligurian coast, she thought a lot about Marc. Maybe she should have followed her first thought when Willem had asked where she would go. Head straight to the airport, buy a ticket with cash and fly to Detroit. Yes, why not go to Marc, fold herself in his arms and tell him everything? He would probably have a much better sense of what she should do.

And then she had begun to wonder what would really happen if, more or less unannounced, she just showed up on his doorstep? Would he greet her with delighted hugs and kisses, or would it be somehow awkward? Might she even find herself un-welcomed? What if Marc were in fact close to some other woman in Detroit, someone whose existence he has kept from her? She could not be sure what Marc's life there was really like. And with that uncertainty and many others clawing at her, she banished the thought of making that huge leap, flying off to another continent, to a place where she had never been before.

In Lerici she found a room in a building two doors down from where she and Marc had stayed. November was off-season, the prices lower than she expected and somehow in this familiar, beautiful place, now so quiet and even more charming, with less than half the number of people she was used to here, she felt as if she had begun to think more clearly. Around the corner from her building she found a small Internet shop, where she could rent a computer with web access by the hour. Once on line she quickly checked out the websites of the Geneva papers and the TSR television news programs, searching with a strangely avid dread for any indication that she had been charged with a crime by the Banque Privee Morneau. With both frustration and relief, she found nothing.

She opened a Gmail account but then was afraid to write to anyone, thinking anything she sent could possibly be traced back to her, and remembering again Willem's warning that she would endanger anyone by simply letting them know she was still alive. She also thought about buying a new phone, a pre-paid mobile with no contract, a phone the bankers could not know about. Whenever needed she could replenish her minutes with the purchase of a phone card. At first she thought if she owned a mobile that could not be traced, with a record of calls that could not be tracked, she would only be tempted to use it in a risky way that could come to no good. No, she would probably be better off without one.

But she woke Wednesday morning thinking that was nonsense. Even before she had coffee, bread and cheese at her favorite café off the main piazza, she found a shop nearby and bought herself a new mobile, a cheap, basic little Nokia, pre-paid, with no contract and no record that was likely to be traced back to her. She was still not sure whom she might call, but sitting in the café with the phone there next to her on the table, she felt better. If something happened, if she really had to connect with someone, she now had the means to do it, without the danger of giving away her location. She thought about calling Lina's mobile. The professor would be back in Bologna, safely away from Geneva, and maybe Cecile had gotten in touch and told her something about Clara's trouble at the bank. Maybe she could swear Lina to secrecy. Maybe she could even go to Bologna and stay with Lina. Maybe she could get some helpful advice from the brilliant Lina. And then it became clear that the only one to call was the man who already knew she was alive because he had decided not to kill her.

Back at the café after her lengthy walk on the promenade, she has a salad and thinks again that the owner, Signor Schiavone, who is preparing food behind the counter, reminds her of her father. It's the thick frame and large hands, the mostly gray hair and goatee, or maybe it's just that he is a cook, the chef of this little place he's operated for close to thirty years.

Her grandfather, her father's father, and her great uncles had built the house in Speranza. They were common laborers, sometimes construction workers, or ditch-diggers, or barge builders, or even fishermen—whatever it took to make a living in those close-to-the-bone days. But it was something of a miracle that her father grew up to be a chef. The youngest of three, he learned to cook early from his mother and just took to it, for a while in his teens doing construction work with his father but then often cooking for the family as well. Somehow he got a job in the galley on one of the boats that plied Lago Maggiore, and later he moved up to a cooking job on a boat that used to make the trip from Geneva to Montreux and back. In Geneva he met a young Austrian woman working as a nanny for a wealthy family who had moved from Austria to Switzerland during the horrors of war in the '40s. They married and had Clara and Claudio two years apart. Clara was always close to her younger brother, but he passed away from pancreatic cancer 10 years ago, just before he turned 40 and just two months before he was to marry a woman he called his "dream girl."

Thinking of Claudio is always a reminder that life is essentially heartless and that she must never indulge in feeling sorry for herself. She looks around this little place, from Signore Schiavone chopping behind the counter, to the girl Pia, his granddaughter, waiting on a couple at the table next to the window, and wonders what has happened to her resolve to avoid familiar places and people who know her. She has already tired of it is the short answer. It's not her, and besides, there seems no possible way that word of her presence in this little café could ever make its way back to Geneva. And then in walks the old man in the bowler hat.

Once again he nods to her and touches the brim, but this time he comes to a stop in front of her. With a quiet voice in rather grandiloquent Italian, he introduces himself as Marcello Cerni, the mayor of the beautiful town of Lerici.

Clara smiles and, as she did in the Carabinieri office, says her name is Doloro. With a closer look, she notes the unruly white fuzz sticking out from the bowler around the ears, the long black coat over a gray sweater and black slacks, all well-worn and frayed in places.

"May I ask, *Signora* Doloro," he says with a slight bow, "from where you bring us such beauty and charm."

She thanks him and then surprises herself by saying, "Vienna."

"Ah, Vienna, a beautiful city. I hope your stay with us is everything you wish it to be." And with that he bows again and moves off to a table on the other side of the small room.

Pia arrives and says, *"Scusi, signora."* Then she flicks her eyes at the old man. *"Lui e pazzo, ma innocuo."* He is crazy but harmless.

Clara smiles. *"E bene. Non e problema."*

The mayor no longer seems to have an interest in Clara, but a few minutes later Signor Schiavone comes over to sit with her. With his sad eyes the café owner tells her a sad story. About a year ago the old man lost his beloved wife and hasn't been right since. He was a painter — Clara may have seen him in years past working on his watercolors of scenes in and around the town — a man of strong but limited talent, who made a modest living at it. His wife, a sweet woman to whom he was totally devoted, made knitted goods, mostly shawls and scarves, sold through a local shop.

Then one night with no warning she died in her sleep. And Signor Cerni simply could not accept it. He attended the funeral along with practically the whole town, but he was soon telling people she had gone for a short visit to her mother and would soon return. Those close to him tried for a time to keep him attached to reality and encouraged him to take up his painting again, but they soon gave up on both. His wife and his painting had been his whole life, and now both had left him forever.

His neighbors and friends made sure he had food to eat and clothes to wear. And then one day from the window of a resale shop he bought himself a bowler hat in the style of a mayor of the town from many years ago, when the old man was just a boy. He began telling people, whether acquaintance or stranger, that he was the mayor of Lerici. There were a few awkward moments early on, when Signor Cerni was challenged and once even made his claim in the presence of the real mayor of Lerici, thus being forced to explain that, well, he was actually the retired mayor. After that, word spread quickly that the best way to handle this unfortunate situation was to say politely, "Well, good day to you Mr. Mayor," and go on about one's business.

Yes, truly a sad story, says Clara, as Signor Schiavone rises to return to his work. A story, she knows, about the power of love and the kindness of a community toward one of its own. But she soon feels a dark and anxious pall settle over her. She needs to deal with her own fraught and risky life. What about the man she has loved beyond all others? What about Marc? She keeps coming back to Marc and wondering what he would think and say about her impossible situation. She ponders if and how she should contact him. Find a way to sound him out on how he would feel about her coming to Detroit. At the very least she could send him an old fashioned letter by post, with no electronic trail.

No, first she needs to know what is really happening in Geneva. She needs to have a real conversation with Willem. Perhaps by now he has turned his phone back on. She needs to call him again. On the way back up to her room she thinks that when she calls maybe she won't block her number. Maybe if he thinks it's someone else, he'll be more likely to answer.

Sitting on the narrow bed in her room she stares through its lone window at a window in the building across the narrow street below.

There she can see a young mother feeding her tiny child in a high chair, the two of them enjoying each other immensely. She feels a nearly overwhelming urge to call Honore, but finally fights it off. As she punches in Willem's number, she prepares herself to leave a message this time when he does not answer. And then after one ring, his voice says, "Yes."

"Willem, it's Clara. Can you talk? Please don't hang up."

"Yes, I can talk, but why are you calling? You are putting both of us in danger." His voice is not friendly, but he at least sounds calmer.

"I am worried, Willem, frightened about what has happened at the bank. Why have I been charged with a crime? I have done nothing wrong. You know that."

"Yes, and you know why they have done that. I told them you are dead, but in case you turn up, either dead or alive, they have the reason and the evidence for why you disappeared. But how did you learn of the charge? It has not been on the news."

"I went to the Carabinieri…"

"The Carabinieri!"

"Yes, but I did not give them my name, and I did not talk to them."

"You are not making sense."

"Yes, I went to them, but while I was waiting, I heard one officer tell another to go to my house to see if I was there. They had a request from the police in Geneva who said I am accused of a crime. And so of course I left and talked to no one. Now I am someplace else."

"In Italy? Where?"

"Yes. In Liguria. Willem, I am afraid maybe you have changed your mind. Should I fear you?"

"No. But you said the States. Why haven't you gone to the States?"

"I don't know…." She falters. There is too much to explain.

"Look, this is what you need to do. Go as soon as you can to Genoa, the airport, and fly to the States, to your friend in Detroit, or anywhere. Just get out of Europe as soon as possible."

"But won't they be watching for me at the airport?" She has just thought of this.

"No. Maybe, but probably not. They have sent out notices, but even with a major crime, which yours is not, they do not always pay attention."

"Willem, I am so frightened."

"I know. But you will be all right if you do as I say. You have a new phone?"

"Yes. It's prepaid. I don't think it can be traced."

"Don't use it unless you absolutely must. But now I have your number. If I learn anything that would help you, I will call. Otherwise, just do what I told you."

"Yes, Willem. And thank you. Oh, and one more thing. Does Cecile—Madame DeRocheford—know about the charge against me? And what about my family?"

There is a long pause, then Willem says, "No, I told you they have not made this public. They have sent information only to the police. Just remember, anytime you call me you put us both in danger. They are watching everything."

And then there is only a dial tone.

She pushes the end button on the Nokia and glances up at the window. The happy mother and child are gone. Suddenly she understands there is something she must do, something that Willem would forbid in a rage if he learned she was even considering it. Now she needs to go out and buy herself a writing pad.

Chapter 15

On Thursday at noon in the cafeteria of the Clinique de Gervais, Lina as usual checks the messages on her mobile. In the ICU she abides hospital rules and keeps it powered down. Now, before starting on her vegetable salad, she finds three new calls since she checked this morning. One is from Guido Falcone, her family's old solicitor in Catania, the second is from Julian, his fourth call in less than 24 hours, and the third is from a blocked number again. Her guess is this is another from Clara who left a voice mail late yesterday, also without revealing the number. The message was cryptic and a bit strange, not unlike what you might expect from someone on the run:

"Lina, dear, this is Clara. I have been thinking about you and trust you are well settled back in Bologna. Have you heard from Cecile since you left Geneva? My love to you, dear. I will try you again soon."

Picking up the new voice mails, she skips through Signor Falcone's as soon as she hears he needs a word from her on the sale of a property on Majorca. She knows what Julian wants—dinner tonight—and she has been avoiding him. The third message is what she expected:

"Hello, dear, it's Clara again. I'm wondering if you have heard anything strange about me recently from Cecile. Or from anyone else for that matter. If so, please know there is nothing true about what you might have heard. And please, dear, it is important that you say nothing about these voice mails if you do speak to Cecile, or anyone in Geneva. Thank you, dear. I'll try to call you again sometime soon."

So Clara, who has disappeared and cannot be found by the police, is concerned about what Lina might think about the charge against her at the bank, but she doesn't want Cecile to know she has called Lina. Strange indeed. And reason enough to call Julian back finally and accept his invitation to dinner this evening. She wants to hear more about this charge against her friend, something that Clara has now denied but has apparently refused to face by turning herself into the police.

An hour later back in the Cecile's room, nothing has changed. Nothing has really changed since last Friday night when her old friend was rushed to this hospital. As she has so often in the past week while sitting with Cecile, she finds herself drifting back to those awful days in Taormina almost two years ago now. Maybe it is the thought of Clara's trouble with the law, or perhaps the subdued glow from the nursing station in the hallway glancing through the glass wall of the ICU room, but Lina is somehow reminded of the dappled light on the black and tan forest floor high on Mt. Etna's slope. She wonders again, as she has so many times since, how she found her way on that convoluted hiking trail all the way back to her car, parked on the edge of that Sicilian road skirting the volcano's summit. There were several divergent paths along the way, but either an innate sense of direction or the benefit of her childhood memories of walking that trail so many times with her father, brought her all the way back without consciously thinking about the route until she suddenly found herself in front of the silver VW.

Yes, she had been lost all right, tossed in the jumble of her thoughts and feelings about the astounding fact of what she had just done, an act so primal and horrid that she could never have imagined doing it before that very day. Yes, she had her reasons, for Stan had murdered a beautiful young man for whom she had cared deeply, had tried to kill her and the man she had cherished beyond all, poor John, who was then lying on his deathbed. And now this murderous fellow had joined her on this lovely forest walk fully intending, she knew without a doubt, to take her life. She could easily have handed it to him. And nearly had. But after a 40-year abhorrence of violence, she had kissed Stan and then slipped open the yellow-handled box cutter to sink the point of the blade into the flesh of his neck and—neatly, swiftly, surely—draw it across the breadth of his life to end it for good. Rapt in repellent horror, bloody self-disgust and a raw satisfaction so deep there had been nothing in her life to compare it with, she finally left him head down at the bottom of a deep crevice, a narrow volcanic split where nothing, including what some would call his immortal soul, would ever be found.

For a while, sitting close to Cecile in the bed, she reads aloud from a copy of the woman's own book, the most recent one, *Getting On*. Having finished with Rousseau's Confessions, she thought maybe if Cecile were to hear the sound of her own prose, it might stir a response. If it has, Lina has not noticed. She tries again:

> Unfortunately we have had no luck in devising a scientific study of the efficacy of prayers for the dead. Still, my believer friends definitely favor praying for the sick or seriously ill. But will prayer make any difference to their physical future? On this we do have some scientific evidence. Several recent studies have tested whether prayer aids in recovery. Sadly the answer seems to be no.
>
> A few years ago the American Heart Journal published a study in which researchers recruited Christian congregations to pray for two groups of cardiac patients. One group knew the Christians were praying for them, and the other group thought they *might* be praying for them. A third, control, group of patients were also told that the Christians might be praying for them, but there were in fact no prayers raised for their benefit. All three groups had comparable mortality rates, but the fewest complications came to the un-prayed-for group. Such, apparently, is the power of prayer.

She stops, lowers the book and gazes at her old friend's slack and ashen face. It might as well belong to a stranger. The lively wit in the eyes, the quick, subtle expressions, the animated nods and gestures? All gone. She needs to remind herself; this is the same remarkable woman who has been her almost constant companion for the past two months.

Was it this way with John, at least near the end? Not really, not even when she knew his passing was both inevitable and close at hand. Even then there had been moments when she picked up small signs that her lover was still with her, if only for a few seconds here and there. But all this waiting for the end with someone precious, all the conversations with the doctors about options and possibilities, all the private attempts at preparation for the ultimate loss, all of it has stirred in Lina a vortex that has swept her back to those three long months, starting the day after that last hike with Stan, as she watched and waited while John tried to live and then tried to die. She is still certain that is how it was at the end, John trying with whatever he had left of conscious mind (and, who knows, perhaps with unconscious resource as well?) to will an end to the ordeal. Dr. Notaro, Donatella and the other nurses at the hospital in Taormina were good with the physical pain. But without a plug to pull and excluding murder, there was nothing anyone could do to obviate the psychic ache of knowing, fitfully for him and constantly for her, exactly what was happening as those rogue cells in his brain did their efficient and lethal split.

She had set up a small table in his room where she could work to finish her book and still be with him throughout each day. For a time they had been able to talk, share thoughts, memories, even hopes, dreams and desires. As she has with Cecile, she often read to him, from either the novels she was deconstructing or her own writing. And then more and more in the final weeks, as the cancer was clearly advancing, when she read to him, she was often uncertain whether he was hearing or comprehending anything.

There was always a window open on the green Sicilian hills rolling out to the snow-capped and fuming Etna, but she knew he was mostly trapped within the confines of his own head, fighting perhaps with bitter regrets and blasted dreams and staring with certainty at what was coming. On that last day she had sensed it was near. Sitting next to him on the bed, she held his head to her breast, her hand on his chest, feeling his uneven breathing and the soft beat of his heart. And then there was nothing more to feel.

"*Carissimo, ti amo,*" she told him softly and then answered for him: "I love you, darling."

After a while she moved so she could see his face. The deep blue eyes that had so often thrilled her with intelligence and desire were closed forever. The mouth that had delivered both insight and tender kiss was still. He was gone. She had been so lost in the moment that she realized she was weeping only when a tear dropped on her hand.

Later on that bright, fresh spring day, as she walked from the hospital to her empty apartment, she offered herself all the usual bromides. He was at peace. He was free. At last he had the oblivion he wanted. But then she found herself wondering, even if he had fervently wished for it, could he really have visualized his own descent into nothingness? Can any of us truly picture ourselves no longer existing? Can even a suicide actually see his wished-for death as the last true end? And could that failure of imagination reside near the core of religious belief? If you cannot imagine yourself fading to nothing, then must there be something, some alternate slice of consciousness or sliver of spirit, that somehow carries on? And so we debate the so-called immortal soul, perhaps floating about on its own, or sharing in bliss or torment with those similarly judged, or melding, along with a zillion others gone before and still to come, with the great Oneness of Being.

Now she asks herself, at the very end, as Stan began his hopeless fall to forever, did he find the imaginative power to predict his self-obsessed self transformed to nothingness? She finds herself hoping so.

Later, well after seven, delayed by more than a half-hour as she waited for another conference with Dr. Monrovian in which the news was only that there was no news, that nothing has changed, she steps off the elevator in the hospital lobby, knowing she is already late for dinner with Julian. When she finally returned his calls, she told him she wanted to meet at L'Entrecôte because she was in the mood for beef. In fact, she wants a look at the place where Clara and Marc met for the first time four years ago. There are several people waiting to board the elevator, but her eyes meet briefly with those of a stone-faced fellow she has seen before at the hospital.

Late on one of the first nights of her vigil, she was in the room with Cecile and looked up to see this tough looking man in a black leather coat walking slowly past in the hall, staring in at her. He looked away and moved on, to one of the other ICU rooms, she presumed, in this trouble-filled place. Now, she knows, there is only one other patient besides Cecile, still on the unit from early in the week, so this fellow must be visiting the 70-year-old man who had also suffered a stroke. But then that seems unlikely, since Lina spent time a few days ago in the unit's waiting room, talking with the old man's niece, who said she was his only living relative.

The man in black leather looks down quickly and lets Lina pass.

Chapter 16

"Interesting you should mention that Clara and Marc first met here at L'Entrecote. That I didn't know. Though, like everyone else at the bank, I was aware of their 'unusual' love affair."

"So it was common knowledge," says Lina, and he notes how carefully she eyes him in this small, busy place.

His original dinner plan was to persuade her that Madame DeRocheford really should be moved to the Clinique Generale-Paquis. But then Giles finally agreed that Tanner should go in and finish his business at the Clinique de Gervais. And now the idea is to keep the professor occupied here, so the Lout does not have to worry about her appearing at the hospital at an untoward moment. His task, which he wanted them to believe was so fiendishly difficult, should go easier now.

But when she failed to arrive on time, his nerves acted up. He imagined things going badly wrong at the hospital. Maybe the plan they had settled on had fallen apart. Perhaps she had stepped out of the room for a few minutes, and, thinking she was gone for good, he had been caught red-handed upon her return, injecting the follow-up compound into the feeding tube. Yes, he would be in orderly scrubs, the nurses would be busy dealing with visiting families, not just sitting there monitoring in the middle of the night, and the injection would produce only a significant turn for the worse, not instant death. But then the best laid plans....

Finally, she arrived at L'Entrecote full of apologies, and he could breathe again. They spoke only briefly about poor madame's unchanged condition. Now about Clara and Marc he tells Lina, "Oh, yes, we were all so happy for her, and so sad at the same time. Happy because everybody loved Clara. She had been at the bank for so many years, and she was really such a popular gal. And sad, of course, because it seemed inevitable that this would not end well."

"That she and Marc would not end up together."

"Yes. I used to try to help her with English, but it just did not work out."

She sips her cabernet. "And you were surprised when you found this evidence, open and shut, as you say, that she defrauded the bank and disappeared?"

"Not surprised. Totally shocked. As I say, it's interesting you mention the two of them, because the only theory we've come up with that makes any sense at all is that she did it to be with him."

"You mean she would throw away her pension and steal 40 thousand Swiss so she could run off with Marc?"

"Yes, I admit it doesn't make perfect sense, but then people in love do crazy things. In any case, this morning we received a report from the bank's computer expert, the fellow who set up our system and knows how to go in and open her email."

"And what did he find?"

"Well, that they are either very cunning, or that this fellow Marc has had no idea what she's been up to. Everyday this week he has written her a message wondering why he has not heard back from her and expressing more concern. Each time he writes to her, he sounds more desperate."

"So unless they've been clever enough to put you off with his emails, she has deceived him as well."

"It would seem that way. But let me ask, have you heard at all from our friend Clara in the past week or so?"

She seems surprised by the question. "Have I heard from her? Certainly if I had, I would tell you about it."

"Yes, but I thought perhaps as a friend, she might have sworn you to secrecy."

Her smile takes on a strange cast. "No, we are not friends that way. I have known Clara only for the past two months and have met her only a few times. But may I ask something that will change the subject? I find all this talk of Clara and what she has done both sad and distasteful."

"No, of course, by all means."

"So, on our visit to Annecy, you spoke very little about yourself growing up. You mentioned that as a boy you preferred math and science, were skilled at drawing and enthusiastic about soccer. But you said little about your parents."

"Yes, well, I think I mentioned that my mother was beautiful and doting, and my father was missing. I really have no recollection of him at all. Mother always referred to the man as 'a beautiful loser,' inordinately handsome, with absolutely no work ethic, who left — after years of promising marriage — more or less upon my arrival. He then married a wealthy widow, whom he soon divorced to wed another well-to-do woman.

"At that point Mother completely lost track of him. She was the daughter of a poor tradesman. She was fond of saying, 'My father, your grandfather, was a mason, as thick as the bricks he laid.' She had left her family at 17 to find her way in Lausanne and at 18, late one night in a restaurant, met the man who would become my father. She told me once, 'It was love at first sight for both of us, the only time it has ever happened to me, and it did not work out so well. Something to remember, my beautiful little boy.'

"Later she traded on her beauty and charm to become, as I understand it now, a kind of courtesan, pleasing and supported by a series of older men, most of them bankers and most married. She doted on me but must have squirreled away money, because she always sent me to good schools, preparing me, I'm sure she thought, for the kind of earned success in which my father was never interested. Growing up, I was never of any use or concern to the men in my mother's life. I was never close to any of them."

And that is about as far as he wishes to go with this smart and beautiful woman who seems to have a knack for getting him to talk more than he wants. The rest of his story he has shared with Giles and almost no one else. Because by age 11 or 12 — mostly from watching TV in their small town outside Zurich — he already knew he was gay. His first experience was with a secondary school art teacher and soccer coach. The man asked him to pose for life sketches and then thought he had seduced the boy, but Julian had planned the whole thing. Their private sessions continued for a year before the man was transferred to another school, and Julian later had a fling or two with older boys. By his senior year he was often going to a gay bar in Zurich, getting himself picked up or invited to what could only be described as orgies. Then one night he made an unfortunate choice and got himself badly beaten by three fellows cruising the city on the hunt for their special kind of prey. After that he was much more careful.

When he was 19, early in his first term at the University of Zurich, his mother died of a heart attack at 41. He was devastated for a time, but she had left him enough to get through college without working, and one winter evening at a gallery opening, he picked up Giles, who was then in the graduate banking program.

From the start their lovemaking was exhilarating, "liberating" Giles called it, beyond anything he could have imagined, and within two months they were pledging their love for each other. Giles claimed this was his first real love affair, having tried only two tentative, guilt-ridden couplings with fellows who meant nothing to him. During the two years it took Giles to earn his masters, they fucked almost as much as Julian studied, experimented with drugs and spent a lot of time debating what Giles should do with his life. Should he take the easy path laid out for him at the family bank, or do what he really wanted — return to school, start over, almost from scratch, and study to be an architect? Giles said he had always denied himself this path out of family loyalty, an annoying but prevailing sense that fate had carved out the banker's life for him, and perhaps also out of a fear of failure.

But according to Giles, their two years in love had fostered a new sense of possibility. Julian's mantra was, grab the freedom to be and do whatever you wish. And that passion for personal liberty was the basis for everything between them. Now Giles wanted to hold hands and kiss in public, to "shout our love from rooftops," and he was surprised when Julian often advocated privacy and discretion.

Finally, when decisions had to be made about plans for the future, Julian argued that Giles should do what would please his father. Go back to Geneva, join the bank and do what was necessary to fulfill his legacy and claim what was rightfully his: substantial wealth and the power to control his life. And once he possessed those vital things, Giles could do whatever he liked, follow any whim or desire. Take the other path, and you might always be hemmed in and limited by practical realities. You might never achieve the freedom you will always long for.

Ultimately, feeling betrayed, Giles took this argument as proof that Julian no longer loved him, perhaps never had. Their quarrels and fights became long and bitter. In the end Giles seemed crushed and returned to Geneva.

Alone for a while, Julian then twice surprised himself. First he majored in the banking curriculum, and then he started dating young women. He told himself that banking was the quickest, surest way to extravagant wealth, and with the girls, he was exploring "openness and universality." The sex was infrequent and seemed mostly to lack point and pleasure, but once that had been established, he found a few genuine female pals whose company he truly enjoyed.

In his senior year he took up with a nerdy freshman named Eric Boll, a freakishly skilled hacker and digital wizard who taught Julian a number of tricks, shortcuts and methods of manipulation that would, years later, turn out to be especially useful. The affair with Ricky turned out to be quite satisfying, right up until it ended, early in his graduate year, when they were caught trying to manipulate Julian's grades. To save himself with university officials, Julian gave up Ricky as the sole culprit. Actually the enterprising young fellow was doing his hacking and grade-fixing thing on a commercial basis for a number of student clients and continued his business even more successfully after being expelled. Julian did not last much longer, dropping out in the middle of his second term.

With something still left from his mother's estate, he decided to travel. On the cheap he moved through Europe with his laptop in a backpack, trying to play the market, then trying to learn how to play the market, neither a great success.

Then in Moscow, of all places, he met Jacob, an elderly American businessman, who brought him back to New York, made him a personal assistant and installed him in the old guy's penthouse on Central Park. For two years it was a beautiful deal, long on travel, short on demands, but when Jacob croaked, Julian was left with a decent investment account and no way to stay in the States.

Finally, passing back through Geneva, after six years of total silence, he just picked up the phone and called Giles, who sounded quite pleased to hear from him. They met for lunch at Brasserie Lipp. It was awkward at first, but with Julian taking the lead, each admitted his own culpability and bullheadedness at the end of their relationship, each admitted the other had probably been right, and Giles invited him to his wedding two weeks hence. This news came as a shock to Julian, but he did not let it show.

There was so much catching up to do. Giles took the rest of the afternoon off so they could walk in the brilliant summer sun across the Mont Blanc Bridge and past the exuberant water cannon, the Jet d'Eau. Along the lakeshore, they continued past the luxury hotels all the way up through La Perle-du-Lac, talking non-stop until they paused in a kind of rapt silence to gaze at the giant steel horse prancing with the naked boy, his pretty prick poised for pleasure. Chattering away again, they moved on to the Parc Moynier, the loveliest place in Geneva, lush with flowers in light and shade, the lake glimmering in front of majestic Mont Blanc.

Yes, of course, Giles had joined the bank upon his return from Zurich. Really, what else could he have done? But those first four years or so were truly awful, marked often by bitter scenes with his impossible father. With clients, the old man was cordial and solicitous. With his only son, he was rigid, suspicious, tight-fisted and dictatorial. Like many of his old-line investors, he was absurdly narrow-minded and rabidly homophobic. Giles had rebelled, drank too much, did too many drugs and with Albert Morneau fought battle after battle he had no hope of winning.

Finally, a year-and-a-half ago, his beloved mother died of breast cancer — yes, they had both adored and lost their mothers so young — and because of her passing, or because he had just turned 30, or for some other well-hidden reason, he had grabbed hold of himself and transformed the way he functioned at the bank and dealt with his father. He even became meticulous and deferential. Before there had been furtive affairs with meaningless men. Now he began dating young women, the culmination being his engagement to sweet, petite Hilde. His father had begun to trust him at the bank, and Giles could actually foresee the day when he would take over operations and run things in a way that made modern banking sense.

He and Giles were sitting on a bench in the shade of a beautiful old oak, and his old lover's sad face was lit with such earnest relief, that Julian quickly glanced about, then pressed his hand and kissed him softly on the lips. And at that moment, it felt like Jules and Giles in love again. Attending the wedding, Julian marked the happy occasion by finding a very private little room on the Morneau mansion's second floor to give his old lover a "celebratory" blow.

He stayed in Geneva for a while and continued seeing Giles until he was certain the man was more in love with him than ever. And then he took off again, this time for a tour of the Far East, where he learned a number of things, including where to meet the wealthiest, most sophisticated guys in Singapore and how to pick up the best-looking traders in Mumbai. And finally he learned that none of these experiences came close to matching the simple yet certain satisfaction of sharing his love with Giles Morneau. Then one day he was on-line at a Starbucks in Bangkok, when an email arrived urging him back to Geneva. Giles had finally taken over the bank from his father, and there was a job waiting for Julian as Chief Investment Manager. In short order Julian had concocted a dazzling resume with successful stops at firms in Hong Kong and Tokyo, knowing, of course, not a word of it would ever be vetted.

Neither of them had been anything but mediocre students in school. Not surprisingly, Julian thinks, neither is a very swift banker. Yes, Giles had made what must have been a bold move to grab hold of the bank five years ago. But he had only done so when his 80-year-old tyrant of a father was in a very weakened condition after a heart attack. Giles has never spoken candidly about it, but Julian has wondered if Giles might have pulled the plug on old Albert in the hospital to complete the take-over.

Whatever, it was only then that Giles fully realized that what he had grabbed was mostly trouble, that because of the way it was originally set up and stubbornly run by both his grandfather and father, the bank was poised to fail. And perhaps worst of all, Giles' own trusts, his own financial future, had already been badly depleted.

No, there is nothing about this story, Julian thinks now, chewing the last of a savory steak, that he would wish to share with anyone. Certainly not with this razor-sharp redhead, whose looks remind him a little of his poor dead mother.

And then his mobile vibrates in the breast pocket of his suit coat. On its screen, he sees that it's Giles. Is the job at the hospital already completed? Or did something go wrong there?

"Sorry, I need to take this," he tells Lina and then listens as Giles imparts the news. Unsure of his success, he tries to keep the emotion he is feeling from flickering across his face.

Finally, he ends the call and tells her, "They've found Clara. In Italy."

Chapter 17

When the call comes from Dubonne's office asking if he can be there at noon, he's already had a full morning. He didn't really plan any of it, but he isn't especially surprised that it happened.

Earlier in the week he had picked up the girl with those mismatched eyes and brought her to a dark lot not far from the airport, a place he knew the cops cared not a jot about. They hardly spoke, but with that avid little mouth she was surprisingly skilled and enthusiastic, not taking nearly as long as he thought she would. When she was done, in his dark Mercedes after midnight, his anger was still beating, but a wave of exhaustion poured over him, and it was all he could do to drive back, drop her near the lakefront and head to his house.

Last night he started earlier, right after finishing at the hospital. Everything had gone like clockwork, the two nurses called away to deal with the emergency giving him more than enough time to feed the feeding tube and bid the old gal adieu. He found Peanut again at the bar. In a little tank top and ruffled mini-skirt, she looked even younger than before. He bought her a drink, and they actually talked for a while. So why did she call herself Peanut? Was it a name she had growing up, or a street name?

Both, she said.

Not a very sexy name for the street, he pointed out.

"Sexy is as sexy does," she said, sounding more pert and cocky now that he had come back to her twice.

He asked how much for the night.

She said, "I thought you didn't like me."

He said, "I like you a little."

"Then fifty," she said. "If you liked me more, I'd charge you less. Besides, you're a cop, no? So I'm already giving a discount."

She had some attitude, and he thought that might be good. When they walked into his place, she said it was "sweet" and "stellar" and "much too nice for a clean cop."

"Who said I'm a cop?"

"I did. But I'm just a stupid little cunt. If you are not a cop, then you get the works for free. I don't hardly ever get taken to such a nice pad."

The works started in the shower, where he took her from behind with a kind of fury, and all she offered were small, pleased-sounding cries. Later in the bed he wanted that rosebud of a mouth again, and she gave it to him so slow and thorough that he felt nearly crazy before she switched gears and he came with a crash. The third time was after they had slept for a while. She woke when he was rubbing down hard on her bald little snatch and moving his finger inside. She turned and said, "No, I want to play with this unbelievable horse thing here."

He let her go on for a time, then pushed her down and shoved it in the old fashion way, slamming until she was screaming. Afterward they lay on their backs, getting their breath back. Finally, with a long sigh she said, "I think I'm in love."

He put his arm under that thick neck of hers in a show of affection. And without thinking about it for more than a few seconds, he turned quickly and, with a brutal twist, felt and heard the snap. It happened so fast her face still held a kind of startled smile.

The anger was finally slaked. Now there was just a foul annoyance that he would have to clean this up. Instead of simply dropping her off downtown, he'd have to shove her into one of those heavy-duty, oversized trash bags, move the car to the backdoor, and stow her in the trunk. Then it would be 40 minutes in the dark to the place he knows on the French side where he can put her for good.

On the way back, he stopped at his favorite small cafe outside Geneva where he had a big breakfast. He lingered over a newspaper and more coffee than was good for him, before getting on the road again. And then came the call from Thoma, the chief's secretary.

"No problem," he says. "See you then."

He'll have more than enough time to go home, clean up and change before the meeting. Good thing, since he looks far less than professional, with mud on his shoes, old worn jeans and a day's worth of beard. He'll ditch the leather and wear a sport coat and tie, the way the chief likes to see him. It fits the man's conception of Willem's role in all this, a trusted bank security guy, who can offer assurance that all is well with the accounts of interest. He figures that's what this is about. In fact, he's surprised it has not happened sooner, with all the talk of Clara defrauding the bank and on the run. No matter what Morneau has said, Dubonne has to wonder if this woman might constitute some kind of threat to the integrity, shall we say, of those two special accounts.

At five minutes to noon he pulls into the spot in the garage they still reserve for him. Upstairs he pokes his head into the squad room where he almost always finds Savoneau and Tremelyn, but they aren't there. Two officers he knows only slightly tell him his old pals are on holiday. In the chief's suite he is ushered right into the large office he knows so well. Everything, from Thoma's shapely ass twitching it's way out, to the sweet smell of the chief's pipe, to the cracked leather of the chair he always sits in. All of it brings back memories that seem a lifetime ago.

Dubonne greets him warmly but then seems rather distracted and says the piles on his desk are for a report due the mayor. He asks about the accounts, but only in what seems a perfunctory way, and is quickly satisfied when Willem says there have been no inquiries from the Supervisory Commission, no expressions of interest or concern about the Chilean and Brazilian accounts.

Then Dubonne says he's been wrestling with naming a new deputy chief, and it's down to Willem's old pals, Tremelyn and Savoneau. With strong factions backing each, he could use a more detached, objective view. Willem knows if history had been just a bit different, his own name would top the list, but he gives quick thumbnails of his friends and then says the choice should come down to leadership qualities. He'd go with Savoneau.

"Interesting," says Dubonne. "That's how I'm leaning."

They finish quickly, but as Willem gets up to leave, the chief says, "Oh, by the way, tell Morneau there is nothing new on the woman."

"The woman?"

"Yes, the woman who worked at the bank. I believe she was a friend of yours actually, at one point."

"Clara?"

"Yes, Clara. No word on her since Monday. Well, actually Thursday, yesterday, was when we heard about it from our friends at the Carabinieri. But it was Monday when she was last seen."

"Seen."

"Yes, I would have thought Morneau would have you in on this."

"Well, frankly, he doesn't always keep me in the loop." Willem sits back down on the cracked leather. "Maybe he thinks I see you all the time and that you give me updates. So Clara was seen on Monday in Italy."

Dubonne nods slowly, as if he's now wondering if he should have mentioned this. "At her home in Speranza. It was second hand, but a neighbor told an officer who stopped back yesterday to check further that she had seen Clara over the weekend."

"Interesting. But nothing since?"

"No, we don't know where she is now."

Willem wants more details but shouldn't seem too interested. The chief starts again: "Yes, I wondered if you'd be available today. I thought you might be in Italy or somewhere looking for this woman. Morneau seems very concerned about finding her."

"Yes, well, they have me working on other things here. But you say the report from the Italians is second hand. Any chance there might be a mix-up?"

"I don't think so. The officer who went to the house on Monday said everything was closed up, and there was no one around to talk to. But he said he was a little 'suspicious' because of some broken cobwebs on the door. You know, the fucking Carabinieri. So when he happened to be in the area again yesterday, he stopped by and spoke with this woman who lives down the hill from the house. The woman said this Clara arrived on Saturday, said she was not feeling well, but was gone on Tuesday when the woman returned with her husband from a visit to Milano. That's literally all we have."

Willem gets to his feet again. "I'll give Morneau the latest. And if you settle on Savoneau, you won't go wrong."

"Thanks for coming in. Take care of yourself."

Back in the Mercedes he slides the key into the ignition but doesn't turn it. There was something strange about this meeting, especially the way it just ended, and he sits there unmoving trying to decide what it was. In all the years, decades really, he has sat in that office with Alain Dubonne, discussing work assignments and specialized activities with a wide variety of risk, has the man ever advised him to take care of himself? He can't remember it happening, even once.

As he waits for the gate to let him out of the garage, he thinks it's good advice. But there are several questions now. Would Morneau actually tell the chief he had ordered Clara's termination? Would he talk about Willem's failure to carry out orders? Did the chief play-act that whole scene in the office? Do they already know he's been in touch with her? Does he even have time to go back to the house and toss some things in a duffle bag? Probably not. At least his two guns are in the car, the SIG-Sauer in its compartment under the seat, and the Russian shotgun in the space between the backseat and the trunk.

Driving away from headquarters he watches the rearview mirror for three blocks, then circles the next, still checking behind. And then he remembers how well he's equipped this vehicle. He hasn't even had a reason to look at it in more than a year, but now he opens the glove compartment and pulls out the small black bug detector. Wondering if the battery is still good, he switches it on, and sure enough the green light glows. Not even a flicker from the red. The Mercedes is clean.

An hour later in France, near the entrance to the tunnel under Mont Blanc, he's still certain no one has followed. But after moving through that enormously long tube for close to 15 minutes, and by the time he finally sees daylight ahead, he is in a full-blown rage. At the girl for being so stupid that she went with him, not once but twice. At Clara for letting them find her and for calling him on his phone. But most of all at himself for blowing the deal of a lifetime. All because he went soft and silly at an old woman's smile. Was there any way to fix this? To get himself back to where things were with Morneau before his own stupidity fucked up everything? And if not, was there a way, maybe, to turn all this to his own advantage, so that he might even be better off? Could he actually make something happen beyond, in fact, his wildest dreams?

First, he needs to find Clara in Liguria and get her out of the way once and for all. But then it will be a special treat to deal with those two faggot assholes he has spent the past several years trying to please.

Chapter 18

Sitting alone at this table in the corner and sipping a local white from Colli di Luni, does she look as nervous and worried as she feels? What does Laura Baroni see, bustling about with her sisters, Simonetta and Alessia, keeping everyone happy in their popular little wine shop and bar on this Friday evening? Does she think, ah, good old Clara, coming in here for years with her girlfriends or with her black boyfriend, always smiling without a care? Or does she see the cracking shell of a woman collapsing inside? One week on the run, and whatever her appearance, her true feelings have ranged from badly jangled to about-to-explode. Where is she now? Maybe somewhere in the neighborhood of numb-with-fear.

If she lived in Lerici she would probably come here everyday to shop at this wonderful little place filled with pastas, condiments, liqueurs and wine. But this is her last night here, if everything goes as planned.

Yes, and when was the last time everything went as planned?

If Willem walked in that door right now, a half-hour early, would she be able to give him a smile? She's been unnerved ever since his phone call this afternoon.

She opens her large black leather bag and digs out several folded over pages of lined writing paper. In there also is her thick letter to Cecile, sealed in its stamped and addressed envelope. Earlier at the post office, she paid for the stamps, then asked the clerk for the letter back, saying she would mail it later. With all her painstaking time and effort on that letter. After buying the writing pad yesterday, she worked through the day and into evening, and this morning she was at it again. Writing and re-writing, fussing with changes and then writing again, putting it aside to search her memory and coming back to find it lacking in this or that. She did the same with her letter to Marc, but finally at the Internet shop, just before coming here, she actually faxed it, flying it across the Atlantic to her beautiful Marc.

114

Has he found it on his machine yet? Has he typed it into the auto translator and learned its shocking news?

But the letter to Cecile remains in her bag. Is she worried about some glitch in the system that would send it, not to her deeply-wronged friend, but to some forsaken pile of lost mail? And what if something happens to her, and it is never sent? She needs to get hold of herself and start thinking clearly. Taking another sip and unfolding the pages covered with her spare, careful handwriting, she finds the copy she made of the final draft.

> Dearest Cecile,
>
> Please forgive me. I am writing to tell you things that I now think I should have spoken with you about as soon as I learned of them. My only excuse is that I have been so frightened and confused, so uncertain of what might be the best course, that I have done nothing. Nothing but run like a frightened rabbit, trying to hide long enough to come to my senses and decide what to do.
>
> My plan now is to fly tomorrow to another continent, to a place that hopefully will be safer for me. But it is finally clear that in case something happens to me, I must write down all that I know about events at the Banque Privee Morneau and about my experiences during the past week.
>
> Your accounts are in serious jeopardy, and it occurs to me now that perhaps you are as well, my dearest Cecile. And so below you will find my attempt to tell you, as I say, everything I know about what certain people at the bank have done to you and your accounts and what they are trying to do to me. But please read this next part very carefully:
>
> You must not tell anyone about this information. Not your friends or acquaintances, not my family or friends at the bank. Because I have

been warned that anyone who knows about this will be in serious danger. As you will learn, police agencies may be a party to this plot. So what you can or should do with this information I do not know. I send it to you with the hope that you will find some way to protect your wonderfully generous funding to many important charities.

One last point: when you finish reading this letter, it will be clear why the bank has charged me with a crime, and why I have fled in fear of my life.

With grateful affection for every kindness you have shown me,

Clara

She followed this personal cover letter with five stern pages she tried to fashion as a kind of legal document, starting with today's date, Friday, November 6, 2009, and beginning, "To Whom It May Concern." Then came an account as precise and complete as she could make it, beginning with that fateful evening visit to the bank to send Marc an email from her office computer, what she saw on the screens on Julian's desk, her meeting with Giles the next day and the visit from Willem that evening, with heavy emphasis on what he said about strong, illicit connections between the bankers and the Geneva police. Included along the way were details as tiny and perhaps inconsequential as how she told Giles that white lie about the Toblerone to explain why she had moved all the way into Julian's office. Then she covered her flight to her home in Speranza, her visit to the Carabinieri in Verbania, where she learned about the charge against her, and finally her escape to Liguria, along with Willem's confirmation on the phone that police agencies were looking for her everywhere.

Reading carefully through these pages now, she wonders again why she did not leave the letter with the postal clerk and send it on its way to Geneva. The account here is certainly as thorough as she could make it, and Cecile should have had it a week ago when the most important events occurred. So why the hesitation? What is she afraid of? What could they possibly do to her that they aren't already trying? At the bottom of the last page were her signature and her current location, Lerici, Italy. Was that a mistake? Not as long as she actually leaves tomorrow, as surely she must.

She glances at the next page and then looks at the small gold Bulgari the bank gave her last year to honor her three decades of service to the Banque Privee Morneau. Fifteen minutes before Willem is due. She does not want to be reading these things when he walks in the door.

The fax to Marc is all on one page. The Italian open and close are what they always use with each other. The body is in French, for which he will need the auto-translation program.

> Carissimo Marc,
>
> I am in trouble, and I need your help. Please forgive what I am about to ask of you. I think you know me well enough to be certain that it must be absolutely necessary. It could well be life or death for me. I know this all sounds absurdly dramatic, but soon, when I am with you and in your arms, and I am able to explain everything in detail, I know you will understand.
>
> I am in Italy, in a beautiful place we have shared and loved. But I must leave Europe as soon as possible. Something has happened at the bank, a matter you may have heard something about. But what you may have heard is only a small part of what has happened. I cannot explain it all here, not in a document other eyes might see. I do not mean to be mysterious. This is something I must tell you in person.
>
> Thus, I am coming to be with you in Detroit. I know there is much presumption in this. I truly trust and hope that I am not imposing in any great way on you or on your life in Detroit. I would not ask this, if there were any other way. I will arrive at Detroit Metro Airport at 2:30 pm

tomorrow, Saturday, 11-7-09, Delta flight 276 from Amsterdam.

I know this comes as a shock. I know you have probably tried to reach me by email, maybe even by phone. That has not been possible for the past week, and I am certain you have worried. I can only tell you it will be heaven to be in the shelter of your arms, to feel the touch of your lips and to tell you with every fiber of my being how much I adore you.

Carissimi baci.

Ti amo.

Clara

And so she wonders again why she did not write and send this a week ago, why she did not fly to him immediately, why she was so filled with doubts and fears about how he might receive her in Detroit. She thinks the truth is, it was mostly a matter of her own failure of faith, her own lack of trust in their love and in their future together.

One more glance at her watch and she refolds these pages and stuffs them back in her purse. Willem, she knows, is almost always on time. His call came when she was sitting on a bench on the promenade with an especially lovely view of the harbor, trying to decide again why she had changed her mind at the post office. She was startled by the ring in her purse, frightened really. Her first call on this new phone. Unless it was a wrong number, someone must have somehow traced her purchase of this mobile. No, of course, it must be Willem. He was the only one with this new number and had told her he might call. The two messages she had left for Lina had not included the number. And finally, once she had decided to write to Cecile and then fly to Detroit, she saw no point in trying further to reach Lina.

"Yes," she said holding the mobile in front of her eyes and not recognizing the number.

"Clara, it's Willem." He sounded like he was driving in a car, his voice a bit strained.

"Oh, Willem. Where are you?"

"In Italy."

"Italy! Why Italy?"

"Because I need to see you. I told you I would call if I had news."

"What news?"

"Well, I'm afraid it's not good. Our friends, the banker boys, know you're alive."

"They know? How could they know?"

"Yes, they know at least that you were alive, and in Italy, as of last Sunday or Monday. The Carabinieri came back out to your home the other day and spoke with your neighbor."

"Ah, God, Anna!"

"So they know, the boys know. And their friends with the Geneva Municipal Police know. So you must be even more careful now."

"Willem…."

"You are in Lerici?"

She is silent. How could he know that?

"Clara, you are in Lerici, no?"

"But how do you know? Do they know?"

"I told you, they only know you were in Italy, at your house, last Monday or Tuesday."

"But how did you find out, Willem?"

"I guessed. You said you were in Liguria, and I recalled you loved Lerici. Look, I need to see you. As soon as possible."

"Why?"

"Because I need to get you to the airport in Genoa. I want to make sure you're in the States by tomorrow evening."

Even though he had spared her life exactly one week ago, last Friday night, the thought of Willem finding her now made her teeth grind. But then again, here he was, saying he would help her, and who else had said anything like that lately?

"Okay," she said, "can you be here by 8 this evening?"

"Yes. Tell me where to meet you."

Not at her building, she thought. "I'll be at the Enoteca Baroni, it's a wine bar at Via Cavour 18, near the center. But you can't drive into the center on the weekends now, so go to the Vallata, the main parking lot, and walk to Enoteca Baroni. It's easy."

"Good. I'll see you at 8."

"Willem, where are you calling from? I don't know this number."

"From my new mobile. It's prepaid…like yours."

"But why?"

"Think about it, Clara!" Again his voice sounded strained and impatient. "I just told you, they know you're alive. Where do you think that puts me?"

"Yes...."

"We're in the same boat now. They know I lied about killing you. They can't trust me, and they want me dead. From now on we both have to be extremely careful, and to keep that boat from sinking, we're probably better off looking out for each other."

"Yes," she said again, more firmly.

"At least until I can get you on that plane in Genoa and make certain you're safe."

"Willem, I'm so sorry."

"I'll see you at 8," he said and ended the call.

Now Laura is moving toward her with a smile, no doubt to ask if she wants another glass. Feeling her nerves buzzing again, she would love one. But she is thinking now about that strain in Willem's voice. He twice mentioned the airport at Genoa, and she said nothing about what she had found on line after she faxed to Marc at the Internet shop. Face it, she fears Willem, even if there is no one else to trust.

A glance at the Bulgari: 7:54.

Chapter 19

He drives fast through the night on the A7 toward Genoa, and each time he spots a pair of taillights in the gloom ahead, he shoves his foot down harder on the gas. Each time he thinks it might be her, but often well before he closes the gap, he can see from the shape of those red lights that it is not the Opel.

When he arrived in Lerici just before 8 and found the Vallata car park, he spotted her car quickly and actually parked next to it. He had memorized the plate number, but he hardly needed to check it to be sure this was her red Astra, the one he had put her in last Friday night in Geneva with the admonition to disappear.

It took him less than 10 minutes on foot to find the wine bar on Via Cavour, but when he walked in, she was nowhere in sight. The woman who seated him said her name was Alessia, and he asked for a Peroni. Being just a little late, he figured Clara and her smile would walk in any time now, but after several minutes he pulled out his phone and tried her number. It rang five times before going to voicemail. When he tried again a few minutes later, it went straight to voicemail. He was still carrying his old mobile with the battery detached. When he put them back together and turned it on, he quickly pulled up the photo of her he had downloaded from the bank. He caught Alessia's eye, and she came smiling.

"Another beer, *signore*?"

"No, I was wondering," he said in his limited Italian, "if you have seen this woman tonight." He showed her the screen on his phone.

"Ah, *si*, Clara."

"You've seen her here?"

"*Si, signore*, she was here, but she left about a half hour ago."

"I wonder if you know where she is staying in Lerici."

"No, *signore*. I am sorry."

He nodded, and she moved away toward another woman who had been serving customers. He finished the beer, spilled a few euros on the table and got up to leave. On his way out the door he noticed Alessia's cross face and saw that the other woman was angry, shaking her head. Apparently he had been given information he was not supposed to have.

Back at the car park, he was not surprised to find the Opel gone. Obviously, after their talk on the phone, her fear of him had gotten the better of her, and now she had already left Lerici. He was angry at himself for giving into his growling stomach and stopping along the way at the pizzeria that took forever and made him late. But where would she go now? There was only one place that made sense: the airport at Genoa.

Now as he continues to chase taillights, his mind is roaming. Without being told much by Morneau, he early on pieced together what had happened at the bank. Somehow, with a look at something she was not supposed to see, Clara had learned that the banker boys have been looting Cecile DeRocheford's account. That is probably the source of the cash they have funneled to him from an off-shore account to pay for the project he has overseen for the past year. He has not pressed Clara about exactly what she saw, because knowing what she knows would probably not be much use to him. He has been much too complicit in their schemes to be able use the details for any kind of leverage. Of course she knows he had orders from Morneau to kill her. But that is all she knows about his role, because that is all he has told her. And just as it would be only her word against the bankers, it would also be only her word against his.

As for what Morneau has discussed with the chief, he's quite sure now that Alain Dubonne knows all or most of this story, certainly that he was ordered to kill Clara, failed to do so and then lied about it. And it seems clear that most, maybe all of what happened earlier today in his meeting with the chief was a charade. But the bottom line about Clara is this: if she could find a way to get someone in authority to consider her story long enough to investigate the bankers, the boys could lose badly, and he along with them. From the beginning, getting rid of Clara Marche has been the only safe course, and he still can't believe how stupidly he has acted.

Signs for Genoa's Cristofo Colombo Airport are starting to appear, and now it seems likely he will have to deal with her after arriving there. He has made this normally 90 minute trip in less than 70, but she apparently had enough of a head start. Now he must think carefully about what she will do once she is inside the terminal.

If he were in her shoes? She's been living for a week on what he gave her and what little she had, and the boys have no doubt frozen or emptied her account at the bank. So with only limited cash and not wanting to use a credit card that would give away her location and itinerary? He'd look to pay cash for a cheap flight to one of the major European hubs with connections to the States. Then once at the hub, he would probably have to use plastic for the much more expensive flight to Detroit.

But inside Cristofo Colombo he finally realizes what he's really up against. This is not a mammoth terminal, but to keep his eye on the ticket stations for all the airlines with flights to all the possible hubs, he will have to be in several places at once. And in order to extract her from this terminal, he will likely need to make contact with her before she gets through the security line. Once beyond that check point, things could get complicated indeed. Even if he manages to get himself through security, she could hide in a women's restroom until just before boarding at one of any number of possible gates. And even if he found her in time, she could choose to create a scene that could make matters more than a little difficult.

No, he is going to require help from someone in authority here, and then he will need to free-lance and improvise to make certain she ends up with him and is not simply picked up and held by the Italians. Nobody, not the banker boys, the Geneva police nor himself, wants that outcome.

So now he has to decide between the Carabinieri and the airport's security office. The thought that there might already be a word out with police agencies on a certain Willem Tanner suggests he try security first. In the second-floor office, once he presents his credentials as a security agent for a private bank in Geneva and briefly explains why he's there, a dark-haired young officer named Regina Allesandro is assigned to assist him. She has a plain, rather bored-looking face and a flat, angular figure for which the uniform she is forced to wear does nothing. It's 10:45 pm now, and he knows she is on the overnight shift, usually an uneventful time on this job, with few flights arriving or departing until the morning. But she speaks French quite well and after he outlines the gist of his mission, she perks up a bit. When he mentions that their system should contain a bulletin on this case issued by the Geneva Municipal Police, she begins snapping away at a keyboard in an effort to find it. After a few minutes she does and turns her screen to him. He sees the same photo of Clara he has on his phone and scans the lines about her being a person of interest in a criminal matter involving theft from Geneva's Banque Privee Morneau and asking that she be detained and the Geneva police be notified. Yes, that's her, he says, and begins to feel better about his chances.

The bank has received information, he says, that this Clara Marche was in Lerici earlier today and that she has plans to travel to the U.S., specifically Detroit, Michigan, departing from Colombo on the earliest possible flight. Because she appears to be strapped for cash, it seems likely she will opt for a cheap flight from here to one of the major hubs with connecting flights to the States.

Officer Allesandro says there are no more flights tonight to any of the hubs, so the woman will have to wait until the morning. And to her knowledge, there are no inexpensive flights from here to Frankfurt Main or Paris De Gaule or Amsterdam Schiphol. So the choice, she says, would have to be Rome Fumicino, and in the morning the only airline with cheap fares there is Alitalia.

That makes it easy, he says. But she thinks to be safe she should print out a list for him of all the flights leaving in the morning for all four hubs. Once he has the list in hand on several pages, he notes that the Italian line has Genoa-to-Rome flights basically every hour on the hour, starting at 7 am. He asks if she can provide Alitalia with the name Clara Marche and instructions to notify security if and when this woman buys a ticket to fly from Cristofo Colombo to Fumicino.

Of course, she says quickly, but it will be no problem to send the bulletin to all of the airlines flying to the hubs in the morning and to make the same request. That way there will be no chance the subject will slip past the officers supplied by this office.

He gazes firmly at Officer Allesandro, thinking that he will surely need to make his move before those officers ever have a chance at Clara Marche. He thanks her and says he's most impressed with her efficiency and with the help provided by her office. It is simply what they do, she says and gives him her first smile. And, she says, please call her Gina.

Of course, Gina.

Now, she says, it is likely to be a long night for him. Even if the subject is here in the terminal, there is no telling when she will decide to make her move and purchase her fare. The woman could wait until several hours from now. So rather than wait here in the office, why doesn't he head down into the terminal, perhaps get himself something to eat or drink, and she will call his mobile as soon as she hears something. If he'd prefer, she can give him access to one of the airline lounges, and he can wait there.

He thanks her again but says he'd rather stake out the airline ticket stations, particularly Alitalia, and watch for the subject. Of course, she says but gives him her mobile number and tells him not to hesitate to call or to check back here in the office anytime. In any case, he really does not have to worry: he will certainly be the first to know if the airlines report anything.

Back on the terminal's first floor he finds a clothing shop that is still open. He's been wearing this dark suit and tie ever since he went back to the house to clean up and change this morning. Although he removed the tie when he made the call to Clara to arrange the meeting in Lerici that never happened, he slipped it on again before walking into the security office. Now he needs something to turn him incognito and figures his best bet are items and colors he wouldn't be caught dead wearing. First a heavy maroon coat sweater that buttons up the front and then a brown felt hat with a turned-down brim. He also buys a tote bag, then heads for a men's restroom. With his suit coat and tie rolled up in the tote, he deems his new look a bit eccentric but not likely to draw gapes.

In a group of chairs against an outer wall he joins three other people who look like they're ready to spend the night. He slouches in a chair that has a full view of both a set of entry doors and a dozen check-in stations with Alitalia logos. Feigning sleep, the collar of the sweater up and the hat brim down over his eyes, he watches only a handful of travelers moving across the terminal floor. Only two agents man the Alitalia stations.

After waiting in this fashion for an hour and spotting no one who even remotely resembles Clara, he calls his new friend Gina. "No word, I presume."

"No, nothing yet."

He settles in again. A look at his Movado tells him it is nearly one. Later, with his second look, he realizes he's actually been dozing. It is well after 2, and when he gazes out across the concourse, there's Gina walking past with a male colleague, obviously on a break. So the good news is his "disguise" is working: the woman has paid him no attention at all. The bad news: Clara too could have walked right past him anytime during the past hour.

When he sees the two officers ride up an escalator, he goes in search of a cup of coffee and brings it back to his chair with a view. It is almost two more hours before the call comes.

"Monsieur Tanner?"

"Yes, Gina. You have news?"

"Well, yes, but maybe not so good,"

"No?"

"I have a report from Alitalia that your Clara Marche has booked a flight to Rome Fumicino leaving at 8:25 this morning."

"Yes, so what is not good?"

"Well, a short while ago I began wondering if it might not be possible that Madame Marche had decided to change her plans"

"Change her plans."

"Yes, and so I thought just to be on the safe side, I should check also with Alitalia at Malpensa."

"At Milano?"

"And sure enough they just called to say that a "Clara Marche" has booked a fare to Fumicino — paying cash as you thought — leaving, as I say, from Malpensa at 8:25.

He suddenly feels foolish. "This morning."

"Yes, still, if you are able to leave here right away, you could make the drive to Malpensa with more than enough time."

"Yes."

"Certainly. I have done it myself in the past, in less than 90 minutes."

He says he is grateful for her diligent help. She says when he gets to Malpensa he should go to an Alitalia counter and ask for a supervisor named Fiori. He will confirm that flight 2269 is still leaving from gate D26 and will put him in touch with Officer Orifice with Malpensa Security, who can assist in the apprehending of Madame Marche.

The trip to Malpensa, on the A7 again as it turns north and east, is uneventful. Traffic is light at this hour and he is no longer concerned with anyone's taillights. He just keeps the pedal close to the floor and knows the Mercedes at a steady 175 km/h can handle anything this road will offer. He actually feels refreshed when he parks not far from the terminal, steps out of the car and the cold morning air hits his face. Yes, with a wrong guess and a wrong turn leaving Lerici, he lost her for a time, but now he has found her again. He's confident he will soon escort her out of this airport. It should not be difficult to go from fighting her fears to using them, convincing her quickly that he is saving her from arrest, prison or worse.

Inside the terminal the early morning bustle stirs his hunger. It is just after 6, and he has more than enough time for some breakfast before finding that Alitalia supervisor. Still in his new hat and coat sweater, he sits at a restaurant table on the edge of a concourse and finishes the last sweet roll. He thinks about how frightened Clara must be to mislead him as she has. If she is capable of this, what other deception might she try? And then he spots them.

At first they are walking together quickly as if late for a take-off, and his initial thought is that this is some huge coincidence. Here they are off on holiday, and in this Milano airport he runs into them by sheer chance. He nearly stands and calls to them but then glances back to look for Savoneau's wife and Tremelyn's girlfriend trailing behind. And then he remembers the two women loathe each other. They would never go off together on some vacation adventure. No, this must be a boys-only holiday. Except, as he finds them again, they are slowing their pace considerably and giving each other those matching nods he knows so well. They separate now and move off at different angles, obviously keeping their eyes on their target ahead. He does stand now and tries to search the distance in front of them.

Well ahead he finally spots the dark blue car coat, gray scarf and pert blond hair he knows only too well.

And suddenly the realization hits. He moves away from the table and begins following with care, whenever possible staying behind others heading in the same direction, even as the whole stupid scenario of the past 24 hours unfolds in his head. Of course, while he was meeting with Dubonne, these two were all over the Mercedes, no doubt soon finding in the glove box the bug detector he had bragged to them about more than a year ago. The obsessive tech geek Tremelyn had surely been able to open the little black box and snip a wire, or scratch a contact, or do something just as simple, so they could place their dirty little GPS enabler somewhere under the frame of his formerly immaculate sedan. And thus advantaged, they followed far behind, well out of sight as he checked his rearview mirrors a thousand times and saw nothing.

Ignorant, he has led them straight to the ill-fated smile of the desperate Clara Marche.

Chapter 20

Wheeling the suitcase briskly behind, she turns into the restroom's open entry and moves past an unoccupied stretch of mirrored wall above the sinks. Pausing for a look, she doesn't like what she sees. The hair is lank, the make-up too thick here, too thin there, the knit top and skirt visible in the opening of her unbuttoned car coat badly wrinkled. For good reason she looks as if she has been up all night in these clothes.

In a stall with the door latched, she finds the walls and fittings exactly like those in the other two women's bathrooms where she has spent most of the past several hours. There has really been no other place to feel safe, and so she has even tried to sleep in these narrow little partitions, searching for some position in which to doze for at least a few minutes at a time. Minutes seem about all she has managed, but she can't even be sure of that. A wash of nervous exhaustion makes it difficult to trust her own good judgment.

Over the past two days she has thought and schemed to formulate a plan to cross the Atlantic, and that brief exchange she had with Willem on the phone has often replayed in her head.

"But won't they be watching for me at the airport?"

"No. Maybe, but probably not. They have sent out notices, but even with a major crime, which yours is not, they do not always pay attention."

That halting, faltering attempt at reassurance hardly inspired trust and told her there might well be people ready to stop her from flying to Marc. At the Internet shop in Lerici she searched on line for the best flight options and a way perhaps to divert or mislead, to give herself at least somewhat better odds of slipping through whatever net might be cast.

She was such an amateur at these things, with no talent for deception. But maybe if she thought carefully enough, she could find a way to leave without losing her freedom, or her life. And then just before eight last night, sitting in the Enoteca Baroni waiting for the

129

man who was minutes from walking in the door to help her, he claimed, get to the airport and out of Europe, she suddenly decided the safest thing to do was to move up her plan. As she paid Laura for the wine, she asked that anyone looking for her be told she had not been in this evening.

On the town's dark winding streets, watching for him at every turn, she hurried back to her little room to pack. Next to the Astra in the car park she found his Mercedes, and, thinking of a scene from a movie vaguely remembered, she placed her hand on its black hood and could still feel the heat. With a knot in her stomach, she lifted the suitcase onto her backseat and rushed away from Lerici and the man she now feared too much to trust.

It took her three hours to drive back to Milano, find the airport, park and drag the suitcase into the terminal. She used the time to think through what she would do once she got inside Malpensa. Of course, she knew Willem would soon return to the Mercedes. She could only hope he would chose Genoa, but she had to act as if he instead would head for Milano and was no more than an hour behind, maybe even less. The first thing she did was scout the terminal, locating the spots she needed: a postal box, a fast food stop, the Alitalia ticket stations, the EasyJet counters and three restrooms, one near the food place, and the other two close to the ticket counters.

At the postal box she finally sent the letter to Cecile on its way. As soon as that hefty envelope slipped out of her hand and into the slot, she felt better. And worse. At last, within a few days, her old friend would have all the information Clara could provide on the crimes perpetrated by the Banque Privee Morneau. And yet there was also a new kind of despair now that she had finally told someone outside the bank about what she had seen on Julian's computer.

Despite the late hour, at the Alitalia counter an agent was still available to book her flight to Rome Fumicino, leaving in just over eight hours for a total price of 54 euros. The gate was currently listed as D26, but she should check again in the morning to confirm. She thanked the agent but knew she wouldn't care by then.

By now she was already looking around so often for Willem that she went directly to the nearest restroom and waited for over an hour. Then feeling weak with hunger, she screwed up her courage and moved out, in the direction of the food stand, where, just before it closed, she bought a salami and provolone sandwich and a bottle of San Pelegrino. It was late now, well after 1 am, and there were few travelers moving about. None of them looked like Willem. She was tempted to find an out-of-the-way chair where she could eat and drink and then maybe even lounge for a while to get some real sleep. Maybe she could cover most or all of her face with her scarf. But, no, finally the risk wasn't worth it, and she headed to her second restroom. With something to eat and drink she felt a little better, and that was where she spent most of the night.

When a cleaning woman knocked on the door of her stall, she moved out again and some time after six walked with pace in the direction of the EasyJet counters. Then, just in case Willem had avoided her searching gaze and was following behind, she ducked into this, her third restroom.

And now in the stall she has a decision to make: what to do with the copy of her long letter to Cecile? She certainly does not want it in Willem's hands or available to Giles and Julian at the bank. She could rip it to pieces and drop them into a trash bin, but if she is arrested by a police or security agency, she will want it with her. And if she gets lucky and makes it all the way to Marc? She will definitely want to give him her detailed, hand-written account of everything she knows, so he can type it into the auto translator and quickly know what this is all about.

She digs the folded-over pages out of her purse, both the letter and the fax to Marc, then opens the suitcase far enough to shove them between a blouse and sweater at the bottom. A glance at her watch: it's nearly 6:30, and time to move. Avoiding a look in the mirror she pulls the suitcase behind her and walks onto the concourse. The EasyJet ticket stations are directly ahead.

A young couple gets to the front of the line just ahead of her, and she waits impatiently as the older woman working the counter deals with what seems to be their complicated request. Do they not know where they want to go? What could possibly be taking so long? She feels exposed as she waits. Willem could be anywhere on the concourse watching her here.

Finally, the couple is finished, but now they need to share a prolonged kiss standing in front of the counter. Clara marches forward, and they almost knock into her as they turn to leave. Putting her passport and a 100-euro bill on the counter, she tells the agent she wants a one-way ticket to Amersterdam Schiphol on flight 7789 leaving at 7:15. The woman glances at the wall clock behind her and shakes her head with a frown, but she takes the passport and types in what her computer needs. Actually the agent moves quickly and the process is finished without a hitch, although it takes longer because Clara now wants to check her one bag. Gate C19, they board in 10 minutes, says the woman handing her the boarding pass.

Yes, of course, there is no time to waste, and Clara drops the change into her purse even as she moves away quickly toward the security area. One more obstacle, and one she fears. Maybe she made a big mistake last night, booking that later flight to Rome to throw off anyone watching for her name on flight lists. Even though she has waited until the last minute to book this flight leaving more than an hour earlier to Amsterdam, maybe these people manning the security line will be looking only more diligently for the name Clara Marche. She needs to calm herself. These security people are trained to spot anxiety and fear, and she needs to seem like any other bored and weary traveler.

Maybe it will help if she keeps her mind fixed on the man she is flying to meet, the love of her life, the man who will fold her in his arms and put an end to this nightmare. She loves Marc with a passion so intense it has frightened her at times, but at this moment there is only a consuming desire to be with him now and forever. Her flight is due in at Schiphol just after nine. Then she'll find a Delta counter to book flight 276 leaving at 10:25 direct to Detroit. It will still be mid-afternoon in Michigan when she runs to Marc's huge waiting smile. She feels her own smile relax her face with this thought as she nears the security line entrance.

And now, almost there, she is suddenly aware of a man's presence next to her. His body crowding hers, she feels his hands grip her left arm firmly, one above and one below her elbow. This happens so fast that she feels a stab of fear only when his voice, low, almost reassuring, says close to her left ear, "Madame Marche, we'll need you to come with us."

She tries hard to pull her arm away, and when that proves hopeless, she turns to glare into the man's face. There is something familiar about the veined blue eyes and the stern, thin mouth. She has seen this face before. It is connected somehow with Willem.

"Why?" she says sharply, stopping dead.

And then a second, larger man joins them, this one on her other side. He takes her right elbow in one hand and with the other holds in front of her eyes a polished police badge. "Because," he says in a voice hissing and unpleasant, "we are with the Geneva Municipal Police, and we have an order for your arrest."

She feels tiny and helpless between them but hears herself say, louder now, "But this is Italy!" As if whatever it is they are doing with her simply cannot happen in the land of her long-dead father.

But they are all three walking now, even though she has willed her feet not to move, heading away from the security line, which now seems not a risk-filled obstacle but a longed-for refuge, and toward a set of steel doors leading out of the terminal.

The man on her left, the one she is certain she has seen before, says with a calm reassurance that only deepens her fear, "As stated, we have an order for your arrest. Please come with us now, and we'll be happy to explain everything."

Feeling frantic, she looks back at the EasyJet counter where everything has just gone so smoothly. "My bag," she says.

"Don't worry, Madame," says the one who showed the badge. "We will get it for you later."

As they approach the large exit doors, one of them opens as a middle-aged couple enters. She searches their eyes, but neither gives her the slightest glance. She already feels the frigid morning air. She looks back one last time at the security line, hoping to somehow catch the eye of one of those busy, focused agents. And then standing there watching her is another man she is certain she knows. Yes, it is definitely his large, square frame, his stolid, unlined face, but that brown turned-down fedora and the maroon sweater with buttons belong to someone else.

Even though she has been running from him all night, she wants to call to him now, to plead for his help. But then she knows without question exactly what will happen. In fact, he is already turning to walk away.

Chapter 21

According to Giles, Hilde is fine with the fact that every Saturday morning her husband takes a long walk, usually more than two hours, to "decompress" from the past week and "recharge" for the week ahead. Long ago she came to terms with this, and actually she and the children have weekend routines of their own, play dates for the kids and a gossipy brunch for the mothers. At 9:35 this morning, ten minutes into his stroll, he is standing as usual in front of the small but stylish contemporary home that his Chief Investment Manager began renting when he took the job at the bank.

Through a living room window Julian can see the chairman of Banque Privee Morneau in a jogging suit, as always looking up and down the street before heading for the back door. Julian meets him there and opens it before Giles can use his key.

"Jules."

"Good morning, darling." They share a long kiss. Julian says, "I have news."

"Yes?"

"Professor Lentini just called. Madame DeRocheford is no longer with us."

Giles raises his eyebrows. "Well, that is news."

"Yes, after taking that turn for the worse yesterday, she apparently suffered another stroke, and her life was hanging by a thread. When Lentini arrived at the hospital this morning, she learned the old gal passed away last night about two am."

"For the best, I would say."

"Definitely for the best."

Minutes later they are in the shower together, taking a slow, special pleasure in soaping and caressing each other. By the time they have rinsed, toweled off and sprawled on the big bed with the finely tooled oak headboard, they are both hard, both pointing at the softly lit ceiling, both ready for the scented oils and absolutely

134

anything the other has in mind. The amazing fact is that some of these rituals reach all the way back to their early days together at the university. They both often claim to be astonished at how their desire for each other still flames.

Really, how can this mysterious chemistry remain so potent? How many times in all these years has Giles extolled the size and beauty of Julian's prick. How often has Julian marveled aloud at the sweet tenderness of Giles' kisses and the silky touch of his delicate fingers. How can they never tire of saying and hearing these words and doing these things with each other? How is it possible this electric excitement still arcs between them?

For surely the one-thousandth time Julian hears himself say, "It must be love, you sweet silly fool," as he slides his oil-covered finger into Giles' warm, impatient bottom.

Later, spent, they doze for a time in each other's arms. Julian stirs first and after a few minutes kisses his lover's ear, then takes the lobe in his mouth to savor. It is one of those small moves that never fails to rouse Giles, and he turns now to kiss Julian's mouth, lips pliant and playful, teeth nibbling, tongue exploring.

Finally, he rolls on his back. "Ah, Jules, you are so fucking beautiful I can't stand it."

This is something he says when he wants to stop, and Julian asks, "What's wrong, darling?"

Giles takes his own prick in one hand and Julian's in the other, a gesture they both use occasionally for comforting reassurance. He says, "I want to hear from Dubonne."

"No word yet?"

"Nothing."

"It's only been two days."

"I know but still."

On Thursday, when the chief learned from his friend with the Carabinieri that Clara had been seen in Italy earlier in the week, they had set up a meeting with Dubonne. He needed to know about his man Tanner's betrayal and what it could mean for the bank.

Giles brought Julian along to the chief's office but did most of the talking. The first thing to make clear was that this "problem" had nothing to do with the two accounts in which the chief had a special interest. But there were "potentially serious consequences" for the bank, and this situation might substantially impact all of them and

135

everything they value. The chief simply nodded.

The bottom line was that this woman Clara Marche had by chance, by sheer rotten luck, seen something she should not have seen. And again, although it related in no way to those two special accounts, there was a sense in which she could hold the bank's fate in her hands. That was why Tanner had been ordered to "eliminate" this woman. This was in fact the moment that Dubonne himself had warned about in suggesting that Tanner be hired by the bank, a moment when something unpleasant might be required, a moment when a man with Tanner's special resources might prove extremely valuable.

But for whatever reason, Tanner had not performed as needed and moreover had lied to their faces about it. "With these hands," he had sworn, when asked how Madame Marche had been terminated.

"Have you confronted him?" asked Dubonne. "Does he know she's been sighted?"

"No," said Giles. "As far as we know, he has no idea."

"Good," said the chief. "Keep it that way, and I'll take it from here. I have two men who know Tanner well and can handle this."

And that was basically how they left it. Dubonne frowned throughout and seemed slightly exasperated. But Tanner was the guy he had vouched for and recommended. And the guy had failed and then deceived.

Now the mobile Giles placed on the table next to the bed buzzes and chimes. He picks it up and looks at the screen. He says, "Dubonne."

Julian says, "Ask and you shall receive."

Into the mobile Giles says, "Alain, tell me something good."

And then he listens silently for a long time. Twice he glances at Julian, who is sitting up in the bed and watching him now. Twice he nods. He says "yes" a couple of times, then "no," and finally, "So they will stay with it now?" And then, "Thank you, Alain. Stay in touch."

As Giles puts the phone back on the table, Julian says, "More good news I hope?"

Giles nods. "Things went quite well. Yesterday Dubonne called him in on some pretense and set him up. Acted surprised that we had not told Tanner about the Clara sighting and then figured Tanner would head straight for her current location. He had his guys ready, and they followed him right to a location in Italy."

This doesn't sound right to Julian. "But he is one of them. He was a cop. How could he not know they were on his tail all that way?"

"They put some kind of bug on his car, GPS, I guess. Apparently it was easy."

"And where was she?"

"A town in Liguria called Lerici."

Julian shakes his head. "I should have known. She goes there every year with Emmanuelle and some other woman friend of theirs."

"Not any more."

"So how did they actually get her?"

"Yes, well, I don't have all the details. But when they got to Lerici they found her car and, since she was the priority, moved the bug from his car to hers. They lost Tanner on foot in the town, but when her car left, they followed it right to Malpensa, the airport in Milano. They found her inside the terminal and carted her off without a problem."

"I'm surprised he told you all this on the phone."

"Yes, but there is a kind of basic trust at this point. We're in this together. Cops and robbers."

"I guess. And Tanner?"

"Who knows? They'll keep looking for him."

"Do we think he knows about Clara?"

"We don't know. But he's certainly on the run. I doubt we'll ever see him again."

Julian nods, thinking, wouldn't that be nice, but then says, "I am not so sure."

Giles shrugs, and with his hands behind his head, he leans back against a pillow. "All in all, not a bad morning."

"You were certainly on your game." Julian gives the penis next to him a small tug.

"Oh, that too, Jules. You were fantastic."

They are silent for a while. Then Julian says, "Time soon to mobilize Op B again." Their shorthand for Operation Bliss. The implementation was well underway when the shit storm hit. Literally.

Giles with his eyes closed: "Do you ever wonder whether we'd end up fighting like cats, if we had each other all the time?"

"No." He stares at Giles until the brown eyes open.
"What? Can't a man even ask a question?"
Julian too leans back. "Give me a suck."
"Ah, with pleasure."

Chapter 22

Late Sunday night, unable to sleep, Lina is up with her laptop at the desk next to the bedroom windows. Outside it is black, no moon, no stars. She is writing an email to Marc, something she probably should have done more than a week ago, letting him know about both Clara and Cecile. She asks if he has heard anything at all from Clara. Then, having filled him in on woman's disappearance, the news that the bank has charged her with a crime and that she had apparently been spotted near her home in Italy, she stops, uncertain of what else to write.

She wonders again why her first call yesterday morning, after learning that Cecile was gone, went to Julian. Was she just not thinking clearly? Even though every morning before walking into the hospital she prepared herself for the worst, it was stunning to find the ICU room empty. In her momentary confusion she thought perhaps Cecile had somehow taken a sudden turn for the better and would soon be found in another room, sitting up and talking. And then the ICU nurse explained that Madame DeRocheford had unfortunately passed away in the night.

"Her poor heart just finally stopped and so suddenly there was no time to call madame." Lina remembers closing her eyes and feeling unsteady as the nurse helped guide her to a chair. Over the past two months the attachment to Cecile had become so deep that it felt as if she had just lost some vital part of herself.

So perhaps her thoughts were still jumbled when she called Julian. Certainly he and Giles had been solicitous, trying to be helpful, suggesting the move to a larger hospital. But why Julian first and not one of Cecile's many personal friends who've been calling all week for updates? Maybe because, after those two voice mails and then silence, she was also wondering about Clara. As it turned out Julian could offer nothing beyond that sketchy report from the Carabinieri. No one, including her family and her friends at the bank, had anything new.

At least her second call from the hospital made sense. It went to old Charles Mercier, Cecile's attorney, who had possession of the will and a letter Cecile wrote last year, outlining exactly what she wanted in terms of funeral arrangements and a memorial. The old guy, close to 80 himself, was obviously prepared for what he called "this heart-wrenching news, which has seemed inevitable since that second stroke yesterday." It was Cecile's wish, he said, that her body be cremated and that her ashes be placed "without ceremony" in the crypt that holds her husband's. As for a memorial, he said Cecile wanted an afternoon soiree, a gathering at the villa for her closest friends.

He quoted directly from the letter: "Wine and appetizers prepared by Zazu, just as she has done for us for so many years. The only difference will be that I won't attend. Anyone who wishes to have a little say may do so, and that will be that. And if this can happen without undo inconvenience, particularly for Zazu, within a week of my passing, that will be preferable. There is no point in dragging these things out. People need to get on with their lives."

Lina said she would check with Zazu about the timing of the party but thought the disconsolate little woman would be pleased with the chance to carry out the wishes of her beloved "Madame." Charles said Cecile's letter contained a list of friends to be invited. Once they have a date, his secretary will contact all of them with an invitation. Of course, no problem if Lina should wish to invite anyone else.

As it turned out, she had been right about Zazu: the sooner the memorial gathering the better. And so it was set now for Thursday afternoon. Monday morning, after another night of fitful sleep, she turned on the Dell, and sure enough there was a response waiting from Marc.

> Dear Lina,
>
> I am grateful for your message. I read it on my phone late this afternoon as I was standing in the airport terminal here in Detroit. At my wit's end, I was waiting in vain a second day for Clara. I can't say I feel any less concerned for her or less confused about what's happened, but at

least I know more than I did before and have someone in Geneva who can tell me the latest.

First, my condolences on the passing of Cecile, one of my favorite people in this world. She welcomed me in her home and so clearly cared for Clara. I feel like this warm, brilliant light has gone out, and we all mourn in the dark. Knowing you were close to this remarkable woman, I'm sure this is a difficult time for you.

But about Clara. My last email from her was nearly two weeks ago. There was nothing different about her message, just the usual about the insensitivity of her boss and not getting to 'fitness' as often as she wanted. And then nothing. For several days, a silence unlike anything before between us. I kept writing everyday, each time voicing more concern. But nothing in response. At first I was puzzled and then after a week deeply concerned.

I tried calling her, hoping to have some kind of conversation that would at least let me know she was okay. But her phone always went straight to voice mail, and then her inbox was full. I have no contact info for her family, and at the bank I knew only the name of her friend Emmanuelle. One of her last messages said you were returning to Bologna. So I tried emails to Cecile, figuring she might know what was going on. Now I know the terrible reason she did not write back.

Finally, two days ago, this past Friday, I returned home after a long shoot to find a fax on my machine. I saw the handwriting, and my heart leapt, but her first line was "I am in trouble, and I need your help." I raced through the rest of the fax with lines like, "It could well be life or death for me," and "I must leave

Europe as soon as possible." She said I might have heard something about a matter at the bank, but she could only talk about it in person. And I'm thinking, what?! Finally, she said she'd be arriving in Detroit the next day, Saturday, on a Delta flight due in at 2:30 pm. You can imagine what I felt.

So yesterday there I was in the terminal waiting for Clara's smile. Traveler after traveler walked through those doors, finding relatives or friends or heading off for taxis. After a while I asked one of the last ones off the flight if he recalled seeing someone of her description on the plane, perhaps being delayed by customs. He said no. When I checked with Delta they said no one named Clara Marche had booked a seat on that flight.

Today, Sunday, I did the same thing again. What's that definition of insanity? On the chance that her plans had been delayed by a day, I was waiting at the airport again, and, of course, the same result. I kept calling myself an idiot, but what else could I do except go with the hopeless guess that she'd take the same flight one day later. And then your email arrived.

I cannot believe for a second that Clara would rob the Banque Privee Morneau after working there for more than 30 years. And then I ask myself if we can ever really know another. Yes, I tell myself, of course I know Clara. And yet now you tell me the last time she was seen in Geneva was more than 10 days ago. If she was fleeing for her life back then, why didn't she come to me immediately? Or at least contact me in some fashion?

I can't answer my own questions. I only know I must come to Geneva asap. I am trying to move work obligations so I can leave by Wednesday to arrive on Thursday. Perhaps in time to attend the memorial for dear Cecile. With all that Clara has told me about you and your interest in our unlikely love affair, I feel as if we know each other so well. It will be a pleasure to meet you in person.

With gratitude,

Marc White

Scrolling back to the top of his message, Lina thinks of the place where Marc received her email and read it on his phone. She knows it well, that waiting area in front of the large sliding doors in the terminal at Detroit Metro Airport. That was where one August day two years ago she emerged to find Stan and Father Redding smiling their welcome to Michigan, the beginning of what would be a roller-coaster visit that radically altered her life. And it is where Marc has just spent two emotional days looking in vain for Clara, quite possibly the end, she fears now, of the couple's rare affair of the heart.

She reads again through the email, searching for some sliver of hope. There is only the fact that within a few days Marc will be here himself to look for her. He certainly sounds the same as the voice Lina came to know in reading through those years of computer-translated exchanges between the lovers. Warm, open, thoughtful, unafraid to show emotion or express an opinion. She can see again how Clara quickly became enamored. From the photos she has seen, he is dark brown, not African black, a hint of his Italian grandfather around the eyes and mouth. A quizzical smile and the glasses suggest the look of a scholar. Yes, a smart, capable man who knows Clara well, able to read her inclinations perhaps better than anyone. But with a better chance to find her, or discover what has happened?

What *has* happened to her? Like Marc, she finds it difficult to believe in Clara the criminal. But even if she is guilty, even if she ran off with 40,000 of the bank's cash, why does she apparently fear for her life? *It could well be life or death for me.* Really? For theft? Does she equate prison with death? Perhaps. She hints there is something else behind the charge the bank has brought against her. What could that be?

143

When her mobile sounds, Lina learns she has not quite given up on hearing from Clara herself. The woman has tried twice to connect on the phone, why not a third try? Maybe all this intense thinking about Clara has somehow reached her antennae.

Instead it is the daughter, Honore, calling with condolences about Cecile. She saw the long obit in the Tribune yesterday and felt especially sorry for Lina. Of course, they end up talking about Clara as well. Honore has just called Julian at the bank, and there is nothing new about her mother's disappearance. Everyone in the family is desperate now, completely beside themselves.

"I mean, it makes no sense," she says, her voice pleading. "Even if she committed a crime, which I don't for a second believe, but even if she did, why wouldn't she somehow get in touch with us, to at least let us know she's alive? This silence is not what anyone would expect from my mother."

Not to upset Honore further, Lina says nothing about the two phone messages from Clara. But she feels compelled to tell her about the email from Marc.

After a long silence, the anguished woman says, "Really? She wrote to him?"

"And said she was flying to the States on Saturday. But then she never arrived."

Another long pause. "I cannot imagine."

Chapter 23

On Tuesday, after thinking about it for a while, Lina calls to invite Julian and Giles to the memorial on Thursday.

"We'll both be there," says Julian.

Something keeps her from saying anything about the message from Marc and his coming to Geneva, but she does ask about the latest on Clara. There is nothing, he says, and really they are leaving it behind. If Clara or information about her turns up, fine. But they are moving on now.

"Sometime next week," he says, "I will finally be off to Hong Kong. And how about you? Will it be back to Bologna soon?"

"This weekend, I think."

At mid-morning on Thursday she decides to check on Zazu in the kitchen. Lina has offered to help more than once this week, but the tiny cook has said everything is under control. Now she finds two dark, younger women in white uniforms helping in the kitchen. One is moving a platter covered with anchovy and olive appetizers into the refrigerator, and the other is helping Zazu stuff small, luscious-looking pastries.

"*Bonjour*," she says.

All three turn to her and bow slightly. "*Bonjour, Madame.*"

"Please," she says in French, "Carry on. I don't wish to intrude."

On one long counter several bottles of wine with three different labels are aligned. At the end of the counter is the cardboard box where she knows Zazu places the mail to be picked up by someone from Charles Mercier's office. For some reason she is curious and moves down to glance into the box. There, on top of one of the piles, is a business-sized envelope addressed by hand and with only one line for a return address: "C. Marche."

Her heart already pounding, Lina reaches in to lift it out of the box. The envelope is heavy, thick with folded pages. She looks closely at the postmark. Nov. 7 Malpensa. Saturday from the airport at Milano.

Holding the letter casually, she tells them everything looks beautiful and thanks them for all their work. All three nod to her again, and as she walks past, she notes that Zazu's dark eyes dart to the envelope, then back to her as she leaves the kitchen.

On the stairs she uses a finger to rip open the flap. Half-way up she is already reading Clara's clean cursive, and when she reaches the phrase *"frightened rabbit,"* she slows her climb. The start of the third graph brings her to a full stop, and she sits on the top step of the broad marble staircase.

"Your accounts are in serious jeopardy, and it occurs to me now that perhaps you are as well, my dearest Cecile."

She thinks of Honore and that strange notion that Cecile's stroke and Clara's disappearance might somehow be related. At the line *"You must not tell anyone about this information,"* she glances up, half-expecting Zazu to be heading up the stairs. Then reading that *"police agencies may be a party to this plot,"* she shakes her head, gets to her feet and moves directly to the bedroom. There she closes and locks the door. With her back against it, she finishes what turns out to be a kind of cover letter. She re-reads the line, *"...it will be clear why the bank has charged me with a crime, and why I have fled in fear of my life."* Then she moves to sit on the bed and begins reading the next five pages.

What she finds there is an astounding story told cold, addressed "To Whom It May concern" and presented mostly without emotion or Clara's own response to the events she describes. One of the few times she offers a personal reaction comes early on, after her initial description of what she saw on Julian's computer screens: *"I suddenly knew that my life had changed forever."*

But if most of what Lina is reading is flat in the writing and without affect, she soon finds herself roiling with emotions, at times burning with anger at what the bankers have done to Cecile and with rage at what they are trying to do to Clara. By turns she feels pity for poor Clara caught up by sheer chance in this horrid misfortune, admiration for the woman's courage, resolve and resourcefulness, dread over what seems like the terrible odds against her now, and finally shame at how thoroughly she, Lina, has been duped, even used by these men to further their vicious plot.

There is one thing now she does not feel at all: doubt or

skepticism about Clara's story. Yes, an astonishing tale, but how could anyone imagine this bright, level-headed woman, loyal employee, loving mother and grandmother and devoted friend and lover, fabricating something as awful and unlikely as this? Not once in reading and then re-reading these five packed pages does she ever think, well, no, this detail does not ring true, or that's just not credible, or this part smells of concoction. No, all of it seems honest and true, and so now she fears for herself, for the simple fact that she too now knows this story. And if this new knowledge of hers is ever discovered, she herself will be in certain danger. So now she understands in a deeply personal way what Clara wrote about her life having "changed forever" and the advisability of telling no one. At the windows, looking down on Cecile's winterized garden, she wonders, when Julian and Giles arrive at the villa this afternoon, how she can possibly allow them to walk in the door.

Counting the murderers—her word for them now—along with Charles Mercier and herself, there are 26 in all. Most of the older women are seated on the two couches and four chairs. The rest are arrayed around the large room, a few standing in the archway to the dining room. All of them, except Julian and Giles, are well known to each other, having often spent time here at Cecile's gatherings, either in this room or in the garden, depending on the weather. It is just as their absent hostess had planned, a warm and pleasant affair, brimming with loving memories of Cecile, with friend after friend reading a favorite passage from one of her much-loved memoirs or offering a reminiscence meant to capture something valued about their dear old friend.

Finally it is Lina's turn, and she is grateful again for her habit of writing out anything she plans to present in public. Often she will not even pull the notes from her purse, but on this fraught occasion, she is more than pleased to read.

From the moment the guests started to arrive, she felt on edge, worried, even self-conscious, waiting for the bankers to walk in. Could she really hide her true feelings, so acute and powerful, with smiles and cordial words? Could she deceive them as fully as they deceived her? Now as she glances at them standing in a corner near the door to the foyer, she finds there is something about the way they are looking at her—with a kind of calm self-assurance—that makes her want to reach into her bag on a nearby table and pull out Clara's letter to Cecile. How stunning it would be to read that instead. The urge to do it is powerful, so strong she feels a stab of fear. It is not time, not yet. And so she lifts the short piece she wrote last night and begins.

"Two months ago, in mid-September and not long after I arrived here from Bologna for what turned out to be an extended visit I will always cherish, Cecile brought me along to a lecture. This was not, as all of you know, an unusual activity for Cecile, who was always up on the latest cultural happenings. Whether politics, literature, science or the arts, if it promised to be stimulating, provocative or in any way enlightening, she was there.

"But this particular lecture was the hottest ticket in town, and some 4000 people crammed themselves into 10 different venues at the University of Geneva for a presentation by the world-famous astrophysicist Stephen Hawking. Most of them watched a video feed, but Cecile and I, probably because of her friendship with several scholars at the University, were among the 600 fortunate ones who were in the lecture hall with Hawking himself.

"His body crushed by a vicious disease he has fought for nearly 50 years, this crumpled little man is almost totally paralyzed, able to move only a cheek, which is what he uses to nudge a computerized contraption designed to help him choose the words he wants from a list that flashes on a screen in front of him. This is the only way he is able to communicate. And so we sat there mesmerized for 40 minutes as this brave man with the brilliant brain and giant spirit told us about the origins of the universe. And, of course, he did so without any reference to an almighty creator or god of any sort, because, as it was with Cecile, he has no use for one.

"At age 88, she was stirred, thrilled and instructed by our experience that afternoon. And while there have been difficult, heartbreaking moments since, I choose to recall that moment, when she literally glowed with excitement. That is how I will always remember my wise, dear, beautiful and loving friend Cecile."

There are nods, smiles and soft applause. She too nods and smiles but knows this hardly contained what she truly feels for her brilliant friend. Actually she was afraid to try something more honest and emotional. So this will have to do. In their corner the murderers are smiling, Julian offering a small wave that indicates they need to leave.

She moves to them as a younger woman on the other side of the great room starts a description of an outing Cecile organized two years ago for several of them to visit the large pink villa only about 10 minutes away where Byron and Shelley, with their extraordinary entourage, spent the summer of 1816.

When she reaches the foyer they are waiting. In whispers they praise her eulogy and explain they unfortunately have a meeting at the bank. She thanks them for coming and allows each of them to kiss her cheeks. Her stomach churns, but she continues to smile as the murderers walk out the door.

Back in the great room she stands where they were standing near the foyer. The young woman is talking about the poets' sexual arrangements during that long-ago summer in Geneva, Shelley with his 18-year-old mistress and soon-to-be wife, Mary Wollstonecraft, and Byron with her stepsister, also 18. Ten minutes later the woman was still rolling out the exotic history Cecile had recounted. It was the summer Mary wrote *Frankenstein* and Shelley penned "The Prisoner of Chillon."

And then Lina hears a noise in the foyer. When she looks in, standing there holding a small piece of luggage is a tall black man with rimless glasses.

Chapter 24

"Brilliant, charming, with beautiful red hair and green eyes that miss nothing." That was Clara's first email description of her new friend, the literature professor from Bologna. So he knows her immediately when she moves to him in the large foyer.

She smiles, takes his hand and says softly, "Lina."

He feels a feathery touch and also smiles. "Marc."

There is an awkward pause when she turns back to the archway she came from, through which he sees a portion of the great room and a few of its occupants; a woman's muted voice comes from there. Still Lina doesn't move, as if thinking better of what she was about to do. Finally, she motions him to follow, and he does, through the opening and past some 25 people, mostly women, listening to one of the younger ones standing on the far side of this high-ceilinged room, speaking warmly about Cecile, as he carries his suitcase and tries to walk silently across the beige marble floor. He feels every eye on him as he follows her to the broad staircase and up to a bedroom on the second floor.

Sorry, she says, she thought about introducing him to the group downstairs but somehow it did not feel right. He nods and says maybe for now it's better not to be here, officially. Yes, she says, perhaps so.

She asks if he is hungry, and he says, no, his plane was delayed in Amsterdam because of weather, and he had a big lunch there. "Actually, I'm exhausted and might take a quick nap. I slept maybe an hour on the plane from Detroit and a few minutes in a chair at Schiphol, but otherwise nothing in 24 hours."

"Of course. Make yourself comfortable. There's a bathroom just down the hall. I'll leave you alone for a while, and then we'll catch up." She smiles and moves for the door and then stops. As if speaking to herself, she says, "No, there's something I really need to show you. I will be right back." In less than 30 seconds she returns

150

with four typescript pages.

"I found this today in the mail. It was postmarked Saturday from Malpensa, the airport at Milano. A long letter from Clara to Cecile, of course in French, but I did a quick translation."

He raises his eyebrows. "Thank you. And mailed the day she was supposed to be flying to Detroit."

"Yes." She hands him the pages.

"I'll read it with great interest."

"Yes, I think you will." With a faint smile, she leaves the room.

* * *

Later he descends the staircase to find the great room empty and quiet. Faintly he hears glasses clink in the kitchen on the far side of the dining room. Pushing through the door he finds Lina helping Zazu along with two young women he has not seen before.

"Ah, there you are," says Lina, carrying wine glasses to a counter next to the sink. "Were you able to sleep?"

"No."

Lina nods and removes the white apron she is wearing while he greets and offers his condolences to Zazu. Thinking of the first time he met this dark little woman, with Clara and Cecile, he feels a wave of sadness, almost despair, and wants to hug her and kiss her cheeks. But her wet hands are holding two wine glasses, and he realizes he's never really touched her except for that first stiff handshake more than a year ago.

Back in the great room, Lina, carrying a large purse, glances at a sofa but says there are chairs in her room upstairs. They can talk there. A minute later, they occupy the chairs, he with the translated letter, she with the original.

"So I'm totally shocked." He raises the pages several inches, then drops his hand to his thigh. "And enraged. At one point, when she's talking about this guy Tanner telling her she needs to be dead, I had to stop reading for a few seconds. I literally couldn't breathe."

"I know."

"Then I couldn't stop reading. Four times straight through until I felt I had locked away every damned detail." He feels himself leaning forward toward her in the chair. "I'm so angry I want to walk into that bank tomorrow and beat each of them to a pulp. Until they're begging to tell me where she is."

"Yes," she says, her eyes glinting. "I had so much rage when I first read it, I could not sit still. I was marching back and forth here in tears." She stops for a moment, then starts again. "And they were just here."

"Who?"

"The bankers. I invited them, obviously before I read this. They had seemed so helpful and caring about Cecile, and now I am wondering if they had a hand in what happened to her."

"I was thinking the same thing. But they were in the room when I walked through?"

"No, they had left just before you arrived."

"That's probably good. And good as well that you invited them. We don't need them suspecting us."

Lina shakes her head. "It was all I could do to seem mildly pleasant. I was fantasizing about pulling this out and reading it to the whole group."

He nods at her but thinks that does raise the question: what exactly can they do with what they know?

Their conversation now is intense, wide-ranging, yet hemmed with frustration. First, there's the police. Clara seems to take seriously this fellow Tanner's claim that the bankers and the police are working together, or that they are somehow tightly connected. Lina runs down the different agencies: the Geneva Municipal Police, the Swiss National Police, the banking watchdog agencies, which could be considered police, and of course Interpol. But no matter which agency might be tight with the bank, it has to be assumed that they might all share information and work closely together. And certainly for each, because of the bank's charges, Clara is a wanted person.

Yes, this letter is her version of the facts, but it offers no real evidence. Only her word. And opposed to it will be the full authority of the bankers, who, according to Tanner, have already wiped away any trace of their own fraud and replaced it with clear proof in the bank's records of Clara stealing from her manager's account for the past several years. As for the bankers themselves, they have already ordered one murder, quite possibly two. Why would they hesitate to target others who have come to know what Clara learned?

* * *

Late the following morning they are on their way out of Geneva. He is driving her silver VW, and, once they clear the Mount Blanc tunnel, she is on her mobile. They talked for hours yesterday afternoon and evening, after a while snacking on Zazu's leftover appetizers and sharing a bottle of wine. By the time she caught him nodding off in mid-sentence they had agreed on a basic plan.

For him there is only one place to start: the town that is Clara's last known location. Yes, it was almost a week ago that she penned her signature to the bottom of her letter to Cecile and next to it wrote "Lerici, Italy." Yes, the postmark said Malpensa, but someone else could have mailed it from there, and in any case it seems unlikely she has spent the past week at an airport. Much more likely, if she changed her mind about flying to him in Detroit, that she returned to the place where she had been comfortable enough to spend the previous several days.

Though he admits a hint of desperation about this trip, setting off for Italy has in itself stirred his hope. Still he senses it is not the same for Lina. While they definitely agreed on the priority of searching for Clara, she argued for a time last night for staying in Geneva to look for this Willem Tanner, the person she thinks most likely to know Clara's whereabouts, and, perhaps, even to lead them to her. But she seemed to quickly understand how deeply important it was to him to take some kind of immediate action to pick up the trail of the woman he loves, no matter how cold it might be. After only a few minutes of discussion, and after using her laptop to google Tanner and coming up with nothing, she agreed on Lerici as the place to start.

When she also checked the bank's website the guy was listed as a security officer, but with no contact information. And there was no reference at all to Clara's best friend at work, Emmanuelle.

Now on her mobile she has dialed the Banque Privee Morneau and simply asked for the woman. Within seconds she is chattering away in French, most of which he cannot decipher. But according to the plan devised last night, he knows she is being circumspect with the secretary to the man who ordered Clara's murder. She has identified herself but said nothing about the true reason for her call. And then the call ends.

"It's okay," she tells him. "This is a good time. Morneau is out of the office, but she wants to use her mobile." A moment later the phone rings, and soon, from her smiles, earnest looks and generally warm tone, it seems to be going well.

Twenty minutes later Lina finally ends the call and gives him a smile and a nod.

"It was good?" he asks.

"Very good. She used the mobile so she could speak more freely. She knew who I was and said Clara had spoken highly of me. Though I'm not sure she believed my reason for calling, she was very friendly. Actually she seemed desperate to talk about Clara with someone who cares about her. As we planned, I told her only that I am working on a book that Cecile started about Clara's unusual affair with her American lover."

"Yes, did she know about the book?"

"She did. She said Clara was excited about it. So I told her for the book I was looking for information about the man Clara had been previously involved with, a man who works at the bank named Willem Tanner. And she said, 'Ah, yes, Willem, another of poor Clara's unfortunate choices.' And then she asked me if I had heard about the bank's charges against Clara and her disappearance. When I said yes, she was off and running, talking a mile a minute. She said, 'I am so afraid for Clara. I mean I just don't have a good feeling about what's happened. Clara is of course very bright, but she is also very sweet and trusting and friendly with people. And this is so unlike her, to disappear, without a word. She would never do that to her family, to us, to anyone really. I cannot imagine what or why, but I am afraid something terrible has happened to our Clara.'"

He glances at Lina. "Did she say anything about the charges by the bank?"

"Yes, she said, 'I do not believe for one second that she has done what the bank says. There has been some terrible mistake. But around here you cannot ask, you cannot say anything. It is basically forbidden to bring up her name. You will get all kinds of looks, and they will say you are being disloyal to her and as well to the bank. It's as if they want you to think they are trying to protect her, even though they've put out this awful wanted notice to the police. But what I keep coming back to is, if she has not called her family, if she has not called even me, something very bad has happened to Clara, and I feel sick when I think about it.'"

"Did she say anything more about Tanner?"

"Yes, I asked what she meant about Tanner being another of Clara's unfortunate choices. And she said that Clara over the years had been in a series of relationships with inappropriate men, some who treated her badly, but also a few well-to-do types, who actually proposed marriage. She said, 'At least she had the good sense to turn them down, but from the start I thought Willem was another bad choice. He did not seem her type at all, closed-mouth, not particularly gregarious or even friendly. But she said she liked and trusted him. She called him unpretentious and down to earth. She said she felt safe with him, meaning, I think, she felt protected, maybe because she knew he had been a policeman. When I told her that he had also been in prison, she said he had already told her about it, said he had taken the punishment for someone else, and that it meant nothing to her. I mean, at this point her girls were grown, she was already a grandmother, she had no career ambitions or social pretensions, but then she had never been that way. So she was just really comfortable with him. And then one day he was gone, out of her life, with little or no explanation. And I could tell she was shocked, or deeply surprised and hurt. And it took her over a year to get her spark back. It didn't really happen until she met Marc.'"

He nods but says nothing.

"I asked her when she had seen Tanner last, and she said not for a while, maybe a couple of weeks. And finally, I asked if she had contact information for him, and maybe even a photo. I said it would all help in writing the book. Again, I don't know if she really believed me about the book, but she said she would send me an email with everything this afternoon."

"I'm impressed," he says. "You're really good!"

Over a quick lunch at a rest stop on the A26 not far from Genoa, she asks if it bothered him to hear about Clara's relationship with Willem Tanner.

Not at all, he tells her. He and Clara have never talked about old lovers, and this new information connects some dots in a way that's actually helpful.

Helpful how? she asks, and so he recounts what he saw and thought that night at L'Entrecôte when he and Clara met for the first time. As he and his cameraman Derrick sat down, he noticed the attractive woman sitting across from him at the adjacent table just inches away. He found her pretty with a rounded figure, probably not devoted to regular exercise. She seemed pleasant sitting there but said nothing, as he and Derrick talked non-stop, running through their usual array of topics, from politics to their favorite travel destinations to books and authors to upcoming work in Detroit. Of course, as he would soon learn, the woman could understand almost nothing they said.

Because she simply sat there without food in front of her, only sipping a glass of wine, it seemed obvious she was waiting for someone, he thought probably a man. This went on for a half-hour, and glancing her way occasionally, he noted an air of sadness about the woman and began feeling a kind of sympathy for her. He has wondered more than once if anything would have happened after that evening if he had taken the seat next to the woman, facing the door, instead of letting Derrick sit there. In any case, he knows now that Clara was obviously just coming off the pain of her break up with this fellow Tanner.

Lina smiles at him and after a pause asks if he has ever kept a secret from Clara. The question surprises him, and he thinks for a while. Finally, he says, yes, there is something he has often thought of telling her but for some reason never has. It is simply that when they met again a year later, when Clara and Adele walked into Brasserie Lipp and headed for the table at which he was sitting with Derrick, he immediately recognized Adele, but had no clear recollection of the woman leading the way with her big, glowing smile and a bright wave. Could this slim, beautiful, confident woman be the same plumpish, sad-eyed person he sat across from 12 months earlier at L'Entrecôte? Of course it must be, but it hardly seemed possible.

"And really," he says, "I'm usually very good with faces and figures!"

So that was his secret. He has never told Clara about his confusion. Later, after several months of almost daily emails, he finally gathered that not long before that dinner at L'Entrecôte she had broken up with a man who worked at the bank, and she was still in a kind of grieving process. But over the next year she must have pulled herself together, dieted and put herself on a "fitness" regime. She basically transformed herself into the woman he failed to recognize, which only deepened his respect for Clara and further fueled his love. But he continued to keep all this to himself because he thought it might embarrass her if he brought it up.

Also, he admits with a wink at Lina, he's been loathed to tell Clara his secret for fear that she might think he had found her less than memorable that first night at L'Entrecôte.

And then he adds, "Or I guess that my own visual memory might be suspect."

Her look and those wide eyes hold him as she says, "I don't think you have to worry. Clara adores you."

He drops his gaze to the table. "It's strange, though. There is something about that smile of hers that seems absolutely unforgettable. I mean, it welcomes, encourages, delights. It dazzles, almost like a movie star's smile, and yet it seems totally honest and authentic. It says, 'You can trust me. I want only the best for you.' And yet I failed to recognize her that night."

There is sadness in Lina's look, as if she is recalling something of her own. "Yes, that smile is extraordinary. I remember Cecile saying once that she knew men who would have paid for just that smile. But the human face can have an amazing range, depending on mood and circumstance. I think it's a tribute to the way you made her feel that her look had changed beyond your recognition."

Chapter 25

The closer they get to Lerici, the more the poor man seems pre-occupied. Quiet, lost-in-thought, or just plain worried. The lines in that dark face are etched deeper, the sad eyes behind those spectacles turn to her less often as he drives. Of course she understands. They both know the odds of their finding Clara or even some lukewarm trace verge between slim and none. It is now almost a full week since she was scheduled to fly from Schiphol to Detroit. He cannot say it, perhaps even to himself, but reality will probably not take long to force the admission that they are on a very cold trail indeed.

Earlier in this trip they talked almost non-stop. She asked him about the troubled state of his hometown, the internationally infamous Detroit, and off he went, offering an outline of the past few decades with several cause-effect connections to the city's steep descent. Having read a few pieces on the subject in the Times and elsewhere, especially two years ago when she was lecturing at St. Thomas, a two hour drive from the city, she found his thinking original, his insights keen and his language by turns inventive, charming and profane. But then she was already impressed with this man, from his emails to Clara and from their adrenaline-fueled conversation last night.

As they skirted Genoa he gave her a brilliant riff that drew a line from the city's teenaged drug entrepreneurs in the '70s to its recently convicted and jailed young mayor.

"Same kind of outrageous gangster mentality. Same lure of easy money, big power and obscene trappings. But Kwame and his pals thought they could ditch the shit side of illicit narcotics, all the murder and incarceration, and make it even bigger with the traditional nexus of corrupt public service and business hustle. 'Just scam the damn system, baby.' And the same with those black yuppie assholes who've been looting millions from our broke and broken schools. Their mindset is, 'These stupid black kids and their fucked-

158

up moms are hopeless. So all those millions we take from their abysmal schools will find much better use in our own greedy pockets.'"

It was after this rant that he grew silent, and she thought of what Clara had told her about his younger daughter, the one he had lost to the streets. Was that who dominated his thoughts now? She wanted to ask him about the girl, but the time did not seem right.

And then came the first of two emails to her phone. The one from Emmanuelle, as promised, included contact info for Willem Tanner, and, yes, a photo.

"Let's see," he said, glancing at her phone.

She turned the stern, unsmiling face on its screen to him, saying, "Cordiality personified."

He nodded, and she quoted from Emmanuelle's note: "A very tight-lipped fellow. Good luck getting him to talk about anything."

Ten minutes later a note arrived from her publisher, about her most recent book, her third, the one she had finished in Sicily while John was dying. Translations into Spanish, Portuguese, French and German were being arranged and foreign rights sold. He seemed genuinely interested but remained mostly silent as she rattled on about the book's recurring themes.

Now she too goes quiet, thinking how different yesterday's memorial for Cecile was from the service she attended in Cleveland a year-and-a-half ago. For John she had crossed the Atlantic fully expecting awkward and painful moments from the presence of John's unstable wife Marissa, along with anyone who might ask about Stan. Lina alone had spent those last heart-breaking months with John before he died in her arms, and she owed it to his memory to personally affirm how honest and brave he was at the end.

She stayed three days in the attractive Shaker Heights home of his parents, Dr. and Mrs. Martens. Bob Martens health was failing badly, and John's mother Tammie was clearly worried. Lina and the parents had grown close over the week they had spent together in Taormina after John's brain cancer was diagnosed. Then complications from the father's diabetes forced a return to Ohio, and Tammie had to choose husband over son. Together now in the private room of a large restaurant, they greeted a few of John's childhood friends still residing in Cleveland, a handful of former students he had mentored over the years, and a small contingent from Cedar Hill including

George Rolande, retired and now out of the closet with his much younger friend Sam; John's "running buddy" Bob Bourne; and department chair Fr. Redding heading the religious contingent, having driven down with Sisters Martha and Gertrude. From the University of Chicago came John's star-scholar pal and famed lecher, Marlon Tish.

In all, she thought, a sadly limited turnout, but everyone was friendly and solicitous with her, no one mentioned the obscene pranks that had marred her days at St. Thomas, or wondered aloud whether Stan might suddenly surface here. When the Carabinieri had contacted the university to see if he had returned there, it became generally known on campus that Stan had disappeared in Italy. Thanks perhaps to Marissa and some of the more imaginative department members, rumors flew: that Stan, John and Lina were living in a ménage a trois, or that Stan had murdered John and disappeared, or that John had killed Stan and then taken his own life.

When emails clogged her inbox with this nonsense after John's passing, she sent a note to Redding, asking that it be forwarded to everyone in the department. John had come to Italy, she wrote, knowing about his cancer and not wanting to inflict it on anyone in Cedar Hill. They had toured some of the places favored by Lawrence, one of John's literary lights and the subject of his final book, and they had seen almost nothing of Stan, who claimed he was off doing research in Torino. That was Lina's story, and apparently it had been accepted, at least by the handful of people who showed up in Cleveland.

Nearly everyone in the room took turns speaking about John with warmth and affection. Lina covered only what she could without equivocation. "How lucky am I," he had said on one of his last good days. "Lawrence, the genius, was 44. I've had almost a decade more." He seemed much more concerned about her, and his conviction never wavered: this was absolutely the end, and no stern but caring almighty waited to render judgment. Saying this, she gazed firmly at Redding, who had offered a prayer for the repose of John's soul. As she was finishing, Marissa walked in.

Lina almost did not recognize her. The woman had lost some weight and let her hair go from brassy blond to a natural-looking light brown. Apparently she came alone, which was a good sign. This manic-depressive alcoholic was, according to John, terrified of being picked up again on a DUI and sent back to the county jail. If she drove herself here from Cedar Hill, there was a good chance she was sober.

Marissa shook her head when asked if she would like to offer a few words, and when the eulogies were over, after a stiff hello with her in-laws, she came straight for Lina, who braced for the worst. Was there a pistol in that purse, or would it be perhaps just a hearty slap in the face? Instead, wordlessly, Marissa embraced her. After several seconds, they held each other at arm's length, and Lina found an indecipherable mix in the woman's dull brown eyes.

She said, "You look good, Marissa. I like your hair."

Those comments ignored, Marissa said after a pause, "Look, I know, you urged me to come and be with John, and I wish I had. I just couldn't handle it. You gave him something I could not give, and for that I am grateful." The words were coming slowly, the voice low and even. "But I will always hate you."

Lina felt tears in her own eyes but saw not a trace in Marissa's. There was no alcohol in the air between them, and no affect at all in the woman's look. It must be the meds she took to counter this awful disease that robbed her of any reasonable control over her life's most powerful emotions. Lina felt a deep sadness for her now.

Within a few seconds Redding and Tish, the rake from Chicago, had split them up. There was no problem reading Tish's eyes.

"Well, John always said you were a gorgeous piece of ass, and the poor guy certainly knew what he was talking about."

Lina laughed through her tears. "And he always said you were perfectly charming."

Tish nodded with a smile. "So nobody gets everything right."

They talked for a time about John, about the sad state of publishing and about the politics of their respective universities, a heady conversation that Lina enjoyed, and when he asked, as she expected, if she would like to spend the weekend with him in Chicago, she said thank you, perhaps another time.

* * *

She has not been here in Lerici in nearly a decade and now lets Marc lead the way. There is energy in his step, and he seems to look everywhere at once as they walk. Because he was here with Clara last year, his plan is to start with the places they shared and loved the most. She tries to sound hopeful, and they stop first at the building

161

where the couple took an apartment for a week. The old manager remembers Marc and recalls Clara but says he has not seen her since their visit a year ago. Then it is up to their favorite bar, high above the town and overlooking the sea, a place called Vertigo. He shows the young bartender photos on his phone and asks if she has seen this woman, perhaps served her recently here at the bar. The answer again is no.

On their way back down through streets in the town's center, he takes another tack. Maybe since she was hiding, she avoided places where people might know her. But when they try a restaurant, a farmacia and a small green grocer, all with no luck, they switch back to his original plan. With quick results. Signore Schiavone at the café and Laura at the Enoteca Baroni both say they saw her for a few days last week, but she has not been in since. Then Laura says a fellow who looked like Willem's photo on Lina's phone came in asking for her last Friday evening. But Clara had left not long before he walked in and had asked her not to say she had been waiting for him.

"You're certain it was this fellow?" Marc takes the phone and shows her the screen again.

"*Si, signore. Era quest'uomo.*"

Marc looks crushed. They both know now that Clara's presence in Lerici had been discovered. So whatever happened after she left for the airport, it seems very unlikely she would return to Lerici.

So did Willem Tanner come here to help Clara or to kill her? She thinks Marc is probably wondering the same thing, and she knows he will want to leave quickly for Malpensa. But they need to slow down a bit and sort things out more carefully. How about a glass of wine, she asks, maybe a sandwich or a salad? He says that sounds good.

While they wait for the food, he says, "So, obviously she changed her mind about meeting Tanner."

"Yes."

"And presumably because she finally decided he was someone to fear."

"Even though, as she tells us in the letter to Cecile, he had spared her one week earlier and helped her disappear. 'Willem saved my life,' she said."

"Yeah," he says, "but for some reason, as she waited for him here last Friday, she thought, 'No, do not trust him.' I wonder why."

162

"Well, she said they spoke on the phone, so it could have been something he told her, or something about the tone of his voice."

He sips his wine. "Whatever it was, if she ended up in his hands, I'm afraid we are much too late to help."

She feels the same but gazes firmly at him and says, "I think there is only one way to look at this: If Tanner could not or would not harm Clara the first time around, the same thing could happen again."

He says, "I guess, maybe," but sounds like a man grasping at straws.

"And the next thing we do," she says more brightly, "is find out what happened at Malpensa."

* * *

Six hours later, close to midnight, they are in a small plain room at an airport hotel outside Milano. At the front desk they had asked for two rooms, but the clerk said this was all they had. Something about a strike at Fumicino in Rome and bad weather in Germany. "*Ma due letti,*" he said.

"Two beds," she explained to Marc.

"That's fine," he said. "No problem for me if it's okay for you."

"Of course."

They were both exhausted and not about to go looking for another place. Soon after leaving Lerici on the road to Malpensa, with Marc driving again, she called the number Emmanuelle had provided for Tanner. It went straight to voice mail, and in French she left a message:

"Willem Tanner, this is Lina Lentini. I am a friend of the late Cecile Eaton and also of Clara Marche. I would very much like to talk with you about Clara. As I am certain you understand, the matter is urgent, and we hope you will return this call as soon as possible."

She left her number and said again to call soon. After ending the call, she told Marc, "I said 'we.' I did not want to say 'we.'"

"It doesn't matter. I'm sure what you said was good."

A minute later she sent a text message to the same number, saying basically the same thing. And for the rest of the trip, she kept looking at her phone, willing it to ring or deliver a text. Ten minutes from Malpensa she called again and left another message.

"I will just keep trying until he gets sick of me and calls back."

At the airport it took them three-and-a-half hours of running around, pleading, cajoling and even threatening at times, but they finally secured most of the information they were after. Clara, they learned, had booked not one but two flights last Saturday morning, paying cash for each. But she did not take either one. For the second, on EasyJet to Amsterdam, she had checked a bag and then never showed up at the gate. According to regulations, of course, the bag could not remain on the plane without her on the flight and so had to be pulled off. At some point later, someone, perhaps Ms. Marche herself, had apparently claimed the bag and carried it away, because it was no longer in EasyJet's possession. And as for whether Clara took another flight out of Malpensa over the following few days, a security agent promised to run a check and get back to them within 48 hours.

Near the end of the letter to Cecile, Clara had written that a remark from Tanner on the phone had caused her to worry about being apprehended by airport security or police agents, if she attempted to board a plane. And so they had also spent time trying to establish whether in fact her fear had been realized. Finally, after dealing with three different agencies at Malpensa, they felt reasonably certain that she had not been arrested last weekend. They were also told that no reports had been filed of a woman being abducted or escorted away from the airport.

"Dead end," says Marc. He has just come from the bathroom in a T-shirt and shorts, a trim man moving with an easy manner to slide under the sheet and blanket on his bed. "We're really at a dead end, unless you think it makes any sense to look for her in a major city like Milano."

"No," she says from under the covers on her bed, "it makes no sense. Even if Clara went there thinking she could hide effectively in such a big anonymous place, we could search for weeks and find nothing." She is sitting up with the Dell on her lap. Normally she sleeps naked, but the wrap she fortunately tossed into her suitcase at the last minute is closed firmly over her breasts. Still she feels comfortable with him, as he seems with her. It has been that way since the first moment they met.

"But we still have Tanner," she says and points at the screen where she is writing the man an email. "Maybe he leads us right to her."

"Maybe," he says without moving. "But I've pretty much decided what I should do on Monday back in Geneva. Walk into the Banque Privee Morneau, demand to see the chairman, and then just tell him everything we know. Just lay it all out on the table. I'll leave you out of it, Lina, but I'll show him a copy of Clara's letter and say, 'Tell me where she is right now, or I go to every police and regulatory agency in Switzerland and give them the whole damn story.'"

Chapter 26

Saturday morning, 10:30: a full week now after the encounter at Malpensa, he sits with his computer at a table in the window of the Blue Parrot, a coffee shop in Amsterdam's Old Center, about three blocks from the Red Light District. As he has everyday, he is checking the news sites in Geneva and Milano for any word of Clara, anything really from her apprehension by police to the discovery of the unidentified body of a woman fitting her description. As usual, there is nothing.

His gaze strays to the busy street where a heavy overcast promises rain, then back inside to Ghete, waiting on a line of customers while her two young people dash about filling orders. Hardly an empty chair in the place, it's filled with students, matrons, business and trades people. Just two whores. It's too early for them. As always Ghete is full of small smiles and sly looks, comely nods and, even from across this good-sized room, the same soft, low tones he hears from her in bed. Yes, she is a bit rounder in the face and broader through the middle, but he still likes to look at her.

Not the same as a quarter century ago, of course, when he first saw her in the window, one of the District's most popular girls. Back then it was all the fine blond hair, the delicate features and the trim yet voluptuous figure that started things with both men and women, but what brought them back was the earnest, natural way she had of giving pleasure, something that made you feel she really was kind, tender and a little bit wild. Not just a calculating young woman who knew exactly how to get the biggest tip or most extravagant bonus — though she was surely that as well. And there still seems to be something sweetly unassuming about her, not that he's ever been convinced she is anything close to the proverbial good-hearted whore. From what he can tell, she has never been greedy or grandiose in her needs or plans, and the Blue Parrot seems to make his point.

It came to her in the will of an 81-year-old fellow with one arm, who had spent every Thursday evening with her from 8 to 9 for the previous eleven years. It had been a stable once, then a small warehouse for the man's copper salvage business, then just a dusty empty space when the old guy finally croaked. With it came the modest apartment above and a small garage two blocks down with enough room for seven cars. So a dozen years ago Ghete retired at age 40 and put her life savings into turning the warehouse into a coffee shop and refurbishing the apartment into a comfortable place to live. The garage was always fully rented and added a nice little income, but she always kept one space open for visiting friends.

And that was where Willem put his car 12 years ago when Dubonne sent him to Amsterdam to meet with the cartel. It was the first time he had actually stayed with Ghete and his first look at her new business. In one corner of the place was a large cage holding a very red parrot. Another gift from another admirer, she explained, a traveler from the States, who had picked it up in Madagascar but was now tired of carting it around the world.

"And so," said Ghete, "of course I decided to call my shop the Red Parrot. But the American was adamant. 'No,' he said, 'it must be the Blue Parrot because as soon as she opens her mouth, that's what she is.'"

And just then, as if on cue, as Ghete finished her story while they were standing next to the cage, the creature had screeched so loud that Willem flinched.

"Fuck you, sailor!"

And a few seconds later: "Tits and ass!"

And to complete its repertoire: "Shit on a stick!"

He stares at the bird now, bopping its head back and forth as if trying to decide which way to go, even though the most it could manage in any direction would be a meter or two.

"She's feeling old and cranky," said Ghete earlier.

He told her, "You'd also feel old and cranky if you had to live in there."

Old and cranky is how he feels too. And caged. But then sitting and waiting for someone else's move has never been his thing. It was the worst part of prison. Unable to act, or turn things his way. Just sit there and wait.

He thinks about that scene at the airport again. Watching them

167

move her out the door as she stared back at him made the urge to act, to do something, feel nearly overpowering. Concerned they would follow her gaze and spot him despite the hat and the sweater, he walked a few steps in the opposite direction and then turned back. Outside they each had an arm and were heading her past the cabs and buses toward the parking area. He told himself they were doing him a favor. In fact, the thought of terminating Clara still slithered away when he tried to fix it in his mind. And because they were surely after him almost as much as they wanted her, she was also doing him a favor.

Yet, for reasons he still can't explain, he had followed them, dodging between travelers into the structure, past pillars, ramps and long dense lines of parked vehicles, to lose them, find them, and lose them again. Finally, he had ducked behind a car as they each whipped past, Tremelyn driving Clara's red Astra and Savoneau in his own Volvo. He couldn't see Clara in either car. His Mercedes was close by, and he might have been able to follow, but if they split up, as he suspected they would, he wouldn't know which to follow. Or had they already scrubbed her and left the body under some car in this huge structure? He had suddenly felt sick with exhaustion and wondered if maybe he was acting so strangely because he had been up all night and gone sleepless for so long.

Again not sure why, he ended up back in the terminal, and then he remembered her suitcase. The one she had checked at the EasyJet counter. For some reason he thought he should try to retrieve that suitcase. It was instinct, really. If asked why, he probably could not have offered a coherent answer. But with the help of the information and contacts provided by plain-faced Gina at Cristoforo Colombo, the process of actually securing the bag had been surprisingly simple. An hour after the take off of that EasyJet flight she had booked and missed, he was back at the Mercedes and dropping her suitcase into the trunk.

Then he forced himself to do a slow, painstaking search of the car's interior and underside for the bug they had used to track him. Finally convinced it was no longer there, he drove about 10 kilometers and stopped at the first hotel he came to. He slept the day away, then showered but decided he would not be shaving for a while. He ordered food brought to the room and, once it was dark, went to the car and drove through the night to his home in Geneva.

He spent most of that trip thinking about his former partner Savoneau and their pal Tremelyn. In the decade before he had gone to prison, they had worked together on several assignments for the chief. Willem had come to know both of them well, like brothers, he thought, their strengths and weaknesses, their habits, vices and telling little quirks. And yet he was finding it difficult to decide what they would do with Clara Marche. Promptly carry out the wishes of the banker boys as conveyed by the chief? Or freelance a bit? Both of them had enough stewing anger and simple greed to at least consider holding on to the woman long enough to explore the possibility of extortion. Put her in the ground someplace hidden away, with a breathing tube perhaps, and then send the boys a note saying, hand over a bushel full of euros or we provide the Carabinieri with the precise GPS.

Would they actually do it? Maybe, if they didn't know what he knows about how tight Dubonne is with Giles Morneau. Certainly the dark and devious little Savoneau, with his gambling problem and that skinny, grasping wife of his would be sorely tempted. And the large and geeky Tremelyn would definitely go along.

And on orders from Dubonne, after they finished with whatever they were going to do with Clara, would the two of them seriously come after him? As a sullen New York cop had once said to him in a dark Manhattan bar, "Does a bear shit in the woods?"

He felt a strong sense that he should take all three of them out, starting with the chief. But then maybe that should wait. The last thing he needed right now was the full force of the department coming down on his head.

At his house by 3 am, he made sure no one was staking it out. Inside he changed his clothes and then packed two bags, one with winter things, the other for a warmer clime. He knew he'd be traveling for a while, and widely. He grabbed the two lead-sided containers he used to travel with the SIG-Sauer, and also the Sony laptop the boys had insisted he buy two years ago when he began traveling for them in a major way. From the black iron safe hidden in the basement he took his false ID packet that included a passport, driver's license and credit cards, and a goodly stack of cash in three different denominations. He donned his black leather, set the thermostat low and wondered if he should take the hat and sweater. They had served him well in Italy, so why not? He stowed everything next to Clara's suitcase in the Mercedes' trunk, and it was still dark as he headed out of Geneva for points north. He really did not know when he would be back, but the road ahead he knew quite well.

He had made this trip several times over the years, up through France and Belgium to Amsterdam, whenever time permitted the luxury of two of his favorite things — driving fast and visiting Ghete. Then leaving his car in her garage, he'd fly out of Schiphol and take care of business. How long he spent with Ghete this time would depend on when he heard from his sworn-to-secrecy man at the bank, Marcel. The night security guard had promised a call when either or both of the boys left Geneva. Where they would go Willem was sure he knew.

Still sitting in the Blue Parrot's window he checks his email, something he's forgotten to do this morning, and finds two new messages, both from Lina Lentini. What's this about? The subject line in each says "Clara Marche." This should be interesting.

> Willem Tanner,
>
> I am a friend of the late Cecile Eaton and also of Clara Marche. I want very much to talk with you about Clara and her possible whereabouts. This is a very urgent matter to me, and I hope you will respond as soon as possible. I have also left you both phone and text messages. Please contact me soon in any way that is convenient for you.
>
> Thank you for your prompt consideration.
>
> Lina Lentini

She included her mobile number and sent the message at 12:07 this morning. Eight hours later she sent the second one.

> Please, Mr. Tanner,
>
> I know you have acted as a friend to Clara in the past, and I hope you will act now on the concern I feel we share for her welfare.
>
> I await your prompt response.

Lina

He wonders why this follow-up, more personal response mentions his acting as Clara's friend at some undesignated time in the past. Was it simply a reference to his relationship with Clara four years ago, or could this mean the woman knows what happened two weeks ago when Clara left Geneva? If the latter, he might have a problem.

The phone and text messages she mentions must have been sent to his old mobile, at the moment sitting with its battery detached in the glove box of the Mercedes in Ghete's garage two blocks away. He suddenly wants to check those messages as well. He stuffs the Sony in its bag, swings past Ghete to say he'll be back in a few minutes and heads out the door. On the street a light rain has started.

At the car when he puts the mobile back together, he finds four voice mails and three texts all from the Lentini woman. He attends to each carefully but finds nothing helpful, no other reference to any past connection with Clara. Splitting the phone from its battery again, he slips the pieces into his coat pocket and is about to leave when he remembers Clara's suitcase in the trunk. It's been there for a week, and he hasn't opened it yet.

When he unzips it next to his own bag stuffed with warm-weather wear, he finds, as he expects, her clothes packed with meticulous care, a sheet of tissue paper between each layer. It is how she has always packed, he remembers from those two short holidays they took together years ago. And it nearly drove him to yell at her as she took forever getting ready to leave Geneva, when she was already supposed to be dead. As he lifts each layer, he wonders what the hell he is looking for. Until, under a thin beige sweater that always showed off her chest in a way he liked, he finds several sheets of writing paper covered with her cursive.

Sitting in the car he reads page after page, knowing now he will definitely have to deal with this Italian woman who is suddenly sending him all the messages. And reading further, he guesses there will soon be someone else, Clara's black American boyfriend, also on his agenda. He'll need to find a way to have them both come to him.

As he heads back to the Blue Parrot, it's raining heavily now. He's moving fast as he approaches the front door, and then through the window, in front of Ghete, who is speaking with a big smile and a special animation, he spots the blond head and broad back of

Georges Tremelyn.

He halts in front of the shop's glass door, turns on his heel and strides quickly across the rain-swept street. He stops in the shadows of a low awning covering the large dark wood doors of an apartment house entrance. Turning he finds he can still see into the brightly lit Blue Parrot where Tremelyn, with a wave and nod to Ghete, is moving to the table in the window where he himself was sitting just twenty minutes ago.

Under the awning he slides to the edge of the narrow apartment building and moves into an adjoining alley. From there he can still keep at least part of Tremelyn's torso in view. He pulls out his mobile and dials Ghete.

She answers on the third ring. "Willem…"

He cuts her off. "Ghete, say only yes or no to what I'm telling you. Do you understand?"

"Yes, but…"

"Good. Now do not look at Tremelyn, who is sitting there in your window. He asked about me?"

"Yes, of course."

"And you told him I would return shortly?"

"Yes."

"Good. So tell him when we hang up that I called to say that I'm doing some errands and that I will meet him at noon at In De Wildeman. That's his favorite beer bar. So, at noon. Understood?"

"Yes, I understand."

"Okay, now tell me in full voice that my friend Tremelyn has just come in and is looking for me."

Chapter 27

That she drives fast surprises him. Clara is right: beyond the obvious charm and intelligence, she is interesting in ways you would not expect. A calm, thoughtful kindness makes her easy to be around, and he's grateful for that, since this whole effort to find Clara has produced only angst and frustration. And now as they head north from Milano he's fighting this sinking feeling that the woman he loves is falling away, further and further behind, literally, as if she's been hidden somewhere in Italy, her voice, desperate but too muffled to hear clearly, calling to him but more faint by the minute.

He's back to blaming himself. Clearly he should have dropped everything and got on a plane last Sunday when he received that email from Lina telling him about Clara's disappearance and her trouble at the bank. Actually he should have flown straight to Amsterdam the day before, when she failed to arrive as she wrote in the fax she would. It was already obvious then that something was very wrong. But there he was back at Detroit Metro on Sunday in that foolish effort to make her magically appear exactly one day later. Why didn't he just book himself on one of those evening flights to Schiphol and start his search for her immediately? Not almost a week later.

And now, of course, he knows he's being foolish again. They've just learned that, for whatever reason, she booked two flights out of Malpensa, one to Rome and one an hour earlier to Amsterdam where her fax said she would take a Delta flight to Detroit. But she took neither flight out of Milano. Paid for both but took neither. What sense did that make? Something, or someone, changed her mind about following her plan. As far as he and Lina know, she did not return to Lerici and now could literally be anywhere on the globe. The trail would likely have been just as cold a week ago as it is today.

As she sails them up the Autostrada, his quick glance at the woman's profile—smooth brow, a few tiny wrinkles at the corner of

173

the eye, straight nose, a sensuous curve to the mouth—makes him think about last night in the hotel room. Normally he might have found sleep difficult with a woman so attractive in another bed only a few feet away. The enveloping darkness might have teemed with secret images, thoughts and desires. But last night his mind was littered with broken hopes, and the last thing he remembers was trying to formulate what he would say to Giles Morneau or Clara's hated boss Julian. And then he was gone, taken by a dreamless sleep that lasted the night.

If only, he thinks now, Lina had contacted him as soon as she learned that Clara had gone missing. That would have been a whole week earlier. But that is not being fair to Lina. It was exactly the time she was dealing with Cecile's health crisis, calamity really. No, the real question is why Clara did not get herself on a plane immediately after Willem Tanner told her to leave Geneva and seem dead. Why didn't she just fly straight to Detroit where Marc would have embraced her and helped in any way he could?

He has no answers.

It's almost a relief when Lina asks what he thinks of the possibility that Cecile's stroke did not stem from natural causes but was perhaps induced by someone who came to the villa, while she, on a seemingly spur-of-the-moment invitation from Julian Lyon, was off on a visit to Annecy.

"I've been thinking the same thing," he says.

"I should never have left her alone that way."

So she too is playing the blame game. "And how could you have ever imagined that she might be in danger simply by being alone in her home?"

"She was 88-years-old, Marc. Anything can happen at that age."

"Anything can happen at any age."

"Yes, but…"

"Lina, the woman was wonderfully independent. She would not have wanted it any other way."

"No, of course. But I will always wish I had been there with her."

They are silent for a while before Marc says, "More to the point, I've been thinking that if Monsieur Tanner was assigned by the bank to eliminate Clara, it seems likely he also visited Cecile."

Lina glances at him. "I have thought the same. And now that you mention it, I have been wondering why Tanner in the photo

Emmanuelle sent from the bank looks somehow familiar. I think I may have seen him at the hospital while I was keeping the vigil for Cecile. Maybe more than once."

"Really. Well, I wouldn't be surprised. So how many messages have you sent this guy?"

"I think nine or ten. I am losing track, but I will just keep sending until he responds."

Treading the land of guilt and regret, he finds himself drifting to thoughts of his troubled and troubling younger daughter, beating himself up for serious failures as a parent and husband. Amelia (they called her Amie until she began insisting on Lia, about the time the awful things started happening) was at just the right age and in just the right place to suffer the full impact of all the anger and pain delivered by her parents' nasty, rancorous divorce. In a classic and predictable way that any reasonably in-touch parent would have recognized, she sought refuge with the wrong friends. With two reckless, feckless pals, she sampled and embraced the inviting perversity of the street, moving eagerly through weed, crack, meth and smack, and inevitably trying any means to their risky ends, from petty theft to the sale of self. He knew that world well, having produced a couple of gritty, full-bore documentaries meant as a stern warning to a city on its way to hell. But she had plunged right in, as if to say, " Here you go, Pop, you think you're an expert on this shit. I know it in a way you never will."

And so he blames himself for not loving her enough and for loving her too much, for being too tough and for being too soft, for not grabbing her by the hair and yanking her out of the muck and for reporting her to an old cop friend for her own damn good, for letting her search for her own rock bottom and for intervening in ways she only resented, for bailing her out of jail and for leaving her behind bars to at least dry out, for letting her live alone with her fucked-up buddies in a rat-trap just beyond the city limits and for not moving out of Detroit to a place with better schools and less crime.

Yes, nearly everything he's tried to do for her has turned out badly, but just lately there's been a flicker of hope, and now he is worried about the way he left things at home in his rush to get here. Amie has been living with him for close to three months and has been mostly straight, he thinks, saying all the right things and doing them as well, from what he can tell. But he was not about to leave her alone in his home on the city's west side, where she can walk in five minutes to a fix. Connie, the good daughter, the lucky older one who somehow escaped his toxic touch, agreed to let her sister stay with her and his little grandson in their suburban ranch, but he thinks that's probably not fair to either girl.

And while he is not living hand to mouth, he knows he can't really put paying work aside for any extended time. How long can he go on with this increasingly hopeless search for Clara? He needs to talk to Lina about this, but he can't bring himself to do it right now.

Chapter 28

On Sunday afternoon, they sit together in the great room, each with a copy of Clara's letter in hand. They are going over it line by line, looking for anything they might have missed, misread or somehow forgotten. Anything that might look or sound different in light of what they've learned on their visits to Lerici and Malpensa. Anything at all that might suggest a new way to search for Clara or some new approach to explore the shocking things she claimed were going on at the bank.

They tried this same exercise last night after returning from Milano, but they were soon interrupted when Lina's cell rang with a call from Honore. The desperate daughter wondered if some word had come from Marc or from anyone else about her mother. "Of course," she said, "I know if you had heard anything, you would have already let me know."

From the way Lina shook her head and shot him dispirited looks, he knew she hated not being able to tell the poor woman anything at all about the letter to Cecile or what they had learned in Italy. But he and Lina both understood the risk attached to the information in that long letter, and, as Clara herself had warned, they must be careful indeed about what they did with it. Why put anyone else even potentially in harm's way, especially when he and Lina still don't know what happened to Clara and what really occurred at the bank? The call with Honore soon ended, and they found themselves talking for a time about Clara's family. Lina explained she had told Honore about Marc receiving the fax, that Clara had said she was flying to Detroit but that she never arrived.

"I wonder," said Lina, "if you might meet with them and perhaps find a way to tell them something."

"Not a good idea," he said quickly. "I've met Honore and her husband a few times and Vera, the younger daughter, once, and they're all very bright. They won't stop asking questions, and you'll never keep them from going to the bank."

"Speaking of going to the bank," she said with a soft smile.

"No, I know, you made your point." He too smiled.

On the trip back as they approached Geneva she had tried in a way he found both kind and direct, to talk him out of his stated intention of confronting Giles Morneau at the bank on Monday morning. He had said he would think about it.

"I was being a hothead. I still want to meet with Morneau on Monday, but I'm simply going to ask him for details on the charge against Clara. Nothing more. I know you've met him, and I trust your judgment, but I want to take the measure of the man myself. Decide if I think he could actually order the murder of a devoted employee who has worked at the bank for more than thirty years."

"It is incredible."

Back to parsing the letter, sometimes phrase by phrase, even word for word, they got nowhere fast. Finally, she suggested they give it up for now, get a good night's sleep and start fresh in the morning.

"Maybe something will come to us in our sleep."

"Yes," he said, "that happens to me sometimes. Just in that hazy window between sleep and waking, when there is still a little crack open to the unconscious."

"*Si*, you put it a nice way."

Her English, he noticed, almost always impeccable, could get just a bit stilted, "Italianized," when she was tired.

In the morning there were no revelations. He woke from a long dream in which he was walking empty streets, crossing a cold, barren desert and wandering a huge, endless mansion. He had no idea why he was doing any of it. Out of the warm bed and into the cool room well after nine, he fired up his laptop. Surfing the Sunday papers, he caught up on Detroit's pathetic mayoral saga and confirmed the city's cowardly Lions as a monument to football futility. He answered an email from Derrick about the shooter's availability two weeks hence. Marc had no clue where he'd be in two days, let alone two weeks. And he tried writing to his daughters. He got as far as "Hi Connie & Lia," and then everything came out awkward or cliché-ridden. Before leaving he had said only that Clara had run into some serious legal trouble, a false accusation at her bank, and needed help and support. Their responses were typical.

Connie, who had never been happy about his "trans-world

romance" and had been trying for years to fix him up with accomplished and attractive women: "Dad, you can't be taking off half-way around the world every time your girlfriend has some problem at work. This relationship has been crazy from the start."

Lia, who probably saw a chance to get out from under his thumb for a while: "Cool, Pop. Do what you need to do."

He ended up writing just a few lines: that he'd been busy traveling outside Geneva, that he loved them both madly and that he would bring little Vincent "all the holes from all the Swiss cheese in Switzerland" (an inside joke for his 4-year-old grandson).

Now, in the afternoon, after the tasty frittata Lina made for lunch, they are working over Clara's letter again, and he finally has a thought. At least for now, perhaps they should try dropping Clara, her whereabouts and her fate from their thinking. Try searching the letter for something else, something that might suggest a more productive course of action.

A minute later Lina says, "What about this? We know we cannot go to the bank and expect to hear anything straight or true. According to Clara, the bankers will have already covered their tracks, altered their records, in effect re-written history, so that it would strictly be her word against theirs."

"Right."

"So what we need is a way to check what is real and true outside the bank."

He thinks for a moment or two, and something pops: "The charities?"

"The charities. Yes, good. Of course."

"So do you know what they are? What groups Cecile gave to?"

"No, she never talked much about it, and then only in general terms or categories."

"And her giving was anonymous, right?"

"True."

"So I suppose if it were really anonymous, even the charity would not know the donor."

"Yes, probably so."

"Well, anyway, what we need are the names of those charities. Who would have those records? I mean outside the bank."

"Yes, of course, so that would be Charles. Old Charles Mercier, her retainer, the attorney who handles all of Cecile's legal and financial affairs."

"And the executor of her estate."

"Yes, I am sure."

"So we need to see old Charles."

* * *

Monday morning they are both dressed and ready to leave the villa by 9. Perhaps because second thoughts are sniping at him, he says again, "So I'll just show up, demand a meeting and take him by surprise."

Gently now Lina suggests he can accomplish the same thing if she calls Emmanuelle and asks for a meeting "at the chairman's earliest convenience." And then the two of them can walk in together. Her approach, he finally admits after a pause, has a better chance of getting what he wants.

As for Charles Mercier, the plan devised yesterday is to tell the old attorney they have concerns about Cecile's account at Banque Privee Morneau. Because the woman who worked with Cecile as the bank's representative has recently been charged with fraud, they fear either of two possibilities.

One: the charge is true, and Clara Marche has actually looted another of the bank's accounts.

Or two: the charge is false, which would cast suspicion on the bank itself.

In either case, it would seem prudent to confirm the continuing charitable donations from the DeRocheford account. Hopefully, there is nothing amiss, but that should certainly be established beyond question with a private request for records from each of the charities involved. And of course it goes without saying there should be no contact on this matter with anyone at the bank.

Last night Marc asked, "How sharp is the old guy?"

"Very, I think."

"Will he find us suspicious?"

"We will give him no reason to. We will tell him nothing he could not know on his own."

"And you think he'll say nothing to Morneau?"

"I think we have to take that chance."

And so with their plans in place, nothing goes as planned. When Lina calls Emmanuelle, she learns the chairman is out of the office for the day. They set a tentative appointment for 10 am tomorrow.

"Any news on Clara?" asks Lina.

"Not a word."

When she tries Mercier's office she gets voice mail, and on his home line a woman's exasperated voice tells her, "Monsieur is not well today."

Chapter 29

He and Giles are in one of the smaller buildings on Bahnhofstrasse, Zurich's street of dreams for high finance or luxury shopping. They're in the offices of Hans Krueger Holding AG, a private bank based in Zurich, and meeting with Hans Krueger III, the bank's frail and sickly 75-year-old chairman, and his stunning, blond, 40-year-old daughter, Fernanda, her sexual vibe veritably glowing. As in their previous meetings, Old Hans has hardly said a word, and, of course, it's clear who wears the pants in this family. Then again, as she crosses and uncrosses those shapely legs in that short red skirt while they sit around a low, carved marble table, she may not be wearing any pants at all. "Sometimes I forget my underwear," she told him once, and so he wouldn't put it past the audacious Nandi. She's not a new breed of Swiss banker. She's from another planet.

He imagines her as a little girl of 8 or 9, discovering that her given name means daring and adventurous. Tossing her fetching golden curls, she announces, "Yes, that's who I am!"

The two of them met for the first time late one evening two years ago in the lounge of the Armani Hotel Dubai. She had crossed the room, lodged in the colossal Burj Khalifa, the world's tallest tower, and sat next to him without asking. And without a smile she said in French, "I saw you today at the plenary session and wondered, 'Who is that beautiful creature?'"

He responded, also without smiling, "And I wondered the same about you. Julian Lyon, Banque Privee Morneau, Geneva."

"Ah, I thought so. Your reputation, at least your physical description, precedes you. I'm Fernanda Krueger."

"So. Yes, clearly from everything I've heard, you could be no one else."

With Giles and her father asleep in their suites, and lubricated with a 600-euro bottle of Riesling that she selected and paid for, they gossiped, flirted and talked shop for the next two hours. It was the end of 2007, and they traded tales of the global banking catastrophe, the multi-billions in loser investments soon to be announced by giants like UBS, with thousands slated for lay offs in the months ahead. They asked each other how smaller private banks such as Morneau and Krueger might weather this storm and discussed how there might come a time when they could find certain ways to help each other out.

Actually it was all foreshadowed that first night, everything that's happened in the two years since, from breakfast the next morning and their mutual introductions of Giles and her father ("His friends call him Three," she said with a smile), to their re-acquaintance meeting in Paris, to their now frequent get-togethers in Geneva and Zurich.

The same for the flirting. He quickly learned there would never be a husband or children in her future and that she had no compunction about saying or asking anything at all. That first night he had trotted out a version of his broken-heart story of the exquisite woman with the two adorable kids and the missing husband, but he had the distinct impression that he might as well not bother trying to "bullshit a bullshitter," as the Americans put it. Did she know that he and Giles were lovers? He was pretty sure she had figured that one out early on, but it had not stopped her from the occasional obscene tease. "Are you any good at cunnilingus?" or "I've been told my clit has a savory taste."

As they wrap this Monday morning meeting now, the last one before the accountants and attorneys really dig in and start making things happen, she says, with bright hazel eyes dancing between Giles and himself, "Of course, it goes without saying, please reassure everyone, especially your most skittish clients, that contrary to the pathetic trends in current Swiss banking, away from the discrete and toward the transparent—the craven capitulation, in our view, to the pressure from outside forces to reveal the names of foreign account holders—we at Krueger Holding have a fierce and consuming passion for the privacy rights and privileges of all our customers."

For some reason, her little speech makes him think of one of his proudest recent moments: the secret addition of an obscurely placed footnoted exception to that original by-law forbidding the sale of the bank. On their feet for the leave-taking, she stands close and looks him in the eye. "So the next time I see you, it will be in Hong Kong.

I'm due there in late January."

Without blinking, he says, "I promise a wildly good time, exquisite food and exotic pleasures galore."

She says, "Sounds like fun."

After a limp hand and nod from old Three and a firm kiss on each check from Nandi, they pick up Mersch in the outer office and find Samuel waiting in the Tank outside the front entrance. Actually it's a customized Porche sedan, but Julian decided it should be called something else when he learned the windows were not only darkly tinted but also bullet-proof and the doors were reinforced steel.

The four of them are silent as they cruise up Bahnhofstrasse past the giants USB and Credit Suisse just a block apart. For Julian there is always an emotional tinge to their visits to Zurich, and he knows it's the same for Giles. It is after all where they met and first seduced each other as students, where they explored these streets for hours, feasting on the splendid architecture of this beautifully designed and constructed place. He smiles faintly as they pass the corner where young Giles once sat down on a curbstone and ate a creampuff off the sidewalk. Homage to a city "so clean you can eat off its streets."

With its expansive Alpine backdrop, gleaming river, crystal clear lake and pure fresh air, it is the perfect bourgeois capital of the world, obsessed with all the vaunted values—money, tradition, family, safety, cleanliness, responsibility and prudishness. Everything that annually ranks it as the city with the world's highest standard of living, and everything they loved to mock as devoted students of youthful iconoclasm.

It is also why they have always loved the spot they are heading to next. For one hundred years the marvelous Art Nouveau Café Odeon has been both a compliment and an antidote to buttoned-up Zurich, a place where Albert Einstein brought students from a nearby institute, where Lenin and Trotsky argued, where a young Mussolini hung out and Mata Hari danced, where James Joyce drank, Thomas Mann trolled for beautiful young men and Patricia Highsmith looked for pretty girls. Yes, it has always been a magnet for novelists, poets, musicians and artists of all types.

And now with its flawless marble-and-mirror décor, it serves veal to Julian and sausage to Giles. As usual these days Mersch and Samuel are positioned at a table near the door.

"Our new chauffeurs," Giles said he told Hilde and the children about these two. "The Mutes" is what Julian soon began calling them as it became evident they were men of few words. On the three-hour trip here from Geneva, as Samuel drove and Mersch sat next to him, they said almost nothing to each other. Now even here inside the café, their small cold eyes hidden behind mirrored shades, their dark hair trimmed short, their faces all sharp angles and flat planes, they look like they've just stepped off the screen from one of those convoluted thrillers with two or three more twists after credibility has already been breached. They are certainly ex-military or ex-police. Who else would find work with a personal security service recommended by Alain Dubonne?

At first, ten days ago, on that memorable Saturday morning when the good news arrived that they would no longer have to worry about either Cecile Eaton or Clara Marche, Giles had seemed almost cavalier about the possibility of Willem Tanner coming after them. But it took only a day for the chairman to come to his senses and realize that everything they had planned and worked for over the past several years could all come crashing down if they weren't very careful. Certain parts of Op B must definitely be kept on hold, and they must surely consider themselves easy targets for the highly motivated killer they hired into the bank and who now knows so much about how they live and work and especially about their secret future plans.

And so one week later Giles did not even begin his usual Saturday morning walk but arrived directly at Julian's in the Tank. And even with bodyguards there is no way they'll relax or do any of the international travel they have planned. Not until they are absolutely certain their man Tanner is no longer a threat. There has not been a single word from Dubonne about the progress of the search, but they know the plan was first to make certain the fellow was nowhere near Geneva and then to have his former colleagues on the force widen the circle to places they know to be among his favorite locales. But even with their extensive and long-standing knowledge of Tanner's habits and proclivities, the chief warned this process could well be a long, drawn out, needle-in-a-haystack kind of thing.

Now as the waiter arrives with two forks and one piece of the Odeon's famous chocolate cake, Giles' mobile buzzes on the table.

"Emmanuelle," he says looking at its screen as he lifts it to his ear.

Julian watches his lover's face as he takes the call. There is a puzzled frown as he says to his secretary, "The Amsterdam police?"

Then impatience. "Yes, well put him through."

Then a glance at Mersch and Samuel watching them from the front of the café. "Yes, inspector, this is Giles Morneau."

Then the frown again. "Yes, he deals with security for the bank."

And now a shake of the head with the eyes growing larger. Pulling the phone from his ear to scan its screen, he says into it, "Inspector, can you hold for a second? I'm getting another call."

He looks at Julian and says, "Tanner has been found at Schiphol, shot dead in the trunk of his car."

"Jesus."

"Dubonne's calling. Ring him while I find out more."

Julian is on his feet and heading for the men's room as he pulls his mobile from his suit coat. By the time he finds the john empty and leans his back against the far wall, he has the chief on the line.

"I was just trying to call him," says Dubonne.

"Yes, he's on with the Amsterdam police right now. So what can you tell us? I presume you know about Tanner?"

"Of course, I've been on with them back and forth all day. They were tipped at 5 am, and I received a text about that time from our man there, Tremelyn, saying it was done and that he'd be traveling for a while. I didn't see the text until about 7, but I didn't want to call Morneau until I firmed things up with our friends in Amsterdam."

Julian is impatient. "What do you mean they were tipped?"

"Just that. Tremelyn called them, probably from the airport and just before he boarded for someplace warm, probably South Africa. He likes Johannesburg."

More impatience. "So what did he tell them?"

"Well, according to Amsterdam, he said they might want to check the contents of the trunk of a Mercedes in Schiphol's short term parking. He gave them the plate number."

"And that's all he said?"

"That's all they needed. Sent a car out there, popped the lock on the trunk and found him there. Or most of him anyway."

Julian stares hard at the men's room door, as if forbidding entry. "What do you mean most of him?"

"I mean his head was blown off."

"His head…? Why would he do that?"

"Tremelyn? Well, it's one good way to make certain your man is gone."

Feeling toyed with, Julian is angry, but then the chief gets more serious. "Look, we don't know exactly how it went down. Maybe there was some kind of confrontation, and Tremelyn, being the resourceful guy he is, actually used Tanner's own shotgun, the one he always kept hidden in his car. I wouldn't be surprised, since it's unlikely that Tremelyn was traveling with one. And that KS-23 of Tanner's is Russian-made and one powerful bloody gun. It really did blow most of his head away."

Julian thinks for a moment. "So, but there was enough of the face to say it was Tanner."

"Oh, lord, no. I told you the head was blown off. In the photos they sent, there were just a few tendons, pieces of…"

"But I mean, then how could you tell?"

"Well, I told you. That's why I was going back and forth with them so long. Of course, the car was Tanner's, and so was everything he was wearing and carrying—passport, wallet with the driver's license, bank ID, all his credit cards, and his old department card from back when he was with us. That's why they called me. But in the pocket of his jeans, the silver monogrammed money clip he used, on his wrist the black Movado and around his neck that gold chain he was so vain about. And then also the clothes—his black leather coat and that gray high-collar sweater he practically lived in this time of year. Of course, some of it—the coat, the sweater and the neck chain—were damaged in the blast."

"And you saw photos of all this stuff."

"Yes, they sent me pictures of everything. And actually, just in case my memory was playing tricks, I sent all of it on to Savoneau, who was in Marseilles looking for him down there. He confirmed it was all Tanner's."

For a moment Julian thinks again. "And so you sent them fingerprints to check?"

"No, no fingerprints. There was no point."

"Why no point?"

"Because the hands were mostly blown away as well."

"The hands?"

"Yes, again I saw photos, but I also spoke with one of their forensic guys, who said the damage to the hands was consistent with either the victim putting them in front of his face in a kind of futile defensive posture, or, more likely, with Tanner reaching for the gun's muzzle as it was fired."

Julian begins moving slowly toward the men's room door. "And so, bottom line, you have no doubt at all that Tanner was in that trunk."

"None."

Back at the table Giles is well into his half of the chocolate cake. Julian sits down saying, "He has no doubt it's Tanner."

"Yes, that's what this inspector said."

"And it was one of his friends on the force who did it. Fellow named Tremelyn."

Giles nods silently, then says, "My man was full of questions. Of course, most of them I couldn't answer, or didn't want to. But one or two I had to think about."

"Like what?"

"Well, I told him we had not seen Tanner for a couple weeks. He was on assignment for us in Italy, and we hadn't heard from him in several days. But I said that wasn't unusual for him when he was on assignment. So, naturally, he asked me about the assignment, and I didn't want to tell him about Clara, but I remembered this inspector probably had a report on her in his files — missing after theft from bank — so I figured it would seem strange if I did not mention her."

Julian is rapidly catching up on the cake. "Yes, good thinking."

"So I told him about Clara and that Tanner had been out looking for her and that I could only assume his search had taken him to Amsterdam. And then he asked if I knew whether this Marche woman had any criminal associates, and I said I had no idea. And finally, he asked if I could think of any reason why someone might want to kill Willem Tanner. I said, no, though I imagined that as a member of the Geneva Municipal Police he might have made some enemies on the wrong side of the law."

"Did his stay in prison come up?"

"Yes, he had already asked if I thought it unusual to hire an ex-con for security at our bank. And I said Tanner had come highly recommended by his former chief."

"What did he say to that?"

"Not much. He sounded like he had already talked about it with Dubonne."

Julian swallows the last of the luscious brown icing. "Well, I think my darling is turning into a first-class criminal mind."

On the drive back to Geneva the two guards are again silent in the front. They have no idea this will be their last assignment for Banque Privee Morneau. Giles, next to him in the back, seems lost in thought, so Julian is using this time to plan meticulously everything he needs to do over the next two or three days.

He spent much of the weekend in his office, making sure that all the computer files were exactly as they should be, everything in its place and ready for review, or gone, deleted and destroyed without the slightest electronic trace. He also made certain that all the "vital paper," as Giles calls it, has been properly created, that all the notes, certs, forms and summaries were letter-and-number-perfect and indexed with precision. "The whole damn trail" is what he calls it, and tonight he'll spend the evening going back over everything one more time.

And then he'll pack up. There won't be much to take with him. A couple of the framed photographs he cares about. Maybe those etchings he acquired in New York. Not enough probably to fill a small cardboard box. He'll carry it down the elevator, say goodbye to old Marcel, and walk onto rue de Hollande for the very last time.

Tomorrow he'll deal with the house, on which he's been working, an hour here and there, over the past week. He'll book his flight, pack what little he'll need for now and box up the rest to be shipped later. On Wednesday he'll be gone for good and have only a day or so to wait for Giles, so the two of them can walk naked in the sun on the edge of the sea.

It is astonishing, he thinks now, putting his hand secretly over the one Giles has resting between them on the seat, after all the disasters, setbacks, heartaches and false starts, there is finally nothing, and no one, standing in their way.

Chapter 30

The call from Emmanuelle comes at mid-afternoon when Lina and Marc are walking in Cecile's frigid garden under a leaden sky, wondering aloud who will care for this place in the spring. The secretary tells her that the meeting with Giles Morneau, tentatively set for tomorrow at 10 am, will need to be moved back until sometime later in the week. Having been out of the office today, he is behind on a number of things and won't be able to clear his schedule for a while. As soon as a date and time can be set, Emmanuelle will call.

"But in the meantime," she says, sounding nervous, "I've just heard the most awful news. We got a call here in the office earlier today from the police in Amsterdam, and they said that our security agent Willem Tanner—remember, you asked about him because of his connection years ago with Clara, and I sent you a photograph?"

"Yes, of course." Lina is already guessing he is either in jail, or accused of a crime.

"So, yes, this inspector calls from the Amsterdam police and asks directly for Chairman Morneau, and so I say, 'May I ask what this concerns,' because he never wants me to put someone through without knowing what they are calling about. And also he was in meetings in Zurich, and I certainly did not want to interrupt him with something not important."

"Certainly."

"So this policeman says, 'It concerns the murder of one of the bank's employees,' and immediately I think it must be Clara, because, you know, she's been missing now for two and a half weeks, and I've had such a bad feeling."

Lina feels her breath constrict and takes Marc's arm. "Yes, I know." He's staring hard at her.

"And so I ask the name, and he says, 'Willem Tanner.'"

Lina breathes again. "So Tanner was murdered?" Now Marc is

shaking his head and moving her toward the old stone bench.

"Yes, and of course I was shocked. So I patched the call through to the chairman's mobile. And later as he was driving back here to Geneva, he called to pick up his messages, and I gave him yours, and then I said, 'Is it true that Willem Tanner has been murdered?' And he snapped at me, 'How do you know?' And I said, 'From the Amsterdam police.' And he said, 'Well, then keep this to yourself. Do not tell anyone. The bank has had enough trouble lately because of Clara. We do not need another unseemly story about an employee of this bank.'"

Sorting the implications of this surprise, Lina only half-listens to what the woman is saying, until the voice takes a more urgent turn.

"So, please, I ask you, do not tell anyone that I have told you about this news. Please, say nothing, even though I am quite sure the newspapers and TV will soon hear about this from the police and report it widely, and all of Geneva will know soon."

After the call, ignoring the cold, she and Marc sit in the garden and talk through this news. How was Tanner murdered and by whom? A random killing, a street mugging or a bar fight? Otherwise, who would want Tanner dead? Why was he in Amsterdam? Was he searching for Clara in that major airport hub, or did he bring her there to send her somewhere else? They know he was closing in on her in Lerici and either found her at Malpensa, or did not. They know her intention was to go to Amsterdam on her way to Marc in Detroit, but that was ten days ago, and about her movements since, and Tanner's as well, they know nothing.

Except that Tanner is dead in Amsterdam.

"So I guess this could be good for Clara," says Marc, "or bad. I suppose it's possible she has someone else on her side that we know nothing about, and who did this to Tanner."

"Or maybe she did this to Tanner herself," says Lina, thinking of a sunny afternoon in a forest high on Mt. Etna.

"Highly unlikely."

"Yes, probably so."

"The fact is we have no answers. All we know is that our last plan to find Clara is also dead."

Lina turns her gaze from the snow-covered Alps across the lake to his sad brown eyes. "I have to confess now: I did not really have much hope for the idea that Tanner might lead us to Clara. It was a

191

long shot at best."

He nods and looks away. "But it was our only shot, and now it's gone."

"I suppose we could go to Amsterdam and ask for details from the police. See if they have a report of Clara showing up there and being arrested."

"Maybe." He pauses and then goes on. "I could do that on my way home."

"You are thinking about going home?"

"Yes."

She is silent for a while, and he takes her hand and says, "Look, you've been wonderful, Lina, a true friend, but I can't justify staying here, with nothing to do but wait for something that may never happen."

She is nodding. "I understand, of course."

He gets to his feet, and she suddenly feels chilled.

"I still want to confront Morneau," he says. "And I'd like to help you explain things to old Mercier and get him on the case. But we are dead in the water now with Clara, and I'm in no position to just stay here and hope. I frankly can't afford it. I need to get back to work, and I'm feeling guilty about leaving my daughters in a tough situation back there, especially my younger one."

Rising from the bench she gives him a sad smile, takes his arm and they move toward the back entrance of Cecile's old villa. "I am getting cold."

Minutes later they sit at a table in the kitchen, watching tea bags steep in large porcelain cups decorated with snowy mountain vistas. "I love these old mugs, she says. Why drink tea only from dainty little cups?"

He smiles but says nothing. She thinks again of how bereft she felt when he said he was leaving. "So tell me about your daughters. Obviously you are close to them."

"Yes, I guess we're close, although sometimes I wonder. I don't know that I've been a very good father."

"Why do you say that?"

"Because I really don't know. As I always tell them, I love them madly, and I have always tried to be supportive and understanding. But that has not always turned out well. The older one, Connie, is in most ways successful. She's a prosecutor in Oakland County — well-to-do, just north of Detroit—and she's very tough. Nothing really stops her, not diabetes, not a bad marriage, not being a single mother, not her parents' unpleasant divorce, nothing. She's an excellent trial attorney, one of the best they've got. I've seen her work in a courtroom, and it's kind of scary. She's ruthless. If she were trying to put me away, even if I weren't guilty, I'd feel hopeless."

She smiles at him, recalling a similar line in one of his early emails to Clara.

"Really, she takes after her mother in some ways. As I say, tough, unyielding, maybe too ready to draw a line in the sand. I suspect her of harboring certain Republican values, so I try not to talk politics with her. Let's just say, compassion is not her strong suit."

"You say she is like her mother."

"Yes, Nancy is like that. Tough, uncompromising, and she really is a Republican. And so is the guy she married about five years ago. Near as I can tell, a very successful slumlord in L.A., which is where they live. Couple of sterling buppies, black urban professionals. Both voted McCain-Palin."

"What happened between you and Nancy?"

"I was too consumed with my work and not making enough money. That was her take."

"No divorce is that simple."

"Yes, well, I'm sure I was foolish, selfish and a pain in the ass."

"Somehow I doubt it."

"You're kind, but you don't know. Anyway, the worst thing about the divorce was that Amie, the younger one, was only 13. I'm not sure you want to hear that story."

"Of course, I do. Clara told me a little but…"

"Hell, I forgot that you've read all those emails between Clara and me. You probably remember more about all this than I do."

Her mobile rings in her purse on the counter. Up to get it, she looks at its screen and nods at Marc. "Hello, Charles, how do you feel?"

The old attorney says it looks like he will live, but he is angry at his housekeeper Emma, calling her a "tyrannical witch." He apologizes profusely for not being available to Lina earlier and for taking so long to call her back. The inexcusable fact is that Emma did not tell him about Lina's call until just a few minutes ago, and then he exploded at her. It's true he was not been feeling well, really since last Friday, and spent the weekend unable to keep anything down, actually — forgive the indelicacy — unable to keep anything from coming out either end. A bad case of food poisoning, or stomach flu, though he has long thought Emma fully capable of attempting murder in the classic manner of the mad housekeeper, with a lethal dose of some household cleaning product.

Lina recalls Marc's question: *"How sharp is the old guy?"* And wonders about her answer, *"Very, I think."*

But now old Charles switches gears. Really, he says, he likes to tease the redoubtable Emma, but she actually takes extraordinary care of him, much better than his late wife ever did, keeping precise track of his schedule and making certain he never misses a thing. And when he is not feeling well, such as this past weekend, she becomes fiercely protective and nurses him with selfless care. Now feeling better, he would relish a chance to get out of the house. His driver can have him at the villa in short order, and then they can discuss in person this concern Lina has about Cecile's account.

At 6, an hour-and-a-half later, she, Marc and Charles Mercier are sitting in the great room talking about Clara. At first he looked pale and drawn, but now as he sits forward in his chair, the better to follow what she and Marc are telling him, his complexion is regaining its usual ruddy glow. He was surprised by Marc's presence at the villa but was warmly cordial and switched from French to English when she explained Marc's connection to Clara and his language limits.

"How extraordinary!" exclaims Charles when Marc describes how his transatlantic romance with Clara was made possible by computerized auto-translation. The old attorney says he met Clara once and by chance, right here at the villa about a year ago. "A lovely woman, very kind and charming to an old man."

Lina explains that this woman, indeed charming, has been for more than thirty years a devoted employee of the Banque Privee Morneau and remembers the day when 10-year-old Giles, now chairman, first visited the bank with his father Albert.

"Ah, Albert. Don't get me started on Albert. A stubborn, pig-headed man. I never could see what Cecile's sweet husband Claude apparently saw in Albert and his bank, which I hear, by the way, has had it's troubles lately."

So, says Lina, this loyal employee of three decades, a woman with

194

a perfectly open and above-board life, with strong family ties and without an enemy in this world, has been missing for more than two weeks, and in the wake of her mysterious disappearance the bank has charged her with fraud, with looting the account of the bank's former investment manager who has just resigned for a job in Hong Kong. At this news old Charles shakes his head in amazement.

A half-hour later he is still shaking it at the story Lina and Marc have recounted and at the legitimate questions they think it raises.

"Surely," he says, "I hope all of this will prove a mirage that will melt away as soon as we secure the facts and elicit answers. But until then let's all keep an open mind. While you two continue searching for Clara, I will approach Cecile's charities and ask for their records."

"How long, sir," says Marc, "do you think it might take to get what we need from the charities?"

"Hard to say. In my experience it can vary widely. Some of these groups are highly organized and spend perhaps even more than they should on administrative costs. They may respond quickly, while others who might run things more loosely will take longer. But what I'll do is tell all of them that time is scarce, and as soon as I see what looks like a trend, I will let you know."

Lina asks, "And the bank, Charles?"

"Ah," says the old guy, his eyes sparkling and darting between the two of them, "I say all of us should stay as far away from the bank as possible."

Later in the bed in her darkened room, the world even darker beyond the lattice windows, she thinks again about the meeting with Charles Mercier. It went well. His response was everything she hoped it would be, and even Marc seemed encouraged. Then why does she feel so uneasy? Why so unhappy with the reality she faces now? Cecile gone, Clara lost and Marc about to leave. Is it simply that she will soon be left to her own devices? When has that ever made her feel this way, desolate really?

Then from the desk across the room, the Dell sounds its hopeful little two-note alert. Falsely hopeful, she thinks. Off the bed she ties her wrap and with a touch lights up the open laptop. Her email inbox shows a new subject line: *M'aider*. The message is from cmarche777@gmail.com.

With her heart already racing, she does not trust herself. She pulls the power cord, lifts the Dell from the desk and leaves the room.

Down the hall she can see Marc's door open and a light on. At the jam she peers in and finds him in his T-shirt and shorts, working at a small table with his own computer.

"Marc?"

"Oh, Lina. Come in." He is up and looking at her carefully. "Are you okay?"

From his face she knows she must seem strange, and glancing at a mirrored cabinet door, she sees a look stiff with concern, her hair on one side bent at an odd angle from lying on the bed. "Yes, but I just got an email."

He stands close to her now. "From whom?"

"I am not sure. Maybe Clara." She sits on the edge of his bed, the Dell open on her lap, and he joins her.

"You haven't opened it?"

"No, it is not from her usual address."

He stares at the screen. "Gmail, easy for her to open anywhere. '*M'aider*'?"

"It means 'Help me.'"

A double click and within a second or two they are staring at a message in French. She translates for him as she reads.

> Dearest Lina,
>
> Today is 16-11-09. I am being held against my will, and I need your help. Also, if possible, show this to my dear Marc and ask him to come with you. I am a captive on the island of Eleuthera in the Bahamas. I think near the place called Governor's Harbour. Please do not write back to this email. Do only this: Come here as soon as possible and wait until I am able to write again. It is very dangerous and difficult for me to do this, so I must be careful. Please do only as I say here, or I fear my life will be over.
>
> All my love to you and Marc.
>
> Clara

Chapter 31

At a good clip they are walking from gate to gate through the terminal at Heathrow. From the looks he's noticed from other travelers, they apparently make an interesting couple, the lanky black man with a little gray showing and the striking redhead with the great figure and confident stride. A glance at the glinting, imperfect mirror of a glass storefront confirms this notion, and then she veers off toward a large newsstand. His soft-sided bag on a strap over his shoulder and her small case wheeling behind, he stops. With more than an hour and a half between flights, they have time for whatever has caught her eye.

She moves directly to a large newspaper rack filled with journals and tabloids from cities around the globe. Pulling one from the rack, she unfolds it and holds it up for him to see. He moves across oncoming traffic to get closer.

Pointing to a front-page photo, she says, "Amsterdam. Tanner. Looks like a passport photo." And then she reads the headline, as usual translating for him. "Swiss Man Found Murdered at Schiphol."

He nods and watches as she skims silently through the brief story below. Then she folds the tabloid over, stuffs it back into the rack, and they move on.

"He was found in the trunk of his car. Killed with a shotgun blast. No suspect, no motive."

"Sounds like some mob hit."

"Yes, a cartel execution."

For maybe the fifth time since they left Geneva at 7:30 this morning, he thinks about the email, wondering at the awful, dirty business his good-hearted Clara stumbled into.

Last night when Lina finished reading Clara's note aloud, they both sat silent for several seconds, until he said, more to himself, "Jesus, this is crazy." And then he looked at her and said, "Could you read it again? Maybe more slowly? And make sure you're happy with every word."

She nodded and read again with a slower pace, at times giving him phrases in French before rendering the line in English. He noticed no difference the second time.

Finally, he asked, "So, what do you think? Is it genuine? Is it really Clara?"

"To me it sounds like Clara, but honestly, how can we be sure?"

"Yeah, I don't know. It sounds like her but cold and stiff, unlike the way she is in person, or in all those years of emails. But then, if this is real, she would certainly be frightened and stressed, like someone might walk in on her at any minute. I mean, it sounds like she's stolen a minute or two of access to someone's computer, and she's afraid of being caught."

"Yes, maybe," said Lina. "The writing here is more like the writing in her letter to Cecile and also in the fax she sent to you."

"But if she did not send this, who did? Who could have done this and why?"

"The why is easy. To get us to this island, Eleuthera. But the who? My only guess would be Tanner. He knew we were looking for her. But Tanner is…"

"Dead."

"Yes, it seems so."

"Maybe he wrote and sent it before he was murdered."

"But it was sent today, the 16th. And he was already dead three days ago."

He mulled possibilities for a moment. "So, who else even knows about us and that we're searching for Clara?"

"Well, Charles Mercier, and maybe Julian, or possibly Emmanuelle. But why would any of them do this?"

"No, it makes no sense."

"So the only other answer is that it comes from Clara."

He said, "I suppose someone might have grabbed her at Malpensa, when she tried to take the flight to Amsterdam on her way to Detroit. Basically abducted her and brought her to this island where they've held her, as she says, 'captive.'"

"But why, for what purpose? And why that island?"

"No idea. The usual purpose of a kidnapping is a ransom demand."

"And who would pay a ransom for Clara?"

"Well, her family. But there's been no contact or demand that we know of. And it doesn't really add up. They're not wealthy people."

"What about the bank? What about Giles Morneau? Maybe whoever is doing this is blackmailing him."

"But we think Morneau wanted her dead, and then he charged her with stealing from the bank. Either way, why would he pay anything for her release?"

Lina was quiet for several seconds. "Maybe," she said finally, "it is not for her release. Maybe the kidnapper is threatening to give her to authorities who would then investigate her charges against the bank."

"Well, yes, that would make sense. That's the first thing that doesn't seem crazy."

"But why take her all the way to the Bahamas to do that?"

He shook his head and then felt a new conviction wash over him. "To me one thing is clear. I have to go to this island and do it as soon as possible. No waiting around, no dithering like last time, about coming here. I need to get there as soon as I can and be there for her, no matter what. Otherwise, I'll never be able to live with myself."

And then she surprised him. "So I am coming also."

"Lina, that's not necessary. There's no need for both of us to go. I can handle this on my own."

"But I want to go."

He looked at her closely. "This might very well be a wild goose chase, as we say. It might well come to nothing."

"Whatever it comes to, I think our two heads together are better." She smiled for the first time, and it forced him to smile also.

They quickly divided the tasks suddenly facing them, each with a laptop buzzing, she on his bed, and he back at the table. Lina looked for the fastest way to the Bahamas on the earliest available flight. Probably through Amsterdam or London to Nassau, and then possibly a short flight, or maybe it would have to be a boat, to the island. He googled "Eleuthera" and learned as much as he could about where they might stay, of course as close as possible to this Governor's Harbour Clara mentioned.

They talked back and forth as they worked, their eyes usually never leaving their screens. He asked if she had ever heard of this place, one of hundreds of so-called out islands and cays.

"Yes," she said, "Years ago it was popular with Italians. I think in

Greek Eleuthera means freedom."

"Freedom," he repeated. "Governor's Harbour has an airport, daily flights from Nassau."

"I'm booking us on British Air through Heathrow. If we are lucky we will be there by late tomorrow afternoon."

And amazingly, he thought, within little more than 40 minutes all their arrangements were made. They would need to be at the airport by 5:30 am, so they should pack quickly and grab what little sleep they can.

"Packing will not be a problem," she said, closing her laptop to head back to her room. "Just my thinnest clothes, flat shoes, toothpaste and a brush."

"Maybe we buy T-shirts and shorts when we're there. Sounds like that's all we'll need."

He was traveling light to begin with and just stowed everything in his duffle. This could be his last Atlantic crossing, he thought. It was possible he might never again see Geneva.

In their seats on this 767, separated by an aisle and three rows, (the closest she could find, booking so late), he can sit up, twist back and find her red curls next to a window. They're looking at more than a 10-hour flight to Nassau, so he'll have lots of time to think about some of the things that are still eating at him. Like the fact that Clara would send her email only to Lina and not also to his address. Maybe it was only a time-crunch thing. Maybe she was about to add his address but then heard someone coming. And yet it was "Dearest Lina," not "Dearest Lina and Marc."

Once they're cruising 40,000 feet above the Atlantic, and after a mostly tasteless breakfast box, he declines coffee and tries to sleep. Last night he managed only an hour or so, stirred by this new desperate plea, his mind racing over what fit and made sense and so much that did not. Now he closes his eyes and expects the same. Especially since he never feels comfortable in this sardine-can arrangement in coach, refusing to tilt his seat back into the face of the woman behind him, even though the guy in front is doing it to him.

But when he wakes, he's surprised to feel refreshed. More than three hours have passed. No jumble of half-recalled dreams, no mind bushed from chasing its tail. He pulls his HP from its bag at his feet and starts reading through several documents he saved last night

200

from his visits to websites on Eleuthera and the Bahamas. He sent all these to Lina and figures she has already read them or will shortly. Learning as much as they can about this place can only help. So late this afternoon, if they're fortunate enough to make their connection in Nassau with only an hour between planes, what will they actually find?

One of the first things he learned was that Governor's Harbour was the capital of this oddly shaped island, 110 miles long and only one or two miles wide. Located about midway between the north and south ends of the island, it's one of several villages that dot the coastline and house most of Eleuthera's 8000 residents. In various glowing accounts of the island he notes many recurring lines of hype and tease:

Your own slice of paradise...unspoiled pink sand beaches...the aquamarine sea...rolling green hills...sleepy villages with a church on every corner...a step back in time...a small town feel...everyone seems to know one another...no one bothers to lock a door...crime almost unheard of...passing visitors get a friendly wave...no cruise ship docks...no casinos or nightclubs...no shopping centers...no crowds...no traffic...not a single traffic light.

How to get around? You must have a car, so he emailed a fellow named Stanton Cooper, mentioned on three sites as offering rentals. He listed the expected time of their arrival but heard nothing back. One site mentioned ragged roads and a plenty of potholes, but another reported a recent repaving project. Only one paved two-lane strip, the Queen's Highway, runs the length of the island, and of the side roads that slant from it, some have asphalt, most do not.

The weather? With the Gulf Stream and Trade Winds and typically 300 days a year of brilliant sunshine, someone called it "Perpetual June." Naturally there is the occasional hurricane. Floyd, ten years ago, flattened some things for good, including a Club Med. Places to stay? The preference of most visitors seems to be a villa rental, with lots of attractive-looking homes, most right on a beach, from one-bedroom love nests to sprawling mansions. There are only a few small resorts and tiny hotels or inns, but at one of them, the Buccaneer Club, right in the middle of Governor's Harbour, he booked the Hibiscus Suite, with two queen beds.

Where to eat? A handful of close-by restaurants rated good Bahamian to excellent eclectic, including one at the Buccaneer. But mentioned most is a place called Tippy's, described as a rustic beach bar with a varied and excellent cuisine.

He shuts the laptop and again leans back to close his eyes. Why in Christ's name would someone kidnap Clara and cart her off some 4000 miles to a place like this? He thinks of Lina's answer last night when he wondered what the motive could be, if this whole thing were some kind of ruse.

"To get us," she said, "to this island."

And for the first time he feels a stab of something like fear. When they finally get to this peaceful piece of paradise, he better watch their backs.

Chapter 32

"Have you ever done this?" she asks. "Drive on the left?"

"Oh, yes, once, on Barbados, but that was a right-drive car. Had to shift with your left hand, and I clipped all kinds of things on the left. With this left-drive steering I'm used to, it's much easier."

Well behind them is the bustle of Nassau's busy airport, crowded with oldsters eager to cram in a little more living, married couples ready to recharge, some lovers licit and other not so much, and families with kids crazed for the theme-park pleasures of Atlantis. Once through the long passport lines, they dashed between terminals (their first touch of blustery warmth under bright sun) to the Bahamasair counter, then past another security check to make it just in time to join their 20 fellow passengers on a packed puddle jumper. The props lifted them up and over a sea where you could often spot the bottom through variegated blues to land twenty vibrating minutes later, not in Governor's Harbour but at the North Eleuthera International Airport. It turned out that this long, narrow place has not one, but three international airports, in the north, the south and the middle.

Another 10 or 15 minutes up and down and they were finally at the one they wanted. As they walked out the door of the tiny terminal, there were a half-dozen black men eying them with mild interest. He said, "Stanton Cooper?" and a huge fellow with a smile to match responded with that familiar Bahamian lilt, "Yes, suh. At your service."

Within a few minutes they took possession of the battered white 4-door Jeep he had waiting for them. There was no need for a walk-around; the scratches and small dents were too numerous to note. With the ignition turned, this much-used vehicle fired up promptly, though the check-engine light stayed lit. "Don't worry," said Stanton, "it's stuck. The Jeep will do you good."

And so it seems, as he does the 45 mph speed limit without a problem on this Queen's Highway that looks for all the world like a country road. There is a some rise and fall, several curves, and an occasional straight run through lots of sunlit green vegetation south toward Governor's Harbour. As he recalls, the coast on their left, to the East, they call the Atlantic, and on the right, to the leeward side and the west, is the so-called Caribbean coast. Each is only a half-mile away. Normally, his eyes would roam over this unfamiliar landscape, trying to take in everything at once, but he finds his gaze searching for only one thing now: the house where Clara is being held. From the signage and the side roads and drives, there seem to be several homes along this route, but most of them are out of sight. And after a few minutes, when the first car approaches and sails past, he stares into it, looking hard for that familiar blond head but finding only a driver blacker than himself. Even with every old, apparently unused or abandoned building they pass along way, he does the same.

She says, "I see your eyes go to every house and car. Mine are doing the same, but I doubt we will find her this way."

"I imagine not." This woman often seems to read his mind.

After 15 minutes they roll slowly down a low hill into Governor's Harbour, a welcoming view of this pretty place, their first real look at the sea, calm, mirror-like, to their right, the Caribbean side, at 5:30 the bright ball of sun already low in the western sky. Ahead at some distance he can see a thin line of buildings that must be, from the website photos he's seen, Cupid's Cay, a long, narrow sprit with the town's oldest buildings. Before they can take all this in, they are smack in front of the bright blue and yellow building with the Kalik Beer sign that Stanton told them to watch for.

"And so we take a left in front of the liquor store and go up the hill." He's trying what he deems a clumsy version of the man's Bahamian accent and resolves not to do it again.

A few seconds up the narrow one-way street, past a gift shop with a "Going out of business" sign in the window, and they have arrived. "The Buccaneer Club," he says. "That was easy."

A half-hour later they've stowed their things in the Hibiscus Suite, one of five in a two-story blue building with white balconies and a good-sized pool. Along with two sleepy dogs, a loud-mouthed rooster and three harried hens, each with a line of tiny chicks following about, they have the place to themselves.

Inside the room is large and bright with pink-orange walls, hardwood floors, a decent ensuite bath and a flat-panel TV.

"American satellite," said the bar girl who showed them to the room.

Most importantly, as they sit on a large outside deck, sheltered by a huge tree, a Chardonnay for her and a Kalik for him, Lina has found a web connection with her Dell. She picks up three emails, two from friends in Bologna , one from her publisher in Rome. Nothing more from Clara.

"Unlikely," he says, "she would think we could already be here in less than 20 hours."

He walks to the gift shop only 30 yards away, looks through the window at lots of bright colored clothes but finds the door locked. When he asks the bar girl when it might open, she says, "Oh, I think in a few minutes."

And sure enough when they've finished their drinks and try the shop together, the door is open, an old man waiting behind a counter. They buy shorts, T's, flip-flops and a short-sleeve shirt and blouse, all at 40% off. So far she's put things on her credit card, insisting they settle later. So far it's close to three grand for the airfare for the two of them, 60 bucks a day for the Jeep, 150 a night for the Hibiscus. This trip could burn through his meager savings in no time. But for the clothes he pays with a one hundred U.S. dollar bill and receives back his first Bahamian dollars, the two currencies, he knows, interchangeable. Walking back he wonders how long he can afford to stay here.

After some tasty snapper right there at what they're already calling the Buc, they spend a couple of hours surfing, each propped on one of the queens. From lists of villa rentals, he's taking notes on their locations, how far north or south of Governor's Harbour and on which beaches. She sends him a site called eleuthera.living.com, operated by a Canadian ex-pat couple. Their bio says Mac was a builder, Margo a school teacher, both retired 10 years ago and, fed up with ice and snow, moved to Eleuthera. They built a home and, "to share our love for this place," started the website featuring anything of interest to visitors, snowbirds or full-time ex-pats: a little history, topography, lists of beaches, sights to see, restaurants and grocery stores, weather data and tide charts, interviews with developers and government officials, profiles of long-time residents and stories submitted by visitors about their times on the island.

"Mac and Margo might be people we'd want to know," he says.

"Yes, maybe they could tell us about someone who has brought a lovely blond woman here to hold captive."

He gives her a look, knowing she's teasing. "Exactly," he says. He also knows they both need sleep. Other than what they managed on the plane, they've been up for well over 24 hours.

Chapter 33

In the morning he wakes at 8:30 and finds her already on the Dell checking her email.

Nothing.

After taking the one free breakfast that comes with the room, he is not about to sit around and wait. He takes his Nikon, the little Flip video cam he tossed in the duffle almost on a whim when he left Detroit, and the reporter's notebook with his list of rental home locations, and heads for the Jeep. He leaves her sitting by the pool with her computer. He knows she understands he needs to at least feel like he's doing something other than just waiting for something that may never happen They know both their phones work here, though at what radius from the Buc they have no idea. She will of course call him "if there is any contact."

Driving the Jeep slowly through narrow, bumpy residential streets near the Buc, he passes a variety of small, closely-spaced homes, from ramshackle and impoverished to colorfully painted and well-kept. One thought comes quickly: Clara is not here, not likely to be locked away in one of these places with folks so close they would surely hear a woman's screams.

Once he finds the Queen's Highway and heads south out of town, the houses become larger and farther between. Clara could be in a back bedroom in any one of them. So what the hell is he going to do? Stop, knock on the door and ask for her? Clearly what he's doing is ridiculous.

But for the next two-and-a-half hours he just keeps doing it. With his notes and the map they picked up last night at the gift shop (colorful, full of ads and so basic it shows little more than a thick red line for the Queen's Highway and only a few side roads), he finds his way to a number of villages and beaches, only some of which he can put names to, some with decent roads and others with woeful, pot-holed strips, bouncing the Jeep at weird angles.

On the Atlantic side he finds a long beach called Double Bay, lined with a variety of homes, many of them rentals, but only some of which he can see from the road. At an access he ditches the flip-flops and T-shirt and strolls on a wide expanse of sand that glistens with a pink sheen in the bright warm sun. The surf is energetic in a stiff breeze, the water dark blue with wide aquamarine stripes, waves crashing to send sparkling foam gliding up firm, easy-to-walk sand to greet his feet. After 20 minutes he's passed maybe a dozen places, most with rear decks in view, but he hasn't seen a soul. Ahead, probably another mile up, he finally spots what looks like a couple walking with a dog. And when he looks back at a deck, he sees a gray-haired woman standing there now giving him a wave. He returns it and then heads back. Did he really expect to find Clara sunning on one of these decks? Would her captors ever actually let her see the sun?

There are also homes on a much shorter beach on the Caribbean side called Ten Bay. Again there's no one in sight here, and with the tide out, a wide stretch of white sand reaches out maybe 50 yards to meet light blue water, almost mirror flat. These homes are more modest and closer to the beach. Maybe he could even see a face in a window.

Leaving the Jeep he walks on powdery white sand that soon becomes firmly rippled as he moves out to the waterline. From there he looks back at the houses. A few of them are perhaps separate enough from the others to keep Clara's presence a secret. He heads toward one just up the beach, but something on the flat, firm sand nearby catches his eye. It's a small starfish, caked with sand, and somehow, as he stares at it, this 5-pointed creature assumes an almost human aspect. Yes, there's the head and the arms flung wide, one thick leg spread, the other twisted and curled as if locked in a final agony. Looking closer he sees an indentation in the sand less than a foot away where it had rested earlier. Somewhere he read that starfish move on hundreds of microscopic tube-like feet on the their underside, and he can see the tiny scratches in the sand that trace its lost struggle to get back to the water. For an instant he flashes on an awful image of Clara twisted in a death throes, and then with a small shake of the head he turns away.

This will not do. If there is any chance they might find Clara on this island, he must keep her alive in his mind. He moves back toward the Jeep. Forget the houses. It's clear again that what he's doing makes no sense.

In a village called North Palmetto Point, full of schools, churches and modest homes, four or five people on porches or walking along the road give him a casual, friendly wave. Do they think he's a visitor or someone they might know? Obviously he looks like he's one of them, but if they hear him speak, they'll know he's not.

Thirsty, he stops at what looks like a small country store and buys himself a cold bottle of water. As he pays the heavy-set black woman at the register, on an impulse he says, "Ma'am, may I ask you a question?"

She gives him a serious look. "Yes, suh, you may."

He pulls out his phone and quickly has Clara's photo on its screen. He says, "I wonder if you have ever seen this woman. Her name is Clara."

"Clare?" The woman is studying the picture.

"Yes, Clara."

"No, suh. Never seen this woman. You lose her?"

"Did I lose her?" He suddenly has no idea what he's doing again. Finally he says, "Well, she's been missing for a while, and…"

"Missin'!" The woman looks very unhappy with him. "So then you took this to the police?"

"Well, no, not yet. I just arrived here yesterday."

"Yesterday. So you need to take this to the police. Where you from?"

"Me? From Detroit. Michigan."

"Michigan." The woman is nodding as if this is all making sense now. "And where you stayin'?"

"Staying? In Governor's Harbour."

"Well, right there's the police. Right there across the road from the Shell gas grocery. You need to go there to the police."

He's nodding and backing away now. "Yes, actually, that was my next stop. I was just going to the police."

The woman is looking past him now at someone coming in the door. "Brittany, girl, this man here lost a woman. She's missin'. Suh, show Brittany here your picture."

He turns to find another middle-aged black woman, this one thin, staring at him with big eyes. He will not get out of here without showing her the photo and so gives her a look.

The woman's eyes get even bigger. "What's her name?"

"Her name is Clare," says the woman at the register.

"Clara," says Marc.

Brittany says, "She's pretty. Looks a little like that Miss Marion's mother. You know, those people I cooked for last month? Stayed in the green house on Banks Road."

"No, that's not the Miss Marion's mother. This woman is Clare, from Michigan."

"You know," says Brittany, "maybe my Mattie would know her. She did the cleanin' for that couple last week. They were from Michigan, I think."

"Ladies," says Marc firmly, "thank you so much for all your help. But I really need to get to the police and report this. Thanks again for being so kind."

And he is out the door before either woman can respond.

In the Jeep he turns the ignition and glances in the rear view mirror. There's a light skinned man in a blue ball cap staring his way and opening the driver's side of a red car that's parked maybe 40 yards down the road. As he watches the mirror, the man gets into the car and closes the door.

Still watching, Marc thinks back to his resolve on the plane to watch their backs once they set foot on this island. What happened to that thought? He never once checked to see if he was being followed on his travels this morning. And, of course, he left Lina totally alone without a word of caution. What's wrong with him? Is he just absurdly careless, lulled by the laid-back feel of this place, or so obsessively focused on Clara that he's making himself stupid?

Back on the Queen's Highway, moving at 60 now back toward Governor's Harbour, he watches the red car still behind him, though quite a distance back. He tries calling Lina's cell but gets no answer. When he slows on the town's edge, he feels only mild relief when the guy in the red car turns off on a dirt road to the right.

* * *

Worried when he thought of her being alone and when she didn't answer her cell, and even more worried when she was not at poolside, as he approaches their door now he feels like bursting in but pauses and knocks in case she might be less than decent. "Lina?"

"Yes, Marc," says her voice, "Come in."

As he steps in, she's in her wrap, her hair still wet, the curls

210

clinging. He says, "I called a few minutes ago, but I couldn't tell if I was out of range, or you just weren't answering."

"I must have been in the shower," she says mildly.

"Anyway, I was a little concerned, because I thought on my way back here there might be someone following me."

"Following you?"

"Yeah, I stopped to buy a bottle of water, and a guy followed me from there all the way until I was entering Governor's Harbour."

"But there is only one road, no?" She gives him a smile.

"That's true, and I'm probably being silly, but the guy had a look about him, as much as I could tell from a distance."

"Was he white or black?"

"White, I think. Look, I should have mentioned this before, but I just think we need to be a little careful here."

"Careful why?"

"Well, if it's not really Clara who wants us here, then maybe someone else has plans for us we would not like."

"Who?"

"I don't know. But Clara's been missing for weeks now, and the guy who was supposed to kill her has been murdered himself. It just makes sense, not to be afraid, but to be aware of our surroundings and to look out for each other. You don't agree?"

"Yes, of course I agree. I just wanted to be sure we are both thinking the same way."

Over lunch, once again on the patio at the Buc, he tells her about his adventures that morning, for the most part making fun of himself. She laughs easily, especially when he describes his encounter with the women at the store.

"Anyway," he says, "the people really do seem friendly, and certainly the hype about the beaches here is not just hype. They really are amazing, and I saw almost no one on them."

"Ah," she says, "sounds like it would not matter that we have no suits."

He doesn't know if she is serious, or what to say if she is, but once again he thinks about how much he likes this woman.

When he suggests they take a walk through "downtown," she hesitates, not wanting to be away from the Dell. Then he points out that the town library has computers connected to the web, and they could check for email there. And so they walk down the hill past the bright blue and yellow liquor store and spend the next two hours wandering pleasantly in this quiet little place, strolling down the waterfront, stopping to chat with residents about where things are, finding the pretty coral pink colonial library facing the sea. There's no email waiting, so they move on to the adjacent Cupid's Cay, the oldest European settlement in the Bahamas, said the librarian, with several ancient-looking blackened structures still standing, almost next door to a new duty free wine shop. They buy a red from Italy and a white from Chile.

Then it's back through the town. Children now are walking home from school, all of them in uniforms — the girls in blue plaid jumpers and the boys in white shirts and dark ties — many, as they pass, wishing them "Good afternoon." They stop at a bank machine, Lina using her card to extract some Bahamian cash, then head past the small blue-green police station on their left and the Shell gas grocery on their right and laugh again about his conversation with the women this morning.

Finally, across the street from the blue and yellow liquor store and at the edge of the harbor, they stop to chat with two gregarious young guys named Daniel and Jamie with a table full of fish — some grouper, hog snapper and small tuna — and a whole slew of spiny lobsters of various sizes. On most days, they say, they're here about this time with their catch from that morning. And then a favored customer arrives in a pickup. He's in a white chef's jacket. Speaking with an accent, he negotiates for several items, and as the guys hustle to clean and filet, Lina strikes up a conversation with the fellow in French. They banter, smile and laugh often. On the way up the hill to the Buc, she says that was the chef at Tippy's.

"He says if we come tonight, he will prepare two of those lobsters just for us."

* * *

That evening when they park in a lot across the road, the moon in the night sky looks nearly full. They've decided to dress up, breaking out the short sleeve shirt and her new blouse, but Tippy's really does appear to be nothing more than a beach bar.

"Hopefully it lives up to its reputation," he says, pleased that they've left the laptops behind for a couple of hours, along with the useless speculation about when or whether they'll ever hear from Clara.

As they approach the open front door, the sounds inside are clearly from a happy crowd of drinkers and diners delighted to be exactly where they are. The place sounds packed. Lina pulls open the screen and walks in first, and he can see over her shoulder a large direction tree, with mileage signs pointing to many locations around the globe. And then suddenly she is wheeling in front of him and grabbing his hand, pulling so firmly that he almost loses his balance. Outside he says sharply, "Lina!" but she is not about to stop, leading him quickly back across the road and into the lot.

"Lina," he says again. "What's going on?"

"Please just come." Her voice is urgent, and they don't speak again until they're sitting in the darkened Jeep. They both look back at where they've come from. He sees nothing moving.

He tries again. "Lina, what just happened?"

There's enough moonlight for him to see the deep concern on her face.

"They are in there," she says finally in a low voice.

"Who's in there?"

"The murderers. Julian and Giles."

Chapter 34

"To Tippy's!" he says, raising his Merlot over the table. "Without this place, none of this happens." Well, he thinks, a bit of an exaggeration, but there is much to celebrate. It's their second toast in the past five minutes.

The first was actually a double, Giles lifting his glass to their beautiful new home. And feeling his eyes moisten as they lock on those soft browns, he slipped his hand across the table to cover his lover's and responded, "And to our beautiful new life."

Their hair, usually so carefully tended (Giles' neatly combed and his own artfully teased), is all fluffed, loose, careless and curly in the humid air. The new Tommy Bahamas shirts are a muted salmon with pineapples (his) and a light green with a banana leaf motif (Giles'), both purchased for this occasion in a shop at the Nassau Airport earlier today. Just before they stepped onto the small private plane that zipped them across to Governor's Harbour.

"Yes," says Giles now, "amazing that this little island has made such a difference for us."

"Well, I suppose without it we would have found someplace else."

"I'm sure, but it's all come together so beautifully here. I mean, we've said it before, on this crowded old globe you won't find too many places with this combination of privacy, perpetual sun, gorgeous deserted beaches and just enough civilization to make it all convenient."

Really, where might they be this evening if he had not checked out the travel section of the New York Times that day four years ago, almost on a whim? He'd been thinking they really needed an actual location to boost the fantasy they'd been feeding each other for more than a year, after their pillow talk in London had started everything.

And then his eye had caught the headline, "The Flip Side of the Bahamas." All he knew of the Bahamas was what he had read about

Lyford Cay, the astonishingly wealthy gated enclave at the opposite end of New Providence from Nassau. And also what he had heard about it from Giles, who had visited there at age 14 with his parents, staying at the mammoth beach home of some hugely wealthy Swiss media tycoon.

And so the flip side to all that turned out to be Eleuthera, described in the piece by Tippy's owner as "an untold hidden gem." The writer added that it was being groomed as "the next big thing" and called Tippy's "the epicenter of the island's emerging social whirl."

So on their next trip to New York, they stopped on their way back for a week in a beautiful beach house not far from Tippy's. Everyday they walked the beach and, with no one in sight, slid off their suits to swim and stroll naked for miles. If anyone saw them from the few homes above the beach, no one said a word. Once they had visited other sensational beaches where there were no homes at all, slipped into the free and friendly island vibe and sampled the surprisingly wonderful food at Tippy's, they were sold. They knew this was it, the island paradise they'd been talking about for so long. They pretty much kept to themselves, and no one cared who they were. Except at the airport, no one ever asked for a passport or an ID, and for some reason they began calling each other Josef and Gerard.

When they returned to the island, they came with new passports, driver's licenses and credit cards, all secured by Tanner and identifying Giles as Gerard Bitou and Julian as Josef Simon. In Nassau they stayed for three days and legally established a private investment firm with nothing more than a postal box. It would be their off-shore holding account. Then it was on to Eleuthera to look for property.

Their plan at that point was to find a great piece of beachfront with fabulous views and no close-by neighbors. Then Giles would design their dream home, the likes of which this island had never seen. He had in fact already been "doodling," producing sketches and studies that excited Julian so much that he started thinking about interior design and décor. But it was on this second trip to Eleuthera that they began to move to an alternate plan. They had finally decided they wanted to be there full-time to oversee construction while the home was going up and taking shape, fully controlling and enjoying the process. So the new plan was to find a serviceable existing home, where, after their permanent move to the island, they could live comfortably while they searched for the perfect property and Giles customized their dream house to take full advantage of the contours and virtues of the land. Then they'd select the right builder and check on everything as it happened, keeping the builder under their thumb and the contractors properly terrorized.

About a year ago they found and purchased a home, an excellent home, really, built several years back on a good beach just above Governor's Harbour, and they decided to make it their own by re-doing and refurbishing parts of it. Actually, he couldn't stand the kitchen's granite countertops and wanted marble, Giles wanted different tile in the bathrooms, and they both wanted a wall removed to open up the kitchen to the living and dining areas. One of the four upstairs bedrooms became a movie theater, and another one downstairs was turned into a study for Giles, with two more windows added for more light.

Outside they ripped out the old pool and put in a larger infinity version, added a new deck and upgraded the landscaping with several mature palms and lots of bougainvillea. Tanner had usually been the one down here making sure that all this work was done properly and on time. For him that involved several trips with lengthy stays, during which he checked on everything, sent back photos, and submitted bills and invoices to Giles. Money for payment was moved from the investment firm in Nassau to Tanner's account at the Royal Bank of Canada.

It all went quite smoothly, and when they walked in this afternoon, after a taxi from the airport, they had their first real look at the re-furbished house and were very pleased. It now has their own stamp, a marvelous place to live while the dream house takes shape.

One of the many things he loves about being here is that it often makes him feel like a totally different person. So, while he has never had much interest in history, on their recent visits he's been surprised to find himself fascinated with colorful tales of Eleuthera's past. Now over tuna and grouper at Tippy's, he treats Giles to a whirlwind tour of the island's last 500 years.

From the sad story of the original peace-loving Lucayans, who, after Columbus discovered nearby San Salvador, were slaughtered or captured by the Spanish and then decimated by small pox, or sent as slaves to the gold and silver mines of Hispaniola....

To the landing of a band of Puritan Brits who called themselves the Eleutheran Adventurers, seeking a utopia of religious freedom and finding it right there on Cupid's Cay.

From the swashbuckling days of bully boy pirates like Blackbeard, who terrorized foes by weaving hemp into his beard and lighting it on fire, and the vain Calico Jack Rackam, who by one report soiled his pantaloons while cowering in the hold....

To the influx of slaves and their Loyalist owners after the Americans won their independence, followed by the arrival of more Africans freed from slave ships after the British outlawed that lucrative trade.

From economic times so dire that "wrecking" became a favored endeavor, lighting misleading lanterns to lure unsuspecting ships onto rocky shores where their goods were looted....

To ambitious ventures in pineapples, poultry and dairy that flourished for a time, then mostly died away, leaving a stretch of strange landscape dotted with abandoned silos sprouting bushes from their tops.

From a post-war tourist boom when the pristine beaches became the rage with British tycoons and American movie stars, complete with tabloid snaps of a topless and pregnant Diana....

To another economic foundering in the '80s caused by changes in government rules and regs in the wake of the Bahamian independence from Britain.

And finally from the resurgence of the past decade when a popular travel mag made the island one of its top five up-and-comers, and music idols like Patti Labelle, Mariah Carey and Lenny Kravits found themselves splendid beachside abodes....

To a multitude of resort and condo plans, designed for gorgeous shores lapped by crystal clear water of surreal colors, all stopped in their tracks by the global financial meltdown.

When he's finished, Giles is practically gaping at him with admiration. And when the double chocolate tort arrives — the usual one dish, two forks — he says he's so happy that Giles changed his mind and traveled with him today, rather than waiting another day or two as originally planned. Everything is so much more wonderful when they can share it.

"Well," says Giles, "I'm going to have to be there through at least January, maybe mid-February, to keep Fernanda happy. I mean, I know her place is thriving and she's getting Banque Privee Morneau for a song. And without those stupid antiquated by-laws to deal with, she can get rid of whatever she doesn't want and really make a go of it. But I just want to make sure the sale goes smoothly."

"Of course."

"But there was nothing really keeping me in Geneva this week. So why not spend every minute I can down here with you and enjoy a full ten days together in our new place, helping you decorate and put our things on the walls and fucking your brains out every chance I get."

On the way home he drives the 3-year-old GMC SUV that came with house and tells Giles that he called Albert and Abigail, the Bahamian couple Tanner found to be their caretaker and housekeeper-cook. They'll be coming tomorrow afternoon for an interview. And as they approach the gate, which they left wide-open, he explains that he also tried calling Martin LeShore to ask why the electronic opener and video surveillance system is not up and running.

"I talked to his wife who said he's off island, in Miami buying parts for our setup, and won't be back until next week."

"Yes, whenever something hasn't been done, they're always off island getting parts. They think we're idiots." Giles almost sounds unhappy.

"Sweetheart, you need some sleep."

In the morning they're up relatively early and stand on the deck off the master suite, gazing at the green sea and the bright blue sky streaked with thin white clouds. The sun is already warm on the skin, the light breeze ruffles their hair and the surf here on the Atlantic side is calm today, with only small, soft, lapping waves.

"Incredible," says Giles.

He simply shakes his head.

By eight they climb down the steps to the beach, drop their suits and do their favorite morning thing, walking the beach on a highly competitive sand dollar hunt. The nearest house is a half-mile away, and there are no footprints on the smooth sand. As they move slowly, heads down, near the waterline, their eyes scour for one of those distinctive disks, always with those five narrow slots arrayed around that star relief. Frankly, he knows his lover is better at this, somehow less distractible, and soon, as if to prove it, Giles calls out,

"Yes!" The man is standing there, smiling proudly, naked as a baby and holding up a large one, bleached white. With that happy little dick free in the breeze, the man is pleased as can be, without a care. He loves seeing Giles this way.

And then as they move on, something unusual happens. He's visited by an unwanted thought, a feeling really. He's almost always transported on these beach walks, out of his mind, no matter how busy or confounded, and into a region of bliss. But now a scowling Clara seems somehow there, hidden somewhere along this lovely beach and watching them. He even looks up at the thick green bushes, the fringy Casaurina trees and the occasional palm lining the sand. And then, of course, he knows this is nonsense.

Maybe it comes from their little talk last night before falling off to sleep. Exhausted and a little drunk from that second bottle of wine, Giles asked what would happen with Cecile DeRochford's account if the loss of her funding to the charities were ever discovered.

But it won't be, he said. No one but Clara knew anything about it, and Clara's gone.

But what if it is? Giles insisted.

Well, if it is, as they both well know, they have arranged a record trail that casts the blame solely on Clara, a record trail that ultimately goes so cold that the funds she's been looting all these years must have been stashed somewhere so cleverly that they will never be found. And so their very own Clara Marche will instantly become one of the most infamous and admired criminals in the long and sordid history of banking. Giles murmured softly and within ten seconds was sound asleep.

Back from their walk, they're out on the new deck, staring at the perfect watery edge of the infinity pool. "I must say," says Giles, "everything considered, Tanner did an excellent job of making sure it was all finished well. Must have been the German in him."

"You think he had some German?"

"I always thought so, but I asked him once, and he denied it."

"Ah, Gerard, you had a crush on that lout. It was that big fat cock you thought he had."

It's funny, when they're on this island together, they love to tease each other in a way that never happens anywhere else.

Giles says, "So, you're jealous, my sweet Josef. And envious of his big one."

"Envious? We were in the men's room once, and I said, 'I'll show you mine, if you show me yours.' And, of course he couldn't resist. But then he was so tiny, so minute, that he could hardly get it to stick out of his pants."

Giles giggles like a teenager. Of course, their plan all along was to have the big shit eliminated once they no longer required his services. But that unfortunate episode with Clara and Tanner's failure to follow orders forced them to move things up. Now all that matters is how wonderful this world is without Tanner in it.

Chapter 35

At 10:30 Thursday morning, finished with breakfast and sitting with Marc in the shade of the tree over the deck at the Buc, she hears the Dell announce a new email. They glance at each other. She pulls it up and says, "Not Clara."

"Who then?" Marc sounds almost angry.

"Charles Mercier." Again she translates for him as she reads.

Dear Lina and Marc,

Just a brief missive to inform you of the initial results of my contact with Cecile's charities and my queries about the status of her donations over the past decade.

As of today, November 19, 2009, I have answers from just two of the ten charities so important to our generous and delightful Cecile. But the answers I have received appear at first blush so troubling, that it seemed clear I should not hold off informing you.

In each case, starting approximately five years ago, Cecile's contributions to each of these organizations were reduced to about 10 percent of what they had previously been, and they have remained at that level to the present time.

The most important and disturbing thing about these figures is that when compared to those contained in the quarterly and year-end statements provided to Cecile by Banque Privee Morneau, they match up without deviation until about five years ago, when they begin to diverge by close to 90 percent less on each and every statement of account.

It may be sometime before I am able to secure an accounting from all of the remaining eight charitable organizations. Some of them may well insist on clearing the release of this information with Banque Privee Morneau. Of course, with all these donations being shrouded in anonymity, the bank has been the only entity with whom these organizations have dealt.

I regret being the bearer of such unpleasant tidings, but given the concern you have expressed, I wanted to provide you with the earliest possible look at this information. Needless to say, as we have agreed, for the moment I will make no approach to anyone at Banque Privee Morneau concerning this matter.

Please let me know if you have need of any further, more detailed information that I might provide.

All the best and truly yours,

Charles P. Mercier, Esq.

Marc looks at her and shakes his head. "So Clara was exactly right about what she saw on Julian's computer screens."

"It appears so."

"And the murderers are here in the Bahamas because this is where they keep the millions they looted from Cecile and her charities."

"A good guess."

"And they're here on this out-of-the-way island because, in addition to being thieves and murderers, they have a secret life together."

"Also very likely."

They have been going on like this since last night, after Marc spent more than an hour in the three-room beach bar called Tippy's, and she walked the beach in the moonlight trying to make sense of what she just saw when they entered the place. Perhaps, they think if they keep talking about these things, saying them often enough, what has surely become obvious will finally seem less bizarre and incredible.

Last night, both of them sitting low in the Jeep's front seat, Marc said, "You're certain it's them?"

"Yes, of course. They look different, but it is them."

They sat in a dense silence for a time. Then he asked, "Does this mean they have something to do with Clara being here?"

Still feeling shocked and confused, she shook her head and said nothing. Marc asked exactly where she saw them, and they talked for a few minutes about what they could remember of the layout of the place after their brief look from the entrance.

Finally, Marc said, "Look, they've never seen me, and anyway they'll probably take me for a local. I'll go back in and try to sit as close to them as possible. I've got my phone that takes decent photos, and I still have my little video cam in my pocket. I'll do what I can to get some pictures. You just sit tight here and keep the doors locked."

She said okay, but after a few minutes, feeling unhappy and claustrophobic, she slipped out of the Jeep and moved back toward Tippy's. Perhaps she could manage another look at them from the back of the place. But when she approached a spot on the beachside deck where she might grab a glimpse of them, she knew they could easily turn and see her, and so she headed off down the beach. It would not be good if they saw her.

Inside Tippy's, Marc told her later, he quickly spotted the two men she described, "one of them among the most beautiful you might ever see." They were at a 4-top next to the wide opening to the back room, and, with the place crowded, he was fortunate to be shown to a table in that back room close to the murderers sitting there, quite oblivious to him. Also in that back room was a party of 10, and that was both good and bad. They were tourists, loud, boisterous at times, taking photos of each other, flashes going off frequently, then sharing their pictures around the table and producing shrieks of laughter. And so he was able to take shots with his phone, even with the flash going off, without his targets noticing. But for a long time he could hear almost nothing of what the two of them were saying. Finally, after he got two or three useable shots, the tourists left, and he could actually overhear a bit of the conversation.

"They were, of course, speaking French, so I couldn't understand much. But when the waitress came, they would speak English, and at the end when she brought the check, they were being friendly and asked her name and introduced themselves. But the one you say is Julian said his name was Josef, and his friend was Gerard."

"So they are using assumed names."

"Yes, and they are definitely lovers."

"Lovers?'

"Oh, yes, they were holding hands at one point, and I nearly got a picture, but I was just too late."

"Really. Lovers. I did not think of that. Morneau has a wife and two children."

"I know, but there's no question. Even when they were speaking French I caught a few words, like *Je t'aime*, and *belle nouvelle vie*. They were like newly-weds, all excited about a new life together."

"You used the video cam?"

"Yeah. At one point I just stood it up on the table, pointed it at them and let it run. It's small but actually takes pretty good movies."

Marc explained that sitting in there he began to think they should follow these guys home. And so he waited them out, even though he was long finished with his lobster pizza and kept nursing his second Kalik, while they were heading through a second bottle of wine. And even though he was starting to worry again about leaving her alone. He tried calling her mobile, but it went to voice mail.

Yes, when she left the Jeep she was so preoccupied she forgot her purse with the mobile in it. And when it finally dawned on her that he might want to call and coordinate, she moved carefully back to the parking lot, thinking they might come out of the restaurant at any moment. She grabbed the purse and quickly headed back to the beach.

Finally, when he called again from the Jeep, he said he was relieved to hear her voice. But the bankers had already driven off, and there was no chance to follow them. He wanted to go back in to get her something to eat, but her appetite was gone.

In the morning on Marc's laptop, they were looking again at his photos and video from last night. Yes, the hair was almost unrecognizable, their faces glowed with a careless pleasure unseen in Geneva, and she had never encountered them in sandals, shorts and pastel print shirts. But whatever they called themselves, Josef and Gerard were without question the murderers Julian and Giles.

Alone on the beach last night, she wondered about the fact that to her they were surely murderers now. She had no proof at all. She also had no doubt. Would either of them personally raise a hand to another human being? Their hand was not needed with Cecile. It took only a word. The same with Clara, except according to her story, the dead man Tanner chose not to follow the word. There seemed no question that Clara's email was connected with the murderers' presence here, but the nature of that connection was a clueless puzzle.

Suddenly it seemed astonishing that she was thinking about such things while walking a beach in the Bahamas. It felt so long since she had functioned as a scholar, and there were times lately when she wondered if she had lost her bearings, even lost herself. As if she had somehow slipped away from what had always defined the core of her being. She felt almost like a different person at times. And yet, she was forced to admit, there were also times when she actually felt she was only now discovering her true, authentic self.

As she carried her sandals, the sand felt soft and fine, and then so firm as she moved close to the small waves curling and spreading up to her. If this were another time, if the murderers were not right up the beach, she would be out of her clothes and into this surf, her skin reveling in its total caress. But she already felt vulnerable here, and this was no time to make herself feel more so. As Marc said, it did seem as if there could be danger for them in this place. There was definitely uncertainty here, but also, she had to admit, a kind of excitement. She felt totally focused here, as she usually did only when she was writing, and constantly alive to her surroundings in a way that seemed akin only to those special times in a classroom with her most talented and inquiring students.

A lovely beach was always one of her favorite places on earth. Yet it had been a long time since she set foot on one. Was it Rimini? Croatia? Mykonos? And under a sky like the one last night, with a full moon laying a vivid, rippling shaft on the sea, and with a clear, cloudless expanse that went on forever, gleaming with bright stars beyond number, in spite of everything she felt an amazed glow in her heart.

On the Buc's deck now she wonders why she has forgone this pleasure for so long. Is she is holding out to share it with a treasured someone else? There has been no one in her life like that since poor John.

Another email arrives at 11 am, this one with the subject line, "On

Eleuthera?"

"From Clara," she says and begins turning the message into English:

Dearest Lina and (I hope) Marc, also Willem.

She stops and looks at Marc. "Also Willem?" he says. "She doesn't know he's been murdered."

"Yes. She sent this to his address as well." He shakes his head, and she goes on:

> Today is 19-11-09. It has not changed for me. I hope you are on Eleuthera. This is my captor: a small thin man, says he is Geneva police, and drives a red car. About my location: We exited the airport to the right. Sign to Governor's Harbour. Then a blindfold. Drove more than 20 minutes, some turns, different speeds, last minutes on a dirt road. I can hear the ocean. If you are on Eleuthera: only within 2 minutes click on reply all and write "yes."

> Please nothing more.

> All my love.

> Clara

He stares off, clearly trying to decide what to make of this. She reads it again to herself.

He says, "At least it sounds like I might have been driving around in the right area yesterday."

"And the red car?"

"Yes, maybe that was the guy following me. I couldn't see him very clearly. You should write back 'yes.'" She does, and he asks, "Is the address she used for Tanner the same one you sent messages to?"

"Yes," she says, and five minutes later another email arrives from that same address.

> Meet me in GH. Walk down the hill. You will see me sitting on the seawall at the water's edge, behind the baseball field. We will save her.

> Willem Tanner

Marc says, "Christ. So now we're supposed to meet a dead man?"

"Apparently so."

"Yes, well, it's like we've walked through a mirror or something. People show up where they have no business being, or they suddenly come back from the dead."

Chapter 36

In Norma's Gifts, the shop right next to the small building housing the police (and Eluethera's one jail cell), he finds a good-sized beach bag. In red, white and blue canvas, this one has letters stitched in the side that say Kalik "It's a Bahamian ting." It has a zipper to close it up over all those euros.

As he walks out and hits the sun, he lifts his wrap-arounds out of the pocket of the light blue shirt he wears over his jeans. He slips on the black glasses, then glances at his left wrist. The Movado is not there. Of all the things he left with Tremelyn, that was the one he regretted. Moving off the porch, he turns left at the corner and heads down the street along the seawall. He doesn't need a watch any more, not with the phone he always carries. He pulls it out: 11:32. More than enough time to think everything through one more time before they arrive.

When he woke this morning, he immediately felt wide-eyed and alert, as if all night he'd been wrapped in a bright, cogent dream, one that made perfect sense and clearly signaled the start of a special day. His big day, the day when all his careful scheming would click into place, the day when those faggot banker boys would finally get fucked, the day when he'd take whatever he wanted from those pricks. Maybe their new beach house, certainly their secret fortune and definitely their useless little lives.

The only thing left will be to shuck these other two, and that should pose no problem. Not after getting them to travel thousands of miles here to attend their own murders. That was a brilliant stroke, finding a way to get them all together on remote, peaceful Eleuthera, with no crime, few cops and easy access to a multitude of places where a body will never be found. No, this island is perfect for a murder, or four. In almost every way, the polar opposite from busy Amsterdam, where less than a week ago he needed the police to find a shot-gunned Tremelyn.

On Saturday, waiting to meet his former colleague at the beer bar In De Wildeman, he really had no plan, knowing only that he needed to do Tremelyn before Tremelyn did him. Only when the guy came through the door and called, "Hey, Twin!" did the plan begin to take shape.

"Twin" was what certain members of the force called both of them back in the day. Yes, they were both blonds and wore their hair very short, and while he was maybe a half-centimeter taller, they did have similar body types. But, he had always considered Tremelyn, though a tech geek, a bit dense and so loathed the nickname. That of course only spurred its use by a cadre of jealous cops who resented Tanner's position in the department and his closeness to the chief. It was typical of Tremelyn that he soon decided the way to disarm the slur was to embrace it, which led to, among other things, absurd phone messages that began, "Hey, Twin. Twin here."

As they drank their way through three rounds of their favorite lagers, Tremelyn claimed to be on holiday, visiting friends in the city and, since he was in the neighborhood, had stopped in at the Blue Parrot to say hello to Ghete. Savoneau and Tremelyn had known he and Ghete were tight ever since that business trip the three of them made to Amsterdam several years ago for Dubonne. About Savoneau, Tremelyn said he was in Marseille visiting Bibi, Tanner's cousin with the big boat. While he did have a sleek 50-footer, Bibi was not his cousin. He was a boyhood chum who had dealt in stolen securities and had an occasional need for certain favors that Tanner could supply. On two memorable occasions the three of them had partied on that boat, and Savoneau had probably gone to the other obvious place to look for him. Maybe they drew straws to see who'd get the more pleasant climate.

What about Clara, his old girlfriend from the bank? Anything new on her disappearance? Tremelyn played dumb (not hard for him to do) and said he and Savoneau had heard nothing.

Tanner suggested lunch at a café they knew in another, quieter part of town and his old colleague quickly agreed, probably thinking it would be a better place to take care of business. On the way to the Mercedes, still parked in Ghete's garage, they walked a half-dozen blocks and crossed a canal. Tremelyn said he'd love to live on one of those big houseboats looking so peaceful lining the canal. As they entered the garage, which at the moment held three cars and no owners, Willem pulled the SIG-Sauer from the pocket of his black leather and gave him more peace than he ever could have wanted. The shot to the head echoed like a backfire, and he quickly popped the Mercedes trunk, pulled out his suitcase, and replaced it with Tremelyn.

Then a long, leisurely drive out of the city to a rural area where he soon found a large tract that seemed abandoned, with a falling down house and a big empty shed. Behind a line of trees that hid the place from the road, he backed the Mercedes up to the shed, unloaded the body and undressed it. Then he shed his own clothes, donned a shirt and jeans from the warm-clothes bag he still had with him, and on an afternoon that had turned dreary, damp and cold, he was happy he had brought along his crazy-looking disguise, the sweater and fedora. Once Tremelyn was in Tanner's clothes, including the black leather, and in possession of the personal items, from the passport and wallet to the gold chain and the Movado, he took time to arrange the body precisely, hands propped in front of the face. Working fast but with care, he made a small bonfire of everything that belonged to Tremelyn, except his mobile, then pulled the KS-23 from its hidden compartment in the Mercedes and made absolutely certain that one blast took out everything he wanted gone. He carefully wiped down the shotgun and tossed it into the trunk along with the remains, now minus most of the head and hands. Then he drove to Schiphol.

At the airport with his suitcase and his laptop, he walked into the terminal a new man, literally. With the new identity he had brought from his safe in Geneva, he was David Marcuse from Lucerne, and the first thing Marcuse did was book a flight to Nassau leaving the next morning, Sunday, at 7:30. He spent the rest of the day and evening in the terminal restaurants, bars and public areas, thinking about who this Marcuse guy was, his background and history, his parents, schools, jobs, and ex-wives. In his ugly hat and sweater, he obviously had shitty taste, but that would change, and he even gave himself a son, an adventurous young man working as an Amazon tour guide. It was an amusing exercise but exhausting, and he slept soundly most of the night in a lounge chair with his feet up. Just before 5 he woke and used Tremelyn's phone to call the Amsterdam police and then text the message to Dubonne.

Once on the island he picked up the car from Stanton and in Governor's Harbour took an apartment at the Laughing Bird, the first place he ever stayed here, before the boys bought the house. The Bird was a run-down property with no Internet, but there was a view of the bay and Cupid's Cay, and he could walk a few steps to the library when he needed a connection.

On Monday he was reading again through Clara's long letter to the old woman when he noticed that on the back of the fax page she had scribbled her Gmail address and its password. And then he knew how he would get the Italian professor and probably also Clara's American lover to Eleuthera. He was already convinced that the boys, thinking he was dead, would be coming soon. And, sure enough, on Tuesday a note arrived from Marcel at the bank, saying, "Julian has officially departed the bank, and Giles leaves tomorrow for 10 days."

Then it was just a matter of staking out the tiny airport at the right times. On Tuesday the red-headed woman he had seen at the hospital arrived with the black man, and he followed them to the Buccaneer. He had a mind to go ahead and take care of the black guy when he followed him around from beach to beach yesterday. But he finally decided that would only alarm the redhead. Better to play them off against the boys, and more or less do everyone at once.

Chapter 37

Sitting on the cement seawall that borders the side road along the harbor, he sees them at the bottom of the hill, walking past the liquor store about 100 meters away and heading in his direction. He's worked over the details and rehearsed a few times what he'll tell them and the deal he'll offer. He feels good about his story and about the chance they'll buy it, even though a few small things might seem shaky if they think about them too much.

The difference-maker is the chance to save Clara. They haven't come this far, so many thousands of miles, to say no to that chance. The one thing he's not sure of is whether they'll know him. He ditched the blue cap to give them a better view, but do they even know what he looks like? And if not, and with no genuine ID, how much will he have to tell them?

As they approach, he gets up from the wall and throws the beach bag straps over his shoulder. The woman moves a step or two ahead, staring at him with her head cocked slightly. "*Êtes-vous Willem Tanner?*"

He pushes the wrap-arounds up on his forehead. "*Oui.* That is me."

"You speak English?"

"Not well, but yes."

The black man says, "The Amsterdam paper said you're dead."

"An exaggeration." He gives them something between a smile and a smirk.

"Mark Twain," says the black man, his dark eyes boring in.

"I apologize," he says. "My English...."

" A famous American writer," says the woman, her green eyes curious. "I have your photograph, and I saw you at the hospital where my friend Cecile died. Why were you there?"

So much for concerns about his true identity. "Because my boss, Giles Morneau, told me to go there to find out her condition. He was very concerned."

"Yes, I know he was."

"Look," says the American, "we know what Clara has said about you, and about the bank and its owner. We might as well cut right to why we're all here."

"Okay, good."

"So why are you here?"

"Because I have business here. With Morneau. He owes me money. And also for the same reason as you. Because of Clara. I was already here, but I got probably the same message asking to help as you. And then this morning she writes again to us both."

The Italian woman glances at the American and then back at him. "Do you want to stay here and talk, or go somewhere for coffee."

"The picnic table over there is free, and there is no one to hear. This is a small place."

"Yes," she says as they head across the road toward the table. "I understand."

The man says, "So how is it that you're not dead, when everyone thinks you are?"

He stares at the American. "I stayed with a friend in Amsterdam. And then a man I knew for a long time with the Geneva police, a fellow named Tremelyn, came there to kill me. He failed, and I allowed him to take my place."

For a moment they look at each other. Then they sit at the table across from him. The woman finally says, "And so now you are someone else. What should we call you?"

"I think just Willem."

"Okay, Willem," says the man. "So do you know where Clara is on this island?"

"Yes."

"You do." The man sounds surprised. "How do you know?"

They are both watching carefully, and he says, "This is the story that Tremelyn, the man who came to Amsterdam, told me. He and my old partner on the Geneva police, Claude Savoneau, took her from Malpensa when she tried to fly to you. Then they made a plan to exchange her dead for money from the bankers."

"Exchange her dead?"

"Blackmail," says the woman.

The American nods. "So why would this fellow tell you that?"

233

"He did not want to, but..." Tanner lifts a hand from the table and makes a small gesture, twisting the palm up.

The American eyes him and nods again. The woman says, "But why would this man Savoneau bring Clara here?"

"Because he knows this is a quiet place, not many police, and they know the bankers were coming here soon."

"How would they know something like that?" the woman asks.

"They know because the bankers are very close to the police in Geneva. The chief."

"The Geneva Municipal Police."

"Yes."

"Okay," says the American, "go on. So where are Savoneau and Clara on this island? And how do you know that?"

"First, because I have come here many times for the bankers, I know the people here. I know the ones here that rent cars and run taxis. There are not many. And so I ask them when I come here on Sunday. I describe Savoneau and then Clara, and I ask them. And the first one I ask, he knows them and where they stay. You know, most of them don't care about the license or ask you to sign a paper. They just want to know where you stay."

"Was it Stanton who told you?"

"No, another one. He says they are at a home by itself on Banks Road. I know it. Not so far from here."

"Have you been there?" the man asks quickly. "Have you seen Clara?"

"No, I went there, but you cannot see her from outside. And to go inside, I want you to help. If you agree."

"Of course we agree," says the man.

"Agree to what exactly?" says the woman, giving a quick rub to each of her forearms. Her skin is freckled, but he also notices a number of small red bumps.

"You have no-see-ums," he says, nodding at the bites.

"No-see-ums?" she says.

"Yes, small insects that bite. So small you do not see them. Usually around the beach, at night."

"Yes, I have them on my ankles also. I was on the beach last night, at the restaurant, Tippy's. We walked in, and I saw the bankers there and turned right around and walked out. They did not see us, and because they do not know Marc, he went back in. And I walked on

234

the beach."

"So you know they are already here."

"Of course," says the man. "I took photos of them inside Tippy's."

Tanner stares at him. "So, if you agree, I will take you to their home, and you can make your photos of the house outside, and maybe the inside also."

"And how would we do that?" says the man. "And, again, agree to what?"

He eyes them both. Everything has gone well so far. Now he must try his plan. He points to the man. "I need you to go to the front door while I go to the back."

"Why would I do that? And what do I say?"

"You say anything you want, to keep them busy with you for a few minutes. Maybe say you are from some magazine, and their home is so beautiful you would like to come in and take photos for the magazine readers. If they say yes, you go in and take the photos. If they say no, you can still take the outside, from the front and also from the beach."

"And you will go in the back. Why?"

"Because if they see me, they know I am not dead, and there is trouble." He reaches below the table and brings up the beach bag. "So, to make it easy, I go in the back, bring this and fill it with euros from a safe I know."

The man glances at the woman and then says, "So how do you know this safe?"

"As I told you, I have come here many times for the past year or two. To oversee the work on the house they buy. They wanted many changes. In the kitchen, in the bathrooms, other places. And I told them to put in this secret hidden safe. It is in the laundry room near the back door. With electronic controls. State of the art."

"And how much is in this hidden safe?"

"One million euros. Just-in-case cash, ready for emergency."

The woman shakes her head. "You know how to open it."

"I know exactly how to open it. I found this for them and had it installed."

The American says, "So why not just wait until the bankers are away from the house. Out to dinner or doing errands?"

"Because the whole place is wired with alarms. And surveillance cameras. If anyone tries to enter when they are not home, the power for the electronic safe is automatically to shut down. Then there is no way you get in until the whole system is reset. And this can be done only with a computer program I do not have. It is a system I read about in a bulletin from Interpol that was set up for the mansion of a Russian billionaire who was a criminal. I brought a guy here to design it and set it up."

The black man glares off at the harbor, then gets to his feet to stand in front of Tanner. "Okay, so you help us rescue Clara, and then we'll help you make your haul from the bankers."

Tanner says, "Yes, okay, but not in that order. First, we go to the bankers' house, and then we go to the house with Savoneau and Clara. I am not asking so much from you. Only go to the front door of each house and talk to the bankers for some minutes, then the same with Savoneau. And then you get Clara safe and sound."

The woman asks, "What happens at the house where Savoneau is holding Clara?"

"Same thing," he says. "My problem is that I cannot approach either the bankers' front door or Savoneau's. They will know as soon as they see me something is wrong. The bankers will not let me in, and Savoneau will probably shoot me right through the door. But none of them know this man, and all I need is for him to go to each front door while I get in the house through another door or window."

The black man shakes his head. "Okay, we need your help to save Clara, and you need me to get what you want from the bankers. So we get Clara first."

"No, the problem for you is I don't need you. I can get someone else to go to their front door. No problem. No, you come with me to the bankers' first, or no deal."

The American is obviously angry, dropping his gaze to the table, then staring at him hard. With his own gaze unwavering, Tanner tells him, "Yes, you don't trust me. And I don't trust you. But unless we trust each a little, this will not happen. If we do trust, when we go to go to Savoneau's place, I will handcuff him, and rescue Clara. Then you and Clara can return to Geneva with Clara's story and the information I can add, and you will clear Clara and bring down the bankers."

The man stares at the woman, who says, "Handcuff him? Why not wait until he leaves the house and then take Clara?"

"Because I know Savoneau. He was my partner for more than 20 years. He is devious and dangerous. I want to know exactly where he is at all times. Once we have all left here and have all we want, I will call the police here and say where to find him."

He pauses and watches the man and woman once again look at each other. Then both turn their gaze at him. "So we have a deal?" he asks.

With angry eyes the American sits back down. In an even voice he says, "We have a deal."

Chapter 38

"Helpful fella," he says, the sarcasm dripping.

They are walking back in the direction of the blue and yellow liquor store, and she says, "Yes, an interesting killer."

They have just left Tanner, and he has a strong urge to glance back and see if the guy's still sitting there at the table, watching them walk away, or if he too has moved off and, if so, in what direction. Not wanting to seem worried, he resists the urge.

They've spent the last 15 minutes, after agreeing to the deal, talking mostly about the bankers. What Tanner has been doing for them, what they've done with the money, what kind of connection they have with the police in Geneva, and what their plans are now for a new life together. Most of the questions came from Lina. Again he noted how nothing gets past her.

Of course she wondered about Tanner's line that he might provide information to help clear Clara and bring the bankers down. Just what might that be?

Tanner said maybe that should wait until their deal was done.

No way, said Marc. Not when they had no idea what might happen in the wake of their little heist and rescue operation. They might never have a chance to talk again.

Tanner stared at them for a long time and then said, "Well, one thing you should know is they have new identities."

"Josef and Gerard," said Marc.

"So you know."

"No, that's all we know. I heard them using those names last night at Tippy's. What are their full names?"

He nods. "Josef Simon and Gerard Bitou. I got them everything. Passports, driver's license, credit cards, everything."

Lina was clearly making mental notes. She said, "And I assume you got yourself everything as well. So what is your new name?"

"That I should not tell you. It is safer for you, better for me."

"Then," said Lina, "tell us about what you have been doing for them down here? What about this house?"

And about this the guy opened up: about the role he played in the purchase of the house, and all the changes made to it; about the bankers' long-term plan to buy seaside property and build a mansion of their own design. When she asked how all this work was paid for, Tanner said the boys would send funds through a Nassau bank from the private—secret, he called it—firm they had set up also in Nassau, to his own account at the Royal Bank of Canada with its branch in Governor's Harbour. And then he would pay the contractors. What was the name of this secret firm? she asked. This, he said, he didn't know. Marc found that hard to believe. It would surely be something Tanner would make a point of learning.

So, said Lina, talk about this long-term plan. Obviously the boys wanted a secret life together, but how were they going to pull it off? Tanner smirked and said they were simply going to disappear. As far as he could determine, Julian, or Josef, was down here for good now and Giles, or Gerard, would soon follow.

Leaving behind his wife and kids? asked Marc.

Oh, yes, said Tanner.

Lina asked how they were going to keep up this ruse. Sooner or later they were going to run into someone who knew them. By changing their appearance, said Tanner. Maybe with plastic surgery, maybe with less extreme ways. Morneau had more than once talked about the possibility of staging his own death.

And what about the bank? Tanner said he wasn't certain but had picked up hints that it would soon be sold.

Finally, Lina asked about this "connection" with the Geneva Municipal Police. Again Tanner was forthcoming. Surprisingly so. The connection was something that went back to childhood between Morneau and the chief, a man named Alain Dubonne. The bank, he said, was washing money in at least two different accounts, each fronted by a South American national, including one for Dubonne himself, and the other for a drug cartel. The main thing was not to deal with the Municipal Police. Go only to the Swiss National Police.

Then Tanner said how about if he picked them up at the Buccaneer in 15 minutes. They can all go in his SUV.

Lina asked, "How do you know we are at the Buccaneer?"

Tanner paused before saying, "I have seen you walking in the town."

Marc: "And you followed us there."

"No, I just saw you there."

Marc glared at him. "Well, anyway it will be only me coming with you. Lina will not come."

She looked at him sharply. "No, I want to come."

"No, if you come, the deal is off. Period. Anyway, we'll talk about this later."

They were about to leave, and almost as if he were offering a distraction from their sudden disagreement, the guy pointed at the bites on Lina's ankles and said, "The best thing for those is called Iverest. You can buy it at the Shell. And maybe if you are allergic, they will swell and blister, and you should take some antihistamine."

"Thank you," said Lina and looked at Marc with a displeased smile as they walked away.

Now as they approach the corner where they chatted yesterday with Daniel, Jamie and the chef from Tippy's, she says, "So what just happened back there? Why did you step on me?"

He stops and, surprising himself, takes her hand. He finds anger in her glinting green eyes. "Lina, I'm sorry, but I'm very leery of this guy. I don't trust him at all. I have no idea if we'll see Clara today, or ever again. But I need to do this. I'll go with him and keep my guard up, but there is not the slightest chance I'm going to let you put yourself in harm's way with this guy. You say he's an interesting killer. No, he's just a flat-out stone killer. Nothing interesting about him. I've met guys like him on the street, and I've interviewed them in prison. I can see it in his eyes. They're dead. And we will be too if we're not careful."

She squeezes his hand and doesn't let it go. "Marc, listen..."

"No, you listen. I have no doubt—whether or not Clara is on this island—he has no intention of letting us leave here alive."

Now she surprises him by moving to his chest and holding him close. "Please, Marc. Of course you are right. About everything. Of course he is a killer. And that is why I must come with you. Two against one, you might at least have a chance."

He holds her for a moment, then moves back to see her eyes again. They're pleading now. "I'm sorry," he says, "but I could never forgive myself if something happened to you here. Look, I'm no hero, but I can handle myself. And we'll stay in touch. Our phones work here, even on the beach. I'll keep you posted as much as possible. When we get there and he goes for the back entrance, I'll call and tell you exactly where we are and how to get there. Really, you can be more of a help to me that way. Maybe you'll go to the police and bring them. Or…"

She stops him with a smile. "Okay, Marc, you win."

"Really?"

"Yes, really, but you must call me as soon as you can."

No longer holding hands, as they walk up the hill to the Buc he pulls his phone from the pocket of his shirt. He pushes a couple of buttons, then puts it to his ear. After several seconds, though the volume is low, he can hear distinctly Lina's voice saying, "Êtes-vous Willem Tanner?"

And Tanner's voice replies, "*Oui*. That is me."

Lina: "You speak English."

Tanner: "Not well, but yes."

He hands her the phone and says, "Listen."

She does and is soon shaking her head. "You recorded all of it?"

"Sounds like it."

"Why didn't you tell me?"

"I didn't want to make you nervous. I'll dump it all in your Dell later."

When she hands it back, he peels off the small piece of duck tape covering the corner of the phone where the light is located, the one that was flashing red the whole time with Tanner.

They sit at a table near the deck's center, and she says, "Promise you will call."

"I promise."

"And tell me exactly how to find you. So I can get in the Jeep and drive right there."

"Lina, I promise."

Chapter 39

At a table on the deck close to the bar entrance a couple is eating lunch. Somewhere in their 60s, both sport heavy tans and ample waistlines. At the moment they're both grinning at him. Lina is sitting with her back to them, and he gives the couple a quick smile and nod, then concentrates on Lina's face. The last thing he wants right now is to chat with strangers.

"Hi, there!" says the guy. "First time on Eleuthera?"

Knowing Lina is gregarious and more likely to respond, he quickly mutters under his breath, "Official greeters." He wants to talk about what Tanner said, what made sense and what did not, why he was open on some things and not on others. They have only a few minutes, and he needs to cut this short. He looks at the couple. "Yes, our first. Great place." And then, turning back to Lina: "Are you up for something to eat?"

But the guy will not be stopped. "Mac and Margo McGinnis, Thunder Bay, Ontario. How about you folks? Where you from?"

He looks back at them and doesn't smile. "Detroit. And the lady here is from Italy."

"Really!" The man sounds delighted.

"Italy!" says the woman. "Another beautiful country, so I'm told."

As Lina half-turns, he says, "Yes, it is." And then getting to his feet, he says loud enough for them to hear, "He's going to be here any minute. I need to get my camera."

"Would you bring my Dell?"

"Of course." He's already moving past the couple on his way to the room. Inside he grabs the Nikon in its case and throws the strap over his shoulder. He slips the Flip in the pocket of his jeans and then looks around the room. He wonders if there's anything else here that might help him with what's ahead? Or maybe, he thinks, he's just taking one last look at a place he'll never see again. "Watch your back," he tells himself aloud.

On the deck he finds Lina turned in her chair and talking with the super-friendly Canadians. "Marc," she says, "Mac and Margo here run that website that was so helpful to us. Remember, Eleuthera Living dot com?"

"Oh, right, yes, very helpful." He puts the Dell down in front of her. From the look she gives him, he knows she's found some use for these people.

"Hey, Marc," says his new friend, "your lovely lady here tells us you make documentaries. We could sure use your skills around here to spread the word about our wonderful isle of freedom. There's nothing like movin' pictures to sell a beautiful place."

"Well, right you are, Mac. That would certainly be a labor of love."

About to sit, he sees Tanner pull up at the corner in a blue SUV, an old Honda Pilot, he thinks. "There's my ride," he tells Lina. "See you in a little while."

"Call me."

"Right." And then to the McGinnises: "Great to meet you folks. See you again."

The guy actually stands up, straining for a better look at the Honda and its driver. "Right back at you, Marc."

As he reaches the Honda, he can hear old Mac saying to his wife, "Hey, isn't that Will Tanner?" But when he slips into the passenger seat, Tanner is looking away from the deck and acts as if he hasn't heard his name. He shoves it in gear and takes off.

Marc says, "That guy back there seems to know you."

"Which guy?"

"Name's McGuinnis. He and his wife run a website here."

"Yes, I met him once. Wanted to know more than I would tell him."

"He's still like that."

Two turns on residential streets and they are soon at the Queen's Highway. They head north, away from Governor's Harbour and toward the airport. Tanner drives just over the limit. Marc asks, "So, where is this place?"

"You will see soon. It takes only a few minutes."

"Atlantic side, or Caribbean?"

In his black wrap-around mask, the guy looks pissed. "Atlantic."

Marc wonders again what appealed to amiable, good-hearted

243

Clara about this tough, cryptic ex-cop and ex-con. And killer. He asks, "So what do you think Clara saw in you back when you met?"

The guy shakes his head. "What did she see in you? A black American who does not speak the same language."

He doesn't like the way Tanner made "black" sound but lets it go. "Maybe, as we say in English, there's no accounting for taste."

"Yes, I think so."

"And why didn't you carry out the assignment?"

"Assignment?"

"Yes, to kill her."

Tanner pauses, then says, "I did not want to."

"Yes, but why?"

"Maybe it was the smile."

He nods his understanding and for the first time feels some slight kinship with this asshole. He needs to keep track of where they're going, and he better concentrate on that. And just then Tanner takes a right onto a narrow paved road, and Marc sneaks a look at his watch.

"It was five minutes from the town," says Tanner.

"Yeah."

The guy is a clever animal. Marc turns to look back at the main road. About 30 yards to the north he spots a small cement block structure, half-built and overgrown with bushes. Another minute or so and Tanner turns left on a road that once, decades ago, had some asphalt but is now a backbreaker. The Honda bounces, and Tanner jerks the wheel one way and then the other. Finally, they reach a smoother, packed-sand road that angles off to the right, cutting between trees and heavy shrubs for a while. And then there's a clearing and a pair of old stone posts holding a new metal gate, opened wide. On each post is a small, weathered sign. One says, "The Wrights," the other, "No Trespassing." Obviously an entryway that twists through heavy vegetation to an unseen home. Tanner slows but doesn't stop until they're well past the gate, pulling the Honda into low scrub and shutting it down.

As they get out, Marc asks, "How far up there is it?"

"Three, four minute walk." Tanner carries the beach bag.

With the Nikon on a strap around his neck, Marc powers it on. "And the Wrights were the previous owners?"

"Yes."

He raises the camera enough to see its screen. "So how much did the boys pay for this place?"

Tanner gives him a look. "It was listed four million, but..." The shutter button sounds a soft click. The guy looks angry. "Do not do that. No pictures."

"Sorry." He moves toward the gate waiting for Tanner to say delete it.

Instead the guy says, "You walk up the road. I know a way around they cannot see."

"You're sure they're home?"

"I called."

"Okay, what time do you want me at the front door?" He looks at his watch. "It's 1:06."

"One fifteen," says Tanner and then he leaves the road and disappears into what looks like impenetrable jungle.

Walking up the road to the house, he wants to leave himself time for shots of the front. As he heads around the first bend he begins to see the place. Definitely big, white stucco with a red tile roof, a large two-floor section flanked by single-floor wings. He can hear waves breaking on the beach. There's not much breeze on this side, but the taller palms are rustling. A large porch has steps leading up to a pair of handsomely paneled doors with no windows, and parked in front is the black GMC Yukon they left Tippy's in last night. He stops to takes several shots, moving up and back and side to side, having trouble getting it all in.

As he gets closer, he checks out the large sliding windows, four across the second floor, one on each side of the front doors and two in each wing. None of them show coverings. No blinds drawn or curtains, and no one seems to be watching from them. As he reaches the front steps he glances at his watch. It's 1:14, and then he remembers the call he promised Lina. It's too late now. It'll have to wait. He snaps a few shots of their SUV and the driveway to the house, then pushes the doorbell button and hears a chime inside.

And suddenly he wants to confront these guys, call them murderers and frighten the shit out of them. Soft, unhurried steps approach the door, and then it opens.

Standing there is Julian in bare feet, a teal tee and tan shorts, the curly hair disheveled, that beautiful face red and blotched, the eyes bloodshot. He's been crying, or maybe still feeling the effects of a terrible row.

Disoriented by the guy's look, instead of confrontation he says, "Hello, sir."

Julian looks him over, then says something that sounds French: "Al bare?"

Uncertain, he says, "Yes?"

"Albare, this is not a good time. Please come back later."

So he's been taken for someone else and says, "Yes, sir, but…"

"Thank you," says Julian and swings the door firmly shut.

He stands there feeling stupid. After a few seconds, he turns and heads back down the steps and past the GMC. And then he stops. Has he carried out his part of the deal? Tanner wanted a few minutes, and that little fiasco just now took no more than 20 seconds. If they discover Tanner in this house, there is no telling what might happen with the rest of the deal. On the chance that Clara is really on this island, he needs to go back to that door. And so he does.

Once again he pushes the button and hears the chime, and this time he waits for quite a while before there are faint sounds of an approach inside. He's thinking the hell with confrontation, just do what you can here and then save Clara. The door opens, and Giles Morneau is standing there in a skimpy red bathing suit. The face is somber, maybe sad, but with nothing like Julian's raw emotion.

"Yes?"

"Hello, sir, my name is Marcus, and I'm a photographer." He raises the Nikon a few inches and watches Morneau's gaze move there. He tells himself to speak slowly and says, "I often do work for the web site Eleuthera Living, and Mr. McGinnis, who runs the site, asked me to come out and see if you might allow me to come in and take a few photographs of your beautiful home."

Morneau says quickly, "Yes, we appreciate the thought, but…"

He pushes ahead. "I realize this might not be a good time, but it would only take a minute or two, and we've heard so many wonderful things about what you've done with this great home. The beautiful additions and elegant touches, and people, of course, are dying to have a look." He actually finishes with a nod and a smile.

"Interesting," says Morneau. "But thank you, this is not the right time. And frankly I cannot say there will ever be a right time. We are private people and do not wish to have it otherwise. So things will need to stay as they are."

He nods again. "I appreciate how you feel, sir, and thanks for your time."

"Thank you for understanding, and good day to you."

With that the door closes again. He looks at his watch. It says 1:19.

Chapter 40

In the laundry room he stands stock still, listening carefully but hearing nothing more. Outside, while he was approaching the locked door and then finding the key in his jeans, he heard the door chime twice. Then the muted, unintelligible voices of Morneau and the American drifted down to him for a while, until maybe a half-minute ago when he thinks the front door closed. Now the black guy is probably outside and moving away from the house.

But can he trust this guy? Is it possible he just told Morneau that Willem Tanner was about to rob him blind? Possible, but not likely. Not when the fellow thinks Clara's life is at stake. And what about the Italian woman? He knows they both have their doubts, could see it in the looks they exchanged when he was talking with them by the harbor. That's why he told them more than he probably should have—to win at least enough of their confidence to pull this off. The woman is smart and sexy, looks and acts like nobody's fool and someone well aware of her sexual lure. Now there's a thought. Give her one last good fuck before he's done. The guy is suspicious and carries himself okay, but word around the bank was that Clara's American beau made TV shows. So, no, not very likely to show much physical moxie, especially with a gun in his face. Overall, their fear factor? Not as high as the faggot boys. Gullibility quotient? They are sharper, more aware than he might like, but the fact is they've crossed an ocean to be here with him. Of course, the bottom line is, none of this really matters. Those two along with the cocksuckers will all stop breathing within the next hour or so.

He pulls the SIG-Sauer from the beach bag, then reaches in past the box of rounds he won't need (one shot each to the head is the plan, but just in case...) and takes the silencer. He twists it into place on the barrel, and he's ready to head up.

There are two ways to the first floor from this bottom level, which, in addition to this laundry, holds a game room, storage space, a

248

utility room and, under the entrance hall, a large cistern filled with rainwater off the roof. Off the game room near the front is the main stairway that continues up to the second floor. And back here from the laundry is the narrow stairs to the kitchen. He uses this one, moving up silently.

At the top of the stairs he pauses, listens, then comes through the door to the open kitchen and dining area. It's all part of the great room arrayed across the beachside of the house, lined with large windows and door walls that open onto a deck with sweeping views of the sea. And there, in front of him, walking now between the new marble counters and looking especially soft and vulnerable in nothing but his red bathing brief, is Morneau.

No more than 10 feet away, the man stops dead and actually jerks his head back with the shock of seeing a ghost. A familiar yet, no doubt, fearsome ghost directly in front of him now and pointing the SIG-Sauer and its silencer straight at his face. He utters a short, piercing, terrified scream and then shrieks, "*Mon Dieu!*"

In a low voice in French, Tanner says, "I don't think He will help you. So speak softly. Where is Lyon?"

"What?" Morneau is shaking and seems unable to comprehend a simple question.

"Your precious Jules. Where is he?"

"He's…" A pause, a blank, drained face, with two stunned blinks, then, "On the beach. We, we…had a fight. He went for a walk."

"So then, already trouble in paradise."

Morneau holds himself, arms across his chest, apparently trying to keep from shaking. "No, no. It will be nothing." He nods his head quickly. "But we thought you were…" He can't finish.

"Dead. Yes, you did. But now, as you see, I am here, and you will do exactly as I say."

Morneau says, "Yes," once and then again.

"Where's your laptop?"

"My what?" He looks completely unraveled.

"Your computer. Your laptop."

"Oh, it's in the study."

"Then that's where we go. Move." He gestures with the gun.

The faggot seems still so frightened that he moves as if he's forgotten how to walk, twisting back to look at the gun as he struggles forward, stumbling and almost losing his balance. As they pass the large circular staircase on their right, Morneau stops and turns. "Tanner, please!" he says loudly. "I will do whatever you ask. You can have anything you wish."

"Good, but I told you, keep it down. Now the study."

Just two weeks ago still his boss, the guy moves more quickly now, walking into the entrance hall and then to the left. Both doors are wide open to the large study that takes up the south wing of the house. The room has a vaulted ceiling and, with large windows on all three walls, lots of natural light. In the center of the study is a gleaming stainless steel desk with a beveled glass top holding a pad of paper and the black Mount Blanc ballpoint with the gold clip he's often seen Morneau use. Directly behind stands a smaller glass-top table with only the laptop, the lid open, the screen black.

Shoving the banker to the swivel chair between the desk and the table, he sits on the edge of the desk next to him and, pointing the gun at the laptop, says, "Start it up."

Morneau turns to face the computer and pushes the power button. In a shaky voice he says, "Whatever you want."

And what does he want? Everything, that's all, and the moment has finally arrived. After all the shit he's taken from this mousy guy and his faggy lover. After all the poking around it took, first through his RBC branch and then on a two-day stint in Nassau, to find the name of the secret firm that had channeled funds to his account. After all the research into how access is gained to the accounts of super-secret private firms, the kinds of codes and passwords and, most importantly, the custom-built computer programs that usually offer the only way in. After all the scheming to get to this time and place.

The laptop is up, and its blue-green screen shows the owner's name, Giles Morneau, along with the password box. "What now?" asks Morneau.

He moves the pad and pen from the desk to the table. "First," he says, "write down the password on this pad, then slowly type it in. And let me explain something to you. Any attempt to do anything other than what I tell you will result in the loss of a body part."

"The loss...."

"Right, and we'll start with that little thing you've got there in your Speedo."

"Jesus! I said anything you want!

"Good. Here's what I want: a demonstration of exactly how to get into the accounts of your private firm ChevalGarçon Capital. And then we'll go from there."

Morneau's head begins to turn toward Tanner, who is sitting behind and to his left, looking over his shoulder to follow everything the banker does.

"Just do it!" he shouts and shoves the silencer into the man's neck.

Morneau cringes. "But how do you know...."

"I know everything. Except what you are about to show me. So let's get started. Just remember, every address, code or password, you write it down first." Again he shoves the silencer, this time into the back of Morneau's head. "Do it!"

The man lets out a small cry, leans forward and starts printing on the pad.

Until they get to the part about making transfers, he won't mention the one million euros to be sent to his RBC account. And until then he needs to pay close attention, so that later he can take the rest of the millions, certainly more than 100, in the ChevalGarçon account. Yes, he could have just brought the laptop to his hacker freak, but this way is faster, safer and more certain. Once they're finished here, he'll put a bullet in Morneau's brain and slip the laptop and the pad of paper into the beach bag. Then another slug in the pretty boy's head when he returns, and the same for the American when he calls him in to take photos.

And he's already decided where the bodies will go. Rather than dump them in some remote, hard-to-reach location, he will simply drag them to the closet off the central hall, the one that has in its floor an access to the cistern, and drop them through the hole. Yes, the house may well have a stench after a time, but once he locks the place up and leaves for good, there won't be anyone with a reason to enter this house for months or years to come.

Then it will be back to the Buccaneer to give the Italian woman some cock-and-bull story about how Clara and her lover need help. He'll bring her back here, fuck her on the floor of the entrance hall, give her pretty neck one last hug, and slip her also into the cistern.

And then? He hears French Polynesia is nice this time of year. Once he thought about making this house his own, but that was part of a silly notion about taking over and living out their dreams. Now he knows he's about to have everything they ever wanted. And he will never see this house or this island again.

Chapter 41

At the top of the broad circular staircase, he's gripping the wrought-iron railing so hard his hand begins to hurt. His body feels numb with fear, but his brain is teeming. From the occasional string of words he can hear from the study, he thinks he knows what's going on down there. As for what will happen next, he has no doubt. Tanner will murder both of them just as soon as he's got want he wants.

When that first piercing scream came from Giles downstairs, Julian was sprawled on their big bed in the master suite, weeping into his pillow, still raging at Giles and at himself, but mostly at a situation, a reality, he obviously should have foreseen. The scream and the horrified *"Mon Dieu"* brought him off the bed and to the doorway to the hall. And then, in the kitchen, or maybe the living room, there were voices he could not quite decipher. One certainly belonged to Giles, but the other? He couldn't tell. His first thought was the guy standing at the door when he opened it 10 minutes ago. The guy, Albert, coming about the caretaker's job. Only after closing the door in his face did he remember seeing him at Tippy's last night. The guy had wanted into the house. Maybe to rob them. Maybe he was tracking them last night.

But then as he moved to the top of the stairs, he heard Giles say, in a voice shrieking with fear from almost directly below him, "Tanner, please! I will do whatever you ask. You can have anything you wish."

And then, though it was impossible, from a quiet but unmistakable voice came the clear, terrifying tones of a dead man: "Good, but I told you, keep it down. Now the study."

No, it cannot be. But it is. The disgusting Tanner has duped the police agencies of two European nations and is standing now in the study of their new home, no doubt pointing a gun straight at poor Giles. From what little he can hear, Tanner is forcing Giles to show him something on the laptop, and he can easily guess what that is.

Once the lout has the access to everything they've got, there is no way he leaves without taking their lives as well.

So how to save himself? How to get out of this house unseen and unheard? Only one way: down this staircase and out the back, and then a desperate run up the beach to the nearest house. A half-mile. But wait, what about his phone? He moves back toward the master suite and gets all the way to the door before he remembers the mobile is on the counter in the kitchen. Abandoned there after he stalked out of their fight. He can grab it on his way out and use the back stairs off the kitchen. Then he can call for help. But does he know any local numbers, most importantly the one for the police? No. And then he remembers Albert at the door. The one for Albert and Abigail should be stored in the phone. They will call the police.

At the bedroom door he looks in and on a chair spots the hammer he was using to hang the paintings and framed photographs Tanner brought down two months ago. Maybe if the lout sees him, he can at least throw the thing at that fat head and hope to get lucky. And one good thing: in his bare feet on this cool tile floor, it seems like he can move without a sound.

Back at the top of the staircase he stops. It's one thing to think through and visualize what he's going to do. It's quite another, he knows now, to actually get your body to do it. Once he starts down these stairs and for the several seconds it will take him to reach the kitchen, if Tanner comes out of that study and sees him, he knows he will die on the spot.

Dead, after just one morning in their new life together, a morning filled with bliss and despair. How beautifully it began, how wonderful the promise for this day. The excitement of their love-making upon waking. The pure pleasure of their walk on the beach. Their plans for an afternoon drive north to the water taxis for Harbour Island, just a 10 minute boat ride to a place so totally different from Eleuthera, so larded with money, wealthy visitors, boutique hotels, tasteful shops and charming colonial homes. And then, after dinner at one of their favorite restaurants, on the way home a stop at Elvina's, the little dive of a bar in Gregory Town, where musician's of every stripe, from big time pros to willing locals, drop in on Friday night for a joyous, raucous jam.

But first, with no food in the house, Giles suggested brunch at

Cocodimama, the new Italian place right up the road on Alabaster Bay. And everything was perfect: the water a gorgeous mirror, the breeze light and fragrant on the deck, the food delicious and delivered by the owner, a sharp looking guy from Rome. Perfect, until the moment when Giles chose that very public spot to drop his little bomb. No doubt because he thought that in front of an old couple and a young party of five sitting close by, some measure of decorum would have to be maintained. And so it would foster the quiet, rational discussion this serious matter deserved.

Instead, he stood and shouted at Giles, "You fucking little liar!" And then grabbing their celebratory bottle of champagne, he threw it off the deck to the beach, where it stuck neck-down and emptied in the sand. Brushing past the shocked guy from Rome, he stalked off the deck, and by the time he reached the Yukon he was weeping uncontrollably. He sat behind the wheel for a while, then turned the ignition and started to drive away. As he passed the restaurant's entrance, Giles came down the steps waving for him to stop. Instead he accelerated and left the little shit behind. But then about 40 meters down the side road toward the Queen's Highway, he stopped, put it in park and watched in the mirror as Giles half-ran, half-walked to catch up.

As he got into the Yukon, Giles said, "Jules, I'm so sorry. There was just no good way to tell you."

Staring straight ahead, no longer crying but tears still wet on his checks, he said nothing.

"Really," said Giles, "I assure you I feel the same or worse."

He tossed him a withering glare, put it in gear and drove home, never saying a word. Once they were back in the house, Giles went upstairs, while he sat in the great room and with ugly, angry thoughts stared at the beautiful green sea. When Giles came down in his Speedo, he said he was going to try the new pool.

"How can you act like nothing's happened?"

And then the big fight began. Really in a way this had always been his deepest secret fear, one that most of the time and without making a concerted effort, he avoided thinking about. Only once in a great while, only at certain rare times and in a certain few places would it ever take him over. When he angled himself a certain way sitting in the chairman's office, and sometimes gave himself a glimpse of petite Hilde and little Eric and Isabelle in that framed photo on the shelf behind Giles. When, maybe once or twice a year, the beautiful children showed up at the bank with their tiny-breasted, narrow-hipped mother for a grown-up lunch with Father at Brasserie Lipp. Or when the Herald's society columnist offered a line about the generous and civic-minded Morneaus at a symphony gala.

Then a dark, desperate mood might descend. He'd actually try to imagine Giles playing with that young boy's body of his wife, wondering how the guy could have ever managed to do it even once, let alone twice in making those kids. And he'd finally allow himself to wonder, in spite of all the denial and delusion, if Giles would actually do what he always said he longed for with "every ounce of his being."

And now that it's happened, after all those fervent words and gestures to the contrary, after all those shared dreams spun in bed, over sumptuous meals in world-class restaurants, on long walks together in some of the world's most beautiful places, he knows that his hidden fear meant only that he really knew all along this day would come. The day when Giles would hold his hand and say with love in his eyes, "Jules, I must be truthful to you: yes, maybe some years from now when they are older and away at school, but now there is simply no way I can leave my children for good and forever."

He knows he was dreadful in their fight, screaming obscenities, throwing things—a half-filled tea kettle clattering across the tile floor, a large decorative dish splashing into pieces against a wall—and calling his lover horrible names. But the injustice of it carved up his heart.

"None of this," he screamed, "would have happened if I hadn't come up with my ingenious little fix. Your fucked up family's bank would have crashed, and you would have been ruined. I saved you, gave you everything, held nothing back. You had all my love, and now you turn on me in a way that is fucking despicable."

And with accusations both vile and undeniably true, Giles fired back: "You have no idea what it means to bring a child into this world!"

And: "You are being cruel, vicious and totally self-obsessed!"

And: "You act as though only you can have what you want and need!"

But at one point Giles actually tried to reason with him: "Look, it won't really be all that different. With the bank sold, I'll be retired, able to come and be with you almost anytime. We'll still do all the things we've talked and dreamed about. We'll just have to wait for a while sometimes. You'll just need a little patience."

"Patience?" he screamed. "After five bloody years you talk about patience! You are such a fucking cunt!"

That's when he threw the dish and with a fury beating in his chest, walked out.

"Jules, please!" Giles voice was almost plaintive, and despite everything, he could still hear the love in it. But he kept walking away, knowing the only thing to do was to shun his lover and pay him back for all the pain he had caused today.

And now he finds himself moving down the stairs, the hammer heavy in his hand. As he reaches the bottom step he hears Tanner in the study say, "Okay, write that down too. I told you, I want a full road map through all of this." So, yes, he was exactly right about what's going on with Tanner, Giles and the laptop. When the lout is finished with them, he'll take that computer and have total access to their fortune.

Stepping off the staircase, he bumps against the railing with the back of his left hand, the one holding the hammer. There's a soft, dull thud, and he freezes, but in the study Giles is saying, "And after that, there's this." No sound of movement comes from Tanner.

And then he shocks himself by turning not left toward the back of the house but right toward the front. He's moving slowly toward the entrance hall, but his body is so tense he's afraid he'll drop the hammer. He carefully moves it to his right hand and makes sure of his grip. Then, stepping lightly, and, yes, without a sound, his bare feet move deftly across the tile, until he's at the edge of the front hall where he'll be able to peek into the study. He stops and wonders what can possibly be moving him to do this. He has never possessed any measure of physical courage. When those gay-bashing thugs cornered him that night in high school, he pissed in his pants and whimpered like a girl, which only enraged them more. But now, even with his body almost numb and the taste of fear rancid in his mouth, he knows he will continue moving forward, no matter what. No, it's not courage but maybe some potent mix of loathing, rage and despair that finally makes him move his head forward, just far enough for a glimpse into the study. And there he sees just what he hoped for: both Giles and Tanner intent on the laptop screen, their backs to the wide-open study doors.

He takes a deep, silent breath and steps forward and then to the left toward the study. They have not moved, Giles in the swivel chair and Tanner on the edge of the desk behind and to the left. Both are staring intently at the laptop screen. He wants to run, to leap, to fly to the desk and to Tanner's ugly head, but he continues to move slowly, silently into the large room. His gaze locked on the lout, he wills him, with every last ounce of resolve, not to turn around.

And just then Tanner says, "Okay, got it. Keep going." And he moves his right hand with the gun in it, a few inches up and down, as it points at the laptop.

Transfixed by the gun, he stops dead. He feels paralyzed, but finally blinks and looks away. Somehow he manages to steel himself. After a few seconds, he's moving again, and as he approaches the front edge of the desk, he raises the hammer well above his eyes, focused like a laser on the short blond and white hairs on the crown of Tanner's large, hateful head.

There is no hesitation. With every ounce of strength he can muster from all his hate, rage and fear, down comes the hammer straight at that head. But something—peripheral vision, a sixth sense, the sound of Julian's arm and the hammer cutting through damp, tropic air— something makes Tanner begin to turn, and the black iron head of the hammer lands not on the crown, but high on the right temple with a blow of such force that it brings the sweet, satisfying sound of the lout's skull cracking

Chapter 42

The Jeep pitches and rolls, and she brakes sharply in front of a pothole that is more akin to a crater, the asphalt here crumbled and pitted over decades and washed out by a thousand heavy rains. Marc on his mobile called this road "more like the moon," and now she thinks the turn she took off the Queen's Highway was correct. That was the one he seemed unsure about. "Maybe five minutes out of town if you keep it under 45. When you come to a paved road off to the right, look ahead and I think you'll see a small half-done building, cement block, abandoned, hidden in weeds." She had passed a few roads on the right with no unfinished construction in sight and passed this one too, but then she glimpsed the structure, someone's dream dashed, and did a quick U-turn.

Now she twists the wheel to skirt the hole and, looking ahead, keeps to the right, half on, half off this obstacle course, bushes and trees scraping the Jeep's passenger side as she drives as fast as she dares, the right side relatively smooth, the left bouncing and rocking. His last word on the mobile was "Hurry."

She had waited 30 minutes before calling him, wracked with nerves because he had not called as he said he would, but afraid his phone might go off in the middle of something crucial. Finally, after she learned about Clara on the Dell, she dialed his number, now deeply frightened for him, and got no answer. To his voice mail she said simply, "Marc, call me. You are in danger."

Two agonizing minutes passed, while she told herself that he was nobody's fool, that he was smart enough to take care of himself, but then she thought, "I should never have allowed him to go off alone with that killer." And she tried him again. This time on the fourth ring he answered, "Lina, I was just about to call you." He sounded like he was running.

Marc, are you okay?"

"Yes, but you need to come and get me. Now."

"Marc, Clara is dead. They found her in Italy."

"Oh god." And then there was silence, and all she could hear was his breathing, heavy, agonized. She wished she had not told him so soon.

Finally she said, "I know. I feel so awful. But this is clearly a trap for you. Tanner will kill you."

"Tanner is dead."

"Dead?"

"Yes, Julian killed him."

"Julian? You are sure?"

"Yes, I'm sure. He hit him in the head with a hammer, several times. He's dead."

"I can't believe it."

"I know, I'll show you the movie. Please come now and get me. Also, find the number for the cops and bring it."

"Okay, but I can just go to them. They're a block away."

"No! Just bring me the number, and hurry!"

Feeling admonished, she said, "Of course. So tell me how to find you."

Now with this broken road looking a bit less treacherous, she accelerates and hopes she has not failed him. She has gotten to this point as quickly as she could, but it has felt like forever. Searching the heavy scrub to the right for the sandy road he talked about, she finally spots an opening about 30 meters ahead. And then she sees him, emerging from the opening at a trot, one hand on the camera around his neck and the other holding his mobile. He's waving it at her now.

When she reaches him, he looks grim as he opens the passenger door and climbs in. "Good Girl! Now turn around, and get out of here."

She wonders how long it has been since someone called her a girl but feels so relieved about having him safe in the Jeep she wants to take his hand and kiss it. Instead she backs around to retrace the route. She asks, "Do you want the number for the police?"

"No, not until we get to the Queen's Highway. They shouldn't see us anywhere near here. They do, and we could be implicated in what happened back there."

"So what did happen? I know, Julian hit Tanner with a hammer, but how did all this happen?"

"Yeah, so I went to the front door, and Julian answered. But he looked strange, like he'd been crying."

"Crying?"

"Yes, he said it was a bad time and slammed the door in my face. So I waited a minute and tried it again, and then Morneau answered. We talked for a while, but he wouldn't let me in."

"What did you tell him?"

"That I was a photographer for those folks we just met back at the Buc, and they wanted a spread for their web site on this beautifully refurbished home."

"They do want a spread."

"So while I was doing that, Tanner with his beach bag circled around the side of the house through this heavy vegetation to the back and I guess went in through the laundry room. But that whole thing about a million euros in a fancy hidden safe was apparently a crock. I mean, when I left the front, I went back out to the road, found the way Tanner used to get around to the back and did the same thing. But as I'm getting there and about to look in the laundry, I hear someone, I think Morneau, scream and yell, '*Mon Dieu!*' And it's coming from one floor up. So I find steps up to one side of the main deck.

"And then after a while I hear voices inside, Tanner and Morneau, and I think they're coming from one wing of this house. So there are two big windows across the back of this large room, and I slide up to the nearest one and take a peak. And then I got very lucky, because there's Morneau with Tanner holding a gun on him, a gun with a silencer on it, and they both have their backs to me, and they're both looking at a computer, a laptop sitting on a table. And then I remember I've got my little Flip Cam in my pocket. So I pull it out, hit start and reach it around to the windowsill. I put it there and point it right at the two of them, while they're still staring at the laptop. Now at that point all I could do was hope the light was okay, and I wasn't just getting a reflection off the window. I mean it looked okay, but I couldn't really tell."

"Marc, that was crazy. If Tanner had turned for some reason, you would be dead now."

"But he didn't turn. I told you I got lucky. Anyway, I wasn't in view either time for more than a second or two. So then I moved back to look from the deck into the center of the house, and since no one was in there, I slid open a door and took a couple of quick shots of the kitchen and the living area. Then I went back near the window where the Flip was and crouched against the wall there, where they couldn't see me even if they looked out the window. And after a minute or two—I'm not sure how long it was—I hear another scream and a commotion in there and more screams. And then Morneau and Julian are yelling at each other. So I wait for a while, and finally I reach around and grab the Flip. I don't even look in the window at that point. I just grab it and take off, back down to the lower level and out the way I came in, through all the trees and bushes. That's when you called."

"I also called a few minutes earlier."

"I had the phone in my pocket and, I guess, couldn't feel it vibrate."

"So you got a movie of everything that happened in there."

"Yes." He pats the Flip Cam in his jeans.. "Actually I watched it while I was waiting for you. It's incredible what I got. Pretty gruesome but I'll show you when we get back."

Finally at the Queen's Highway they turn left toward Governor's Harbour. She asks, "Now you want the police?"

"Yes, I need to report a home invasion and a justifiable homicide."

"You think they will say it was self-defense?"

"Well, that's what it was. Anyway, I want the cops out there before they can get rid of the body."

As she gives him the number, he punches it into his mobile and says, "Tell me how my accent is." He waits, then into the phone with an excited, worried edge to his voice: "Yes, police! I have home intruder. He try to kill us. Rob and kill us! But we kill him."

A pause, and they glance at each other as he listens. He's trying for a French accent. Not great, but she nods that he is doing okay.

"Yes," he says. We kill him with a hammer. Please come now!"

Another pause and then: "We are at our home. The old Wright house. North Governor's Harbour, five minutes, off Queen's Highway, Atlantic side."

A pause again and he makes a face. "Not white. The Wright house. We bought from the Wrights. They are from England. Please come soon!"

He ends the call, and she asks, "Will they have your number?"

"I blocked it. How did I sound?"

"You were fine."

"I just hope they get out there quick. I'm sure they don't get many calls like that one."

They are silent for a several seconds. She finally says, "Marc, I feel so terrible about Clara."

He says nothing, and her glance finds his face mournful and angry as he stares straight ahead.

She says, "What they did was so awful. I feel so horrible for her. And for you."

She feels his gaze turn to her. "What did you learn?" he says. "And how?"

"I was looking through the Geneva news sites — I will tell you why in a minute — and the Herald has this headline: 'Geneva woman found dead in Italy.' Apparently Clara's body was found in her car at the bottom of a mountain near Cinque Terre. It was heavily wooded, so the car was hidden and not found for almost two weeks. According to the story, the Italian police theorized that she drove off a road high on the mountain and landed several hundred feet down. And because there were no skid marks, they think it was either at night and she missed a turn, or she did it on purpose."

"On purpose!?"

"I know. There were quotes from Dubonne, the chief of the Geneva Municipal Police, and from Claude Savoneau, the fellow Tanner said was holding her here."

"Really. Saying what?"

"Dubonne said this was a sad and unfortunate case, in which a woman who was a trusted employee at the Banque Privee Morneau looted a substantial sum from one or more accounts at the bank and then tried to disappear. He claimed his investigators had been closing in on Madame Marche in the Liguria region of Italy before they lost her trail. He speculated that she may have been wracked with guilt and thus took her own life."

"Unbelievable. What about Savoneau?"

"He supposedly went to Italy to work with the police there and said the body showed no signs of foul play. Her fatal injuries were all consistent with what he called 'the catastrophic impact of the crash.'"

"Those fucking pigs!"

Lina says nothing and squeezes his hand for a second as she drives. As they pass the "Welcome to Governor's Harbour" sign, two police cars sweep past on the right, no lights flashing or sirens wailing but moving fast, two men in each car.

Marc says, "So they're on the case."

After a while she says, "Is it possible that everyone in this sordid story might get what he deserves?"

"That only happens in fairy tales."

She nods. "Maybe this will be different."

"So why were you looking at news sites in Geneva?"

"Because of our new friends Mac and Maggie and their website. As you were leaving with Tanner, Mac stands up and says, 'Isn't that Willem Tanner?' And I am surprised and say, 'Yes, do you know him?'"

"Yeah, I heard him. Tanner said he ran into them a while back, and they were curious about the boys and their house, but he wouldn't give them any information."

"Yes, they called him 'a taciturn fellow,' but they were very interested when I said we were friends with the bankers."

"Friends."

"Yes, they said a local contractor told them some great renovations had been done to that house, and it was wonderful news in this down economy that someone was 'investing in Eleuthera.' So I told them that Julian and Giles were fine people, just a little shy, and I thought there was a good chance they would let us interview them about their move here and take some photos of the house. Mac said, if we could do that and write a little profile, he'd get it up on the site 'lickity-split.' He said, 'You send me something today, I'll have it up first thing in the morning, guaranteed.'"

"I've got the photos," says Marc as she turns in front of the liquor store and heads up the hill. "But I guess you can forget the interview."

"No, I already started writing the profile, complete with quotes from both of them. Remember, we are talking about the Web here. Truth, fantasy and flat-out lies all live happily together. And I started making a list of news sites in Geneva and all the relevant police and regulatory agencies in Switzerland. The Swiss National Police, the Swiss Banking Commission, all of them."

"So you started with the Herald and found the story on Clara."

"Yes." She parks in front of the Buc and turns off the ignition. They shift in their seats.

"But, Marc, think about this. What if Eleuthera Living publishes, so to speak, our profile of the bankers, using your photos, and including their real names, their real IDs, and telling their real story? How the bank is being sold and how they are retiring here to Eleuthera, and how they are looking forward to living here together for the rest of their lives."

"Totally blowing their cover."

"Yes, totally. The profile would be the truth, not the lie they are hoping to live."

"Exactly."

She watches his dark face brighten and says, "So what if we start by sending a link to that profile to everyone on our list, all the news and police agencies. And then, think about everything else we have now, all your photos and videos, including the bankers killing Tanner. Think about the recording of our meeting with Tanner, who was supposed to have been murdered in Amsterdam but who talked about murdering his old police pal there instead. Think about Clara's letter to Cecile and everything that it lays out, and everything old Charles has already learned about the real fraud at the bank. Think about...."

"Lina," he says, stopping her with the beginning of a smile, "What I think is, you're a bloody genius."

Chapter 43

When the door chime rings for the second time in 10 minutes, Giles, still in his red Speedo, snaps his head back to glare at the study's vaulted ceiling and growls in a whisper, "Jesus, what now?"

They are standing in the doorway to the entrance hall, where they've been arguing almost non-stop from the moment he delivered that final blow to Tanner's mushy, caved-in head, stopping not because Giles was nearly hanging from his back and screaming at him, but more from sheer exhaustion, the hammer finally falling from his hand into the small pool of blood already forming on the off-white tile floor.

Ten minutes ago when the door chime first interrupted their argument, he peeked out a front window to find a middle-aged black man and woman, dressed as if for church, standing on the front porch and gazing up at the house. He told Giles calmly, "Don't worry, it's the caretaker and the cook. I'll send them away."

And before Giles could say a word, he was at the front door.

"Wait," called Giles finally. "There's blood on your shirt."

Julian looked down at himself, then quickly lifted the tee over his head and tossed it in a corner. When he opened the front door, the couple was posed there with matching smiles.

"Albert and Abigail, I presume."

"Yes, mon," said the man.

"Thank you for coming, but this is not a good time. Can you come again tomorrow? Maybe a little later, about 3."

"Yes, mon."

"Good, and thanks so much. See you tomorrow." And he shut the door.

From the window he watched the couple get into their dusty old Suburu, saying something to each other and shaking their heads. Then he and Giles resumed their fight. The issue was what to do with Tanner. Or rather with the body of the man Tanner had become after he was murdered in Amsterdam. From the back pockets of his jeans they had taken both his passport and his wallet and discovered that this was, officially, David Marcuse, a Swiss national from Lucerne.

"So, nobody we know," said Julian, "but somebody who certainly knew about us and tracked us here where he seemed to be under the impression that we had a million euros stashed away somewhere in this house. Someone who invaded our home with the intention of robbing and murdering us and leaving our bodies behind to rot. Someone therefore we had every right to protect ourselves from, using every means at our disposal, including, of course, violent force. A totally justified homicide, an open and shut case, as our friends with the police would say. We have our new identities, our fool-proof IDs, and every reason to simply call the police and report this home invasion, attempted armed robbery and attempted murder."

"No, Jules, this is crazy." Giles' voice quickly rose. "Yes, everything you're saying is true, but you're forgetting certain crucial things. Those new IDs of ours are fool-proof only according to the guy laying there dead after trying to rob and kill us. We have no true idea how much scrutiny those documents will stand. And you know the first thing the police will do is take those passports from us and check them against every record they can find."

"No, no, look, you told me when Tanner got us those documents, you passed them by Dubonne and he said they looked good...."

"He took one quick glance and said that. It means nothing under these circumstances. Besides, he's the one who got us to hire this guy, a guy who then betrayed us, lied to us and finally tried to kill us. And you want us to trust his word?"

"No, I'm saying the police here will have no reason to put us and our documents under the kind of scrutiny you're talking about. This is open and shut. It is self-defense."

Giles was shaking his head as if he thought him hopeless. "Jules, even if it goes the way you're saying, even if all they do is a perfunctory check, even if our new passports pass muster without a problem, this is a case, a story, involving three Swiss nationals, a rare and sensational case for this quiet little island. Don't you think it's likely that some kind of account, maybe even with photos, will end up getting back home? Admit it. That's a real possibility."

"I don't admit anything of the sort. They'll probably keep everything quiet here, because it's bad for the tourist business. The only damn business they've got."

They went on and on this way, each of them making the same points over and over. He wanted to call the police to report the crime, and Giles argued the only smart and safe thing to do was to wrap the body in a blanket, stuff it in the back of the Yukon, and drive south.

"There are a million places down there where we could dump him," said Giles, pleading. "And you know he'd never be found. No one would ever know about this, and we could just go on with our dream."

Actually, he was finally beginning to admit that Giles might be right. Keeping this whole thing secret might be the safer way to go. And as his resolve diminished, he wondered if his rage over Giles' refusal to leave his family completely behind in Geneva was somehow playing into this dispute. Maybe there was part of him that saw this as a chance to lock Giles back into their original plan.

And now the door chime has sounded for the second time. He moves to the edge of the nearest window and peers out. Startled by what he sees, he suddenly knows the argument has just been settled, the decision made. Standing there next to the Yukon, trying to look through its darkened windows, are two young men in crisp blue uniforms with red trim. The Royal Bahamian Police Force. One or two more are no doubt waiting right now at the front door.

He looks at Giles and says quietly, "The police are here."

In a whispered scream: "What! How can that be?"

He puts a finger to his lips, then says softly, "I don't know, but we have to deal with them now. It's the only thing we can do."

"No!" Giles goes to Tanner's body and grabs a foot. "Help me. Drag him to the closet."

Collecting his shirt from the corner, he whispers, "No, look at the blood. There's no way we can hide him now and clean this up." He goes to his lover, takes his arm and pulls him away. "Look, I'll handle this. You just go upstairs and get dressed. And in a few minutes I'll come up and get you, and we'll synchronize our stories."

Giles doesn't move. He looks terrified.

"Darling, we'll be fine. You just follow my lead. I know exactly what to say."

Giles gives his head a woeful shake and moves for the stairway. When he has climbed far enough to be out of sight, the door chime rings again, and there is a loud rapping on the door.

With his shirt back on, the blood-soaked front feels cool now against his skin. At the door he takes a deep breath and swings it open. Two more uniformed officers stand there. One is maybe 40, very dark and with an ample gut, his hat tilted back on a round face. The other is lean, lighter-skinned and half his age. The other two are still back near the Yukon.

"*Oui?*" English, he reminds himself. "Yes, officers."

The older one with a quick glance at the dark wet spots on his tee, then up to his eyes: "Sir, you called about an intruder and a killing here?"

He feels a sudden loss of balance and tries to steady himself with his hand on the door. His mind is racing. Did Albert and Abigail see something? Was the black guy who came earlier working with Tanner? His opening line was going to be that he was just about to call them. But what now?

Finally, telling himself to speak slowly, carefully, he says, "Yes, called. I think my partner, he did that. He is upstairs. We are both so stunned and shaken by what has happened. Obviously. But it is good you are here. Please, come in."

"Yes, sir, thank you. I am Chief Inspector Gibson, and this is Officer Ferguson."

The polite response helps him. "Chief Inspector. Officer." He makes a point of looking each of them in the eye as they move into the entrance hall. And then he gestures toward the study and Tanner on the floor. "It happened in here. As you see."

"Yes, sir," says Gibson, standing in the entrance hall and looking at the body. "And your name is, please?"

"My name? Josef. Josef Simon."

"And who else is in the house?"

Ah, in the house is only my partner, Gerard Bitou. As I say, he is upstairs. Would you like me to get him?"

"In a moment, sir. But first we will look here."

As they move into the study, he says, "Of course. As you can see, the man has a gun, one with a silencer. Well, naturally the gun was in his hand, until I hit him on the head with that hammer."

"Yes, sir." While the younger officer stands erect and watches, Gibson leans over Tanner for a closer look. "Did you know this man, sir?"

"Did I know him?" A glance at Gibson's face shows only a stoic look as he gazes at the mangled head. "No, I have not seen him before in my life. But he certainly knew about me and about my partner. He had the misapprehension, however, that we had a large sum of money here in the house. Actually, one million euros. He was demanding that...."

"Sir," says Gibson, "we will get to that in a moment. First, please tell me if you have touched this body or moved it in any way."

"No." He shakes his head. "Well, yes, after I stopped hitting him with the hammer, which was several times—as you imagine, I was very frightened since he was pointing that gun at my partner—I think I did touch his neck to see if there was a pulse. Frankly, I was pleased there was not one."

"Yes, sir. Anything else?"

"Oh, and from his pockets we took his wallet and passport, which you see there on the corner of the desk."

"Yes." Gibson looks displeased.

"I am sorry, Chief Inspector, if we should not have done that. But, of course, we wanted to know who this man was who came here to rob and kill us."

Having moved his gaze to the desk, the inspector nods. "And you say the other man here, your partner, is upstairs."

"Yes."

"I would like you then to go upstairs and ask him to join us. And if your passports are there, please bring them with you. Officer Ferguson will accompany you."

"Yes, of course."

He is already scheming about how to communicate with Giles in front of this fellow. As they climb the stairs, Gibson opens the front door and calls outside. "Constable Saunders, please bring the camera."

At the top of the stairs, he quickens his pace slightly and heads for the master suite. Once in the doorway he finds Giles, dressed in a polo shirt, shorts and sandals, sitting on the bed. He looks stoned. Maybe a double or triple dose of Lorazepam? Moving to him, Julian makes the small hand gesture they always use between them to say everything is fine.

"Gerard, you are okay?"

"Yes."

He sits next to Giles on the bed. "Have you taken your

270

Lorazepam?

Giles looks at him. "Yes."

"Good. Gerard, this is Officer Ferguson."

"Yes, hello, Officer."

The young man nods from the doorway.

Trying his most reassuring tone: "So the chief inspector downstairs would like us to tell him just what happened. It is so good, Gerard, that you called the police, and they got here so quickly."

"I called." Giles looks at him and raises an eyebrow.

A quick nod. "Yes, that was very good. I was so scattered, but you knew what to do. Also we need to bring our passports."

"I have them here." Giles lifts them off the bed next to him.

"Excellent. So I will change my shirt, and we will go down to speak with the chief inspector."

* * *

A half hour later, when the van arrives and two more officers come in with a body bag, he and Giles and Chief Inspector Gibson are sitting in the great room facing the sea, continuing what now seems more like a pleasant chat than an interrogation. At some point about 10 minutes ago, he noticed the change. Early on he offered all the officers something to drink. Kalik and ice tea were all they had in the house, but the officers were welcome to either. As he expected, the answer was a polite no thank you. But when he made the offer again 20 minutes later, though the answer was still no, he could tell Gibson was tempted.

Yes, he was proud of Giles, but really he should have known better. His lover was quick to pick up on everything, using their argument earlier to pluck lines here and there to add appropriate sentences to the discussion. They were entirely on the same page on everything, and as Gibson moved them methodically through the sequence of what happened, there were no contradictions, no confusion at all. In fact, it was a simple exercise, because really they were just telling the truth. Except for those few minor items: that they did not know the intruder, who was demanding, not access to their entire fortune, but only a million euros cash; and that when he came down from upstairs with the hammer, he found Gerard and Marcuse, not staring at the computer screen, but at each other, with the intruder's back to the study's door and the gun pointed directly at his partner's forehead.

Of course, they had those new names to remember, and early on he nearly slipped once, and so did Giles. But after a time he thought they sounded quite comfortable with their new IDs. And now they're even boasting a bit, telling this chief inspector, who, despite his fancy title, was sure to be limited for life to very modest means, something about how they assembled their remarkable fortune.

Investment bankers originally from Zurich, a few years back they were among a tiny handful of smart, savvy and, yes, deeply fortunate players who sniffed out what was happening as the world's bloated economy began its collapse. They understood just one important thing: real estate prices don't inevitably go up forever, and there would be terrible risks for those betting billions they would. So while others bought into the fictitious value of all those arcane securities based on piles of mostly rotten mortgages and were sucked into a giant black hole of nightmarish debt, Josef and Girard carefully placed their contrarian bets and eventually ended up with close to a billion between them.

Gibson is shaking his head now. He asks so what are they going to do with all that money. Well, a couple of things, they say. Having decided to spend the rest of their lives right here on Eleuthera, a paradise whose glorious beaches they love almost as much as its wonderful people, they purchased and renovated this marvelous home. And while they are certainly happy with it, they have much bigger plans. First, to design and build their true dream home on a site not far from here, a house whose looks, utility and ambience will be unlike anything the island has ever seen, a genuine model for the future. And second — something Julian is actually making up on the spur of this moment — to develop a major resort that will nestle splendidly, but with profound respect, into the God-given beauty of one of southern Eleuthera's most astonishing beaches.

They cannot reveal the exact location at this point, but Chief Inspector Gibson can rest assured that, unlike other recent projects, rumored or half-started and then abandoned, this one will definitely happen, employing hundreds of Eleutherans in its construction and, of course, hundreds more to help it serve all those thousands of happy tourists who will flock here to spend their money.

Gibson first shakes his head and then nods at this wondrous thought. He says that God will surely bless each of them for what they are doing here. When he finally looks at his watch, he explains, almost with regret, that department rules require that he bring them in to the station in Governor's Harbour to record a statement from each of them. He will try to make this happen as efficiently as possible and send them promptly on their way. Unfortunately he will have to hold on to their passports for a short time while perfunctory checks are made.

There's a glance from Giles, but Julian says quickly, of course, no problem at all. Will they be able to drive their own SUV into town, he asks, so they can do a little grocery shopping afterward? Having just arrived on the island yesterday afternoon, they haven't had a chance to get anything in the fridge.

"Of course," says Chief Inspector Gibson. "I would say you two gentlemen have been through just about enough for one day."

Chapter 44

When he first opens his eyes, Lina is sitting on the edge of her bed, the Dell on her knees. He doesn't move, and it's several seconds before she catches him looking at her.

She smiles. "Good morning."

"Morning," he mumbles, feeling groggy.

"It is up." Her smile is glowing.

"What's up?"

"Our profile of the boys."

"Already?"

"It is almost 9. He said he would do it first thing."

Almost 9. They have slept only a few hours. After working through the night, fueled with coffee, chocolate bars and adrenaline, they fell into their beds with their clothes on and told each other to sleep fast. Now she's up off her bed and sitting on his so that, propped on his elbow, he can see her screen.

"Is it all here?" he asks.

"Every word. And all four photos. You were right, old Mac apparently did not check a thing, did not make a simple phone call, or drop by the house to see if even the basic facts are right."

"Just gave it to the world as is."

"Yes, in the now time-honored tradition of internet journalism."

Marc glances at one of his photos and the caption she added: "Giles Morneau and Julian Lyon, formerly of Geneva, enjoy their favorite restaurant, Tippy's." Then he starts reading.

> From Geneva to Eleuthera, with Love
>
> By Clara Bianco
>
> Giles Morneau and Julian Lyon were private bankers in busy, cosmopolitan Geneva, Switzerland. Soon to retire, they have come to

their beloved Eleuthera to build a new life together, sharing their love on this isle of freedom, reveling in the beauty of its sun, sand and crystal clear waters.

"This is truly a paradise for us," says Giles Morneau, chairman of Geneva's Banque Privee Morneau.

"And we love the people here. They are so friendly and always helpful," adds Julian Lyon, who recently left his position as senior investment manager at Banque Privee Morneau.

Lyon will facilitate their move to full-time residents of Eleuthera, while his partner Morneau presides over the pending sale of the bank.

Having purchased a large home on the Atlantic side north of Governor's Harbour from the Wright family of England, they have made extensive renovations to the already beautiful abode. "Just to put our stamp on it and make it reflect our taste," explained Lyon.

The changes include new decking and an infinity pool, new windows and bright new paint for the exterior walls. Inside there are new marble counters in a new open kitchen and several other changes as well. And yet the happy pair's commitment and contribution to Eleuthera will not stop here.

Said Morneau: "We know we have been very fortunate at a time when many are in difficult straits, including those right here on Eleuthera. But we are going ahead with plans for a new, even larger and more beautiful home here on the island. We are in the design stage right now, but this will happen."

"When it does, added Lyon, with a twinkle in

his eye, "it will be something that all Eleutherans will appreciate and take pride in."

He glances at the other three photos, the front elevation, the pool and the kitchen and shakes his head. "I love your little touches, like that 'twinkle in his eye.'"

"It was almost fun."

He struggles to get himself upright, his head feeling woozy. "I guess we better get moving. With this on line, we've got a lot to do."

Actually they started yesterday afternoon, right after she picked him up on the road near the house and returned to the Buc. They've hardly stopped since. Camped in their room, she began writing the profile while he dumped the photos he took at the house into his computer. His favorite was the one of Tanner glaring at him. Then he moved them to her Dell. He did the same with the audio recording from his phone and the video file from the Flip Cam.

At one point he looked up from his tasks just as she stopped her typing and gazed at him. "What?" he asked.

"So remind me. I know we did not want to be connected with what happened out there at the house, but why is it better for us to stay anonymous now?"

"Because I don't want anything bad to happen to you, or me, for that matter. We know the Geneva Municipal Police have somehow been in cahoots with the boys in all of this. Maybe we can't prove it, but they murdered Clara. If they find out we're behind an effort to expose the boys, then we become a target. At least until we're able to put all this information out there and make it public. And as for Tanner's killing here, there is no need for us to be entangled at all. We can set the cops here straight anonymously, so why not keep it that way. All we need now is a pseudonym for the writer of the boys' profile you're doing."

"I already have one," said Lina and then told him the story of what happened when she promised good old Mac the profile. "So he is giving me his card, and he asks for my name. And something tells me — maybe it was your voice in my head — not to use my real name. So for some reason I just said 'Clara...Clara Bianco.'"

"Interesting. Clara White."

"And now in one stroke we have married the two of you and given poor Clara a chance to speak from the grave to name her murderers."

So Clara Bianco would author the profile, and he would open a Gmail account in her name. They would send everything out from cbianco321@gmail.com, and nothing could be traced back to them.

And, finally, the awful reality of Clara's death hit full-square, like a vicious punch to the chest, and he just sat there staring at the large print of a beautiful pink hibiscus on the wall of their room. But instead of the flower, he was seeing Clara's lovely body mangled in the wreckage of her red Astro, the car crumpled under a screen of splintered trees.

He stayed in this deep, crushing funk for a long time, and the only way he managed to stir himself out of it was to ask Lina for the link to the Herald's story of the body's discovery. When he read it, he found that her summary in the Jeep had been complete, not a detail missing. The story was short and, to anyone who did not know Clara, more or less inconsequential. Just one more bit of unneeded proof that our sad old world was awash in trouble, evil and woe.

After a while he got himself moving again by opening the video file from the house in the simple editing program he had on the HP. He cut some from the head and tail and faded up and down on those vital 62 seconds that showed the whole gory story of the killing.

When he was finished, he felt a strong need to learn what was happening to Clara's murderers. Maybe they'd already be at the cop shop down the hill, offering their accounts of what happened at the house. To make himself look different from the guy standing at their door, he changed into a black tee, pulled his old Michigan ball cap with the block M down low over his face and donned his shades. He told Lina he was taking a break, and she said she was just about done "fussing" with the profile.

As soon as he turned the corner at the blue and yellow liquor store he knew his timing was good. There, parked in front of the little teal police station, was the big black Yukon. He found himself a spot in the shade in front of the bank across the road from the stationhouse, sat on the low porch and waited. He started counting in his head all the various documents and files they'd be sending later across the sea, from the profile, to Clara's letter, to the homicide video. When he reached 8 going on 9, he saw the station's front door open. Julian Lyon walked out first, nodding and smiling, followed by Giles Morneau, also looking pleased. Then came a grinning cop, his hefty belly stretching his uniform. As they turned and shook the cop's hand, Marc could hear Morneau say, "Chief Inspector, thank you for everything."

And the chief inspector said, "No problem, Gerard, God bless. And Josef. It should not take long with the passports."

A wave, more smiles, and the bankers were in the Yukon. And then they traveled all of 30 yards to park in front of the Shell Gas Grocery. They both glanced Marc's way before heading up the steps to the store, but the two shared a laugh and headed inside. Obviously Josef Simon and Gerard Bitou were in the process of being fully exonerated.

He was sorely tempted to go into the store and somehow let them know that their lives would soon become hellish. He wanted them to feel the terror and despair that Clara must have felt at the end. And with that thought his rage beat up again so powerfully that he got to his feet. And then he walked away in the opposite direction. The only smart thing to do right now, and he moved along the harbor, past the library and all the way to Cupid's Cay to stare for a time at the bay.

Back at the Buc after an hour, he told Lina that Josef and Gerard were so far in the clear. She was full of news. Soon after he left, she had sent the profile off to McGinnis and within 20 minutes got his reply: "This is great, Clara. As promised, it'll be up on the site under 'What's New,' first thing in the morning. Thanks!"

And then she called Charles Mercier. It was close to 10 pm in Geneva, but she knew the old attorney often read late into the evening. When he answered, they had a long, detailed conversation about everything that had happened. A man with extensive dealings with Swiss banking over the decades, he was shocked at the probable murders of Cecile and Clara and at the bankers' secret new life in the Bahamas. But he was quick to understand their criminal manipulation of accounts at the bank and the full implications of their ties to the Geneva Municipal Police. When she explained the plan to make all this information public along with considerable documentation, old Charles quickly agreed to serve as the "contact person" for the entire effort.

"Tell them," he said, "to respond to me with all questions and requests. And by the way, I just heard from another of Cecile's charities. That's three, and it's the same story. Within an hour I'll send you a statement of what we know so far. You can add it to your list of documents."

With nothing to eat since breakfast, they were both famished and brought dinner from the Buc to the room. Talking non-stop through the broiled grouper, they decided who would do what on each of the several tasks ahead and exactly how their "package" should come together.

Later Lina started on the comprehensive narrative that would put all their supporting files and documents in context. Marc would write the last, "Eleuthera," part of the story, but first he spent a long time on the transcript of their talk with Tanner at the seawall. It was tedious work, but typing out the whole exchange would facilitate dealing with an audio recording not always easy to decipher, especially for a reporter or a cop not fluent in English.

When he finished, it covered more than a dozen pages, and back at the top he added a title: "Transcript of audio recording: A conversation between Willem Tanner and two friends of Cecile DeRocheford and Clara Marche on November 19, 2009, in Governor's Harbour, Eleuthera, the Bahamas. (The two friends are designated as Man and Woman.)"

Then he scrolled through, reading snippets of the crucial information it covered. From what happened in Amsterdam:

"Tanner: And then a man I knew for a long time with the Geneva police, a fellow named Tremelyn, came there to kill me. He failed, and I allowed him to take my place."

To how Clara was caught:

"Tanner: Tremelyn, the man who came to Amsterdam, told me. He and my old partner on the Geneva police, Claude Savoneau, took her from Malpensa when she tried to fly to you."

From the whole Clara-held-hostage-by-Savoneau fiction concocted by Tanner to lure them to Eleuthera; to the bankers' new IDs, their "secret" investment firm in Nassau, and their plans for a new life together; and perhaps most importantly their connections with the Geneva Municipal Police.

He was still wondering why Tanner had divulged this chunk of info about his former cop friends — about the chief, Dubonne, and his early ties with Morneau, and the money-laundering accounts at the Banque Privee Morneau:

"Tanner: Yeah, arranged by Dubonne and opened by two South Americans, one for the chief himself.

"Man: And the other?

"Tanner: Drugs.

"Woman: A cartel?

"Tanner: Yeah, a big one."

Maybe Tanner couldn't contain his rage at his old friends on the force, who had tried to kill him. Or maybe he figured it didn't matter what he told Lina and Marc. They'd soon be dead.

Shortly before 5 in the morning it was still dark outside when they finished all their tasks. The last was Lina's translation into French of his conclusion to the narrative. As she finished, he completed the list of email addresses to which the package would be sent. First on the list was, of course, Charles Mercier. Everything else would wait on his response.

In five separate emails, to accommodate all the attachments — some of them very large — they sent everything off to old Charles. It was getting close to noon in Geneva, and within 40 minutes Lina received his two-word reply:

"Incroyable! Bravo!"

Now, after a shower and a change of clothes, they gulp a quick breakfast and ask the girl who serves them if Eleuthera has an on-line newspaper, something that would have daily news.

"Oh, yes," says the girl. "The Eleutheran, but it's not always up to date."

Lina opens the Dell and quickly finds the site. "Yes, they have the story!" She angles her screen so they can both read.

Home Invasion Results in Homicide

(Governor's Harbour, Eleuthera) – The Eleutheran has learned of a homicide that resulted from a home invasion on November 19, 2009. Governor's Harbour Police report that a Swiss national, David Marcuse of Lucerne, Switzerland, was killed when he invaded the home of Josef Simon and Gerard Bitou, also Swiss nationals, on the Atlantic side north of Governor's Harbour. Marcuse was found dead at the scene with a gun, and the police say his intention was armed robbery and quite possibly murder.

> According to the police, one of the homeowners acted with "great bravery" in striking the intruder in the head with a hammer.
>
> Police say their investigation of this highly unusual event on peaceful Eleuthera will be completed shortly. No charges are expected to be brought against the homeowners.

"Good," he says, "So now we know the name on Tanner's phony passport."

Back in the room they add "David Marcuse" to their narrative and to Marc's note to the cops. And then they begin the careful, methodical process of sending off their package to each of four news outlets in Geneva, including the Herald and the TV channel TSR, and to the Swiss National Police, the Swiss Banking Commission and three other regulatory agencies. Everything is copied to Charles Mercier.

Each receives five emails with the subject line, "A Story of Fraud and Murder" and numbered 1 through 5. Each email is tagged "Highest Priority" and has two or three attachments, a dozen in all, including the profile, the Banque Privee Morneau website (with its bank officer photos), the Eleutheran story on the homicide, the Herald's stories of Clara's death and Tanner's murder in Amsterdam, typed versions of Clara's letter to Cecile and her fax to Marc (with a note saying the handwritten originals will be available in Geneva within 24 hours), old Charles' statement on the charities, yesterday's photo of Tanner on Eleuthera, the audio file of their chat with Tanner and the transcript of that file.

Inside each email #1 is their cover note, directing all inquiries to Cecile DeRocheford's attorney and estate executor, Charles Mercier, followed by the narrative entitled "The Truth about Banque Privee Morneau...A Story of Fraud and Murder." It's complete with references to each of the 12 attachments.

Marc says at one point, "I think if I were a news guy or a cop who received all this, I'd feel like I died and went to heaven."

Having hit send one last time, Lina manages only a weary smile.

There is one last item. He addresses a new email to the only chief inspector he found listed for the Eleuthera police and in the subject line types "Important information on the Wright house homicide."

He attaches the profile, the bank's website and the video clip and then skims one more time through the message he wrote last night.

Dear Chief Inspector Gibson:

A close look at the two websites attached here will move you to question the true identities of the 3 principals in yesterday's homicide at the former Wright house. All 3 traveled to Eleuthera on false passports. Homeowner Gerard Bitou is in fact Giles Morneau, chairman of Banque Privee Morneau in Geneva, Switzerland. Homeowner Josef Simon is in fact Julian Lyon, also connected with Banque Privee Morneau.

And the victim, David Marcuse, was in fact Willem Tanner, an employee (security officer) at the same bank. Because Willem Tanner was a convicted felon who spent 18 months in a Swiss prison, if you send his fingerprints to the Swiss National Police, they will confirm his identity. As for Morneau and Lyon, a thorough search of their home and possessions is likely to uncover their true passports.

Along with this information on the identities of the 3 principals and the true relationships between them, the third attachment, a video file from a hidden security camera, may cause you to investigate further exactly what happened at the former Wright house yesterday.

Finally, in addition to sending Tanner's fingerprints, we strongly urge you to share all the results of your continuing investigation with the Swiss National Police as well as with the Swiss regulatory agencies listed below. What you are about to uncover will begin to expose and unravel a deplorable series of crimes that include murder and the looting of many millions of euros from an account at the Banque Privee Morneau.

Sincerely,

Friends of Justice

Reading it last night, Lina said, "Great...'a hidden security camera.'"

"Yeah, they'll probably search all over for it and then think the boys got rid of it."

They left this email for last on the chance that Chief Inspector Gibson might call their friend Mac to ask about this Clara Bianco. And then the police might show up at the Buc.

But as they're about to close their laptops, Lina says, "Wait, there is one more. We should send everything also to Emmanuelle at the bank."

"Okay, I'll start packing."

With this one she adds a personal note, and for the last time she translates for him:

Dear Emmanuelle,

Here is information that will no doubt astound you and everyone at the bank. It should ultimately clear the name of our poor, dear Clara. Also it means you will soon be swamped with contacts and inquiries from the media and the police.

Thank you.

A Friend

Finally, half-expecting the arrival of the chief inspector at any moment, they quickly finish packing, check out of the Buc and toss their things in the Jeep. Exhilarated and exhausted, he drives carefully and says only "Yeah" when Lina says, "I wish we could go to a beach."

Instead they head directly to Governor's Harbour International Airport and arrive just in time to catch the Bahamasair flight to Nassau leaving at noon.

Chapter 45

On a frigid late January afternoon in Bologna, the wind is whipping, snow swirling, even under the porticoes on Via San Vitale. Walking from her department office at the university, she carries a leather bag full of books and papers over one shoulder, her large purse over the other, and clutches to her throat the russet wool scarf covering her head. Close to her building's entrance she passes an old woman she has seen often in this neighborhood, bundled in black, about her own height but stooped against the wind, her face unhappily lined under a heavy shawl. Lina wonders, *"In quanti anni saranno che io sia?"* How long will it be before she looks like that?

Upstairs in the warmth of the apartment, she scolds herself for negative thinking. A few days ago in Geneva, waiting to be deposed by the Swiss National Police, she read a piece in the Herald about the importance of attitude in the aging process. And what better example than the lively, incisive octogenarian Charles Mercier, with whom she had dinner later that evening. The old guy talked almost non-stop for close to an hour about the latest in this extraordinary case that has so stirred him to life, making him so animated it almost felt as if he were flirting. And now she wonders why all this absurd concern about getting older? She is still months away from age 42. Hardly decrepit.

The two-day visit to Geneva also included a lengthy interview with agents from the Swiss Banking Commission and lunch with Clara's two daughters. Bright, pretty women, though neither with Clara's beauty. They were both still obviously in mourning, but the younger one, Vera, seemed to be having a harder time coming to terms with her mother's death.

The time in Geneva has plunged her back into the events of the past eight weeks, starting with her parting from Marc at the Nassau airport. It took considerable effort, but she finally convinced him to fly back to Detroit while she returned to Geneva. Yes, of course, when the time came, they would both cooperate fully with Swiss authorities, but for now it was better for him back home in the States, where he could take care of his daughters and resume his business.

Fifteen hours later she landed in Geneva, took a taxi straight to Charles' office and dropped off the originals of Clara's letter to Cecile and her fax to Marc. Then it was on to the villa, where she picked up her clothes and her car and drove to Bologna. Relieved to be back in her own apartment for the first time since early September, she nonetheless found her focus riveted to news reports in Geneva.

First to break was the story of the prominent local bankers involved in a killing on Eleuthera in the Bahamas and their use of false ID's. Bahamian police were tight-lipped about the puzzling case, in which the victim, Willem Tanner, also held false identification. There were more questions than answers, since this was a man who had apparently staged his own murder in Amsterdam just a week earlier. But within a day the bankers were being held in custody in Nassau for entering the Bahamas on false passports, and authorities there were voicing questions about why the bankers had entered the country illegally, about their account of the Tanner homicide and about the legality of transactions at their private investment firm located in Nassau.

Considered a flight risk, the bankers were held without bond. Within two days a high-profile Swiss attorney arrived in Nassau to take up their case and soon hired a top Bahamian firm to work with him. Their first order of business was to get their clients extradited back to Switzerland, and within 10 days they reported making progress on that front. But by then a surge of sensational stories was breaking back home in Geneva, and the investigations initiated by both police and regulatory agencies in Switzerland had caused the bankers and their attorneys to re-think extradition. They might be better off dealing with Bahamian justice.

After three weeks of examining all the materials sent in those mysterious email packages — determining their authenticity, pursuing their details, investigating all of their implications (and no doubt after some feverish sessions with corporate attorneys) — the Geneva Herald published a 3-part investigation into what it called "sensational and appalling allegations." That same week TSR presented a prime-time one-hour special report called "A License to Loot...Accusations of Fraud and Murder at Banque Privee

Morneau."

In both reports, as well as in a non-stop stream of follow-up stories, the mystery Man and Woman in the audio recording with Willem Tanner were identified only as friends of the late Clara Marche, deeply worried friends who had gone to Eleuthera searching for her. Knowing the police would eventually identify them through interviews with Emmanuelle at the bank and with Clara's daughters, Charles Mercier had made a deal with authorities, guaranteeing the full cooperation of both Lina and Marc and arranging extensive phone, video conference and in-person interviews. In exchange, police and regulators gave assurances that their identities would be withheld from the public until they were needed in a Swiss court to testify against the bankers.

Following all this from Bologna, Lina stayed in touch with Charles almost daily by phone or email. From his "inside sources," he explained how the role of the Geneva Municipal Police was playing out. Clara's letter, of course, revealed that Tanner, a former member of the force, had told her the bankers were closely connected to "the police" and warned her not to go to them. But in the audio recording, which Charles called "a gold mine," Tanner amplified significantly: about his former colleagues Savoneau and Tremelyn picking up Clara at Malpensa, about the childhood connection between the Municipal chief, Alain Dubonne, and Morneau, and about money laundering at the bank in accounts fronted by two South Americans for both Dubonne and a drug cartel.

Clearly, said Charles, there was enough in the conversation between Tanner, Lina and Marc for the police to put the right questions to the bankers as well as to Dubonne and Savoneau. The plan was to squeeze each to give the others away. And after five weeks, with the extradition process complete and the bankers returned to Geneva, the interrogation process began in earnest.

So who will break, asked Lina. Not likely Dubonne or Savoneau, said Charles. And of the bankers, his guess was probably Julian. The guy the press called "the light-fingered Adonis" would try to lay every serious charge on his boss, Giles Morneau.

The most devastating items, the ones that could send all of them away for good, were of course the murders of Clara and Cecile. Since the video of the homicide on Eleuthera showed Tanner with a gun, Julian was probably okay there, but the murders were something else. To save his own skin, Julian could admit to having a hand in the looting of Cecile's account, but he could also claim that his boss Morneau had ordered him to do it. And then Julian would offer up the following scenario: when Clara, by sheer god-awful chance, discovered that night on Julian's computer exactly what they were doing, Morneau ordered Tanner to kill both Cecile and Clara; and when Tanner failed to kill Clara, Morneau then went to his old pal Dubonne who directed his own men, Tremelyn and Savoneau, to hunt down and kill both Clara and Tanner.

Over their dinner in Geneva Charles reported that, indeed, Julian's confession and cooperation were threatening to bring everyone down. Julian had also told bank regulators about the secret investment firm in Nassau, where most of the funds looted from Cecile's account were still locked away. Ultimately they would be moved to her charities according to her wishes. Yes, Julian would finally get substantial prison time, but it would be a ride in the park, said Charles, compared with what Giles Morneau, Alain Dubonne and Claude Savoneau would be facing.

In Bologna, she has been catching up with her closest friends. Tonight she has dinner scheduled at the apartment of Aldo, the professor of practical ethics, and his wife Rena, the African-Italian poet, who again for close to three months collected Lina's mail, watered her plants each week and then read them her new poems. Also invited are the Zabbinis, Vito, the hopelessly idealistic professor of law, and his pediatrician wife Bianca, along with Bella and Edgardo, the sweethearts about to take their doctorates. Everyone she spends time with these days appears happily paired off. Even the love-shy and fickle Marta seems devoted to her new boyfriend Filippo, a rising chef at a new restaurant in town, who may, or may not, be another romantic disaster.

Now with the new term at the University underway, she is teaching again, though her evenings are usually spent working on the Clara/Marc book. Its working title: *Romance Language…The Love Emails of Clara Marche*. Months ago, around the time she left for her visit with Cecile last September, she had made the commitment to teach, and she felt honor-bound to keep her word. But she had also promised Cecile she would complete this book, and the fact is, with the Banque Privee Morneau murder and fraud scandal exploding in Switzerland and beyond, the book had suddenly become a hot property. Lina's publisher wants it asap and plans to rush it into print.

Before the holidays, fixed on the progress of the bank expose, she had not really started on the book. And then she had to concentrate on preparing for her first classroom stint in several months. But a few days after New Year's, she lunched with an editor from her London-based publisher, a woman named Dottie Armitage, who was traveling through Italy. After a discussion of the slow but steady sales of *The Novel in an Age of Terror*, the book Lina had finished as John lay dying in Taormina, their talk turned to the big bank scandal in Geneva. Lina mentioned she had access to an unusual, auto-translated email exchange covering more than two years between Clara Marche and her American lover, neither of whom spoke the other's language. She was thinking about turning it into a kind of epistolary novel. Dottie became very excited.

"But, Lina, darling," she exclaimed, "why fiction? You have in your hands a unique window on one of the hottest stories in Europe and a rare and tragic love story to boot. Just write a prologue to set it up, an epilogue to bring it up to date, and in between lay out the two years of emails with some smart editing. Then boom, you have yourself a bestseller!"

At that point there was no stopping Dottie, who was famous in the business for her wild enthusiasms. She practically guaranteed a six-figure advance, and within days there was talk of a joint venture with Lina's French publisher. A week later reps from both companies arrived in Bologna with a contract for Lina to sign. It included a bonus provision for delivery of the manuscript within three months. Lina agreed to sign only if the book employed a pseudonym for Marc and changed certain details to protect his identity, and only after Charles Mercier asked for and received permission from both Marc and Clara's family, with the understanding, at Lina's insistence, that each would receive half of the advance and all subsequent revenues from the sale of the book and its subsidiary rights.

Just a week before her lunch with Dottie, Lina had received a thank you note along with Marc's check for $4000 to cover his part of the expenses incurred in their travels, most of which Lina had paid for at the time. Knowing now that he won't have to worry about his privacy or about money for a while, she could feel better about cashing his check.

And then there are those surprising feelings that developed for Marc over that week and a day they spent together. Yes, together everyday, and most nights, sleeping in the same room with him. And now she often finds herself day-dreaming about the black man with his grandfather's Italian features, fantasizing about him on a beach in Eleuthera, on Lerici's promenade or even on the gritty streets of Detroit. She felt vaguely disappointed when it was decided he would not need to be deposed in Geneva but would instead do a video-conference in Detroit. Frankly she is surprised by how much she is thinking about him, wanting to know what he is doing, how he made it though the holidays with his daughters, whether his documentary work is picking up, and if a new job with one of the car companies might bring him to Europe any time soon. She resists the strong urge to write to him.

When she works on the book she generally does not think of these things. The emails and the frame she is writing for them are, of course, all about Marc and Clara. But when she finishes with her writing for the night, she is often prey to stray thoughts that somehow plunge her back into questions about Marc.

The real question is what she will do with the rest of her life.

Once again it feels as if she has been working her way through some kind of identity crisis. Teaching and her scholarly work will always be there, but can she find a way to re-kindle her passion for them? Her department head and university administrators have been extraordinarily patient with her, but she knows their indulgence will soon come to an end. She will have to make up her mind.

How about another job in the States? Perhaps at a place like the University of Michigan?

"*Basta*," she says aloud. Then silently: "*Sei pazza.*" She knows this is crazy. Still she wonders if the U.S. might actually be the right place for her. What might it be like without all the duplicity with John, the conjoined insanity of Stan and Marissa. What if it carried a chance to start something with the bright and beautiful Mr. White?

She thinks again of his parting kiss in Nassau, a light and tender touch on the lips that made her duck beneath his chin and press against him to keep from trembling.

Probably just the potent but passing, and not uncommon, connection felt by two people who have worked intensely together for a time to achieve a deeply challenging purpose, one that demanded and received their best.

Ultimately, she tells herself one more time, probably nothing all that special.

###

From T.V. LoCicero:

Word-of-mouth

It's vital to any author. If you enjoyed this book, please consider leaving a review at Amazon. It may be only a line or two, but it could make a big difference and would be deeply appreciated.

Be the First to Learn of a New Release

If you'd like to receive an auto email when the next book is released, please sign up at: http://eepurl.com/z26Vv

Your email address will never be shared, and you can unsubscribe at any time.

Say Hello

My website (http//www.tvlocicero) offers info, thoughts, photos, videos and much more. I'd love it if you come by and say hello. You can also get in touch on Facebook, or send me an email: tvloc1@netscape.net